D0286837

Books by Jess E. Owen

BOOK III OF THE SUMMER KING CHRONICLES

A SHARD OF SUN

JESS E. OWEN

five elements press

Marysville Public Library
231 S. Plum St.
Marysville, OH 43040
(937) 642-1876

DISCARD

Copyright © 2015 by Jess E. Owen

All rights reserved. No part of this publication may be reproduced, distributed, or transmitted in any form or by any means, including photocopying, recording, or other electronic or mechanical methods, without the prior written permission of the publisher, except in the case of brief quotations embodied in critical reviews and certain other noncommercial uses permitted by copyright law. For permission requests, write to the publisher, addressed "Attention: Permissions Coordinator," at the address below.

Five Elements Press
Suite 305
500 Depot Street
Whitefish, MT 59937
www.fiveelementspress.com

PUBLISHER'S NOTE

This is a work of fiction. Any references to historical events, real people, or real locales are used fictitiously. Other names, characters, places, or incidents are the product of the author's imagination, and any resemblance to actual events, locales, or persons, living or dead, are purely coincidental.

Cover art by Jennifer Miller © 2015
Cover typography and interior formatting by TERyvisions
Author photo by Jessica Lowry
Edited by Joshua Essoe

FIRST PAPERBACK EDITION

ISBN-13: 978-0-9967676-0-6

Hardcover Edition Library of Congress Control Number: 2015904776

To the libraries and bookstores I have known.

Table of Contents

"Only the long day brings rest
Only the dark of night, dawn.
When the First knew themselves, the wise will say
They took their Names to the Sunlit Land
But their Voice in the wind sings on."

A Shard of Sun

Jess E. Owen

A gryfon's view of

The Silver Isles

Starward

Nightward

Dawnward

Windward

Pebble's
Throw

Talon's
Reach

Star Isle

Crow
Wing

The gryfon colony of
Windwater

Sun Isle

The White Mountains

Black Rock

The Nightrun River

The Nesting Cliffs

The Windward Sea

1
THE CAVE

S HARD CROUCHED AGAINST THE INNER wall of the crystal dragon, digging at an edge where the diamond-hard scales met the ground. He'd already worn two talons dull against the hard earth and volcanic rock. His back ached from his prolonged crouch and he made sure to open and stretch his curved, gray wings and his hind legs often.

He could see, vaguely, beyond the walls—only light and shapes, and he paused to check for movement outside.

The glimmer of ten thousand false stars filled a cavern massive enough for two dozen dragons to fly. The cavern was the hollow center of a mountain peak, which gryfons called the Horn of Midragur.

Shard knew where he sat within the cavern, knew what any other creature would see. Near one edge of the floor rose a pedestal of stone, squat and oval, and on top of the pedestal coiled the crystal form of an enormous, serpentine dragon of the Sunland.

The crystal dragon's body formed a dome, sealing two creatures inside, one of whom was Shard.

I need a better plan, he thought, stopping to stare at the meager groove he'd created along the crystal dragon's body. He'd discovered that it wasn't connected to the ground, that given time, if he had the strength, he might tunnel underneath and escape the chamber. And he desperately needed to escape. Food was running low and the only water to be had was whatever condensed along the walls of the crystal.

A low, thrumming thunder shuddered the ground under his body and he swiveled, peering again through the crystal. That time he saw warped, winged, dark shapes that loomed beyond. There would be a consequence for escaping, one that he hadn't yet thought through.

But it was not only for his sake that he needed to escape, no matter the peril beyond.

"Shard!"

He startled, scooped loose dirt back into his shallow tunnel, and sat up. "You're done eating?"

Hikaru bounded forward in rolling leaps, his shining black scales catching the eerie light of the million glow worms far, far above them. When the little dragon had hatched he'd been no larger than an arctic hare. Now he was a third Shard's size. They would starve if they didn't escape, or Hikaru would grow so large that Shard feared he would crush them both against the walls. Shard hadn't yet told him of their danger, and didn't want him to know of the tunnel.

"I have a new question," Hikaru announced, and sat.

"All right," Shard said, happy that the dragonet still didn't understand their peril, and hoping he wouldn't ask why they could only eat so much food at a time. Hikaru's mother had left them a store of dried, smoked fish but now there was only enough for a few more days. Shard had lost track of the time in the unchanging light of the cave, but two things kept him aware. One was their hunger. The other was the wyrms, most of which left at night to hunt, and returned at daybreak. All told, by counting their comings and goings, Shard and Hikaru had been in the chamber just under a fortnight.

Hikaru displayed his small, long wing, growing in shape like a swan's, the tips of the black feathers gleaming like the translucent edge of volcanic glass. "Why have I different...different..."

"Feathers?" Shard offered.

"Yes." Large serpent eyes of luminous gold met Shard's. Hikaru would eventually realize that Shard's moss-green eagle eyes were different than his own as well. "Why have I different feathers than you? And no feathers on my tail, as you do?"

"Because you're a dragon," said Shard quietly, but reassuringly. "And I'm a gryfon." He tried to stay calm, but the young dragon had grown so swiftly, and was growing still, speaking, learning more quickly than any young creature he'd ever seen. The mother dragon had said as much, that her son would grow faster than Shard could imagine, like a bird, and would need guidance. As he doubled in size so rapidly, it was becoming critical that they find a way out of their sanctuary before it became their grave.

Shard wondered if Amaratsu had thought that far ahead, either. The store of food she'd left, that he hadn't noticed in the heat of their last confrontation with the dragons, hinted that she'd planned to remain in the mountain for some time.

A dull, far away sound swept a chill down Shard's back. Hikaru flicked his soft, roe-like ears toward the crystal walls.

"What is that?" he whispered. The long whiskers that sprouted from his snout quivered in the air. He hadn't been able to hear the outside noises before. Shard imagined how rapidly the dragonet's senses would improve to levels possibly higher than his own.

"Dragons," he said, trying to sound matter-of-fact. Hikaru's soft ears perked fully forward. Shadows swooped around the chamber like enormous ravens. They had tried to break in, with no luck, and the walls muffled their horrible, blood-lusting roars to dull rumbling.

"Dragons like me? Like my mother?" He peered at his own body, then sat up and arched his head back like an egret. He offered his bird-like, five-toed forepaws for Shard's inspection.

"No," said Shard, forcing his gaze from the glimmering walls of their haven. Soon Hikaru would fill it to overflowing, but escaping it held just as many problems. "Not like you or your mother at all. Those are dragons of the Winderost. Voiceless, angry. Other creatures call them wyrms. Your mother was from the Sunland at the bottom of the world. A place of snow and light and peace." He tried to speak as if he'd seen it himself, to assure Hikaru of his noble birth. Truly though, all he knew of the Sunland or of dragons was what Amaratsu had told him in the last hours of her life.

She had begged him to care for her son. Begged him, in the face of attacking wyrms who wished to steal her egg, or worse. Shard didn't know what they wanted. He'd tried to speak to the wyrms once, tried and failed.

That lingering fear and threat hovered like a storm at the forefront of their quiet time within Amaratsu's coils.

Perhaps still thinking of his mother, Hikaru walked to the wall of the chamber. He touched it gently, as if afraid to mar the scales, though the wyrms of the Winderost had failed to chip or even scratch it from the outside.

"Mother," whispered the dragonet, stroking the unfeeling scales. "Earth." He touched both delicate forefeet to the ground. "Sky..." He tilted his graceful, wedge-shaped head back to peer through the crystal. He wasn't staring at the false sky that was the roof of the cavern, laced with clusters of glow worms and lichens, but at a far, high hole near the top that Shard had once pointed out to him. A crack near the pinnacle of the Horn of Midragur led to the sky. Shard followed his gaze, his wings aching to fly.

He didn't realize he'd opened his wings until he saw that Hikaru's black wings also stretched wide, opening and fanning in exercise.

"Flight." Hikaru's voice was breathless with hunger. One of the first things they'd spoken of was flight, of the sky, of freedom and joy in the wind.

Hikaru continued reviewing words and objects, like a lullaby. He did it often, usually putting himself to sleep that way. Relief filled Shard that the dragon had no more questions, and he simply watched, correcting here and there and thinking of how Hikaru's voice differed from Amaratsu. Her quiet, winding voice had the strange accent of a bird from a land he had never seen and didn't know. Hikaru's voice lovingly mimicked a gryfon's, more rasping, with the soft rolling rhythm of a cluster of islands in the starward corner of the world. Shard's home.

"Fish," Hikaru said, touching the dry, smoked planks of meat on the ground. Shard saw his eyelids slipping and so he settled himself, stretched out on the ground on his belly, and opened a wing. Hikaru slithered forward, purring, and curled against Shard's warm flank. Shard closed his wing around the dragonet.

"Feathers," Hikaru murmured, combing Shard's wing feathers with gentle talons. "Talon. Pebble. Rib." He yawned widely, then his jaws snapped shut. He bared his tiny, sharp teeth in what Shard had learned was an expression of amusement. "Tired." It reminded him of Catori, his closest wolf friend in the Silver Isles, and he longed for home.

"Friend."

Shard waited, knowing it was the last word that Hikaru uttered each night, a word that brimmed with affection and admiration Shard wasn't sure he deserved. Small, articulate dragon talons curled around his foreleg and Hikaru nuzzled his head against Shard's feathered shoulder. His final word for the evening rolled from between his little teeth in a warm sigh.

"Shard."

A dream bore him a vision of a snowy valley lit by a celestial green glow. He'd never seen the valley or mountains in the Silver Isles, nor the Winderost. In the center of the valley, he beheld a ring of stones. A pale star glowing down on the earth darted to and fro amongst the stones, and then away toward the mountains on the far side of the valley.

Before Shard could explore the vision further, something grabbed his wings, shaking him, demanding his attention.

"I'm awake," Shard grumbled, grasping Hikaru's forelegs and wrestling him off. "I'm awake!"

Hikaru laughed and coiled his tail around Shard's chest, baring his teeth in challenge. Groggy, but determined not to lose a playful spar to a dragonet half his size, Shard rolled to his back and Hikaru fell with him, scrambling to stay on Shard's stomach. Shard arched up to kick his hind legs against Hikaru's belly, lifting him off the ground. The dragonet loosed a long, laughing *scree* like a seabird and flared his wings. At full spread they were as long as Shard's, despite his smaller size.

"I'm flying!"

"Well done!" Shard laughed, still holding Hikaru's forefeet. The dragonet uncoiled his tail and set his hind feet on Shard's paws and his front feet in Shard's talons, so he stood braced against an imaginary wind, flapping his wings hard. Shard gripped the little forepaws firmly, encouraging this exercise. The only way they would escape the cavern was to fly, and Hikaru would be too big for him to carry. He had to build his strength.

After another moment of "flying," Hikaru broke free with a shove and leaped, gliding the small expanse from their side of the chamber to the other. Shard flopped over to his belly and watched the little dragon glide, flap and flare. He looked to have the instinct for it, though he flared too late and smacked into the far wall instead. Shard rolled to his feet and trotted over as Hikaru crawled to a sitting position.

"Are you hurt?"

"Oh. No." He ran his little talons nervously down his belly scales, and Shard detected a flush at the end of his soft nose, which was more like a deer's nose, and had no scales. "Mother caught me."

Shard lifted a foot, taken aback, then chuckled gently. "Yes she did. Well done though. Next time—"

"I know." Hikaru's eyes slitted and he lashed his tail against the dirt, "If I *think* it's time to turn or stop, it's already too late."

Shard nodded once. "Well remembered."

"Next time I will."

A tremor vibrated the earth under their feet. Pebbles shivered on the rock, and pure cold washed Shard's skin.

Hikaru perked his ears at the ground. "What was that?"

"Earthquake," Shard said. The tremor stilled, and he managed to keep his voice calm. "This is an ancient volcano, a hollow mountain. It's not uncommon for that to happen."

Hikaru patted his paw against the ground, as if to make the earth shake again. "Is it dangerous?"

Shard hoped not, and to answer he said only, "It won't matter if we get out, soon. Don't worry. I've felt small earthquakes in the Silver Isles. Are you hungry?"

Shard hated such an obvious change of subject, hated to deter Hikaru from his questions or seem to be lying, but he didn't want the dragon to fear things over which they had no control. For the first time, Hikaru hesitated at the question. He glanced at the dwindling stash of meat. "Should we save it?"

Shard drew a deep breath. "No, Hikaru. You're growing fast and you need to eat."

Hikaru's eyes narrowed further, the delicate ridges drawing down in a reptilian frown. "When did you eat last?"

"I'm fine," Shard said firmly. "Eat a fish."

Hikaru's tail twitched again, then he did as Shard told him. Shard tried to remember the last time he had eaten, himself, and when he couldn't, decided he'd better have something. He ate a smaller fish as well, watching how Hikaru made an effort to chew slowly and savor the meal.

I can't wait to show him a true meal. A real fish. Real meat. Judging by his wings, Shard guessed Hikaru might be able to dive and fish, and the prospect of teaching the young dragon excited him.

First things first. He waited for Hikaru to get sleepy, as he usually did, after eating. Then he could work on the hole to get them out. But Hikaru didn't curl up right away. As if he'd been thinking of something for a while, he left the fish pile and pressed his paw to the crystal wall, angling his head to watch Shard closely.

"My mother gave her life for me. And for you." He searched Shard's face. "Why?"

"She was your mother," Shard said, struggling to answer the new, more complicated question. The previous days all Hikaru had asked about were the names for things, and when they might have fresh fish. At last Shard sat, fidgeting his talons against the rock. "She wanted me to teach you of the world, and of dark and light, and the songs, and of her." He took a deep breath, watching Hikaru's quiet, eager expression. He'd known the moment would come, and he'd already decided what to do. Shard's own past had been a mystery to him his entire life, with others secretly hoping for and expecting things that he might do without telling him everything he needed to know.

He had vowed never to do that to Hikaru.

"Hikaru, the dragons of your kind have kept to themselves for many years in the Sunland, not visiting the rest of the world as they once did. Your mother hoped that by bringing you here and letting you befriend other creatures, you might help to change things."

Hikaru tilted his head. "How could I change things? And why would she want me to?"

Shard tilted his head in an unconscious echo of the dragonet, and flicked his long, feathered tail against the ground. "I'll tell you, but it's a long story."

Hikaru nodded gravely, then, stretching his wings, said, "I shall like to hear it. But could I have one more fish?"

"I knew you were hungrier than that." Shard laughed, and reached forward, slipping his talons gently under the dragon's wings to lift and spread them wide. "Yes, but just one more or you'll get too plump to fly!"

"Ha!" Hikaru squirmed back and flapped once, hopping away. A sudden memory blinked through Shard's mind so swift he almost missed it. Himself, being swept through the air, as a laughing, deep, male voice praised the shape and health of his wings, proclaiming that he would be a fine flier.

But the voice in his memory wasn't his true father's voice, Baldr the Nightwing, dead king of the Silver Isles.

Shard caught a breath, and realized Hikaru had wanted him to chase, so he did, pouncing forward. The dragonet squealed in delight and leaped back to the dried fish, his wings still stretched wide.

Shard scrambled for the memory again while Hikaru picked through the fish. He'd been so young—*why didn't I remember this before?* Strong talons had swung him through the air, and when he looked down, he met the fierce, guarded eyes of his nest-father, Caj. Caj, one of the conquering Aesir, wingbrother to the Red King who had committed so many crimes against Shard's pride. Caj, who had also kept the secret of Shard's true parentage from the king himself, and raised Shard as his own.

A number of regrets surged forth and Shard shook himself of them. He had enough things to focus on, namely, feeding Hikaru, and escape. After that would come decisions.

So many decisions.

The weight of his own birthright sat more than ever like stones across his wings, the amount of wrongs to set right and matters to settle.

"I'm ready for the tale," Hikaru announced, dragging a long strip of fish back to Shard.

Shard fluffed his wings, focusing on the one thing that was important in that moment.

"The story of our being here," he began, lifting his gaze to the crystal wall and the shadows beyond, "begins a much longer time ago. In a place called the Dawn Spire."

Hikaru watched him, entranced, and Shard met his eager gaze.

"And a young prince named Kajar."

2

FLOTSAM

WAVES SMASHED AGAINST SHARP, WIND-BATTERED rocks along the inner curve of a crescent coastline. The worst of the storm had already passed, but pale clouds still gusted low, raining on the ruined shore. The rocks hugged small patches of gravel beaches, some ten leaps long, others wide enough for only a single gryfon to stand. Dead and dying sea creatures littered the small beaches, tangled in mats of seaweed or sprawled on the sand. Fish, seals, a handful of unfortunate seabirds.

Four scavengers ranged among the sea-wrack—three winged, and one on four paws. The painted wolf found the first fish and, with an eye to the gryfons above him, bolted it down without offering to share. If they found out, it would be his hide. But they wouldn't find out. He chuckled to himself and picked up to a lope, stretching his full belly and licking his jaws.

The gryfons shouted above and he saw the source of their excitement. A dead seal. Large enough to feed three starving, rogue gryfons, and one painted wolf. The storm had been the worst one all season, but it left riches for those who knew where to hunt.

10

A scent on the wind distracted him. As the gryfons fell on the dead seal, the wolf turned back into the wind, ears perked. Downwind, he raised his nose and followed it.

Rocks scattered at the edge of the beach and lanced out to sea, forming a barrier between him and the next beach. But the scent came from the next beach. Gingerly, not wanting to slip, the wolf climbed up the rocks, ignoring gryfon shouts for him to come and eat. He spotted his quarry crammed in the rocks unnaturally, not as if it had washed up, but as if it had swam, or desperately crawled, at low tide, into the shelter of the tide pools. Oh, he'd been correct. The scent was worth following.

He quirked his head, thinking.

"What's all this?" demanded Rok, winging up to hover over the wolf. "Ha. A fallen exile? We could use more talons. Is he alive?"

Rok didn't land at first, eyeing the gryfon warily, and the wolf shifted, lowering his head to sniff. Both of them studied the washed-up gryfon in the rocks. Large, big-boned, with golden feathers micah-bright against the stone and seawater.

"Breathing," Rok confirmed. He landed near the wolf, carefully gripping the stones. "Healthy. Big. Looks to be outcast from the Dawn Spire, if I had to wager. This could be good for us. Can you haul him out?"

The wolf tilted his head the other way, studying. "Halfway," he grunted. Words were always an effort. He roamed Nameless so often these days..."You can pull him the rest."

"Good enough." Rok looked back over his shoulder. "Hey, you worthless, lice-infested vultures," he called affectionately to the other two in their band, "over here!"

The two gryfons, a young female of plain brown coloring and a male her age with feathers like sand, ignored him to continue eating. Meanwhile, the painted wolf negotiated his way down to the hollow, to the water, and the washed-up gryfon.

As he drew close, something brighter than the feathers caught his eye. He thrust his face under the feathers to loop the strange material over his nose, and tilted his head toward Rok.

"Rok. What is this?"

The gangly rogue cocked his head. "Hm. Is it metal? I think it's called...a chain." A strange light brightened his eyes.

The wolf wrinkled his nose. "A chain? What does it do?" He shook his head free of the delicate metal and clamped his jaws on the gryfon's scruff. True to his estimation, he was able to haul the limp body halfway back up the rocks by standing on his hind legs, then Rok caught the gryfon under the forelegs and dragged him over the rocks to the beach.

"A chain," the rogue confirmed, his expression guarded. "Gold. I've heard stories of it." The wolf's hackles prickled. He knew when Rok was scheming. "I know a few creatures who might have an interest. Fraenir!" He barked over his shoulder, "Frida! Come over here now."

"Can you eat it?" The wolf sniffed again at the gold gryfon and the chain, curious at his foreign scent, his size, and the bright coloring of his feathers.

"No. It's metal. Don't be foolish. You'd just as well eat rocks."

The wolf bared his fangs, then the unconscious gryfon's tail flipped up and smacked his face, just as the other two of their band walked up beside Rok.

Rok slipped his claws through the chain to tug it free from the unconscious gryfon's neck.

Talons locked on Rok's foreleg and the golden gryfon coughed seawater. "...that...is mine."

"Ha," Rok growled, lifting his wings in surprise at the challenge. "Why, I'll skin you and line my nest with gold feathers. Everything that washes up on this shore's mine, including your chain there."

"Who are you?" asked the wolf of the gold gryfon, almost remembering his own name—realizing, just then, that he had forgotten it. It slipped away again and he let it, unworried. With the name came some dark memory, a fear greater than he wanted to remember.

The gryfon hacked again and Rok chuckled, lifting his ears. "Kjorn," wheezed the gryfon. "Son-of-Sverin. Prince of...of..." Either he couldn't remember, or couldn't decide, but he didn't finish, and his gaze slid between the three gryfons. Fraenir stepped in front of Frida as if to shield her from his gaze, and she dipped her head, peering at the stranger with narrowed eyes.

"Ha! Hear that, my friends?" Rok looked at all of them to make sure. Fraenir chuckled, Frida didn't and Rok looked back to the stranger. "Lucky for you, I'm a prince too. Prince of all you see here on the border of Vanheim. Prince of this mudding cranny between the high-beaks of the Reach and the stuff-beaked Vanhar. What brings you here?" He chuckled, as if it were a delightful conversation on a sunny afternoon.

"Starfire," whispered the gryfon who called himself Kjorn. "Shard. Have you seen...?"

"Shards?" Rok repeated. "What kind? Rocks? We've got plenty."

Shard. The wolf twitched one ear back as something nagged his mind, like a flea. He sat, scratching vigorously as if that could relieve his head. A name, not his own name, which he couldn't recall, but another. He remembered a rainstorm and a thick sense of terror. He shut it out, stood, and shook himself of drizzle.

Nothing to be frightened of, there. Nothing he needed to remember. He had food and a pack, even if his pack was made of gryfons.

Kjorn tilted his head back, gaze rolling to behold the littered shore. Then he looked up and down the three gryfons, and the wolf. His eyes narrowed. He uttered something. The wolf heard it, and laid his ears flat. Rok didn't, and leaned forward.

"What?"

"Poachers," Kjorn croaked again. "You're part of no pride. That I can see." He tried to push himself up, quivered, and fell again. The wolf saw blood oozing from a wound behind one wing. He must've been dashed against the rocks before finding his safe hollow.

Rok's hackle feathers lifted at the word, and his tail lashed. "Oh, is that the way of it? Well, son-of-Sverin." He grabbed the golden chain again and yanked, snapping the delicate links and making Kjorn grunt in pain. "Consider yourself poached." He stalked off, the chain in his fore claws, and said over his shoulder, "Take him."

The wolf exchanged a look with Fraenir, and they braced for a fight—but the large golden gryfon had fallen unconscious again on the sand.

Kjorn opened his eyes. He lay on cold rock inside a cave that reeked of old fish and brine. Swiveling his ears, he determined the sea now lay below him, that he'd been hauled to a cliff-side den near the shore. Bright moonlight washed everything, showing him mostly rock and a night sky.

Voices made him alert, and his instinct for danger flared. He recalled the exiles.

"He's awake!" reported a female.

Kjorn tried to sit up, but something bound his forelegs and his hind paws. By the scent, it had to be thick ropes of seaweed. He squirmed and twisted his talons but he was tied so closely to the digits that he could neither slice through the thick vines nor pull free. He managed to scoot up to a half-sitting position, leaning on his bound forefeet, by the time the leading male approached him from the back of the cave. Kjorn, his eyes adjusted to the dark and moonlight, looked around to see the female who'd spoken. He was surprised to see that she stood smaller, compact and thin, built almost like a Vanir. Her eyes, when she met his, were guarded and hard.

"Welcome awake, Your Highness," said the lanky male.

Kjorn growled low, spying his chain, tied roughly and glinting around the arrogant poacher's neck. "Release me. I have no quarrel with you."

The gryfon tilted his head, then sputtered a laugh and mantled his wings, mocking. "And I have no quarrel with you." He mimicked Kjorn's speech—his own was rough, but his eyes were keen. "But I do have a use for you."

"Return that chain. It was my father's."

"Oh? Well now it's mine. The price for saving your carcass. You'd have bled out or drowned at high tide if not for us."

Kjorn growled, trying to flare his wings, and found they, too, were bound by seaweed. He knew he'd been foolish to take anything from his father's old nest, especially a golden chain that was an icon of the very war that had started all the wrongs Kjorn hoped to right. But he'd seen Sverin wear it often, the gold against the crimson chest, and it helped to have a little piece of his father close by.

Serves me right. He took a slow breath. At first, no one had wanted him to go, seeking Shard, except perhaps for Ragna. When it became clear that Sverin would likely not return to threaten the pride, that everyone was weary of fighting, and that Thyra and Ragna could handle any disputes which arose, Kjorn had decided to go. He had to find Shard, and make amends, and decide, together, the future of their prides.

He decided it would not do to make enemies his first day in the Winderost. Though he was bound, he was alive, and perhaps what the outcast said was true, and he would've died without help.

He managed to keep his voice neutral. "I do thank you for your help. You have my gratitude. But the chain is of no use to you and neither am I. I'm here…seeking a friend." He decided not to tell them the rest. If he'd had his wits about him before, he wouldn't have named himself a prince at all. He'd let them decide if that was true or part of sea-washed delirium. Kjorn shuddered at the memory of the storm closing on him over the sea when he'd been at the end of his strength, and the final wind that had shoved him into the sea.

But bright Tyr bore me to my homeland. At least part of the way. The rest, it seemed, would be up to him.

"What friend?"

Kjorn could see no harm in telling them that, at least. Knowing Shard, he might very well have made allies of scoundrels like these. "His name is Shard. Rashard. A gray gryfon, about your height." He nodded to the female, who darted her gaze away, tail flicking. "A Vanir."

"Vanhar? No, they don't come this close to the Reach."

"No," Kjorn said, curious at the similarity. He didn't want to test Rok's patience by asking, though. He felt he had a limited number of questions the rogue might answer. "Vanir. From a group of islands far starward, the Silver Isles."

Rok looked suspicious. "Never heard of them. Or your friend. You?" He asked the female, who shrugged her wings. Kjorn saw another male, closer to the back of the cave. He merely grunted a negative.

Perfect. The wolf seer said Shard landed and found my kin, was welcomed into the Dawn Spire with open wing, and I land among scruffy, honor-less thieves.

Kjorn tried to fluff his feathers and look proud, though he was certain he looked no better than any of the dead creatures that had washed up on the shore. "Take me to the Dawn Spire. They'll give you a reward for me there." He wasn't strictly certain that was true, but all that mattered was what he could make them believe.

That gained the big male's attention. "Food?"

"Of course. Lots of food. More and fresher than you'd find here. Red meat, not fish."

The leader cocked his head, calculating. "What about this?" He slid his talon along the gold chain, admiring it against his dull brown feathers. "Is there more of this?"

Kjorn switched his tail, meeting the hard, keen gaze. "No. My pride took all the gold from the Winderost. You hold all that's left."

"Ha! So why should they give me anything for you at the Dawn Spire? Hm? Are you high tier? A good warrior? Not from what I've seen."

"Look at his eyes, Rok," burst out the female, as if she couldn't stand the big gryfon's ignorance any longer. "You fool. Look at his eyes."

Rok snapped his beak at her, lifting his wings, then settled in front of Kjorn and peered at his face in the moonlight. Kjorn knew what he saw. Gold feathers, bedraggled but true in breeding, and the rare eye color of bright sky blue. What it meant to them, he didn't know.

"I see," Rok murmured. "I see now. I thought it was a trick of the ocean."

"What do you think the queen will give for him?" the female asked eagerly, and Kjorn wished she'd stayed silent after all.

"I don't know." Rok stood, stretched luxuriously, and scraped his talons across the rock floor of the cave.

Kjorn's tail twitched. "Enough to satisfy you, I'm sure. Take me there and I'll reward you myself."

"You're alone," Rok said. "You washed up half-dead. I don't think the Dawn Spire even knows you're here and alive, and I don't know if they'll want you." His eyes glittered. "But I'll let others figure that out. I think I know someone who'll pay more."

Kjorn's belly dropped out.

"Don't look so forlorn, Your Highness. Consider the good part—we don't have to travel as far as the Dawn Spire."

"Where will you take me?" Kjorn demanded. "To whom?"

"Feed him," Rok said to the female, stalking away. "Let it never be said that I was responsible for letting a prince go without his supper."

The female eyed Kjorn, then tossed a fish at him. It smacked him in the face before he could snap his beak to catch it. Rok and the other male broke into coarse laughter, taking up the game and pelting him with small fish.

"Stop this!" Kjorn roared, flinging himself against his bonds but succeeding only in throwing himself to ground. The younger male exploded into laughter again, and Rok strode forward, planting his talons on Kjorn's shoulder.

"You should stay down for a while."

"I have no fight with you. I've earned no disrespect. Free me and I'll help you hunt, and you can help me find—"

"I've no desire to help you with anything," Rok snarled, squeezing his talons against Kjorn's shoulder. His eyes gleamed in the moonlight, and for the first time, Kjorn recognized not just a desire for food and gain, but true contempt. And recognition. "You, or any other relation to the Dawn Spire."

Kjorn hesitated, studying the gryfon's hard, bitter expression. "Why—"

"Check his binds often," Rok said, and shoved away toward the back of the cave. Kjorn watched him go, then tried to catch the female's eye. She looked away, leaving Kjorn to consider his situation, half buried in fish in the moonlight. Not quite idly, he wondered what Shard would say, to see him bound and treated so, and wondered, with apprehension, if his once-wingbrother wouldn't think he deserved it.

3

THE STAR DRAGON

"WHAT ARE YOU DOING?"

Shard jumped at the voice, bashing his head against the hard, gleaming scales of Amaratsu's side. "Hikaru. I thought you were sleeping."

"What are you doing? Are you digging? Are you digging out?" The young dragon slipped forward, peering at the shallow beginning to Shard's escape route.

"That was my idea. I don't want you near it, though. The wyrms might get a better scent of you."

Hikaru sat up on his haunches, arching his head back. Shard marveled at his size. In another two days, he would be as large as a gryfon. Their sanctuary grew crowded indeed.

"I want to help."

"You don't need to help."

The ground under them shivered and they both tilted their heads back, looking toward the shadows outside. The wyrms, back from hunting a meal, filled the cavern again. Their muffled roars pressed against the walls and Hikaru reared up to place his paws against the shining scales.

"What do they want, Shard? Can they speak like us? Can we talk to them?" His large eyes searched hard against the shadows, then he tilted his head to look at Shard, waiting for all his answers. Shard wished he had more to give.

"I don't know. I tried to speak to them once..." That horrible night. He ruffled his feathers. "I know they want you, and they hate me."

"Why?" Hikaru relaxed back to sitting, his long tail twitching. He narrowed his eyes. Shard tried not to look surprised at the new, growing depth of his voice. "Will they try to kill us? They seem so angry."

"I don't know. I told you everything that passed between them and the gryfons, and the dragons of the Sunland. That's all I know."

"Nameless," Hikaru murmured, not to Shard in particular. "Voiceless. It's not right, is it? It's not right for them."

"No," Shard said quietly. "It's not. Tyr and Tor gave all creatures under their sky life and purpose."

"I want to help them," Hikaru said firmly, and love and fear strained against each other in Shard's heart. He briefly forgot that the dragonet was only two weeks old, and would live only one year.

How his heart must race. Shard thought of all that had befallen him in only a year—not even a year yet—and understood a little how a dragon of the Sunland must think they lived a long, rich life indeed.

"So do I," Shard said belatedly. "And I'm certain we can. And if we can help them, I know it will help all the struggles I've told you about in my own islands, the Winderost, and maybe even your homeland."

Hikaru turned large eyes to him, scrutinizing with frightening maturity. "Truly?"

Shard straightened, opening his wings. "Truly. Together, we can. Maybe I couldn't make them hear me, alone, but together, I know we'll find a way."

Hikaru nodded once, then his ears turned back and he lowered himself to the ground, crawling toward Shard and looking quite young again. "I'd like a song. A new song. A dragon song."

Shard flexed his talons against the rock, thinking. They'd gone through his entire knowledge of gryfon songs, into wolf songs Shard had learned over his short autumn before flying to the Winderost, and the Song of the Summer King, the songs of First and Last Light. He struggled to think of a dragon song.

A rich, wry, gravelly voice came into his head. He shut his eyes, trying to block it and the sadness that came with it. Distracted by Hikaru and their predicament, he had managed not to think of it. Now it threatened to push him to the brink of sorrow.

"I've told you how stars form the history of the world in the sky?" Shard began, his voice quavering. In his mind he saw a cliff overlooking a cold starward sea. He saw bright stars sweeping across a black sky and heard a low voice telling him the tales of each one. The remembered voice threatened to break his strength.

"Yes?" Hikaru asked, hungry for knowledge.

The dragonet's face and curiosity dragged Shard from the brink, and he focused on him.

"I remember," Hikaru said, inching forward, swiveling his head to peer out of their chamber toward the hole in the top of the mountain, past the glowworms and glowing lichens where Shard had promised him the real sky existed, filled with real stars and the light of the sun. "And how they turn in their season, and hunt each other across the sky, how we may use them to guide our flights, and how bright Tyr burns away the dark, and Tor protects us when Tyr is away. And you followed a starfire to find my mother and me."

"Yes," Shard said, proud and a little sad. So much joy and eagerness, and so short a life.

It is Tor who commands the sea, rang an indignant, growling voice in his head, a black gryfon under a star-swept sky, teaching a more ignorant Shard all the things he hadn't learned. *She who brings the thunder when Tyr brings the wind and rain, Tyr's mate.*

The memory of the gryfon who'd first told Shard that tale threatened to push him to the brink of mourning again, and so he focused back on Hikaru.

"Tyr and Tor guide us. And the stars tell all our future and our past," Shard managed, "all the way back to the First Age when the First creatures came from the Sunlit Land, learned their names, and made the world."

Hikaru coiled up at Shard's side and watched him with so much hungry adoration that guilt gnawed at him. He wasn't so special. All Hikaru knew of the world was what Shard could tell him, and he seemed to think Shard knew everything when he knew very little at all.

But I can tell what little I know.

"Across the sky," Shard continued, "you'll see a serpent of stars, a bright band that wraps all the way around the world." In the telling, he found himself calming down. "It's my favorite, actually. The star dragon is called Midragur." He paused, surprised for a moment. He realized, in that heartbeat, that the myth he told couldn't be from the Sunland or the Winderost, as he'd once thought. The timbre of the name was wrong, different than Amaratsu and Hikaru. He wondered where the myth came from—gryfons, or dragons. Or perhaps the wyrms themselves....

Hikaru tugged his wing, impatient for the tale. Shard flexed his talons against the ground and shook his head.

"Those who believe that the earth was born from Tyr and Tor also believe that a great dragon coils around it, protecting it as a mother dragon would her egg." Inspired, Shard retrieved the broken halves of Hikaru's pearly, discarded eggshell, lying all that time near the wall of the chamber. Hikaru perked his ears as Shard fitted the two largest pieces back together, and leaned forward.

"The wise say that the egg that is the world will still hatch one day." He turned the egg slowly, like the world turned, as if he and Hikaru were the sun and the moon, with all the stars of existence behind them. Shard leaned closer as Hikaru held his breath.

"That day, that glorious and terrible day when the egg of Midragur hatches, will be the end of the world."

He popped the eggshells apart.

Hikaru jumped.

Shard laughed and the dragonet shrieked, romping away in long, rolling leaps around the chamber.

"I am Midragur!" he cried, his wild laughter echoing around and around the chamber like bird calls. The loud, overwhelming sound of joy smoothed a balm over Shard's heart. "I am the dragon made of stars!"

When the echoes of laughter faded, Shard's ears twitched back and forth at a strange sound. No, not a sound. A lack of sound. He angled his head to peer out of the crystal walls. He still saw the dark, stalking shadows of the wyrms, but they were silent.

Chilled, Shard wondered if they'd fallen silent to hear Hikaru's laughter. Shard watched him playing, coiling around his own eggshell as Midragur, then "hatching" the egg as Shard had done, and rolling away into oblivion at the end of the world.

Amaratsu had hoped that somehow her son would help to form peace with her wrathful cousins in the Winderost. If they fell silent in the face of his laughter, perhaps that could be a start.

"The Nameless shall know themselves," Shard whispered, watching Hikaru turn his eggshell around to hatch it again. "And the Voiceless will once again speak…"

The boom and crack of a wyrm's roar split the dark. Shard flinched, the ground shuddered and tiny bits of eggshell skipped across the chamber. Hikaru fell still, then cast a petulant glare upward, his luminous eyes narrowed to slits.

We have to escape, Shard thought, bleakly following the black dragonet's gaze.

Hikaru reared up on his hind legs, flaring his narrow wings to their full length, and bellowed at the shadows outside.

"I AM MIDRAGUR!"

A shock thrilled down Shard's spine. He could only stand, amazed.

"I am the mountain born, son of the earth, son-of-Amaratsu of the Sunland! I stand with the Summer King, the mighty Shard of Sun, and I don't fear you!"

Hope and worry curled in Shard's chest. Somehow, Hikaru was learning courage, if only from the songs they sang. *The mighty Shard of Sun*. Amaratsu had told Shard he seemed like a shard of sunlight in the cave, when he couldn't remember his own name. He'd told Hikaru all of it. All that had passed. How large and powerful Shard must seem to him now. How small and pathetic he would seem, soon, when they faced the large world outside.

To Shard's surprise, the roars fell silent for a few heartbeats again, perhaps in shock that any sound came from the crystal at all.

A rumble shook the cavern, but it was not wyrms.

"Earthquake!" Hikaru cried, and laughed as if thrilled, perhaps thinking he'd caused it.

Shard looked at the ground as the tremor grew, shaking the crystal chamber so that the seam where it met the ground rattled, but it didn't move from its place. He feared what the quakes might mean, since the Horn of Midragur had once been a volcano.

The ground stilled. Then, as if fueled by the knowledge that Hikaru was growing strong within, the wyrms shrieked and fell upon the chamber, smashing claws and horns against it, biting, ramming, to no avail.

Shard sat slowly, eyeing the walls, and the shallow groove he'd dug. Hikaru crouched a moment more, wings wide, jaws open in a low hiss. Another wyrm smashed its body against the chamber. Hikaru winced and fell back, folded his wings and slunk over to Shard, twining up to coil around him and perch on his shoulders as he'd done when he was smaller.

Shard braced against his weight even though he was lighter than he looked, like a bird or gryfon, his bones light as any flying creature. Shard didn't discourage him, wanting the dragon to feel safe as long as he could.

"I am the star dragon," Hikaru said again, his coils loose and gentle around Shard's wings and chest, his delicate claws nervously combing the feathers of Shard's neck. Shard closed his eyes, letting Hikaru's voice soothe out all others in his memory, the dragon coiled warm around Shard like the stars around the earth.

"I am Midragur," whispered Hikaru. "And Shard, you are the world."

A nightmare.

Shard knew it wasn't real, yet could not fly out of it. He veered through a chaos of wings, talons, and massive snapping jaws, the wyrms smashing into the towers and arches of the Dawn Spire, killing. Black feathers rained around him and he shouted for his uncle. He shouted for Stigr, then for Asvander, for Brynja. For a moment the ruddy gryfess winged beside him, and his heart thrilled, beating hard, but when she looked at him, her pale golden eyes only condemned.

He thought he saw Kjorn, below, sprinting across the plain with a pack of painted wolves behind him.

He screamed for Tyr to intervene, begged for the sun to rise. A sharp, high pitched voice answered him, calling his name.

Shard rolled and bumped into a warm, scaled body.

Hikaru loomed over him, wings hunched around them both in a protective mantle.

The world seemed to tilt and reel as Shard found his breath. Real wyrms, not his nightmare, screamed out in the dark and beyond them, the silent, false sky glowing with splashes of the glowworms.

Shard lay on his side, panting, staring up at Hikaru, now the size of a mountain cat—much larger than a gryfon fledge. His length made him seem larger. When he saw that Shard was awake, he lowered from his crouch to coil his body in a circle around him.

"What did you dream?" His voice flicked like a winter wind, warming toward a new depth. Shard yearned to hear the accent of the Sunland, Amaratsu's warm accent, but Hikaru had learned his speaking from Shard, and his speech was the half-lilted, rough burr of a gryfon. "You were crying out so loudly I thought the wyrms had broken in."

Shard shut his eyes. "I dreamed the battle at the Dawn Spire, when the wyrm cut down my uncle." He stood slowly, stretching inside Hikaru's coil. "Or maybe it was a battle to come."

"I hope not." Hikaru loosed a strained chuckle. "It sounded horrible."

"It was," Shard agreed, closing his eyes briefly as he remembered Stigr, motionless in the red mud.

"I'm glad you're awake," Hikaru said, averting his gaze and seeming, Shard thought, to purposefully change the subject. "I want to show you something." Hikaru slipped out of his coil, and Shard realized he was losing some of his youthful awkwardness, coming into the strength and grace of his delicate bones and his serpentine body. He tried to determine if it had only been another day or if he was losing track of time entirely.

"What is it?" Shard followed him to the crystal wall, to the shallow groove Shard had managed to create by wearing his talons dull.

Hikaru crouched, and, his eyes on Shard, dug his paws against the dirt and rock.

"Don't," Shard said quickly. "I know you want to help, but let me. You'll wear your claws dull and then where would we be? Hikaru…"

He trailed off as Hikaru's gaze became sly. He held up a paw, full of dirt and rock, then dropped the dirt to the ground. Where Shard struggled to carve the shallowest groove in the ground, Hikaru dug steadily. Easily, he scooped another paw full of dirt, and another. Shard stared, then grasped one of the dragon's forelegs, holding it up to examine the claws.

In the false star light they gleamed, sharp as shaved obsidian.

"I think," Hikaru murmured with suppressed delight, "my talons are stronger than yours now."

"I think you're right," Shard breathed. He'd been a fool. Of course Hikaru's claws would be sharper, stronger, and Shard needn't have been so protective.

"We can escape," Hikaru said quietly, his gaze moving to the dark beyond the walls.

"Yes," said Shard. "Let's fill the hole again. I don't want the wyrms to suspect. Not all of them leave when they hunt. A few stay, to wait, but they do sleep. We'll wait for them to sleep, and dig more." He pressed his own talons to the rock, relieved and then terrified. He shivered, brightening his voice. "Are you ready for the rest of the world, Hikaru?"

"Yes." Every little pointed fang showed. "I'm ready for everything."

4

MOURNING

"Only the long day brings rest
Only the dark of night, dawn.
When the First knew themselves, the wise will say
They took their Names to the Sunlit Land
But their Voice in the wind sings on."

GRYFON AND WOLF VOICES ROSE with the gusts of winter wind on the smallest, barren island of the Silver Isles, called Black Rock. Snow covered most of the surface of the isle, which was true to its namesake. On a high slope amid a half ring of broken boulders stood an odd gathering, a mix of Vanir, Aesir, half-blooded gryfons born from each, and several wolves from the Star Isle.

Caj stood at the back of the gathering, more keenly aware than ever how his feathers stood out against the snow, unnatural in that land—unnatural in any land, feathers the blazing hue of a sea in summer. Other Aesir stood just as bright, their feathers somehow divinely or sorcerously stained in outlandish hues. Supposedly it was a sign of their right to rule, their forefathers' victory in a war with

28

dragons at the bottom of the world. Caj had begun to doubt, and wondered if anything that he'd ever been told was true.

"Einarr's voice will sing on." Ragna's declaration carried across the wind, and Caj shuddered at the sight of her. Gone was the false humility, the meekness, the quiet Widow Queen. Standing before the gathering now was the ruling regent, proud and powerful as the moon. She commanded the Vanir of the Sun Isle until their king returned.

Until Shard returned.

And what will I be then? Caj wondered, unsure how his nest-son felt about him, in his deep heart. When first he'd heard that Shard survived his plunge into the sea, he'd felt relief and joy. Now, only doubt. Everything was doubt.

Ragna called out the other names, those who had fallen that winter, either to starvation, the cold, or the final clash with the mad Red King. Caj lowered his gaze to behold the bodies laid out in the snow, their wings stretched out as if they might, at any moment, lift from the snow and fly to the Sunlit Land. Pitiful keening made his ears twitch, and he looked over furtively to see Einarr's widowed mate, white Astri, huddled between her wingsister Kenna, and Einarr's mother, a full-blooded Aesir.

Caj looked away before any of them lifted their eyes to see him. He had failed the pride, failed to restrain his own wingbrother, and now they stood singing songs of mourning for the dead.

Sigrun pressed to his side, offering wordless reassurance. Caj shifted his wing against his mate, attempting comfort, then flinched at the pain. Hard mud and splint still bound his wing to form, the break not yet fully healed. He'd had to walk, following Sigrun and a wolf through the labyrinth of underground tunnels that connected all the islands. At least Sigrun had walked with him. At least he hadn't borne the humiliation of being ground bound alone.

His gaze flicked to the wolves on the far side of the group. If not for them, he too would be among the dead.

Ragna finished her recognition of the fallen—Einarr, another elder of the Vanir who'd succumbed to hunger, another who'd died in the sea attempting to fish. She turned her attention to the largest wolf of the gathering, a tall, strapping male with black shoulders that blended down into gold and cream on his chest. Two gryfon feathers, braided into the thick fur of his neck, flicked in the breeze, gray and gold.

The feathers of future kings, Caj thought, poetically, and managed not to scoff. It seemed a vain tradition, the wearing of gryfon feathers, that was growing in popularity among the younger wolves, but there were many things about wolves that Caj still didn't understand. Still, they had saved his life that winter, and had asked only for his friendship in return. He supposed he didn't need to understand them completely to befriend them. His sense of honor begged tolerance and curiosity for their ways, rather than disdain.

Ragna mantled to the young wolf king. "We thank you, Great Hunter, for attending our farewell. It honors our fallen. We hope you'll join us for feasting on the Sun Isle. We know your hunting has been not much better than ours on land, but now that we've returned to the sea, we eat well."

Ahanu, the wolf king, dipped his head.

Ragna cast a look to several fledges, who straightened to attention, then with her nod they trotted away to fetch something from behind the tall boulders at Ragna's back. "And we also offer you a gift."

Ahanu raised his head, as did the other wolves. The fledges reappeared from behind the boulder, dragging heavy pelts. Wolf pelts. Ahanu's gaze drifted to them, then back to Ragna's face, neutral, reserving judgment.

"The act of skinning was a desecration of your fallen kin," Ragna said, her gaze slashing over the Aesir gryfons in the gathering. "We return these to you to lay to rest as you will. All those who fell under the conquerors' reign."

She will never stop punishing us, Caj thought, meeting her gaze when it swept by him. He wondered how Shard would act when he returned— if he did return—if he would work toward restoration and harmony. He had grown up with the Aesir, after all. It was, apparently, what his true father had wanted, for Shard to be raised among the Aesir as a brother, so that when he learned his birthright, he could bring peace to the prides. Privately, Caj thought Baldr a coward, leaving his son a legacy he himself couldn't bring to pass.

I made him strong, Caj thought, a sense of injustice heating his chest. *I lied to Sverin and to Per, and took him under my own wing as my son, even if he never recognized it.*

If Shard thought that justice would mean exiling Aesir who had made the Silver Isles their home, or more likely, kill them, Caj knew it would only be the vengeance of war. But, when he thought more reasonably about it, he couldn't see Shard giving an order like that.

He wasn't so sure about Ragna.

Caj couldn't read wolf faces well, but thought Ahanu's looked deeply troubled at the sight of the skins, but moved by the gesture nonetheless.

"Thank you," murmured Ahanu. After a moment, as if he listened to some suggestion from the wind on the rocks, he said, "Let them rest here." His gaze searched the face of the Widow Queen, then drifted to each wolf and gryfon gathered. "Let it all rest here. All that has passed. Black Rock is a place for the dead. Let our enmity be dead, here."

The fledges exchanged glances, then respectfully bore the wolf skins to lay beside the dead gryfons. Caj shifted his feet, chilled without the warm down of a Vanir.

A waste, all of it. A dead wolf had no use for its skin and they'd done better lining gryfon nests.

But then, he reasoned, *how would I feel to know that my father's feathers lined a wolf den?*

The wolves raised their voices, and the gryfons shifted uncomfortably as the long, low notes soared through the air. Caj wondered how many, wolf or gryfon, would actually lay their prejudice to rest on that black isle. He'd had to leave his in the snows of Star Island, that night he'd awoken among caring wolves to find that they'd saved his life.

"Let us return," Ragna said. "Those who wish to learn fishing, or still remember the ways and would help me, come to the Star Cliff. Others, shelter and keep warm. I fear another storm brews."

With that dismissal, Ragna opened her wings and bounded into the sky. The fledges followed, eager for the adventure of the seashore and the strange art of hunting fish, as did several of the old Vanir. Caj noted, with interest, that Einarr's mother left with them, after a last comforting word to Astri.

A coldness grew in Caj's chest, the tight, horned discomfort of unfinished business.

The pride was well in wing, sorted out enough that Caj needn't worry about anyone starving, nor fights breaking out. The Aesir who were left followed his daughter, Thyra, who carried Kjorn's heir in her belly. The Vanir followed Ragna, Shard's true mother. Though tensions and uncertainty strained them, Caj felt confident there would be no violence.

It was time. He took a deep breath, hoping it wasn't too late.

"Will you make the rounds with me?" Sigrun murmured, brushing fondly against his feathers. "Your presence calms the females."

She was happy, no longer torn between loyalties, relieved that she could provide the pregnant females of the pride with hearty meals of fish, though the regular hunting remained poor. A healer's dream, Caj thought. Peace time, good hunting. He wished he could feel at peace, too.

Perhaps soon.

When he didn't answer, she drew back to look at him. He studied her dove-brown feathers, her face, an older, more refined version of Thyra's, her brown eyes strained from long years of worry. "What is it?"

"I won't be going back to the nesting cliffs with you."

Sometimes, he thought she could see inside his thoughts. Her expression darkened. "What are you planning? Your wing isn't fully healed. Where are you going?"

"Some of this is my doing, Sigrun. I have to make right what I can."

"You have. We're at peace!"

"Not all of us," he said quietly, his gaze lifting to the sky.

Her gaze followed his, and she drew a sharp breath. "No. Leave it be. It's folly, it's too dangerous. He's witless and mad with grief, my mate, please, it's too dangerous. There's a reason that Ragna has not sent warriors after him. Let him return to you instead, if he ever comes back to his right mind."

Caj rounded on her, raising his wings sternly. "What would you do, if it were Ragna? I don't forget Sverin's sins and mistakes. But I also can't forget that he's my wingbrother, my friend, and that I also left him alone and I lied. What part I played in his madness, I'll never know. We all have mistakes to accept."

"You're too good for him," she whispered. A few gryfons paused to watch their argument openly, then, at Caj's sharp look, they moved along, either to walk with the wolves or lift into the sky. Sigrun butted her head against his chin. "Please..."

"I'm going to find him," Caj vowed, ears swiveling forward in determination. "On whatever isle he shelters, or out at sea, or if he flies all the way back to our homeland. I cannot leave my wingbrother again, just as you would never betray Ragna." He drew back to meet her eyes, firm. "I stood by you while you remained loyal to her."

It was the right thing to say, though he felt it was cheating. She looked struck, then the cool, controlled look of the healer stole over her face. "Then, I'll come with you—"

"No."

Her hackle feathers ruffed slowly, showing her displeasure.

"My mate," Caj murmured. "You see the sense of it. The females of the pride need you. And it's better if I'm alone. If Sverin is witless, he would see two gryfons coming to attack. If he's not, he sees you, who he...who..."

"He hates," Sigrun supplied, matter-of-fact.

"Yes. And you're not to send anyone else, either." At her incredulous look he added, "I know it would be faster. But say someone spies him from the air, he could see and be gone, or attack. He sees only enemies, only threat. I'm his wingbrother. I have a chance, and I won't risk anyone else in this."

She was quiet for a moment, and Caj could nearly hear her trying to think of another way in. She almost found it. "What about Halvden?"

Caj flexed his talons against the snow and rock, a growl bubbling in his throat. "I would be very glad to meet Halvden again."

She wasn't impressed. "How will you search, then? You can't fly yet."

"I'll use the tunnels to reach the different islands. The wolves are happy enough to lead us through."

After another moment looking grim, he watched her expression relax. She realized, he knew, that he'd been planning to go ever since he learned that Sverin had flown, mad and Nameless, away from the pride.

She reached up to run talons gently over his mending wing. "Be cautious." Her voice rose in pitch, trying too hard to sound light. "I won't have my good work go to waste. I would hate to have to break your wing again."

Caj laughed weakly and began to lift his wing, then thought better of it. "As would I."

Before, when they'd all thought him killed by a boar, Caj's wing had started to fuse wrong. To force it to heal correctly, Sigrun had to break it again. He would still fly again, but only if he let her splints do their work.

"I'll stay," she murmured. "But please, if it comes to a choice between danger and safety, between risk and caution—"

"Between him, and you?" Caj offered, glancing at her sidelong. Twilight dimmed the day. It would take Caj most of the night to walk, through the tunnels underneath the islands, to the next isle where he could search. It was time to get moving. "Only think what you would do in my place, and try to understand."

Sigrun looked away. She had chosen her wingsister over him, once. Surely she couldn't begrudge him this quest to find and save his wingbrother. She slipped her head under his chin and Caj nuzzled down, aware of wolf eyes on them, and the laughing calls of ravens in the distance.

"Just return to me," she whispered. "I lost you once—"

"I'll return," he promised, and savored another moment close to her before drawing away, letting the cold come between them, and walking away.

5

EARTHFIRE

S HARD PRESSED HIS EAR AGAINST the crystal and closed his eyes, listening for the faintest scratch or rumble. Hikaru, sitting behind him, peered through the ceiling of their chamber. Already his senses grew sharper than Shard's own, and Shard relied on his hearing.

"I think they're asleep," Hikaru murmured, his tail sweeping slowly across the ground. He lowered himself to a crouch on all fours, pressing his paws against the earth. "Does the ground feel warm to you, Shard?"

"It's from you, I think," Shard said quietly, pulling back from the wall. Hikaru shed warmth like a fire, and the ground had warmed steadily under their feet for the last few days. The other possibility, that the volcano was waking, wouldn't matter once they fled the mountain.

"I don't think so," Hikaru said. "I think it's something else. You said that volcanoes sometimes make earthquakes."

The short feathers between Shard's wings stood on end like wolf hackles, as if skyfire crackled near.

Nerves, he thought.

36

"It won't matter in a few moments." Shard crept to their tunnel and began drawing out the dirt as quietly as he could. "We'll be out of here soon."

"You're sure we shouldn't leave at night, while they're gone hunting?"

"No. The moment they realize we're gone, they'll hunt us all night. In the day, they won't follow. We'll have a head start."

Shard slipped his talons down through the loose dirt, and dug it back out. They'd tunneled through to the other side of the crystal wall and refilled the dirt each day so the dragons wouldn't suspect their plan. The last of their fish was gone. With Hikaru shedding heat, the air dried up and they needed water. Even if Shard had wanted to wait another day, they couldn't risk losing more strength to hunger and thirst.

"Only in the stillness the wind," Hikaru was murmuring, eyes closed, "only from ice the flame."

"Are you ready?" Shard asked as he pulled dirt from the tunnel. "We'll have to be swift."

Quietly Hikaru answered, "I'm ready." Hikaru's claws clicked together. A new habit, a nervous habit of threading his digits together and wringing his paws. "Shard?"

Shard paused at the note of fear in his voice, and wriggled back out of the tunnel to meet his gaze.

"What is it?" He shook dirt from his head. "Don't worry, we have a plan."

Hikaru's gaze drifted up. "What if…what if I can't fly? What if I'm not strong enough?"

Shard flicked his ears, moved by the earnest, nervous expression on the young dragon's face. He trotted forward and butted his head against the scaled chest. When Hikaru sat up on his haunches, as he was then, he already stood a good half-length taller than a gryfon.

"Never fear, Amaratsu's son." He drew back, opening his wings to draw Hikaru's gaze back to him. "We are born to fly."

"Born to fly," Hikaru echoed. He nodded, his gaze locked on Shard's face. "Born to it." His breath seemed short as he opened his wings.

The ground trembled under them and Shard looked down, perking his ears.

"That's not wyrms," Hikaru murmured, a serpentine hiss creeping into his voice. At once, Shard realized his hind paws and forefeet did feel hot, as if the subterranean floor had baked for a day under summer sun.

The ground shuddered. Then a larger tremor made Shard stumble, and Hikaru's eggshell rolled across the ground. The scent of hot rock and sulfur suffused Shard's next breath.

"Bright Tyr," he breathed. "It's—"

"Earthfire!" Hikaru's tail whipped and he perked his ears at the ground. "Shard—"

"Out, now!"

Shard dove into the tunnel, talons flailing to throw dirt out of his way. He broke through to the other side and shoved his head out, shaking it free of dirt. He forced his breaths to stay shallow and silent. The wyrms slumbered on, at least a dozen of them, great hulking shapes ringing Amaratsu's body. Shard had hoped for fresh air, but their thick, reptilian scent drenched him and the cavern felt hot and thick. Something nudged his rump and Shard wriggled forward to give Hikaru room.

"Ready?" Shard whispered, and lifted his beak to point out their escape. Hikaru slithered out beside him, shook off dirt, and peered around. High at the top, far away, gleamed a narrow beacon of sunlight. A dull-gray, male wyrm shifted, loosing a giant huff of air. The ground shivered and, within the crystal chamber, Shard thought he heard cracking stone.

"Shard, I think it's going to erupt. The air smells bad." Hikaru looked around at the hulking beasts. "If they don't wake, they'll die."

A low thrumming and a great wash of heat made Shard lift his talons. "We have to fly, Hikaru. We have to fly, now. They'll wake at the commotion and they can leave through the tunnel."

"The heat," Hikaru mumbled, his gaze darting around the sleeping wyrms. "I think the heat lulls them."

"Hikaru!" Shard snapped. All around, the great wyrms shifted, but, like the sick, drugged by herb or weariness, they did not wake. *True reptiles,* Shard thought, *lulled by heat or cold.* "Follow me."

Shard lifted to his hind legs and leaped nimbly into the air, wings nearly as silent as an owl's. A sense of freedom and joy shimmered from his heart to his wingtips to leave the ground, to push down the air and feel the stretch of feather and sinew. For a little time, he'd almost forgotten what it was to fly.

Hikaru bared his teeth in excitement and watched Shard rise, then crouched, opening his wings to fly for the first time.

Then the earth exploded.

A blast of air and noxious gas knocked Hikaru against the crystal wall.

"Don't breathe!" Shard ordered, diving to land hard next to the dragon. Hikaru clamped his jaws shut, eyes huge. "Are you—"

"Not hurt," Hikaru grunted, and flexed his wings.

Panicked, Shard looked past Hikaru into the crystal chamber. An second explosion of gas rocked Amaratsu's form. Earthfire bubbled up from a widening crack in the ground inside the chamber. A rush of sulfur, air, and fire shot straight up and smashed against the crystal dragon.

The heat shattered Amaratsu's body.

Twinkling scales and ice-sharp fragments shot in every direction and sent Shard and Hikaru rolling away. Shard grabbed at Hikaru's legs, curving his wings to shield the dragon.

"Jump jump *jump!*" Shard lunged into the air, wings beating hard. Hikaru followed, liquid fire lashing at his heels. Lulled by heat, the wyrms slumbering on the ground shifted and growled but didn't stir. Poisoned air rolled toward them. Where the crystal form had rested, now glowed a long crack of roiling lava. Shard gulped for the cleaner air above the wyrms. His wings, at first stretching and working with joy and relief, threatened to cramp. Hikaru bobbed beside him, staring at the mess below.

The crack in the earth engorged with fire and sulfur.

"Follow me!" Shard commanded. "Don't panic." He circled Hikaru once as the young dragon struggled first against the dead air of the cave, then the strange currents of heat created by the fire below. "Work your wings smoothly, pretend it's a spring day—" Shard gagged against the noxious fumes of the earthfire. The hole of sunlight in the mountain seemed leagues and leagues away. With a glance over he saw that Hikaru was managing to figure out his wings and a good rhythm to undulate his long body, and looked as if he could swim through the air. "Don't look down. Only the sky…"

"The sky," Hikaru gasped, but he did look down, his gaze raking over the Winderost wyrms. Shard banked, turning a long arc to look down also, and a knot twisted his chest. Hikaru beat his wings hard, looking up to meet Shard's gaze, and Shard knew they had the same thought. The wyrms couldn't die like this. No creature deserved that.

"We'll warn them," he called to Hikaru, his voice pitched in attempt only to carry to the young dragon. "But let's get a little higher—"

"Yes," Hikaru agreed, and flapped up to follow Shard.

They were halfway to the top and escape and Shard glanced back again to see smoke pluming and fire splitting from the earth.

"Hikaru, now!" Shard loosed an eagle cry that echoed around the cavern and Hikaru dipped below Shard, and his deepening voice boomed.

"Cousins! Wake up! Wake up or die!"

A wyrm stirred, blinking up at them in confusion. Then a splattering of earthfire splashed his wings. His roar shook the cavern. He looked up again, saw Shard and Hikaru, and screamed his rage. The others woke in a daze, panicked by the liquid fire around them, and lumbered to their feet. Enormous, leathery wings flared and flapped and the wyrms rose in a furious swarm.

"There," Shard panted to Hikaru. "They're awake. They've got a chance. *Fly. Now.*"

"Yes," Hikaru gasped, and they turned together. The hole gleamed closer, a circle of sunlight.

Below, the writhing mass of wyrms split toward the tunnel halfway up the cave wall, and others, toward Shard, Hikaru, and the sunlight at the top of the cavern.

"Faster!" Shard shouted, as the wyrms with their powerful wings lunged higher, closing the deep gap.

Hikaru shrieked with the terror and thrill of it and shot up and ahead, wings pumping fast and deep like a swan.

Shard gave his wings a mighty stroke—but claws snapped shut around his tail and yanked him down. Long days and nights of fighting practice made him relax his body rather than struggle. He let himself fall with a battle scream onto the face of the dragon who'd grabbed him.

Hikaru wheeled in a circle. "Shard!"

"Fly!" Shard commanded, raking talons against the leathery paw that gripped him. A heavy, sour scent washed him. Then, odd familiarity. Shard's gaze locked on the wyrm's, then flicked down the length of her. Dark brown hide. A dead, baleful stare.

Stigr, cut down by a lashing spade tail.

"You," Shard hissed. His feathers stood on end in fury and he sank every talon and hind claw and the razor edge of his beak into the stone-hard hide.

Her angry roar sang in Shard's bones.

A wild, higher, musical shriek followed it. In a daze, overcome by the stench of death in the dragon's jaws and the fumes from the earthfire below, Shard saw Hikaru diving.

"Release him!" Hikaru slammed into the wyrm's shoulder, slashing his talons through the leather hide. Dark blood welled and dripped down toward the earthfire explosions below. Her grip loosened and Shard broke free, soaring up to gain height for a dive. The wyrm swung her freed claws around to lash at Hikaru. He yelped and flapped straight up, shooting quick as a salmon through water. Claws caught his hind leg, sending a few black scales sprinkling down like rain, but he jerked free.

Shard dove to attack, but the wyrm tore away with a sudden, surprised bark of pain.

Shard flared to a hard stop in confusion, to hover between the wyrm and Hikaru. Blood dripped from the young dragon's hind leg, blood that steamed even in the hot air. Shard saw with shock that blood had splashed in a crescent under one of the wyrm's eyes, and every spot it touched now gleamed a rich, iridescent red.

"Bright with dragon's blood," Shard couldn't help but choke out the words he'd heard before.

She dropped and wheeled away, clutching her eye as if it burned, and melded into the tumult of wyrms that blustered toward a tunnel on the far wall of the cavern.

Shard grasped a tendril of clean air and caught himself, flapping hard. Hikaru winged in beside him.

"Shard—"

"I'm fine," Shard panted. "Are you? You're bleeding..." But it looked as if Hikaru's wound had already closed and begun to scar.

"I think I'm fine too."

Shard looked toward the fleeing wyrms at the far wall, and those wheeling in confusion around and below them. A fiber of him longed to chase down the cold she-wyrm and avenge his uncle or die trying.

Likely the latter, he knew grimly, and Stigr would not want that.

He turned and soared high, Hikaru close behind. "Up, up, now! The mountain!"

Earthfire swelled and shot up in great geysers, and the air grew thick with poison. The Winderost wyrms flocked madly around the cavern, some crowding toward the top entrance with Shard and Hikaru, others for the tunnel through which they and Shard had first come.

Hikaru's flight was awkward but they were still smaller and swifter than the wyrms. They raced up, and up. The wyrms' breath heated the air behind them and the poisonous earthfire swelled.

Their escape beckoned, a gleaming crack of sky.

For half a breath Shard feared it wouldn't be large enough....

Then they burst through into cool, open air with a feather's breadth to spare, breaking rocks loose, and the glowworms that clung to the roof of the mountain.

The frosty air shocked Shard's body and sunlight dazzled pain over his eyes.

Beside him, Hikaru shrieked, blinded, thrashing, assaulted by cold and light as if he were hatching all over again.

Shard fumbled for and grabbed the dragon's foreleg. "Close your eyes."

Hikaru whimpered agreement. They wheeled together, blind, flying higher and higher in the already high, thin air. The sudden rush of clean, cold wind knocked the blackness and stench of the cavern away from them. Shard tugged Hikaru to follow the scent of trees, gliding back down. They had to fly in lower air or risk falling unconscious, for they had emerged at the very peak of the Horn of Midragur.

They soared down along the mountain face, high enough to be safe, low enough to take great gulps of cool, clean wind. Shard's eyes streamed but he kept them shut against the daze of sunlight on white snow.

"I want to see it," Hikaru panted.

"Soon," Shard promised, and released his grip. "Follow my voice. This way!"

The mountain thundered behind them. They heard the wyrms of the Winderost break through the top of the mountain and scream in their own pain at the sunlight. Shard didn't dare look back, didn't dare open his eyes yet. The sun would stop the wyrms. Or the mountain would.

"Don't stop," he called to Hikaru. "This way!"

They turned from the dazzling sun, banking in a long turn until Shard felt sun at their backs, and soared nightward, leaving the erupting mountain and the raging wyrms behind. Shard waited to hear roars again, but they remained in the distance. He kept their flight nightward. Windward, he knew, lay the Dawn Spire and more problems than he had answers for. They wouldn't go there. Not yet. Shard had no plan beyond fleeing the mountain and getting Hikaru to safety.

After another moment, the blaze beyond his eyelids darkened as clouds passed over the sun. Shard risked peeking, found his eyes beginning to adjust, and studied the land below them.

Out in front of them and as far as he could see nightward, the land slowly crawled away from the desert of the Winderost and rolled back into grassy foothills lined with juniper and pine forest. Shard squinted, scanning the far horizon. When he'd first flown there he'd been lost, Nameless and bent only on survival and following a small inner tug toward Amaratsu. He hadn't paid attention to the land. He did now.

Far starward, beyond the Horn, rose another low mountain range, white with snow, and a cold wind buffeted them from that quarter. Nightward, far in the distance, it looked as through the land grew more lush, wooded and hilly. Windward, and dawnward, lay the Winderost, plains of grass and red rock, canyons and the ruined Outlands where the wyrms usually dwelled. Shuddering, he turned his gaze away. They would fly nightward.

The sun still stood within first-quarter mark. The wyrms would be distracted by the volcano and the sunlight, and would have no time to pursue until night, if at all. Shard thought of the she-wyrm, wondered if she'd escaped—if he would have a chance to avenge his uncle or if the mountain had claimed her.

Wind buffeted them from all sides. Wind, sunlight, and a view of endless land.

After a moment, when the fresh wind hit his face again, Shard laughed in hysterical relief, brushing other worries aside. He looked over to Hikaru, feeling triumphant.

"So, now we..." He closed his beak slowly, watching the young dragon's face.

He stared at everything, everything, eyes huge and glowing in the light. With every breath the black dragon took in the bright sky, the roll of sweet scented trees and the brown, waving grass, the ring of white mountains on the starward horizon. He looked hungrily in every direction, gasping, ears perking, his talons stretching now and then as if to point out a new wonder. Shard looked again, and through the dragon's awe, saw everything for the first time.

"It's even better than I thought it would be," Hikaru whispered.

"The land?"

"The *world*." Hikaru swiveled to look again at the sky, the spires of trees, the pale light slanting on the sides of the mountains. "Everything you said is true."

A warm tightness closed Shard's throat, the same as the day Hikaru had first broken out of his eggshell. "Yes. And welcome to it, Amaratsu's son."

On impulse, they glanced back at the Horn of Midragur.

They saw that it wasn't clouds that had covered the sun, but smoke and ash. Shard stared at the column of heavy, white and black clouds that crowded into the sky. Now and then red fountains leaped and fell from new cracks in the slopes, earthfire splashing out of the depths. He couldn't see any of the Winderost wyrms, and a strange part of him hoped they'd all escaped. Bleakly he thought of the Dawn Spire, but was sure in his heart that their sky would only be dimmed, that they were nearly four days' flight from the mountain and would see no poison or fire.

Ash and smoke closed over the sun. "We have to keep going," Shard said, drawing Hikaru's attention. "We have to fly as far as we possibly can before you tire."

"I could fly forever!" Hikaru beat his wings, soaring around Shard in a loop, then settling alongside him again. He seemed to have grown even since leaving the cavern, as if his body knew he had more room.

"Let's hope so." Shard laughed as the cold breeze picked up, giving them a strong tailwind. They lifted high again, to cover more ground, and Hikaru followed him without question, nightward. Shard harkened to a small, quiet instinct that drew him away from the mountain, also away from the Dawn Spire and the wyrms, away from all of it, as the sky darkened and ash flurried around their wings like snow.

6

SHARD OF MEMORY

KJORN WATCHED AS ROK PEERED at the horizon, making a low, grumbling noise.

They'd kept Kjorn bound, trussed like a fly in a spider's web, with long ropes of seaweed tying his wings to his body, and separate binds wrapping his forefeet and hind feet together, respectively. Unable to fly with him bound thus, they all traveled on foot, and dragged Kjorn across the ground using more seaweed tied in knots to the main binding on his wings.

For days they'd trekked roughly windward across the barren coast, beset by cold rain and salty wind. It reminded Kjorn of spring in the Silver Isles. *Spring. Thyra...* All the females of his pride would whelp in spring, of course, but only one of them was his mate. Only one had made him vow, under threat of talon, to return in time to behold the birth of his kit.

Kjorn managed to flop onto his belly and see what the poacher saw. A thick haze hung over the far, distant horizon, strangely pale and dark at the same time, more like fog than cloud. His heart seemed to thicken in his chest.

"Storm?" The female, whose name, Kjorn had gathered without official introduction, was Frida, walked up beside Rok and cocked her head.

"No," said Rok in a low voice, and his feathers prickled up.

"Earthfire," Kjorn offered, and the other male gryfon of the band, Fraenir, growled a warning.

Kjorn snapped his beak in return, weary of being treated as a lowly prisoner, as a fledge who should remain silent. *This land is my birthright. My great grandfather's father ruled the Dawn Spire and all the gryfon clans of the Winderost.*

So the elder Aesir in the Silver Isles had told him. More than his father had ever told him. Sverin's version of their leaving the Winderost, since Kjorn's kithood, was that they'd left with honors to conquer new lands and claim them in the name of the Aesir. Now he knew the truth. Kajar had lost his war with the dragons, stolen what treasures he could, and brought a blight upon his kingdom in the form of Nameless, Voiceless, terrorizing beasts. Per, Sverin, and all those whose families bore the curse had fled the beasts to live in exile.

My birthright, Kjorn thought. He shifted his talons against the tight seaweed binds. He'd hoped as it dried it would become brittle, but the long ropes only grew rubbery and tough, and if any of the band of poachers caught him gnawing at it, either he received no food, or a sharp cuff to the side of the head that left him reeling.

"Rok," Fraenir began, in a note of complaint. "His Highness won't stay still."

But Rok was still gazing at the far horizon. "Earthfire, you say. Yes. An eruption. I've never seen the like."

"What does it mean?" Frida sounded breathless, and opened her wings.

"Nothing," Kjorn said, shortly. Like his father, he put little stock in omens—or perhaps his father did, and hid the superstition from him. Kjorn didn't know anymore. He felt he didn't know his father at all, had never known him, and swallowed a bitter taste. Kjorn *had* followed one sign. A starfire sign that led him to the Winderost.

Or maybe it was only Shard's sign, he thought. *Maybe I stole that from him too, as I stole the Silver Isles.* Perhaps so, but he had come to make things right, in his once-homeland, with his wingbrother, if he ever found him again.

"Volcanoes erupt," Kjorn went on when Frida cast him an irritated look. "It's the way of the earth."

"The Horn of Midragur," Rok murmured, as if none of them were there. "Has to be. It hasn't erupted in…well." He faced them, raising his wings. "At least an Age. Not in the history I know of. Perhaps it is a sign."

"Of what?" Fraenir asked, ears perked.

"Who knows. The world's end, maybe." He shrugged his wings, as if he were either prepared for such an event, or unconcerned about it. "Let's move on. I can see His Highness is growing weary."

He strode forward, looped seaweed around his own chest, and tossed some to Fraenir. In that way, they dragged Kjorn across the ground. The thick ropes of seaweed cushioned Kjorn from the worst of it, though the gryfons didn't take much care to avoid large rocks or uneven footing. Frida walked alongside to make sure Kjorn didn't try to chew through the binds. When he tried to talk to her, to reason, she only huffed and looked away. It seemed a lot of work and trouble. Kjorn wondered what Rok thought he could gain.

He ducked his head as they dragged him over a series of short, sharp rocks.

They traveled windward along the coast and Kjorn lost track of the sunmark under the cold gray cover of rain. He tried to track his surroundings and how far they had gone, but much of it just rolled on in wind-swept cliff tops that reminded him of the Sun Isle.

After a rest at one point near mid-day, Kjorn managed to roll to his other side and instead of the inland scenery, he watched the sea bump and drag by. Eventually the cliff top sloped down in a hill that graduated into a long, sandy shoreline.

It was then that the painted wolf returned.

Kjorn had nearly forgotten about him. Upon hearing the wolf's greeting warble, Fraenir dropped his seaweed vine and flapped away to meet him. Kjorn wriggled, managing to prop up on his side, and watched with interest as the wolf and gryfon greeted like pride mates, or wingbrothers, pressing their shoulders together and laying their heads briefly on the other's back.

"Lazy oaf," Rok snapped, stumbling forward against Kjorn's dead weight. Kjorn took note of the fact that Rok couldn't haul him on his own. He hadn't had a chance to stand up next to Rok but suspected he was taller than the rogue, and heavier. If he could take leadership of the bedraggled band, it could be a great help. But it had to happen before they reached wherever they were going, before Rok traded off Kjorn to whoever he planned to meet.

The elder Aesir back in the Silver Isles had reminded Kjorn of the borders, the different claims and boundaries. Once, they'd all been united under a single rule, a single bloodline of powerful kings that stretched back to the first gryfon to claim a kingship in the Second Age. Kjorn's bloodline. But with Kajar's quest came the madness of the dragons, the Dawn Spire splintered, and the clans broke away and returned to their own lands, under their own rule. Kjorn couldn't count on a warm welcome anywhere, not even the Dawn Spire. Perhaps especially not the Dawn Spire. But if Shard had gone there, then Kjorn would too.

As Rok, Fraenir and the wolf exchanged news, Frida watched over Kjorn. He sat still, thinking. If loyalties and schemes and tier-climbing and poachers infested the Winderost, then Rok thought he could take advantage of Kjorn's tie to the Dawn Spire. As near to the coast as they were, Kjorn could think of only one place the poacher would be headed, and that was the Vanheim Shore.

What kind of gryfons dwelled there, and what link or enmity they had with the Dawn Spire, Kjorn didn't know. His father had left him nothing of his true birthright, no knowledge, no heritage. Only a false kingship in a conquered land. A creeping, hollow sense of insecurity carved its way into his chest when he realized that finding and reconciling with Shard would mean that Kjorn himself would have no true place in the Silver Isles.

If we are friends, what then? I can't still claim his land as my own.

Rather than mire in a line of dark questions, Kjorn knew it would be wiser to focus on the situation at present.

The wolf's return seemed to signal their stop for the day, and they dragged Kjorn down to a scant shelter along the shore. The rain slacked as the sky dimmed toward evening.

"We'll start fresh tomorrow," Rok declared. "Make a good impression." He stalked a quick patrol around the area, checking for rogue gryfon or other threatening scents. Fraenir and Frida left to hunt or fish, whichever yielded better food. The wolf cleaned his paws some leaps away.

Rok returned from his brief patrol and sat a wing length from Kjorn, gazing out to sea, and Kjorn watched him quietly.

"When I asked of Vanir, you mentioned Vanhar. I thought they might be the same as my friend, but I don't think so. Tell me about them."

Rok gave him an incredulous look. "For a prince, you've got very little idea what's going on."

"Tell me about them, then," Kjorn challenged.

Rok huffed and shook his feathers of drizzle. "Not my duty to tell you. I don't owe you anything."

Duty. Kjorn perked his ears. No born-and-bred poacher would use a word like duty. "That's true," Kjorn said slowly. "You don't owe me anything. But perhaps we can help each other. Will you tell me why you hate the Dawn Spire? What crime did they commit against you?"

Kjorn managed to keep his tail from twitching. He attempted Shard's method—not jumping to a conclusion but instead, hearing out the other, taking his side. In his own pride, Kjorn's word was law. Here, as far as he could see, there was no law except what gryfons made for themselves. And wolves. Feeling watched, he peered around and saw the painted wolf had stretched on his belly, his gaze locked on Kjorn. His head tilted round a fraction, as if studying a riddle.

Kjorn looked back to Rok, who appeared mildly surprised at the question. For a moment, he thought he'd broken through Rok's shell.

Then the rogue scoffed, and his tail switched back and forth. He lifted his beak to the wind, sniffing. "The usual. Nothing to concern yourself with."

"What's the usual?" Kjorn asked. "I'm trying to make a peace. We've never met, I've committed no crime against you."

"Be quiet. I've had enough of your smug voice. Windbrother," he called to the wolf, who stood and shook himself, padding over. "Watch our prince. I'm going to fish."

"I will."

Kjorn tried to catch Rok's eye again but he turned away, shoved up, and glided out over the water. For a moment Kjorn watched him. Then he sighed, and let his gaze drift along the wet shoreline.

"Son-of-Sverin."

Jolted by the address, Kjorn swiveled to stare at the wolf, eyes wide. He hadn't seen him since the day they took him prisoner, and had barely heard him speak then. "You remembered my name?"

The wolf tilted his head, the strange whorls of white and brown like snow and mud across his flashy pelt. A black mask over his face gave him a shadowed, sinister look, but his eyes gleamed bright, aware, and knowing. "Yes. I remember everything now."

Kjorn just watched him, wary, and waited for him to say more.

"The first day," said the wolf. "The first day we found you. You said you were looking for Shard."

Kjorn shifted, his blood quickening. "Yes."

"You're a friend of Shard?" the wolf asked. "The Star-sent, the wolf and lion brother?"

"Yes," Kjorn said cautiously, thinking Shard had been busy indeed. "Though we've made mistakes against each other, he was my closest friend and my wingbrother. I've come to find him and make amends. I am a friend of Shard," he confirmed again, since it was what the wolf had asked.

The wolf's gaze flicked in the direction Frida and Fraenir had gone, then toward the water, where Rok was now a distant speck over the gray waves. Kjorn's muscles bunched, ready for anything. The wolf stretched out on his belly so that his powerful jaws were a talon's breadth from Kjorn's throat.

"I am Makya, of the Serpent River pack." Dark eyes considered Kjorn's face. "I, too, am a friend of Shard, though I forgot myself for a time."

"I'm honored," Kjorn managed, smelling old meat on the wolf's teeth. "How did you know Shard?"

"I watched as he faced down a great wyrm and tried to avenge the death of my leader and pack mate, Nitara. Then fear overcame me and I forgot myself, and I ran. But now I remember," the wolf said quietly, "and I remember Shard, and I hope he survived."

Kjorn shuddered at the mention of a great wyrm, recalling a nightmarish vision he'd had earlier that winter, and tried to picture Shard standing against such a foe. Cautiously he said, "Then we are friends, you and I."

"Yes," Mayka agreed, baring his teeth wider. "Now, you must do exactly as I say."

He bent his head in, jaws opening to reveal long, sharp fangs. Kjorn flinched—then perked his ears as Makya set his teeth to the seaweed binds.

7

THE NIGHTWARD COAST

S HARD AND HIKARU HUDDLED UNDER a sprawling pine, escaping the worst of the rain. It turned out that Hikaru couldn't fly forever, though he'd done his best. It was Shard who had called a halt, when it was clear Hikaru might drop from the sky in exhaustion. Ash coated the air for leagues and leagues, though they'd flown for an entire quarter into the early afternoon. Shard caught a rabbit, and now they waited for Hikaru's wings to stop aching, and the rain to slack.

"This is delicious," the dragonet purred, again, crunching the last of the rabbit bones. Shard watched him, certain he needed five times the food. "Much better than dry fish, much better." He sat back on his haunches, licking his front toes and claws clean.

Shard watched him in a weary, mesmerized daze. Everything about him was like watching water—liquid and graceful. Or fire. Shard remembered the sight of the dragon's blood, steaming in the hot air, and how it had burned the murdering wyrm's hide bright red.

Has he grown larger? It seemed impossible.

"Thank you, Shard." Hikaru dipped his head to bump against Shard's wing.

"Of course." Shard blinked to alertness, realizing he'd almost dozed. "And don't worry. We'll find much more food." He didn't know quite where, for the forest so far had only boasted small game, but if they both hunted they'd do better.

Hikaru's eyes seemed to glow at him through the dim light, and Shard felt keenly, once again, that he did not deserve the young dragon's admiration. "I'm not worried."

Shard fluffed his wings and chuckled. "I'm glad one of us isn't. Why don't you take a little rest? I'll wake you before long, and if you feel like pressing on, we'll fly more."

"Or walk," Hikaru said, even as he rolled himself into a neat coil around Shard. He *had* grown larger. "If we really must keep moving, then I am happy to walk, and learn everything about the ground that you know." He laid down his head and shut his eyes.

Shard sat within his coils and peered out into the gray. Under the large pine the ground was dusty, dry, and cool. Gray mud, tainted by volcanic ash, slithered in rivulets around the rest of the forest floor. They did need to keep moving, to stay ahead of the wyrms if they eventually tried to follow. Shard could not lead them to the Dawn Spire again. The land starward seemed barren and inhospitable. He would follow his instinct nightward, hope it was Tyr and Tor who led him, and teach Hikaru as quickly as he could.

"Shard?" the dragon murmured. Shard looked down, but Hikaru's eyes were still closed.

"Yes," Shard said, at first thinking the dragon only wanted to be assured Shard still sat within his coils.

"I don't understand something."

"Ask anything," Shard said quietly.

A great sigh heaved the black-scaled ribs, but Hikaru's eyes remained closed. "When you spoke of meeting my mother, you said she told you the Tale of the Red Kings, the tale of Kajar that you told to me."

"Yes." Shard cocked his head, listening to the forest for danger with one ear and Hikaru with the other.

"You said you didn't understand why Kajar chose power over friendship, but then when my mother offered you the choice, you hesitated."

"Yes…" Shard remembered the moment. He looked down.

Hikaru's eyes were open now, watching him. "Why?"

Shard pressed his talons to the earth, then sat back and raised them to gently stroke Hikaru's wing. "That's a very good question. I think it sounded easy when it was happening to someone else. We think we know what we'll do in any challenge. But then when it happens…" Shard recalled multiple times he'd made decisions that may or may not have been the right decisions. Speaking to the wyrms. Lying to his wingbrother.

Releasing Sverin and diving into the sea.

Hikaru's whole body reverberated with a warm, rolling sound that mimicked a gryfon's purr as Shard combed talons through his feathers, but his gaze was intent on Shard's face, waiting for a better answer.

"When something like that happens," Shard said, "you realize it's harder to make the choice than you thought it would be. You realize all the things that could go wrong, you realize how your choice will affect other things."

Hikaru shifted, his gaze flitting out toward the rain. "You thought she might deceive you."

"Yes. In the moment she challenged me, I doubted everything. But I decided to trust her."

Hikaru raised his head so quickly that Shard jumped. He loomed over Shard, his whiskers twitching, testing the air. "I'm glad you did."

Shard chuckled, resettling his feathers. "So am I."

Hikaru's lips pulled back in fanged amusement like a wolf, then he dipped his head low, looking worried. "Shard. What are we? That is, I know that I am Amaratsu's son, but you were the one I saw when I hatched. What are we?"

Shard shifted, lowering his talons to the earth. Rain pattered on the boughs above, only a few drops slipped through to hit the ground, or their backs. "You and I?" Hikaru's head bobbed once in a nod. "Well, it wouldn't really do to call you my nest-son, although that's what gryfons do. In few months you'll be able to pick me up off the ground with one paw!"

Hikaru laughed, then the concerned expression returned.

Shard let his laughter fade. "You and I," he said firmly, "are brothers."

"Brothers," Hikaru said. Pleased with the word, he laid his head down again and for all Shard could tell, surrendered to sleep, satisfied with his new answers.

Shard remained awake in the dragonet's black coils, staring out into the rain, listening for the sound of anything, anyone, who might wish them harm.

Freed from the mountain and his primary concern of escape, his thoughts delved toward difficult things, friends he'd left behind, the choices he'd made that were wrong. He wondered what had happened to Brynja, the huntress to whom he'd offered his heart. He could see her face, bright as morning, with fierce eyes and freckles of vermillion on the pale feathers under her eyes. Sometimes, she fluffed with laughter at his wit or her wingsister's antics before returning to quiet dignity again. Vividly Shard recalled her voice, the night he had tried to pledge to her, to offer her everything he had if she would stay by his side until the end of their days. He also recalled her voice, regretful, saying it couldn't be. She had duties, and she was promised, like a rabbit pelt in a trade, to another.

But she had also spoken of caring for him.

I've fought for my family, for my islands, for my friends. I will fight for her, if I must.

He drew his talons through the pine needles, knowing that wouldn't be easy, for the gryfon who was promised to Brynja was also a friend. Asvander, First Sentinel of the Dawn Spire.

He wondered what had become of all of them—the gryfons who'd aided him and Stigr, who'd offered even to betray their own king—Valdis, Asvander, Dagny.

And Stigr. Shard closed his eyes for a moment, seeing it again. For one brief moment, his uncle laughing, triumphant in battle, then felled by the brown wyrm. His wing, sliced clean from his shoulder. They'd called healers.

Shard opened his eyes, curling his talons into the pine needles.

If they'd called healers, there was a dim, distant chance that his uncle was alive. That would be reason enough to return to the Dawn Spire. When the time was right. Shard looked down at Hikaru's peaceful face.

For the moment, he had other responsibilities, and Stigr would not want him to shirk a promise he'd made.

For three days they traveled through the expanse of forest night-ward of the Horn of Midragur. Alone, Shard would have covered twice the distance—but they went at Hikaru's pace. The young dragon flew valiantly during the day, sometimes as long as three marks of the sun before he tired or grew ravenously hungry. During the day, they flew and hunted. Shard knew the dragons of the Winderost hated the sun, or were shamed by Tyr, and wouldn't travel during the day. At night, he and the young dragon walked as far as they could before their muscles gave out and they slept until dawn.

Shard taught him the basic hunting that he knew, though he sensed that Sunland dragons, like Vanir, were built better for fishing. They found a single deer on their trek, ran it down and killed it. Shard taught Hikaru to honor any creature he killed, whether for food, or in battle.

"Do you think I will ever see a battle?" Hikaru consumed most of the deer before a mark of the sun had passed.

"I hope not." Shard ate his fill and was amazed at the dragon's appetite. His body from shoulder to rump had grown to twice the length of a gryfon, and his neck and tail stretched well beyond that. His whiskers drooped handsomely from his snout and the budding horns between his ears shone silver in sunlight.

They sat in a sunny clearing ringed by towering cedars. The forest—Shard recalled an eagle of the Winderost mentioning the Forest of Rains—boasted dense ferns, crawling greenery and bright songbirds. Shard smelled a fox trail here and there, but no wolves, no gryfons or other large predators. No wyrms.

After appearing to think about Shard's answer, Hikaru asked, "Why not? They seem exciting."

"Some creatures like to fight, and they're good at fighting." Shard thought of his rival, Halvden, who before Shard's self-exile had become a deadly foe. "Some think it's better to do everything possible to avoid a fight."

"What do you think, Shard?"

The weight of Shard's answer sat heavy in his chest, for by Hikaru's bright gaze, he knew that whatever he answered could become Hikaru's answer too.

"I think it's important not to fight for the sake of fighting."

Hikaru bobbed his head, as if that made sense. "Because you could be hurt."

"Yes. Or you could hurt another, and that's another kind of pain."

"Then," Hikaru began slowly, "if you don't fight for the sake of fighting, what do you fight for?"

The question was so innocent, yet so wise, Shard laughed, then butted his head against Hikaru's shoulder. The sunlight of the clearing felt good after the dark cave and the cold rain, the dense trees like a green cavern over their heads. "That's a good question, and no one has the truest answer."

Hikaru shook his short mane. "What do *you* fight for, Shard?"

Shard thought back. "I have fought for my honor—which isn't always worth it, depending on who you're fighting. I fight to defend the weaker, I fight for my family and my friends."

"Your gryfon pride," Hikaru said eagerly, and Shard fluffed his feathers. "Because you're a prince."

"Yes." Shard had a pride waiting for him, hoping for his return so that he could be their king. With that thought and the sun shining on him and Hikaru's gaze shining at him, he did feel like a prince, though his pride was far away. "Well, yes, that's right. My pride."

"And you fight for truth."

Shard tilted his head. "Truth?"

"Yes. You told me you hoped to find the truth of why the wyrms are angry and hateful, that you've argued for them. You fight for truth. I will, too."

"Oh, Hikaru. You're brave. Your mother hoped you could bring peace and friendship to the Winderost wyrms, but it won't be easy. They seem more interested in fighting and spreading fear, and we don't know why."

"They're angry," Hikaru said. "I wish they would say why, instead of just attacking. But I will learn the truth, with you."

Shard picked at a bit of bone from the meal. "I'll need all the help I can get. I tried to speak to them once, but they didn't listen, or they didn't understand." The stormy night came back to him, the terror, the attacking wyrms and their pursuit of him all the way to the Dawn Spire.

Hikaru's tail coiled around Shard's feet—to comfort Shard, or himself, Shard wasn't sure. "They didn't listen to me either," the dragon murmured, "in the cavern."

"Well," Shard said, ruffling off the memory of the battle. The last time he'd seen his uncle, his friends, and Brynja. "You might endure a battle yet. Aesir gryfons like battle. They win acclaim and honor, and titles."

Hikaru considered that. "I don't want all that. I just want to be with you, and to help the wyrms find peace." He lowered his head on level with Shard's. "But I would fight for you, Shard."

Shard touched his beak to Hikaru's nose. "I would fight for you, too."

It occurred to Shard he'd never sparred with the dragon or attempted to teach him anything about it. He made a plan to do so.

Hikaru lifted his head, then stood and stretched his wings. After glancing at what was left of the deer carcass, scraps of hide and the bones sucked clean of their marrow, he looked at Shard. "What should we do with her?"

Shard twitched his tail, surprised. "Do?"

Hikaru hesitated. "Yes. It doesn't feel right to eat of her flesh and then just leave her there." His brows scrunched down, as if he was trying to remember something.

"Oh." Moved, Shard stood and looked down at the bones. "It's all right. She'll feed the crows and return to the earth in her own time. It is the way. In the Silver Isles, the Vanir leave their dead on the isle called Black Rock."

"I see." Hikaru considered his own toes for a moment. "Do we return to the earth when we die?"

"All flesh does. Our Voice sings on, in the winds, in the sky. Our spirit flies to the Sunlit Land of Tyr."

Hikaru sat back, considering the bones of the deer, then the clear circle of sky far above. "I don't know if dragons go to the Sunlit Land."

Shard cocked his head. All spirits went to the Sunlit Land. It was a very strange thing to say. "What do you mean?"

Hikaru folded his claws together. "I feel as if…well, I don't know if I can explain. But I feel as if I'm remembering things from… from other times I've lived." His large eyes focused on Shard. "I think dragons are born again, and again. I think our spirits dwell here forever."

Shard flexed his wings, and tilted his head, indicating that they should walk on, under the cover of trees. He didn't know what to say at all, so he spoke carefully. "That could be, Hikaru. I know that dragons are different. Your blood is like fire. You…well, what kinds of things are you remembering?"

Hikaru walked by his side, in graceful, undulating movement like a rising and falling wave. "Songs, mostly. Songs you didn't teach me. Sometimes I remember other dragons, or things. I had a dream of a red stone gilded with bright gold."

Shard navigated a path through the damp ferns, shaking off the dew every few steps and pondering. Privately, he thought that Hikaru might be a seer, like himself, that they weren't memories but visions. But dragons were very different, and who was he to say?

"What songs do you remember?" Amaratsu had said that the songs of the Sunland would be in Hikaru's blood. Shard hadn't realized he would actually *remember* them, from a past life, through what power he didn't know. If he was remembering them at all, and not hearing them through some power in the wind. It had happened for Amaratsu, and for Shard himself.

Hikaru's warm voice broke the silence like a deep birdsong.

> *The noble draw wind from the water*
> *The brave will call fire from stone.*
> *The foolish seek gold in the mountain*
> *The last know that wood grows from bone."*

"It's beautiful," Shard murmured. "I've never heard it before."

"It's a dragon song," Hikaru said, certain of himself. Shard wasn't going to argue. "Where are we going?"

"Nightward."

"Yes." Hikaru trailed him through the ferns, up a long slope through the hulking, ancient cedars. "But where?"

Shard climbed, opening his wings and checking the position of the sun that glinted through the pine needles high above. "For now, just away." He pondered whether to tell Hikaru his true destination yet, for he wasn't certain how to get there, or if it was the best idea. At that moment, it was the only idea he had. "Away from the Winderost," he continued, "away from the wyrms, and the Dawn Spire."

"And then?" Hikaru rolled and hopped after him, seeming to enjoy the freedom to stretch and work his growing body.

"And then..." Shard wove around a tumble of moss-covered boulders. Perhaps, if they crested the slope, they'd have a good view of what lay beyond the forest. He paused, looking at Hikaru.

I promised myself I wouldn't keep things from him.

"We can't speak to the wyrms. I have more enemies than friends in the Winderost now. We know that the wyrms are angry with gryfons and Sunland dragons alike, so—"

"You want to go to the Sunland," Hikaru said eagerly. "Yes, I think that will be a good plan. There will be answers there, and friends."

Shard chuckled, relieved. "Let's hope so. But I don't know the way."

"I'm certain I can find it, when I remember more."

"It may be a very long flight."

Hikaru fluffed his wings. "I'm growing strong."

Shard stepped forward to butt his head affectionately against Hikaru's shoulder. "I knew you wouldn't be afraid."

He was glad Hikaru agreed with his plan, though he couldn't shake his own feeling that he was just running away.

It'll be best for Hikaru to see his homeland, and he's right, Shard tried to convince himself, *we may have friends there.*

Together they turned and trekked up the remainder of the slope, where a line of trees marked a low ridge. Shard paused at the top. The ground swept back down in a wash of shale, toward yet more forest. Beyond, in the blue haze, he made out a long, flat plain with marsh grasses, and beyond that, more forest. He didn't want to walk through a marsh, and Hikaru had eaten an entire deer. He looked up at the dragon.

"Ready to fly?"

Hikaru laughed and launched from the ridge, shooting ahead like a serpent. Shard leaped and glided after, soaking in the warm sun after the chill of the woods. Every so often he checked over his shoulder. The wyrms must have been hunkered down away from the sun. There was another possibility, though Shard guarded his hope. It was possible that the wyrms may have lost them completely when the volcano erupted, and hadn't followed at all.

"Let's race!" Hikaru challenged, looping back around Shard.

"Ha! All right."

Without hesitation, Shard narrowed his wings and shot ahead, twisting his body like a falcon to streamline his muscles and feathers. Hikaru took a sharp breath, then loosed a warbling shriek of glee. They raced.

Shard gained height and then darted ahead, using altitude and wind for his advantage, working as he had never worked before, holding nothing back. Hikaru, forced to keep up with the swiftest gryfon known in the Silver Isles or the Winderost, tested his wings to the utmost. In that way, without words, Shard helped Hikaru learn what he was capable of, and pride warmed him every time the young dragon pulled ahead of him by a nose.

Now and then they laid back, gliding on high winds to save energy, then they resumed the race and mocking, challenging calls.

Far below, the birds chattered about them. Alternatively racing and gliding, they crossed the rolling cedar forest and the long, flat marsh. The land bumped up into wooded hills again, and though it was winter the plants bloomed green and Shard spotted flowers. They smelled only earth and rain, not snow, and thought the mountain ranges must affect the weather and create a bowl of warmth.

"I'm getting tired," Hikaru said, and it had been almost a quarter mark. The sun slanted low toward afternoon.

"A little farther," Shard urged. "You can do it. You won't be able to rest at sea, when we fly to the Sunland."

Hikaru looked uncertain, then narrowed his eyes and set his gaze forward.

They flew another mark, and Shard was about to call a rest when he caught a familiar scent. Sharp longing ached in his every muscle. Hikaru smelled it too.

"What is that?"

Shard shook himself and answered, as calmly as he could manage, "The sea."

At last he understood what instinct had guided him nightward, what pulled him from the Winderost. The vast land did have an end, after all.

They came to a silent agreement to keep flying until they reached the shore. The young dragon followed Shard doggedly through the final, long stretch. The sun lay across their backs, then sat in front of them by the time they reached the promised shore. The scent was so woven into the strange, ancient green woods, infused in the trees and in the sticky, warm mist that shrouded the temperate land that Shard had expected to see the ocean over every ridge. But it was long in coming.

At last, when Shard thought he only dreamed the tantalizingly familiar scent, the evergreen forest broke.

Hills and cliffs stopped short and lunged down toward a crashing sea. The sky stretched beyond, gray and pink with sunset.

Breathless, exhausted, Shard keened in pure joy and dove, tucking his wings to glide and roll along the faces of the foreign cliffs. Confused gulls scattered and scolded him. Waves crawled onto the broad, sandy beach before the battered rock abutting the sandstone cliffs. Juniper trees clung stubbornly to the shoreline, roots mixing with mountain and salt water.

Without thinking, Shard snapped his wings out and soared over the water. The scent of fish clouded the air. He searched for only a few moments to find a school, dive, gulp down a fish, and dive again.

After a moment he remembered that he'd left Hikaru behind.

Blinking saltwater from his eyes with chagrin, Shard spun in the air. Water flew from his wings in silver drops that turned gold in the light of the dying sun. A fat fish wriggled in his talons. He could have eaten three more, but this one was for Hikaru.

The black dragonet sat on the shore, his forepaws in the sand just where the littlest waves would roll over his front toes. His tail was coiled around his haunches, his wings open against his back, but drooping, his head dipped down to stare at the water. Shard raced back to him and thumped in the sand, laughing as he offered the fish.

"Hikaru, eat!" Shard sank his talons into wet sand and the feel of it brought a rush of bittersweet memories of his home.

Hikaru swung his head and stared at the fish, blinking. Shard realized the young dragon hadn't been studying the water, he was simply so exhausted that he couldn't raise his head. Then his jaws snapped out to gulp down the fish in one bite.

Shard made a sympathetic noise. "I'm sorry. I should have let you rest. You'll feel better if you eat."

Hikaru smacked his jaws together, tasting fresh fish for the first time, then turned his gaze toward the setting sun. His soft, deer-like ears perked. "The sea," he whispered. "I wanted to reach the sea. I know you missed it." His talons flexed against the sand. "The sea. Sand. Water. The sun." He dipped his head low, but his gaze lifted to the clouds of pale pink and marigold, feathered across the pale blue horizon. Shard listened quietly as Hikaru reviewed, leading himself to sleep. His wings trembled.

"Let's go up shore," Shard murmured, leaning into Hikaru's shoulder. "The tide will be in by dark."

"Tide?" Hikaru murmured, absorbing everything as fast as he could.

He has to learn enough to keep up with his size, Shard thought wryly. So Shard explained the tides and the moon as they walked up the beach to one of the cliffs, and climbed it to curl up in the shelter of a squatting juniper grove. Hikaru coiled around Shard, creating a warm, black nest of his scaled body. His enormous eyes barely blinked as he stared at the sunset. Every word from their travels was quietly reviewed as Shard let himself be lulled by the dragon's voice.

"Earthfire...flight. Fear. Ash. Forests..." He yawned, jaws stretching and snapping shut. "Brother," he mumbled, resting his head on the ground, eyes closing. The words rolled on and on and finally the last, always the last. "Shard."

"Rest well." Shard turned his face to the setting sun, and closed his eyes to breathe in the rich smell of the ocean. With that scent came a desperate longing for the Silver Isles, the crowding thoughts of the family and friends he'd left behind, and the resolve to do whatever he must to finish his growing quest and return home.

8

A COLD WELCOME

S NOW BLINDED CAJ AS HE dragged himself across the frozen peat
fields of Crow Wing. Named for its shape from above, the isle
actually had very few crows that Caj had seen. Rather, the scent of
wild horses wafted with every breath, and their round, sliced tracks
stamped the snow in every direction. The packed snow made for slick
walking, but it was easier than wading through chest-high drifts, so
against his better judgment, he followed the horse trails.

His wing ached. His muscles protested in sharp twitches and
melted snow soaked the fine feathers of his face. He needed the warm
down and long winter feathers of a Vanir for this kind of expedi-
tion—but he didn't have that. Only his will. Only his need to find and
redeem his brother.

"Sverin!" He ducked his head against a blast of wind that rattled
his core. Snow stung like tiny stones. He thought of Sigrun and Thyra,
cuddled up in their family den to wait out the blizzard.

Curse you, Sverin. Or curse me.

But he'd found the red feathers. His first day exploring the
open, nearly featureless isle, and he'd found feathers near a pile of

snow-covered boulders, where his once-king had obviously found shelter. To his relief, he'd found no green feathers—though perhaps Halvden knew to carry his away to avoid being tracked, if he'd dropped any at all. If so, Caj reasoned, he would've picked up Sverin's as well. Or not. He could never tell if he gave the arrogant young warrior too much credit, or too little. A spasm shot through his wing.

Too little, he though ruefully. A growl built in his throat as he shoved forward against the wind and snow. The next rush of wind drew the breath from him in a gasp.

Time to shelter out the storm.

Caj paused, waiting for the wind to calm before he peered around. A gray mass stood out in the dimness of the snow, and he trudged toward it. Rock, tree, giant drift—it didn't truly matter, as long as it blocked the wind.

The scent assaulted him in the same instant he realized what the shape was.

"All winds," he breathed, staggering forward, ears lifted. At the top of a short rise, the mangled remains of a pony yearling marred the snow. Its short, fluffy mane ruffled with every shift of the wind, giving it the illusion of life. Caj climbed the rise and looked down at the carcass. Normally his appetite gnawed at the sight of a kill, but not since the vow. He and the others had vowed, before Ragna, Tyr, and each other, to take no more red meat from the land of the Silver Isles, unless it was for special reason with the wolves' blessing, and unless they properly honored the animal they killed. There were only two who had not taken that vow.

Caj opened his good wing, his stomach roiling not in hunger but an eerie nausea he'd never felt before at the sight of a dead creature of prey.

Did this young hoof beast have a name? Awareness? Fear?

Surely, fear. Long talon marks slashing the hide gave no doubt as to the breed of killer, and Caj knew of only one who would hunt on the Crow Wing Isle.

"Oh, my king," he murmured. If Sverin was still mad, still Nameless, of course he would be hunting on land. Of course he would have no awareness that their sun had set, the tide turned on the Aesir and what was once the only acceptable hunting was now forbidden by conscience and by law. The creatures of the Silver Isles already hated them. Caj feared what more damage this might do.

A strange drumming, a warm, thundering sound lifted his hackles. Yes, the yearling had a name—and a family.

Slowly Caj turned, his good wing still open but in a gesture that he hoped looked peaceful, as a dark line of horses pounded toward him through the storm. His instinct roared at him to ramp up, to flare, to challenge, to intimidate the ground-pounding foe.

Try my ways, Sigrun had asked of him after he took the vow. *Try our ways. I have tried yours. There can be balance yet.*

The indistinct line became individual beasts, flashing all different colors—gray, dun, red, splashes of black and spots, all coats shaggy and soft for winter. They broke into two lines and drummed in opposing rings around Caj, trumpeting challenges, tossing their heads. Their eyes rolled to reveal white rings when they caught a whiff of the blood of their fallen yearling.

Caj realized he looked challenging, not welcoming, and closed his wing. For a moment he stood very still, only breathing, noting with relief that their warlike dance at least blocked the wind from him for a few moments. They spoke a different tongue, a guttural, whickering, whistling language. Caj closed his eyes, listening to the throbbing of their hooves on the packed, frozen earth.

Then he bellowed from the earthy part of his heart, in a language he knew they would hear. "I come here peacefully!" He crouched back, lifting his talons to show they were clean. "I didn't kill this young one!"

A mare nickered her disbelief, and all of their anger washed over Caj in waves. He shuddered, mantling his good wing as if he could block it. "Hear me! I seek out the one who did this, to bring him to justice."

"*Lies!*" screamed a plump, spotted mare, whose coat matched the dead colt at his feet. "You killed my son! Poacher, thief, blasphemy under the eye of Tor!"

Caj lunged aside as the hysterical mare broke the ring and charged him. He whirled, ready to dodge again, but she shied at the sight of her own dead son, then her knees buckled and she bowed before the carcass, whinnying grief toward the earth.

"I will find the one who did this," Caj said, raising his voice again over the thunder of the hoof beats. "If you can tell me if you've seen him. Him, with feathers like blood, or a younger, with feathers like spring grass—"

"No." Another broke from the ring, a tall, well-muscled stallion that Caj judged to be middle years for a hoof beast. At his word, the horses began to slow, and turned inward, forming a dangerous wall of hooves and teeth. He tossed his pale head. "You are not welcome here. Not welcome to hunt, not welcome to walk, to fly, or to speak." He stamped a hoof.

Caj curled his talons against the snow, savoring the feel of them breaking through the frozen pack.

A mare, older and the color of mountain stone, joined the stallion. To her, all the others bowed their heads.

So, Caj did too.

Her voice sounded like wind in a pine bough, high and breathy. "The Red Scourge has done enough here and on every other isle. You are not welcome."

"I am friend to the Vanir," Caj began, and the mare flipped her forelock out of her eyes in what he could only think was an expression of disdain.

"The Vanir are weak for allowing you here, and they are not welcome either. I will grant you this chance to leave and to never return."

"Honorable...friends. I..." He swallowed hard against a lifetime of knowing a certain way of things, and a lifetime of pride. "Allow me to search this island. I'll rid you of the...the Red Scourge. I am friend to Vanir, and to you. To the Silver Isles. I am Caj, son-of-Cai. Honor me with your name."

"So humble!" trumpeted the mare, and her male consort nickered. A rustle of stamps and tail flicks indicated the herd's agreement. Black, large, cold eyes focused on him, a ring of contempt. "So humble, when you cannot fly—yes, I see the mud cast on your wing. I hear from the birds that the son of Lapu would have killed you, if not for the mercy of wolves. So humble, when you have nowhere to run, Caj, son-of-Cai. So humble, when you have no friends."

"I wouldn't run from you." Anger ate away at his calm. He smothered it. *What did I expect? They would fall to my feet and make peace?* At least he had tried. Perhaps he should've brought Sigrun after all. But these hard-headed beasts didn't seem to hold the Vanir in high regard, either.

"A proud and bragging poacher from the Sun Isle," said the mare. "If you will not leave, and you will not run, then you will die fighting. We don't need your help ridding our isle of the Red Scourge. We don't fear him, and we don't fear you."

"My lady—"

She ramped, hooves flashing, and three half-grown stallions whinnied their approval, broke from the ring, and charged Caj.

"I offered friendship!" he bellowed. "I offered peace!"

"We refuse," shouted one of the half-growns, surging into a hard gallop. Caj judged distance, the horse's height, and if he could make the leap and take his throat.

He crouched, muscles tight and ready, tensed—then thought of Sigrun's face if she heard he'd killed an island horse.

With a grunt he rolled aside as the stallion trampled past. The second stallion, dusty gray, pivoted and charged Caj's new position. The lead mare encouraged them, promising them glory and honor for a lifetime if they killed an Aesir conqueror.

Caj held his ground, breath short, and when the gray's hooves touched down close enough, he shoved himself straight up, wings closed. He slapped a forefoot against the gray's back, talons flat to leave no injury, his hind paws hit and he launched himself off the horse's back toward the third attacker.

That one had less stomach for a full-grown gryfon warrior flying at him, broken wing or no. He shied away and instead of landing on a running horse's back, Caj hit the snow and rolled. He groaned as pain shot up three different ways across his wing. No time for that. He spun and flung out his good wing, hissing warning at the three young stallions, who minced uncertainly, tails whisking, heads bobbing in challenge.

"I thought you wanted to kill an Aesir today!" Caj slashed his tail through the air. At his back and all around, the double ring of the giant herd hit their hooves against the snow to encourage the stallions. "Well? Shall we have words, instead?"

For a moment, Caj thought they were ready to speak, thought they acknowledged that he could have killed the young male horse, and hadn't.

Then the wind stirred the scent of the dead colt.

"Never," said the queen mare from afield. Her voice imbued the stallions with new vigor. They exchanged glances and murmurs, then split, readying a triad attack. Caj waited, but they did not charge. A silence that sounded strange after all the shouting and drumming settled over the herd, and they all held still. Caj did too. They were prey beasts, their senses heightened. They'd heard or smelled something he hadn't.

Then, he did.

And he never, in life up to that day, had been more glad to hear the low, long howl of a wolf in the distance.

"Don't panic," commanded the queen mare. Her consort left the ring and butted his head against the others, giving them confidence, encouraging them with his powerful height and his strength.

Caj couldn't think of a single wolf in the Isles who would be stupid enough to charge a herd of horses in search of a meal, when deer were more easily gotten on the Star Isle, and the Vanir offered shares of their fish. Unless the wolf was not there for meat. Unless it had come for some higher purpose, some duty beyond instinct.

Unless Sigrun, in her worry, had sent someone after him.

Caj strained to hear the calls of more wolves, but heard only the one, and his relief soured. One wolf. One wolf against a vengeful herd of warrior horses. He watched though, amazed that they reacted as if it was a giant pack. Eyes rolled. Muscles twitched to flee. The next low howl sent three yearlings thundering away into the blizzard.

They caught a scent and more fled, leaving an open space through which the wolf could enter.

And he did, appearing out of the snow and springing through the broken ring lithely as a fox.

His long, almost mocking howl sent another shiver through the herd, though Caj admired the queen mare for standing her ground, then stepping forward.

"This is no affair of yours," she told the wolf. "Go back to your island."

"Proud fools," sang the wolf, a young male.

Caj tried and failed to remember where he'd seen him before, or if he just looked familiar because most wolves looked the same to Caj. His pale, golden coat repelled the snow as he padded up to the queen, who, lock-legged, met his friendly bow with a curt jerk of her head.

"Do you not know the nest-father of Rashard, prince of the Sun Isle?" The wolf stared around the ring. "Do you not know Noble Caj the Just, friend to Vanir, to wolves, nest-father of Shard, the Summer King?"

Don't overdo it, Caj thought, watching the mare's dark eyes.

She looked unimpressed. "I know poachers," she declared. "Murderers, thieves—"

"Harm him," snarled the wolf in a different tone, "and I will name you an oath breaker."

Caj's talons clenched unconsciously against the snow, and probably would always clench at the sound of a wolf growl. But he didn't interrupt.

The mare shifted, tail whisking uncertainly against her flank. "Of what oath do you speak?"

"Your allegiance to the caribou Aodh of the Sun Isle, your dam's and her dam's vows to Aodh's father, and him, and his sons to always stand where the cloven-hoofed stand when needed, as one herd."

She tossed her forelock out of her eyes, and the certainty slipped from her voice. "What do you know of our oaths?"

The wolf bared his fangs as if amused, but Caj thought it was not entirely on accident that this put the mare further on edge. "I know everything."

"I have not heard from Aodh since the Conquering. I know not where he stands."

"He stands with the Summer King."

This sent a flurry of disbelief, head-shaking, and hoof-stamping through the herd. "Ask the wind, ask the birds," said the young wolf, "if you think I have a reason to lie to you. But until you know for sure, I would not kill this warrior. He's here to help you."

The mare snorted steam. The blizzard began to wear itself out, and instead of wind, only heavy, fat flakes of snow fell around them. The mare considered Caj, then the wolf, and Caj heard her teeth grinding.

"Very well. You have our leave to stay. But you will hunt no game on this island, and you will leave if it's clear your Red Scourge is no longer here."

"I will," Caj said, mustering as much respect as he was able. It wasn't much, but it was enough to mollify her. With a piercing whistle, she ordered the herd away.

The grieving mother, lying all that time beside her dead colt, rose unsteadily to her feet.

"I will avenge him," Caj called to her.

She shook her head hard, tossing snow from her mane, then stared at Caj, her eyes dark and searching. "If you do," she said, "then count me a friend."

Caj lowered his head. Thunder beat around him, and when he looked up again, the herd had vanished into the snow, and the young gold wolf was panting in his face, then sniffing along his flank.

"You're not hurt, I hope? I'm not too late? You look as if you need a meal, and a sleep."

"No." Caj ruffled his feathers against the snow, his muscles nearly seizing at the wolf's proximity. "No, I'm not hurt. Yes, I need a meal... and a sleep. Who are you?"

"Oh." The wolf closed his mouth and tilted his head, then displayed his teeth. "I am Tocho. Friend to Shard. And to you."

"I see. And why are you here, alone?"

"Oh," he said again, and he sounded even younger, and uncertain. "I've come to help you?"

Oh, how merry, thought Caj. "It's too dangerous."

Tocho was unmoved. His face broadened again into a pant. "I won't face Sverin. I'll only help you hunt, or bring you food. I'm fast, so you don't have to travel so far between your hunts."

Beyond the danger, Caj could think of no good reason to refuse the help—but he could also think of no good reason Tocho was offering. *Time enough to figure that out later.* "Fine then. Let's find shelter until this snow lets up."

"Already done!" He turned about and padded away. "This way."

Caj broke into a trot to follow as the curtain of snow swallowed them up with the rest of the island.

9

THE VANHAR

D ARKNESS CLOAKED THE SHORELINE AND the wind rose, driving
a chill through Kjorn's damp feathers and straight to his bones.
He remained on the ground, still as he could manage, as Rok and his
band hunted well into evening.

"I should break now," he grumbled to the wolf Mayka.

Mayka slowly laid his ears back, and in the darkening, drizzly
gloom, Kjorn could see his lip twitch to reveal the point of one fang.
"No. No. We must do nothing at night. Remain still. In the morning.
I'll take the last watch, and wake you as the sky lightens."

"I trust you," Kjorn reminded him. "I'll do what I can to repay
you for your help."

The ears perked again, twin outlines in the dark. "I ask only that
you would do the same for me, if needed. When you see Shard, tell
him I remember him, and thank him."

Before Kjorn could respond, they heard gryfon voices in the wind.
Mayka rolled up to his feet and chirruped a warning, sounding almost
like a gryfon. Fraenir answered him, and Kjorn listened as all three

gryfons landed, feathers rustling, murmuring darkly about the storm and the volcanic ash raining farther inland.

A warm hunk of red meat rolled across the ground and struck him in the shoulder.

Kjorn looked up to see Rok. "Thank you." He sniffed the meat, found it fresh, and ate as Rok lumbered forward to stand over him.

"Don't say we didn't treat you well."

Kjorn paused, swallowing a strip of meat and furtively taking the gryfon's measure again. He decided he could best the rogue, in a fight. "Say to whom? Those at the Dawn Spire? These new captors you're taking me to? Those who know my father would have been heir to rule this land?"

Rok shifted, then scoffed. "I know who you are, exile. They masked it with pretty tales of exploration, conquering, and glory, but I know the truth."

Kjorn's heart thumped. He scarcely knew the truth himself, but the elders of the Aesir in the Silver Isles told him what they knew, and he could guess it. "You believe Per fled."

Rok stretched his broad wings, for a moment hiding the stars from Kjorn's sight. "Per fled with the cursed. And all those who would have served him loyally in this land were left to the usurper."

Kjorn's appetite fell away and he bunched his muscles to stand, then remembered he was still supposed to appear bound. He shifted instead, feigning discomfort. "Was your family loyal to my grandfather? Is that why you're in exile? I can—"

"I'm not in exile!" The rogue's tail lashed. "I was born free of the Dawn Spire. My father refused to serve the new *kings*." He put a sour twist on the word, and Kjorn's mind soared. If he could play it right, here could be an ally instead of a foe.

"Rok—"

"Stay quiet, Highness. It's what princes are good at."

"Your father would've served mine." Kjorn tried one last time. "Will you not make amends, and be my ally?"

Rok's head tilted in the dark, then he chuckled. "No."

"Why? What happened to make you so bitter?"

"Eat your food. We'll arrive at Vanheim in the morning. You'll want your strength to argue with them, instead."

He turned, tail flicking across Kjorn's face before he could say another word. Stifling frustration, Kjorn clenched his talons into the mud, and ate. He would need his strength in the morning, though not for arguing.

"Were you being honest?"

He nearly jumped out of his binds as Fraenir slipped forward. Kjorn hated the dark. "I'm always honest."

He spoke, hushed, head tilted as if listening for Rok's return. "He tried to return to the Dawn Spire, a long time ago. They wouldn't have him. King Orn called his family disloyal, oath breakers, exiles, and never gave him a chance."

"Ah," said Kjorn. Then, "You care about him?"

"Of course I do," he growled. "He's like my brother. He practically raised me." At Kjorn's silence, Fraenir continued. "He's good, but because of his father's act, he's stuck with this life. He could have been a great warrior at the Dawn Spire, honored."

Kjorn peered forward, trying to see Fraenir's face, but clouds hid even the stars, and they spoke in blackness. The only other sound was the crash of the sea below. "It's for all of us, in this life, to either live up to, or redeem the acts of our fathers." He inched closer to Fraenir through the mud. "You could talk to him for me."

A moment of hesitation. "No, I can't do that. You have nothing. You can't promise him anything. Even if you really are the grandson of Per, you're in exile too. You've got no pride with you, no warriors, nothing to prove who you are or what you could give him if you succeed."

"Honor means keeping your oaths, Fraenir, not for gain, but for the sake of your own heart. Loyalty means following those you've pledged to, even if they have nothing to offer. He'll understand it as a matter of honor. Tell him that," Kjorn urged. "If what you've told me is true, tell him, and he'll understand that."

From afield, Rok called Fraenir's name. The younger gryfon drew back a step.

Kjorn tried to keep him close. "Fraenir—"

Fraenir hesitated, watching Kjorn, one ear turning back. "I shouldn't have told you."

Wind brought the smell of more rain, and Kjorn braced himself for a long, chilly night.

"Fraenir," Rok barked again from closer by. "First watch." He seemed in a black mood, and didn't bring up any kind of plan to look for shelter. Fraenir edged away a few steps, watching. Perhaps he, or Rok, would have a change of heart, but Kjorn didn't set store in it. He would be gone by morning anyway.

Even through the cold, wet night, he managed a little sleep, chaotic with dreams of shadowy, fanged beasts and multiple gryfons who all looked like Shard, but spoke with frightening, voiceless howls.

True to his word, Mayka woke Kjorn at the first dull light of morning, when the wolf was on watch. Before moving, Kjorn looked around to get a bearing on the other rogues. Frida and Fraenir huddled, asleep in a tight pile like siblings, and Rok had curled up alone a single leap away.

Mayka nudged Kjorn, assuring him they were fast asleep. Kjorn slithered forward out of the seaweed binds. They fell and flopped away with soft thumps on the ground. Kjorn paused, ears twitching. Fraenir grumbled in his sleep before nuzzling in closer to Frida. Kjorn let his breath out.

The dull light glinted off the delicate golden chain that Rok wore around his neck, though brown feathers hid much of it from sight. Kjorn stared at the chain. Perhaps he could slip it loose, and still creep away without risking a fight against three gryfons. He took a step toward Rok.

"Son of Sverin," Mayka breathed. "Don't be foolish."

Kjorn's tail twitched, then he turned away. It was only a thing. Only metal. It wasn't his father. He looked up. Above him, the sky stretched cloudless and dark, still pricked with stars. A rosy gray over the sea marked Tyr's horizon. For the first time in many days, he opened his wings. Wary of debilitating cramps, he extended them slowly, feeling the long muscles uncoil and warm. He crept away, still stretching his wings so that when he lifted off the draft wouldn't wake his captors.

"Fly," Mayka urged, padding up beside him, a soft whine creeping into his words. "Fly!"

"Thank you," Kjorn said, crouching. "If I ever have a chance to repay you—"

Mayka butted his head against Kjorn and he shoved up, flapping hard in the cool air. He would fly inland. He knew that the Dawn Spire lay inland, and if he flew high he'd either spot it, or be spotted by a patrol. Beyond that, he could only have faith.

Shouts drew his gaze down. Rok had woken. Fraenir and Frida shot into the air like falcons and Kjorn wheeled up high, finding a sliver of warm air to help him.

Fraenir, faster than he appeared, gained air and snagged Kjorn's tail feathers in his claws. Kjorn tucked down and stooped, his battle cry piercing the morning. Fraenir ducked, yanking free and sending one golden feather fluttering toward the ground.

Rok barreled up toward them, wing beats hard and deep. Frida climbed the sky a leap above Kjorn, surely planning to dive on him.

"I offered you a chance!" Kjorn shouted, banking sharply away as Rok leveled with him, fury in his eyes. "I still offer you redemption and a chance to serve with honor."

Rok only hissed. Fraenir fell away in deference, and Kjorn, refusing to flee, flared his wings to meet the lanky gryfon's charge. He had a longer reach than Kjorn, but Kjorn was heavier, better nourished and muscled.

If I'm to prove I'm a prince, let it be here.

He hissed, and thrust his talons out as Rok crashed into him. They locked claws, wings beating at each other, and Kjorn's muscles thrilled at the challenge. After a long, helpless, restless winter and a solitary flight over an endless ocean, now was battle.

He would show these rogues the line of Kajar.

Rok shoved his weight forward, trying to turn Kjorn upside down. Kjorn obliged, relaxing and falling back, then kicked the big gryfon's

stomach as they toppled wing over tail. He kicked again as Rok gasped
and knocked a wing toward the rogue's head, slicing flight feathers
toward his eyes. Rok threw his head back and the strike caught his
neck, making him cough. His talons loosened.

They fell fast, Rok's wings beating Kjorn's sides as he strained to
keep flying. Kjorn yanked on their locked talons to throw Rok off balance, then let go as Rok flared to keep from bowling forward. Kjorn
wrenched his talons free, flapped twice and twisted around to land on
Rok's back.

Fraenir and Frida had hung back, wary of impeding their leader,
but now the gryfess screeched and shot forward, aiming for Kjorn.
He clung, talons dug into Rok's shoulders as the big gryfon writhed
and sank with each wing stroke, unable to bear Kjorn's weight and
unable to throw him.

When Frida was a mere leap from them, Kjorn rolled off Rok's
side, kicking Rok's ribs hard to send him toward Frida.

Fraenir dropped toward him and Kjorn managed not to laugh like
a maniac. *Caj never thought to make us spar three-against-one, mid-air. He'd
be proud.*

A long warning call broke through their fight. Just as Kjorn whirled
to meet Fraenir, voices pierced wind, and a strong scent chased them.

"Halt, trespassers!"

"Halt, poachers!"

"Land and answer for your presence!"

Rok shouted an obscenity. By silent agreement Fraenir and Kjorn
turned from their own impending duel to see the newcomers.

Ten gryfons soared at them fast in a precise formation like geese.
Just as Kjorn looked at them, the sun broke the edge of the earth
and the first rays of light dazzled his eyes. He shook his head hard.
Surely bright Tyr had seen him face the first challenge with honor and
courage. Kjorn didn't pretend he could face ten healthy gryfons alone.
He glided toward the ground, heart thumping. The voices who'd
called to them sounded disciplined, firm, like gryfons who belonged
to a pride, not rogues. Kjorn thought that explaining himself would

be better than attempting to flee. He would have more success with honorable gryfons than with Rok and his ilk.

The arriving gryfons shouted again at Rok and his company. Fraenir hesitated, and followed Kjorn down. Frida pleaded with Rok, but the rogue shouted challenge and five of the new gryfons broke off to wrestle him down. Kjorn didn't watch, and was surprised when Frida didn't attempt to help, but stooped and landed meekly beside Kjorn, as if they all went together.

"We would only get injured," she said defensively, to answer Kjorn's curious glance. He looked around as five of the new gryfons landed, reforming into a semi-circle around them. The second half of the group, shoving a bruised and disgruntled Rok up against Fraenir, closed the circle.

Kjorn gazed at the new gryfons. They were not Aesir. The tallest of them stood a head or two shorter than himself, and he watched as they folded their wings, the long, sculpted wings of sea eagles. Their colors ranged from gray to a variety of pale hues, almost white, and soft, dove browns. They weren't Vanir either, he knew at once, there was something quite different, but a resemblance lingered.

Perhaps, Kjorn thought as a pale female stepped forward, eyes narrowed, *the Vanir did originate from the Winderost after all, sometime long ago*. His mind spun, but that was wonder for another time.

"I am Nilsine, daughter-of-Nels, huntress and sentry of the Vanhar." Her voice dipped in a rolling dialect, like the native gryfons of the Silver Isles, but much stronger, older, Kjorn thought. "Declare yourself."

"I am Fraenir—"

"You are known, thief," snipped a male from the ring of gryfons. "Fraenir, son-of-Lars. Frida, daughter-of-Frey. Rok, son—"

"So you know us," Rok said. Two gryfons held him pinned. Nilsine looked mildly from him, back to Kjorn. Her eyes shone almost red, like the forest falcons he'd seen on rare occasion back home.

Home.

This was my home, he thought again. *My true home. This was the first place my talons touched earth, this was the first air I breathed.*

"You are known." Nilsine looked at Rok again coolly. "I speak to the stranger."

Kjorn inclined his head to her. "I am Kjorn. Son-of-Sverin, who is the son of Per."

Her ears perked, tail twitched, but otherwise she gave no expression. "If that is so…" Her gaze traveled between Rok and Kjorn, surely wondering at the story—but she had to have seen them fighting, known that Kjorn had meant no trespass, was not banded with the rogues. "It's an interesting claim."

"My lady," one of the gryfons holding Rok said. "Nilsine, look…"

She looked over and so did Kjorn, and saw that the warrior had lifted the gold chain in one talon. Rok snarled.

"Well." Nilsine looked back to Kjorn. "Perhaps. Time will tell. If it's true, then welcome home."

Not feeling entirely welcome, Kjorn stood tall under her searching look.

Her gaze rolled to the sky, searching. "I see no warriors with you. Lost at sea?"

The cutting edge of her voice didn't seem mocking, but Kjorn couldn't name the tone. It almost sounded like disappointment. That gave him a little hope. *Perhaps there are some who would be happy to see me…*

"I'm alone," Kjorn said.

One ear laid back, then she cocked her head. "This land is in turmoil. Your forefathers chose to forsake it in the hour of need, and others have taken your place. Now you return, declaring your true name and heritage as if you expect to deserve something."

"I don't expect anything," Kjorn said. The female's cool, powerful demeanor reminded Kjorn of Thyra, and his heart ached for home. His old home—the Silver Isles. Or at least his mate. "I'm looking for my wingbrother, Shard, also of the Silver Isles."

"I don't know that name. If he was traveling alone, he might've passed this way like a rogue and we wouldn't have known."

"You would have known," Kjorn said wryly, "if he'd come this way. He's memorable." At her un-amused look, he dipped his head again, remembering that he was not a prince here. "I've come only to search for him and I ask leave to do so in your lands."

Nilsine regarded him again, as if to determine whether he was telling the truth. "It's not my leave to give. The council will deal with you. You'll come with us."

"Good," Kjorn said. "Yes, take me to your king."

Nilsine eyed him sideways and laughed. "King?"

Kjorn hesitated. "Your...leader."

She shook her head, opening her wings. "You have much to learn."

10
BY THE SHORE

"SHARD! I WENT SWIMMING!"

Shard blinked out of a dream. In the dream, he'd stared into a pair of blind eagle eyes, staring hard through him, and had heard a voice whispering, asking if he was the Summer King.

He hadn't been able to answer, in the dream, but he felt as if the milky, un-seeing eyes searched his heart still.

He sat up and shook himself. "Did you?"

Hikaru undulated around him, flicking water from every scale and off his silver mane. "It was wonderful! But I don't like this taste. Is it salt?" He smacked his jaws. "Sea salt? Here."

Proudly, the young dragon deposited a fish in front of Shard's beak.

"Oh!" Shard shook his head of the dream and the whispering voice, invigorated by Hikaru's happiness. Eyeing the horizon, he got his bearing on dawn, still a mark or so off. Like Shard, it seemed Hikaru enjoyed those few dark hours before the sun came up, as if all the earth held its breath and waited. "Well done. Did you go very far out?"

84

"No!" Hikaru coiled around him and told the tale of his early morning fishing, while Shard picked apart the fish. He savored the meat. After their ordeal in the cave, he would always be grateful for fresh meat. Silently, he thanked the fish for its life.

"Must we go?" Hikaru asked when Shard had finished and stood to stretch his legs and wings. "It's so wonderful here, and the more I think of it, the worse it sounds everywhere else, with wars and Nameless wyrms and lies, and all of that."

"It is wonderful here, Hikaru."

"Can we stay?"

"For a little while. So you can get stronger." He eyed Hikaru's growth, the strong muscles forming under his feathers after long days of flying, the long curve of his neck and budding horns. Equal in strength and energy to a gryfon fledge, Shard thought. Soon he would be ready for a flight over the sea.

Hikaru seemed satisfied with staying a "little while" longer, and ruffled his wings happily. "I remembered another song."

"Sing it to me," Shard said, and Hikaru did.

A chilly wind crisscrossed them from the shore, and Shard thought of the warm fires of the Dawn Spire. Perhaps the dragons of the Sunland would know more about fire—if they were even willing to share the information. The memory of Amaratsu's story about the dragons troubled Shard. If they had indeed sequestered themselves away from the world to avoid greed and violence, Shard didn't know what they would think of a gryfon coming to them again. But for Hikaru's sake...

"Come fly, Shard," said the dragon, his face looming down in front of Shard's. "You look worried. And you always look happy after we fly."

Shard ducked his head, and chuckled. "Yes, you're right. You're right of course."

Hikaru warbled and uncoiled, slithering around into a long line before leaping from the cliff where they nested. Shard watched him take off. Still a little rough, finding the wind, and controlling his strokes. Shard leaped out after him, then climbed higher. He soared up, and up, with Hikaru laughing below and encouraging him on.

Shard's purpose was not mere practice or fun. He stroked up until the air grew thin and he could see the vast lay of the forest and the line of the marshland beyond. All lay dark in morning starlight still, and Shard relaxed his gaze, scanning only for movement.

A grim haze still clung to the farthest horizon, the ash and smoke from the Horn of Midragur. He saw no sign of the wyrms. Tilting his wings to bank around, he scanned the distant sea for land or flying creatures, or some other vision he might not expect, but the waves and sky lay empty as far as he could perceive.

With a breath of relief, he tucked his wings and fell down through the cool air. Hearing Hikaru's squeal of delight, Shard folded himself like a falcon so the wind wouldn't stall his wings. Showing off his speed, he adjusted his angle to aim for the water, far out from shore. A sea dive still quickened his heart. Any number of things could go wrong. But he'd done it before. He closed his eyes and stretched out his talons.

The water shocked him, the force like breaking through hard rock. Molded to a compact dive, he shot down through the water like a tern.

Bubbles exploded beside him as Hikaru plunged in beside him, shoving him back in a wave. Shard oriented to the dim light and swam up, up, broke the surface and gasped, streaming salt water. Hikaru's head popped out of the water a leap or two away from him, riding a big wave, laughing. Shard sucked in a breath, and shook water from his head.

"Well done, Hikaru!"

The dragon laughed and made toward Shard with surprising speed. Something large bumped up under him. Hikaru's tail. Shard gripped and climbed up to grasp the dragon's wings gently, for Hikaru folded them and swam like a serpent through the waves. In that manner, he transported Shard back to the shore and bucked him off into the sand.

Shard rolled, snarled playfully and leaped back at him. Hikaru reared his head back, shook the water from his mane and displayed his long, fine teeth. When Shard kept charging, the young dragon whipped around into a coil, using his tail to deflect and shove Shard away.

"Good work," Shard said, prowling around him. Hikaru weaved his head, tracking Shard warily. "But many foes won't attack from the ground." He shoved up and lashed at Hikaru's face, only to catch his claws on a hard, bright horn. Hikaru had ducked his head. "Well done!"

Shard broke off, and they sparred until they were hungry. After another swim in deeper water, with Hikaru giving him a ride to shore, they watched the sunrise. They preened the salt from each other's feathers as Tyr warmed and dried them. Shard combed his talons through Hikaru's wings and mane, and the dragon vibrated with warm noise like a gryfon purring. Shard wondered if dragons did that naturally, or if Hikaru was imitating him.

"Shard," Hikaru began hesitantly. "It's so nice here. What if we stayed here forever?"

"Forever?" Shard twitched his tail, feeling edgy, for the dragon echoed a thought he'd had before.

"Yes, we could stay here, eating fish and swimming and flying, just us, with no wyrms to harry us. I know there's a larger world, but I like it just fine here."

Shard was quiet for a few moments, and Hikaru didn't interrupt his thoughts.

The clear, windy morning should've eased his heart, but it only reminded him of the growing unease in the world. There were things he needed to do, or try, and he didn't know what would happen if he waited or—as he'd thought more than once—didn't do anything at all. But that was a cowardly, selfish idea. He'd thought once of trying to leave Hikaru behind, but the dragonet could help him in the Sunland. More than that, Hikaru's destiny was not Shard's decision, and he'd made a promise to Amaratsu. When he truly pictured the idea of staying at least the single year of Hikaru's life on that safe shore, he knew it might have been wonderful.

But it was also impossible to leave things, forever, as he had. He'd made promises.

Sharp determination swooped through him. He would see Kjorn again and resolve their differences, their kingdoms, and the wyrm's silent war on the Aesir.

He would avenge Stigr. He would see Brynja again.

Cold waves crawled over their hind feet and tails.

"We have to go," Shard said quietly.

Hikaru's claws went still against Shard's feathers. "I understand," he said. "I know we do. But I don't understand why. We have peace here."

"I know, Hikaru." He craned his neck to meet the young dragon's large eyes. "We do have peace. You and I. But not everyone does. And that is why we must go."

Hikaru lowered his head, considering that.

After long moments, broken by the unnerving cries of sea birds that sounded, to Shard's ear, like gryfon kits, the dragon raised his head to a proud angle. Sun broke the horizon in silver and gold, outlining the waves, the cliffs, and Hikaru in light.

"I know you're right. And I'll make you proud, Shard. We'll speak to my kin in the Sunland, and they'll help. They'll know what to do. We'll make everything right. I had a nightmare of the wyrms last night and I was being cowardly, but I know you're right."

Shard nodded once. Not so very long ago, he'd had fine, simple plans like that, too. He didn't dare dim the fire in Hikaru's heart by suggesting it might not be all that simple. He would need every bit of that fire to make the long journey, to keep his hope bright, to say what he needed to say.

"Remember, when we meet the other dragons, you are Amaratsu's son, Hikaru. She told me that's how dragons introduce themselves."

Hikaru's head bobbed, eyes gleaming. Then he stilled. "And I shall introduce you as my brother. I want them to know. I want everyone to know." The dragon extended one long black wing, and a jolt skipped down Shard's spine as he met Hikaru's gaze. "Since we are not brothers by blood, then we'll be brothers by vow. I remember."

"You remember?" Shard didn't open his wing yet, though Hikaru watched him expectantly.

"The wingbrother vow. It was one of the first rhymes you taught me when I hatched. "

Shard had no memory of saying it. He must've sung all the songs and tales he knew and unknowingly included the wingbrother pledge.

But Hikaru was right. If anyone, anywhere, asked him, Shard would say without hesitation that they were brothers.

And there in Tyr's light, he would swear it.

Haltingly, thinking briefly of Kjorn, he opened his wing to eclipse Hikaru's narrow black feathers. In no history or tale that he knew of did a gryfon have two wingbrothers—but neither did any history or tale say he couldn't. Nor did any say he couldn't pledge to someone who wasn't a gryfon.

"Wind under me when the air is still."

Hikaru watched his face solemnly. "Wind over me when I fly too high."

"Brother by choice," Shard said.

"Brother by *vow*."

Tyr's light glowed around them, and Shard pressed his wing to Hikaru's.

"By my wings," they said together, eyes locked, "you will never fly alone."

11

TALON'S REACH

"YOU HAVEN'T ASKED ME WHY I search for Sverin, after all he's done."

Caj followed the wolf, Tocho, through a stone tunnel so narrow it threatened to scrape his feathers bare. He pressed to one side, wary of damaging the splint on his broken wing.

Ahead, Tocho paused to snuffle at the cold rock and Caj stopped short of bumping into him. "I understand the wingbrother pledge."

Do you? Caj's tail twitched, but he managed not to say it aloud. The wolf had proven to be literally worth his weight in food. Rather than having to journey back through the tunnels or hunt when he grew hungry, Caj counted on Tocho departing to either hunt on his own for small game, or return with fish from the Vanir. Without him, the chase would've been much more difficult, and much longer.

"Why do you help me?" Caj caught a whiff of fresh air and pressed forward, urging Tocho to go faster. Knowing that an entire island of earth and rock pressed over his head shortened his breath, but he pressed forward stubbornly.

Tocho quickened his pace. "Your nest-son saved my life."

Caj perked his ears. "I didn't know that."

Tocho laughed. He laughed often, and Caj wished he had a little of the wolf's good humor. "And, I help you because we're in troubled days. At the end of them, I hope to have proven myself well."

Light and wind rushed down the tunnel when Tocho crawled free, and Caj burst out behind him, grateful even as snow blasted his face. "Trying to impress someone, are you?"

Tocho shook himself and didn't answer.

Caj perked his ears. "Ha, that's it. You're trying to impress your king. Do wolves have ranks and favor as we do?"

Tocho looked over at him, earnest. "I help you from my own heart. I owe your family the kind of debt that can't be repaid. If I impress someone along the way, then that's fine." He looked away again, sniffing at the snow.

"It's a female, isn't it."

Tocho's ears flattened, and Caj broke into a rough laugh. Laughing felt strange, impossible, after the long winter. "It is. Well, that's fair enough. I didn't know that helping gryfons was impressive to she-wolves."

"I don't know *what's* impressive to her," Tocho muttered, and Caj laughed again.

At least he knew not everything about gryfons and wolves was so different. He wasn't sure if it was flattering or simple madness that Tocho thought helping him would gain favor with some she-wolf. Of course, there was Shard, the great champion of wolves, and of peace in the isles—Shard, Caj's son.

Nest-son, he corrected himself. Funny to think he had favor because of Shard, when it had been the other way around not so very long ago.

They walked forward in quiet through the snow, heading inland. Caj knew that Sverin would keep as far from the ocean as possible, except if he crossed islands. They knew he was no longer on Crow Wing. They'd searched the entire span and after a few days one of the horses deigned to find them and say they'd confirmed he was gone, and the birds murmured of Talon's Reach.

Caj shook snow from his face, his mood darkening.

The winter hadn't eased when Sverin fled and Thyra and Ragna took command of the divided pride. Some had muttered that indeed, Tyr was not happy with the arrangement, but deep in the pit of himself, Caj felt that all was not right with the world itself. Kjorn, his own prince, had left, perhaps to perish in the sea before ever reaching the windland. No one knew of Shard, if he lived, had fled, or was dead somewhere far from home.

Without warning, Tocho licked the side of Caj's head.

"*Ah*—" he jerked away with a hiss, lifting his good wing to shove the wolf back.

Tocho flattened his ears and stretched out on his belly, curling his lip. "I'm sorry. You looked so troubled. If you were a wolf, I'd—"

"I'm not a wolf," Caj growled.

Tocho pressed himself to the ground and rolled to his side. "I meant no disrespect, Noble Caj."

Caj huffed and shook himself. Snow pelted his face, stinging away the dank, closed feeling of the cave. "Just don't…comfort me again. And stand up. Tyr's wings. This will be a long hunt if you do that every time there's a misunderstanding."

Tocho rolled to his feet, sniffing forward into the blizzard. "I don't know Talon's Reach. We should ask."

"Ask?" Caj just looked at him. "Ask who?"

"Anyone," Tocho said, lifting his head to peer around.

Caj followed his gaze. Dull light filtered through the blizzard, promising that the snow might spend itself soon.

"Birds," Tocho continued. "A hare, if you call in Tor's name and they know you aren't hunting, might answer."

"I don't speak with creatures like that. I don't understand them. They flee."

Bright, hungry wolf eyes focused on him. "You spoke to the horses. You only have to listen." He padded forward.

"I don't need help to find my own wingbrother," Caj called after him, then broke into a lope to catch up. Wolves were swift on the ground. Caj was not, though his strength grew. If he could fly, the whole hunt would've been done by now.

His own father used to say that "if" was the most useless word under the sky.

"They won't help me." Caj caught up to Tocho, caught his bushy tail in his talons. Tocho paused to look at him. "They won't help a gryfon, not me, of the Aesir. Not after everything."

Tocho tilted his head. "Of course they will. You seek your brother, out of love. All creatures understand that. You seek redemption for the Aesir. You love a Vanir. Two actually." He chuckled. "Give the islands a chance, and they will give you one."

Caj huffed, lashing his tail. He caught a scent—red deer? He whirled, ears perking, and saw her, frozen as if her ruddy winter pelt might blend in with the snow. He tried to remember the feeling of speaking to the horses, feeling his feet firmly on the earth, unable to fly, as this creature was unable to fly.

"You there!"

Her ears perked, face blank and shocked, then she wheeled and bounded away into the snow. Caj swore and leaped after her, but Tocho's laughter stopped him.

He whirled and bore down on the wolf. "This is funny to you?"

"Yes!" Tocho dodged away when Caj swiped at him. "I mean it was a good try. But maybe try someone closer to yourself, first. And maybe not so loudly."

"Closer to…"

Tocho tilted his head back. Through the pelting snow Caj thought he made out the form of a bird, flapping fast to seek shelter.

"You there!"

"Would you answer if someone shouted at you like that?" Tocho's quiet question burned under Caj's skin. He splayed his good wing, digging his talons against the frozen ground under the snow just to feel them breaking into something.

"Hail! Little sky brother!"

The bird disappeared into the blizzard.

Caj loosed a breath, and had just turned a glare on Tocho, when the bird swooped back with stunning speed and landed before Caj, looking as surprised as Caj himself did. The sleek, small, sparrow hawk peered up at him and he realized he'd make a mistake calling *her* a brother.

"You called to me, lord?"

Well that's more like it. Caj blinked in surprise at the little falcon, and she stared at him. "Yes, I did. You live on Talon's Reach?"

"My whole life." She looked back and forth between Tocho and Caj. "So it's true! You seek the Red King."

Relieved that she hadn't called him the Red Scourge, and feeling more hopeful, Caj lowered himself to her level, sinking to his belly in the snow. "I do." He didn't even ask how she knew. News of his quest was traveling faster than he was. He glanced at Tocho, smothered his pride, and continued. "And I need help. I mean to redeem Sverin." Caj met the falcon's small, shining eyes. He recalled how Tocho had won over the horses. "In the name of...the Summer King, in the name of Shard, prince of the Vanir...will you help me?"

"It would be my honor."

The quick answer surprised Caj, and he didn't try to hide his gratitude. "What is your name?"

She loosed a little chirruping laugh. "We of the winds have no names."

Caj's ear twitched, and he tried not to be irritated. "Then what will I call you?"

"Call me friend. Come, come, then, slow ones." She hopped into the air and hovered. "We have a large island to search."

12

AT THE VANHEIM SHORE

SUNSET EDGED THE VANHEIM SHORE in gold and red. Kjorn stood on the edge of a cliff within the stronghold of the Vanhar, ringed by their council of twelve elders, half of them male, half of them female, and in their center a thirteenth. She was the oldest, tough and wiry as a falcon, with sharp, orange eyes.

"Kjorn, Son-of-Sverin. I am high priestess of the Vanhar. My council and I share wisdom, seek guidance from Tyr and Tor, and look for signs from the Four Winds, but it is I who have the final say in matters of our law. Do you understand this?"

"I understand." Kjorn bowed low, looking around the half circle of faces. No wonder Nilsine had laughed when Kjorn mentioned a king, but they'd been anything but hostile. His wings were unbound, at his back lay the sea. They trusted that he would not fly. Anything he didn't understand could surely be clarified at a later time. "It's my honor to meet you. I wish only that I could have come upon this shore first, and met you in a better way."

One ear slanted incredulously, but she appeared amused. The dozen elders remained quiet, only exchanging skeptical looks. "You understand that you are here to face judgment for keeping company with the criminal Rok, for trespassing, and to answer for your claim of being Kajar's heir."

"I understand."

The elders conferred among themselves, and Kjorn took a deep breath, casting a brief look to the landscape beyond the half circle of gryfons.

The stronghold of the Vanhar was quarter mark's flight along the coast from where the sentries had come upon Rok and his band. The land changed from barren rock with sparse plant growth into lusher grass slopes that nudged into dunes and slipped into the sea. The Vanhar nested not in rock dens but in those dunes and tall grasses, and now and again Kjorn glimpsed a curious gryfon face peering their way from a distance, or a fledge popping up to practice flight. Wind waved the grasses and sea wheat, seabirds cried, and sunlight sparkled gold over the water.

In all, the effect soothed Kjorn's mood and gave him a hopeful outlook.

He'd been treated—if not like a prince—at least like a guest, fed and respected and trusted not to fly away, while Rok, Fraenir and Frida were guarded more closely. The Vanhar had taken time to reasonably explain their law to Kjorn, taking his word for the moment that he was indeed the grandson of Per and had little knowledge of how things fared in the Winderost.

"What proof do you have that you are Per's grandson, Kajar's heir?"

Kjorn looked to the gnarled, dusty gray male who'd spoken. "My coat and feathers are like my mother's, who was the sister of a gryfess who remained at the Dawn Spire. She would vouch for me."

The high priestess gave him a keen look. "You speak of Queen Esla. Mate to Orn, now."

"Then she fares well," Kjorn said, controlling his surprise. "I didn't know she was queen."

A female hacked a cough. "Didn't know? That's likely. She clawed up to the top to avoid being associated with her sister who fled with a coward—"

"I'll ask you not speak of my kin that way." Kjorn's tail flicked and he rolled his shoulders, re-settling his feathers and pressing his talons to the grass. "Respectfully. I will answer for any cowardice."

"Alone," said the high priestess. "Why do you come alone?"

"I came alone to seek my wingbrother, Shard. A gray Vanir also from the Silver Isles." He searched their faces, but as with Nilsine, saw no sign of recognition. Disappointment twisted in his chest, and he shifted his talons against the ground. So Shard hadn't landed on this shore.

A couple of the elders nodded, accepting his reason. Two gry-fesses bent their heads together, whispering furiously. One broke away from the other to say, "What brought your wingbrother to this land?"

"Tell us your tale," said the priestess.

"It starts much earlier," Kjorn said, glancing around the circle again. The priestess merely dipped her head.

So Kjorn told them all he knew, including what he'd been told that was a lie—that Per led others away to conquer new lands, to expand their pride. He told them of his own mother's death, and with a halting tongue, his father's descent toward madness which even Kjorn couldn't explain, except that he surely harbored secrets, guilt and shame about the way they'd left the Winderost. He told them about Shard, how he'd befriended the wolves and other creatures of the Isles, learned he was the son of the dead Vanir king, exiled himself from the pride. He told them everything.

"What other proof?" demanded a male at the end of the half ring of gryfons. "Anyone could have been groomed up with this story and claimed to be Kajar's heir. We owe him nothing. Just another big out-cast from the Dawn Spire, if you ask me."

"With those feathers, Mirsk? Those eyes?"

"Trickery! I wouldn't trust him on our lands. I'll not—"

"Rok wears a chain," Kjorn said. "A golden chain of dragon craft. It was my father's. It's the only proof I can offer other than my word and my family's story."

The priestess considered that. "We shall return it to you, then—"

"No." Kjorn surprised her and himself. "Let him keep it, when or if you release him. It gives him some dignity and I think he has none left."

For a moment they asked no questions, and Kjorn closed his eyes to listen to the cool wind in the grass. The elders conferred in quiet voices.

After long moments, the priestess opened her wings to silence the others. "Son of Sverin."

He inclined his head.

"My elders have given me their opinions, and the Starwind whispers of new tidings." She studied him closely. Kjorn almost felt as if the gods looked at him, at length, through her old eyes. "It is my opinion that you were raised well, courageous and true. It is my opinion that you're telling the truth, that you were fed lies about Per's history and, the very moment you learned the truth, you wished to make things right. Whether coming here is honorable or foolhardy, I'm not certain, but certainly you are brave. Our trusted sentry told us the very first moment she saw you, Tyr shone on your face. This is not a sign we take lightly. You say your only intention here is to seek your wingbrother to make amends?"

Kjorn's tail flicked against the grass. "It is. With your leave, I'll search your lands and make no trouble here."

The elders muttered among themselves and the priestess fanned her wings to silence them. She folded them neatly on her back again and considered. For a moment, her dignity and strength reminded Kjorn of Shard's mother, Ragna, the Widow Queen. It gave him some hope, for Ragna was a force to reckon with. She was only recently an ally, but a strong one.

"Very well. You have our blessing to pass through this land."

The wind rushed across their backs and bent the grass into shimmering waves. Kjorn shivered at the sensation, then became aware that more Vanhar had crept through the grass to spy on the gathering. Young warriors, older mated parents, fledges—dozens of gryfon eyes gleamed in the last light, watching him, watching the elders.

"Thank you," Kjorn said, his hackle feathers prickling as if something watched him from behind. He resisted the urge to look over his shoulder toward the water.

"You don't know this land well." The priestess cast a look over her shoulder, lifting her wings once again as if to encompass all of the Vanhar who stood behind her. "If there are any who wish to aide the prince in his quest, you have my leave."

A few whispers twittered through the grass.

Nilsine stepped forward from those gathered. "I will help him. I will, and any from my sentries who wish."

Kjorn tried to read her reserved expression, wondered at her reasons, and noted the priestess's look of approval. He dipped his head. "Thank you."

The priestess raised her voice once again, addressing Kjorn. "Hunt, if you need to. Rest where you will." A deeper, keen look came into her eyes as she watched him. "Do no harm, and none will come to you."

Kjorn felt a sensation as of warmth on his wings, but now the air was still, the sun lowering enough to allow the cold of night. "Thank you," he murmured again, the only response he could make.

"You have our welcome," said the priestess. "We shall watch with great interest what will happen, now that the line of Kajar has returned to the Winderost."

13

SEA WOLVES

HIGH, THIN NIGHT AIR SUCKED every breath from Shard's throat. Stars embraced their flight like thousands of distant torches of white fire. That high, the icy ocean below appeared to be only another distant sky, calm and flat with reflected stars.

Shard shook his head, breathing slowly, and looked over to Hikaru. The dragon, now seven times Shard's length from nose to tail, soared alongside him. Free to eat his fill, he seemed to grow as Shard took breath.

It had been Hikaru's idea to fly higher, to cover the leagues faster, and despite his shortness of breath, Shard had to agree. But he saw the dragon's head nod.

"Hikaru."

The dragon flapped his wings once, almost invisible in the dark but for the edges picked out in the starlight, and for the budding silver horns and mane.

"Hikaru!"

"I'm here." He shook his head, Shard heard him gasp. "I'm awake. There's ice on the water. Shard, look, ice!"

"Ice in the air, too," Shard said, breathing deeply again. He had trained himself to high flying, challenging himself always, but he watched Hikaru as sharply as a falcon minded its eggs. He'd taught Hikaru the dynamic soaring flight of seabirds that he'd learned from an albatross named Windwalker, but once mastered, Hikaru had tired of it and insisted on high flight. Now he often drifted in and out of attention, and occasionally dipped in flight so Shard had to slap him awake. "I fear a storm," Shard said loudly to get Hikaru's attention.

"No, it means we're close!" Hikaru scanned the dark horizon eagerly, as if land and friendly dragons and the answers to all their troubles perched just beyond the waves. "We may even see the shore by dawn!"

Hikaru looked up then, at the stars, naming them quietly to himself. Shard kept an eye on the dragon's wings, on his forepaws tucked alertly to his chest, not drooping. "We must keep following Midragur," Hikaru said. "That will lead us. I know it will."

"I believe you. Hikaru, we should save our breath for now."

Below, clouds piled in slowly from the dawnward quarter. If Shard and Hikaru maintained their current height, the storm posed no threat and they could fly over, above it all, if their strength held out. Shard suppressed a shiver at the memory of his last storm at sea.

"I'm hungry," Hikaru announced, and without leave, turned and dove.

"Hikaru! Hikaru, slowly!" Shard shook his head, gasping a breath, and folded his wings to dive. He readied himself for the warmer air, the richer breath, timed his breathing, streamlined his wings to the freezing wind in his face. Hikaru flew well enough, but seemed more eager to get to the places he was going than to perfect his flight. Shard feared for him.

"Hikaru!"

Young, rolling laughter answered him, and Hikaru shot down like a falling star. The first layer of denser air was a relief, a shock, and Shard saw the dragon's wings falter. Like surfacing from deep water, diving too fast posed its own dangers for the novice fledgling.

Fledgling, Shard scolded himself. *He's only a fledgling. I should've kept him closer, shouldn't have agreed to this high flight.*

Shard saw the moment when the wind stalled the dragon's wings—he'd never had so much room to gain speed, never felt the air stall against him.

"Hikaru straighten out! Slow down!"

He saw Hikaru try, lashing his long body to flare, but throwing himself off balance instead. Chest aching, Shard plummeted, hoping to catch him and force him into a flare. The ocean shimmered before him, reflected stars spinning in dizzying array, and he narrowed his focus to the shadow that was Hikaru. Shard knew panic, knew what it was when the world tilted and it was impossible to sort out.

"Use your tail to straighten out! I'm above you, ocean below! Point your nose to the horizon—"

As Shard yelled, he saw Hikaru following his instructions. Relieved, he called encouragement, pushing open his wings a little to slow his own dive. With an awkward, final thrash Hikaru pulled out of the dive, straightening into a glide.

Shard swooped down alongside him and slapped talons against his tail with a hiss. "Never do that again! Do you understand me?"

Hikaru laughed breathlessly. "I had to try it. You told me about all the diving you've done, and I wanted to try."

Shard clenched his talons. "I understand, believe me. And..." He forced himself to calm down, to not act like a mother ptarmigan. They were both fine, after all, and Hikaru had corrected in plenty of time. A wind picked up and the waves sparkled, now only the width of ten gryfon leaps below them. "You did well. You were very brave, and you did just fine."

Hikaru's eyes shone with pride. "Thank you."

"Just remember, I've been flying for many more years than you, and I'd been flying for many years before I ever tried diving into the sea from such a height."

"I know." Hikaru looked over at him. "But I have a much shorter time to practice."

Shard huffed a breath, and could not answer that. *By this time next year, he will be gone from the world. From my world.*

The thought was enough to make him cringe that he'd scolded the young dragon at all.

The wet, frozen scent of snow filled the air. After a moment he managed to answer Hikaru's trusting stare. "You did well. I'm proud of you."

"Thank you, Shard. That means everything to me." Dragon teeth gleamed in the star light. "Though I am still hungry."

Shard eyed the storm clouds rushing in. "We may have to wait. It's safer if we go high again, until the storm has passed."

"But you've flown in a storm, you told me!"

"Not by choice. And I escaped it by flying out, remember?"

"I have to eat," Hikaru declared, a growl coming into his voice, "or I shall fall out of the sky."

"Hikaru—"

Hikaru's gaze darted over Shard and, perhaps realizing Shard couldn't stop him, he spiraled lower toward the waves. Indignity and surprise were a waste of time, Shard supposed, in the face of a hungry young dragon. He angled his wings to follow, keeping his gaze on the storm as Hikaru hunted for fish. Relieved that he seemed to be finding them, if only small ones, Shard relaxed a little.

Hikaru's earlier observation had been correct. Thin, small islands of ice floated around them. Shard watched alternately as Hikaru dove beneath the waves, stopping Shard's heart until he emerged again and either slithered onto an ice floe to eat his catch, or break out of the waves to fly up again.

"You're doing really well," Shard forced himself to call. "I couldn't do that when I was your age."

Whatever his age is. Shard could only compare him to a gryfon by his skill and his range of thinking. A fledge of two or three, at best, and how soon would it be until he seemed to be Shard's age, and older, like Amaratsu?

Shard's own belly snarled in protest at watching someone else eat all the fish. Before he could dive, Hikaru swooped up before him, offering a fresh, wriggling herring.

"Thank you." Shard clenched the fish, flight dipping with the weight of it. Hikaru met his eyes silently and dipped his head. By no means an apology, but Shard remembered what it was to be challenged by an adult as a fledge, the frustration of being told what to do, and let him go again.

The wind picked at the waves and they rose, choppy and large, scattering the reflection of the sky. Clouds covered the true sky, scattering the true stars and turning the ocean black and unfathomable. Shard could barely see his charge. He thought Hikaru had perched on an ice floe to eat, but it was hard to tell in the muddy dark.

He finished as much of the fish as he could, thanked its spirit, and tossed the bones into the water. Squinting, he knew for sure he saw the black dragon clinging to an ice floe, hunched over the water. "Hikaru! We should go."

Hikaru didn't move.

"*Hikaru.*" Shard's voice bounced over the waves, his patience snapping. "Now!"

"Shard, there are creatures!" He sounded breathless, not angry or petulant, but breathless with glee. "Shard, huge creatures under the water! What are they? I can see them easily as I can see you."

Shard strained for patience as the first drops of sleet hit his face. "Hikaru, that's wonderful. I have no doubt you'll see in the dark, and through water, and even underwater in the dark. You must fly with me now. We can't risk a storm. We'll have time to explore the ocean when there isn't a storm. I promise."

"But—"

"Now!"

Hikaru shoved up from the ice floe, rejoining Shard, who drew a great breath of relief. "Up, high now…"

"Oh, look, Shard!"

Sleet and snow slashed against them, and the freezing wind gnawed at Shard's core, even under the long feathers and down of a Vanir.

He whirled to see what Hikaru saw.

Great beasts lunged out of the water with squeals and clicks. Their faces, painted in stark, neat whorls of black and white, seemed to match the patches of ice and darkness in the water. Shard, flapping hard against the storm, closed his eyes with a growing sense of dread.

"What are they?" Hikaru cried, full of awe and joy at seeing something new.

Shard strained to understand their voices, so different from a gryfon, a bird or creature of the earth. He thought of the waves, of salt water streaming around his face when he swam. A memory of a dream came to him, a pale blue king.

Jaarl. Perhaps even Shard's own ancestor, a Vanir king who'd befriended...

"Whales," Shard whispered. But not this kind of whale.

Their voices mingled up from the waves as they breached, crashing against ice and blowing great spurts of air and water against the storm.

"They're calling to me." Hikaru looped around him, seemingly unaware of the driving wind and snow. "Do you hear them? Shard, are they friends?"

"No," Shard gasped against the wind. "Not these. Hikaru, there are some wise sea creatures, but these..." He struggled to breathe against the freezing air, the wind, and could only concentrate on keeping aloft. He'd seen the black and white whales once, as a kit. He'd asked Sigrun about them and she called them sea wolves.

"Sea wolves," Shard said. "Not friends. They could be dangerous. Hikaru, fly higher."

"But you said wolves are friends."

"Hikaru, not these," Shard snapped, his voice cracking. For Sigrun had told him a tale once of her own youth, of seeing the sea wolves for the first time, apparently playing a game in the water. Tossing something back and forth between them. She and Ragna had flown out to meet them, to welcome them to the waters of the Silver Isles.

Then Sigrun had seen what they threw in the water between them. Shard had never seen it happen, himself. But he could imagine it. He could see whales tossing a crying seal pup between them as a game.

Shard couldn't even tell Hikaru. Despite all the tales he'd told the young dragon of his own life, he couldn't yet explain to him the concept of taking amusement in another's pain.

He strained against the storm, running short of breath, his belly aching from the fish and the sudden exertion. "Hikaru, please fly with me, please…" His voice sounded weak and far away to his own ears. He probably wouldn't have listened to himself, either. Hikaru dipped lower, calling out to the whales, unable to contain his curiosity. Shard flew after him, trying to stay close and not fall in the water.

Perhaps they are capable of love as well as cruelty, Sigrun had said, always wary of prejudicing him against any creature unjustly. *Just as a gryfon is capable of great love and great cruelty. Perhaps you could speak to one. But I would not trust them in the water as I would not trust a fox in its den.*

Hikaru landed again on an ice floe and Shard, against his better judgment, dropped hard beside him.

The waves tossed the chunk of ice high and Shard dug in his talons, scrabbling for purchase as they rode down the back of a dark wave. Hikaru looped around him, holding him fast. The dragon's claws dug into the ice as they had dug into stone. As Shard caught a relieved breath, pressed to Hikaru's warm scales, Hikaru loosed a series of whistles and clicks, imitating the whales.

One broke the surface, chattering madly. To Shard it sounded like laughter. Then words.

"Ho, here, what have we?"

A long, creaking note laughed behind Shard and he spun, blind in the freezing dark, his wings drenched. Their voices sounded static, broken, he feared he might never understand them as well as an animal of the land or the air. Half of their conversation took place under the water, and the other half barely audible in the storm, barely recognizable as speech.

"Playmates for my calf?"

"No!" Shard shouted. "Stay away! Hikaru we must go."

"Where is your calf?" Hikaru bobbed as the ice floe surged up and over another wave.

"In the water, lovely sky snake. Here in the water."

Shard sucked in a breath against the sleet. Water loomed over them. He ducked under Hikaru's wing as fast water flowed over their little ice raft.

"Hikaru, they will kill us—fly, now!" Though when Shard lifted his wings they felt heavy, sodden, stripped. *I am a son of Tyr. I will fly. A son of Tor. I don't fear the sea.*

"They won't kill me," Hikaru scoffed.

Arrogant fledge, Shard thought wildly, angry, wondering where his sweet, adventurous, obedient dragonet had gone.

"As one!" sang one of the massive, black whales.

"What?" Hikaru cried, "I don't understand y—"

"As one," echoed the others.

Shard turned in time to see a strange wave bulging toward them. It wasn't natural. "Hikaru, fly! Fly now!"

At last Hikaru heeded and crouched, opening his wings—but four whales shoved a wave over the ice floe, smashed their noses under to up-end it and knocked dragon and gryfon off the ice into the thrashing water.

Something slammed into Shard, driving him under. In the blackness and cold he kicked and flung his talons against anything that felt solid. The taste of salt water mingled with blood. The black waves roiled with whales and Shard clawed through them, seeking the surface. Their voices laughed and shrilled around him, filled the ocean with murderous glee.

"See how he squirms, little one!"

Shard stepped on a slick, muscled back and shoved, breaking the surface for a raw breath. A desperate look around showed him Hikaru, snaking through the water. He tried to make a sound so the dragon could find him. A calf the size of a full grown Aesir flung itself out of the water, laughing, and landed in the middle of Hikaru's back, dragging him under the water.

"Stop it! Stop this now, we're peaceful travel—"

A fin slapped him to silence, driving him backward under the water again. Teeth clamped his hind leg. Shard screamed, shocked by the pain. The whale dragged him through the water by his leg and tossed him into the air. The relief of air almost countered the dazzling pain in his leg. Shard flung out his wings and his muscles nearly snapped in protest from the cold. Water soaked him, too heavy to fly. He smacked into the water again like a stone. Frothing waves rocked him back and slapped his face.

"Hikaru! Get out! Get out if you..." He lurched back as a whale welled up in front of him and surfaced, water spilling down his face, jaws splayed. Shard dove forward and threw himself against the laughing face, slapped his talons out and raked the monster's eye.

With a long squeal the whale thrashed away, shaking Shard off to dive deep again. He could not find Hikaru against the black waves, amongst the black, swimming bodies all around.

"Coward! Let us be! Hikaru, where—"

A female knocked into him. "Wicked, wicked birdie! Come play!"

"Shard, no!" The last sight he had was Hikaru, lashing toward him, only to be driven back by a laughing whale.

The female drove Shard down under the water, down, on the blunt of her nose, until he thought his chest would collapse and his head break from the pressure and the cold.

Lights flickered. He saw strange things. The red she-wolf Catori, sprinting toward him through the dark, howling his name, calling him toward moonlight above the clouds. He saw Stigr falling beside him, then turning, both wings intact, to give him a baleful, challenging stare.

Then he saw the dead. In the ice dark, he saw his father, pale Baldr, lit by a sun Shard couldn't see. The whale shoved her nose against him, nearly breaking his back, and he saw Helaku the wolf king, his son Ahote, saw old gryfon and wolf kings and queens of the Silver Isles. With a shudder he saw the scarlet flash of Per the Red, laughing.

Then, oddly, Einarr. "My friend," Shard whispered, seemingly in his mind alone, surprised. His body, shoved about by the furious whale, seemed a distant thing.

Shard! Einarr appeared to shout.

Why do you stand with the dead? Shard wondered, calmly. And why, he wondered, did there appear to be a vast, sunlit plain just beyond the bottom of the sea...

My prince, he heard the younger gryfon say. *My king. My king.* Einarr opened his copper wings and a strange rush of air came to Shard, sweet as summer, and he took a single breath.

Pain lanced into his awareness. The whale was trying to kill him, which meant he was still alive.

He thrashed around, dragging his talons as deeply as he could through the thick, hard flesh. A squeal of pain filled the ocean, drowning on and on as if it were not water but a vast, echoing cavern. She rolled her massive body away from Shard and he kicked, rising. His head ached. His chest squeezed against itself. Nothing gave him any indication of a surface. He felt he would burst.

My king, my king. The voice called him upward.

Hikaru, he thought desperately. If he never made it alive back to the Silver Isles, he at least had to make sure Hikaru flew out of this cursed place.

Then, just as black and scarlet ringed his vision and it seemed the sea would break him, Shard broke the surface.

Sleet-filled air was the sweetest thing he'd ever tasted. He turned in the water, seeking Hikaru.

A strange sound pierced the storm, a long, hollow, harmonious roar like a lion and many eagles calling together. For a moment, Shard reeled and he thought gryfons flew at them on the wind, for those were the only creatures Shard could conceive of in that moment. But when they called again, he realized the sound was not even close.

A new, unnatural wind chopped up the water around the thrashing bodies of the whales and the chunks of ice all around. Wing beats. Great wings, stirring the wind.

"Petty blackfish," boomed a male...a male...Shard shook his head hard, squinting up into the night. *Could it be?*

"Back to the depths with you!" snarled a female...

It hit Shard like a slap.

"Dragons! Hikaru! Hikaru, dragons!"

He heard no answer. The whales laughed and Shard was aware only of pounding wings, enormous clawed forepaws raking the water. He threw himself across the waves toward a floating chunk of ice.

"H-help," he gasped, at once aware of everything wrong with his body. One hind leg was surely broken, and ached with a wicked pain. The ice beneath him darkened from blood. He dragged himself out of the water, nearly splitting his talons on the ice. "Help! There's a young dragon…"

But it seemed they knew. Whether sentries far out from shore, or dragons fishing and caught in the storm like them, they must have heard Hikaru and come. Shard hugged the ice, fighting the waves and rising nausea. Their beautiful voices, like giant birds, like Amaratsu's, flickered around him.

"Witless bullies! I should skin them."

"None of that, now. They're gone. Where is he?"

"There he is."

"Come, little lost one. Come home. You're lucky we flew out in this storm."

"Shard!"

Shard's ears perked in relief. He tried to cry out again, to respond to Hikaru, but his chest clamped, his body wanted only to breathe. As long as Hikaru was safe, it didn't matter. His charge, his brother. He gripped the ice.

One of the dragons laughed. "He's not so little!"

"Winterborn, but growing strong. That's good. Come now, young one."

From the commotion and wing beats, Shard knew they dragged the young dragon from the water.

"Wait!" Hikaru cried.

"What's that?"

"Shard, my…my brother." Hikaru coughed. At least he was speaking. Speaking, safe, and surrounded by his own kind.

"Did Amaratsu have a second egg?"

"Only one."

"He's delirious. Come home. You need a meal, and fire, look at the state of you. Like a witless, wild beast."

"What of *that?*"

Somehow by the tone, Shard knew the dragon spoke of him. He tried to move but it felt so good to be still, to let the ice cool his wounds. The whales were gone. The storm was passing. Or perhaps the dragons, with their power, drove it away. He bobbed and floated on a calming sea.

"That's Shard. He must come with us," Hikaru pleaded. Shard tried to open his eyes, then didn't bother. It was dark. He couldn't see the dragons anyway. "Please!"

"We can't just leave it to the whales," a female argued, and Shard was grateful to her.

"They won't come back. And the land isn't so far off."

"Yes, he'll drift in. Don't trouble yourself."

"Please, he's my brother!"

"Shhh, you've had a difficult time. Ooh, there you are, heavy young one. You're lucky your wing's not broken, but let us carry you."

"Wing breakers!"

"They don't understand the crime. They're of the sea. Besides, it's not broken."

"I'll break their *tails* and see how they fare!"

"Calm yourself, Natsumi."

"Shard!"

"No more," rumbled the male. "Mind your elders."

"He takes after his mother."

Some halting laughter. Waves splashed at Shard's heels and he clung to the ice, shivering.

"What of the...Shard?" The female again, the one called Natsumi.

"Leave it."

That was the final decision, and the last Shard heard of them, except for Hikaru's low, angry howls piercing higher and higher into the night air.

14

ISLE OF EARTH AND FIRE

THE THICK SMELL OF SULFUR and something akin to sun-baked rock stung all of Caj's senses as he crawled out of the cave.

Despite the falcon's help, they had found no trace of Sverin on Talon's Reach. Wary, Caj peered around for any marks of life, for Pebble's Throw was one of the most dangerous islands.

A raven glided in happy circles above him, riding the buoyant warm air above the lava flows. Caj watched, one ear slanting back. Silently, the bird dipped down and lighted on an outcropping of dusty black rock, watching Caj in return. Ravens were wolf birds, Vanir birds, and he realized he waited with held breath to see if this one might somehow carry a message from Shard.

But the raven hopped up and flew away, almost *oddly* silent, into the mist. Caj sensed a presence behind him in the tunnel and crawled forward to make way.

"I will not go here," whispered the golden wolf, Tocho, still crouched in the entrance of the cave. He'd shown Caj the particular tunnel under the islands that brought them out again to the surface of one of the scattered little isles of Pebble's Throw.

Caj blew a long breath out through his nostrils, drew in again to satisfy himself that the air wouldn't poison him, and turned to the wolf. "I won't ask you to. But I have to search."

Tocho took a moment to watch him, nose quivering. "Be careful. If I don't hear from you by the evening mark—"

"I'll be fine," Caj murmured, surprised at Tocho's concern and at his own growing sense of affection. In many ways, the young wolf reminded him of a gryfon fledge—bold, eager, a bit foolhardy. His help had been invaluable. "Go to your family, take a rest, and thank you. You've done enough today. I remember the way."

Tocho's ears flicked warily back and forward again, scanning the air, then he dipped his head to Caj and wriggled back down underground.

With another slow sigh, Caj turned to face the ragged heap of black rock and smoke. The heat seeping to him from all points soothed the ache in his mending wing and put him in a better humor than he'd been in for a while. Without the wolf, whose scent would either spook Sverin or put him on the offensive, Caj could afford to be less subtle.

"Sverin!" he shouted, and was answered by the hissing of steam somewhere several leaps off as searing earthfire trickled into the cold sea. "Son-of-Per, my wingbrother!"

You will know yourself again if it's the last thing I do, Caj swore silently. A bit of red caught his eye. He swung around, carefully favoring his wing, but the red was only bright trickles of lava. They wormed down from fissures in a jagged peak across a narrow river of seawater, glowing red in the low, gray light. Caj huffed, but was not disheartened. They'd searched Talon's Reach, then tried the Star Isle on the word of a fishing eagle. Then a crow informed them that Halvden and Sverin had fled, driven off the starward edge of that isle by the snow wolves. All the isles, it seemed, knew of Caj's hunt for the mad king, and seemed eager to help him.

For what it's worth, he thought, wondering if the crow had tricked them for some reason.

He walked forward across the surface of the rock on which he'd emerged. It appeared to be the largest chunk of the broken scatter that the Vanir called an island. Caj recalled the final flight of Per the Red. Caj and Sverin had borne the dead king over the other isles and, with the entire pride circling above, cast him into the large lava flow. The red feathers caught and burned, bones flowing down with the lava, burning, and what didn't burn before they hit were buried in the sea, frozen in black rock. Perhaps in his feral state, Sverin had felt called to the last place he would've remembered seeing his father.

Caj shook himself and walked forward, calling Sverin's name. The swirl of seawater between the broken rock islands, the hiss of steam, and the blast of poisonous gases from cracks on distant shores drowned out his calls. Voice hoarse, he finally fell silent. Then he reached the end of his little island.

Wary, he tried to gauge the depth of the narrow channel between the ground on which he stood and the next more ragged, slanting face of rock.

Nothing for it, he thought. He turned and loped several leaps back, reminding himself sternly to keep his wings closed or suffer pain and Sigrun's ire. Then he bolted forward, sprinting to gain speed and momentum, bunched the powerful muscles of his hindquarters and launched himself over the channel of water.

His talons hit the stone, his belly smashed against the curve where the rock broke down into the sea and he gasped. Hind legs scrabbling for purchase, Caj growled and strained, his shoulders cramping and wings screaming to open.

Am I getting old at last? A little jump is enough to do me in? With a final, raw shove, he surged onto the island and rolled, voice cracking out in pain when he crunched his injured wing. The ache faded to dullness after a moment and he hoped he hadn't done too much damage.

When he caught his breath and turned at last to look behind him, he felt satisfied, fairly certain not even the young warriors under his training could have made the leap with wings closed. It would be easier going back, for he realized now he had mis-judged the height of this isle to the next, and he now stood on higher ground.

A blast of steam brought him back to his surroundings and he stared around warily, tail swinging.

The snow that coated the other islands melted against the heat of Pebble's Throw and turned to chilly, misty drizzle. Caj enjoyed the way the drizzle slipped from his newly oiled wings—the wings of a Vanir who fed on fish, he thought wryly—but the moisture dimmed his vision and deadened his calls. Ahead of him the island broke into a series of cracks and small gorges, and out of these, every few heartbeats, issued a blast of noxious steam. The cracks were large enough to stumble over, not fall into, but he knew the steam would be deadly. He watched it for a few moments, counting in alternate rhythm with his breaths and the steam. He could wait and time his leaps around them.

Grumbling, he strode forward, trying to catch a scent of Sverin against the harsh smells of the oozing magma and listening hard for any sound of life.

Blinking against the drizzle, he caught a new scent through the sulfuric air. Immediately he crouched, laying himself as flat against the black rock as he could, though there was no way to disguise his feathers, he slunk along the ground to lower himself behind a ridge of stone.

The low breeze, warm from steam and heavy with sulfur, brought him the new scent again. Feather and fur, warmth and life. It was a scent Caj knew well. It was a gryfon scent, one of his pride.

But it wasn't Sverin.

The memory of battle stiffened his wing and Caj suppressed a growl. He climbed up the stone ridge, silent and low as a ghostly mountain cat around the hissing fissures and shallow gorges. The rock sloped down abruptly into a face of black glass slag for about four leaps, then flattened into a walkable surface again. Surprisingly, the ground there was scattered with pale green and gray lichen, the only growing thing Caj had seen thus far.

Crouched in the lichen, gnawing fiercely at the glistening thigh bone of a red deer, was Halvden. The young warrior who had turned Sverin against him, whose father had stirred trouble with the wolves and died for it, who had harried Shard at every turn and who Caj had for so long dismissed merely as healthy competition for his nest-son.

Halvden, the fluffed up jaybird who, in his blackest, and stupidest, and bravest moment, had tried to murder Caj. Had it not been for the mercy of the Star Island wolves, he would have succeeded.

Halvden had always been the best looking, the best fighter, the best pupil of his age. The price of that was arrogance.

There was only one cure for arrogance.

"Son-of-Hallr," Caj whispered into the drizzle, heart leaping up with hunting thrill. His tail dusted back and forth against the rock behind him. "Time for your next lesson."

15

THE FIRST PLAINS

"WAKE, YOUR HIGHNESS."

Kjorn opened his eyes to the voice of Nilsine, the huntress who'd first met him. Her hushed tone gave him pause. For the last several days she had acted as his personal bodyguard—or perhaps chaperone was more accurate. He wasn't always sure if she meant to protect him, or others from him.

"What is it?" Cold had dropped the night before. Though Kjorn was snuggled deep in one of their best grass hollows, the chill wind off the sea smelled lightly of snow, and there was frost on the grass just beyond his nest.

Nilsine huffed a disgusted sigh. "Rok and Frida have escaped. I don't know how he did it so quietly. My guards aren't stupid."

Kjorn cursed softly and stood, stretching his wings to warm them. He thought of the painted wolf Mayka who'd helped him escape in near silence, but didn't mention it. He owed the wolf a debt. "Will you go after him?"

"No." Nilsine stepped away and looked out over the hills of the Vanheim. "It isn't worth it to hunt him. Not now, when we have more important things to do." He gave her a sideways look and she inclined her head. "We're planning to depart today, and lead you to the First Plains. The high priestess believes that if anyone in the Winderost would know of one foreign gryfon, it would be the lions. And if you want my opinion…"

"I do."

"We should also *try* to meet with the eagles of the Voldsom Narrows. The elders claim there was a time they had peace with the Dawn Spire, but I'll believe it when it happens. Who knows. They might be willing to help you, anyway."

Kjorn chuckled. "Maybe. Thank you. I'll take your advice, and I trust you to the routes. I'd like to avoid any scouts or patrols from the Dawn Spire for now."

"I understand." Her eyes glittered in the gloom of predawn. "If they know of your presence here, it could complicate your search for your friend."

Kjorn laughed. "Something like that." He liked the fierce border guard, and he hoped she liked him. It would be good to have friends in the Winderost.

She dipped her head. "We leave at first light, but I woke you early because Rok's other companion didn't flee with him."

"Fraenir?" Kjorn's tail twitched.

Nilsine shrugged her wings. "He asked to speak to you."

"I thought about what you said." Fraenir glanced uncomfortably between the two humorless Vanhar who stood on either side of him. It was breakfast, and all around, Nilsine's volunteers, the high priestess herself, and younger, stronger gryfons chosen by the elders to represent their council ate fresh fish, waiting for Kjorn's word to depart.

"What, exactly?" Kjorn asked. It had been several days since he arrived, since the Vanhar elders agreed to assist him in his search for Shard.

Fraenir looked embarrassed. "What you said of duty, and honor."

"So you stayed?" He sensed Nilsine walk up on one side of him, and Fraenir crouched back.

But he found his courage to respond. "Yes. I tried to convince Rok, but he wouldn't listen." Fraenir drew himself up, looking first to Nilsine, then Kjorn. "I want to help. I want to…to join you."

Nilsine's tail lashed. "You have yet to recompense for your acts of thievery and mischief."

"He can recompense," Kjorn said without taking his eyes from Fraenir, "by helping me."

"Your Highness." Nilsine glowered at Kjorn. "With all respect, the Vanheim Shore is not your domain."

Kjorn looked down at her, and lifted his wings. "I know that. But he asks to serve me. I'd like to let him try to pay for his crimes and find some sense of honor. He's seen what Rok has become, and surely we don't want him to follow in those foot steps."

Nilsine's expression didn't change. Abruptly she turned back to Fraenir. "I know you better than the prince does, and I have less faith in you. For his sake, you may accompany us, and serve, but the first sign of mischief, the first betrayal, and you'll answer to me."

When Fraenir only glared, Kjorn said quietly, "Yes, my lady."

Startled, Fraenir flattened one ear and echoed him. "Yes. My lady."

"Release him," Nilsine ordered the two guards, and they stepped away far enough that Fraenir could spread his wings and fly if he wished. Kjorn more than half expected him to. But he didn't.

Bright young eyes gleamed at Kjorn. "What now?"

Kjorn eyed the glowing horizon. "Breakfast."

The guards left with Fraenir to seek their share of fish, and Nilsine sidled closer to Kjorn. "You have a good heart, son-of-Sverin, but I don't know if that one does. He could mean to spy for Rok, or take information to the Dawn Spire in return for I don't know what. I recommend you watch him."

Watching the light rise over the sea, Kjorn said, "I thought that's what you were here for. To watch my back. Or watch me?"

It took her a moment to chuckle, but she did. "Aye, my lord. And so I will—watch both of you. See you get something to eat, it's a long flight to the starward border of the First Plain."

"These lions," Kjorn said slowly, "what should I expect from them?"

"Hard to say. They follow only Tor. They believe they are older than us, that Tor placed them first in the world. They dream deeper, and they choose their friends carefully."

"And their enemies?"

She spread her wings in another shrug. "I suggest you focus on becoming their friend."

"If they're honorable, as you say, that shouldn't be difficult."

"Maybe," she said, sounding doubtful. "Just remember as you speak with them that they hunt at night. That is their realm. And for the last two generations the nights have been ruined by the screams of the enemy, the danger and fear of them always lurking." Her gaze fixed steadily on him, inscrutable as a sea hawk. "And it was your great grandfather who brought them here."

They reached the border of what Nilsine called the First Plains by late afternoon, and she ordered them to walk, rather than fly, into the lions' territory, out of respect. A low haze hung like mist across the stretch of land, smelling sourly of smoke, and Kjorn marveled that the effect of the volcano had drifted so far windward.

Despite the haze, vague memory and restlessness circled Kjorn's mind the more scents he caught and the deeper inland they went. Though he didn't remember any of it distinctly, a sense lingered.

As he landed and beheld the long, grass plain and took in the distinct scent of the big, hunting cats that saturated the area, he wondered at Shard's coming here. Perhaps he'd come to find the true history of the Aesir and the Conquering, and why Per fled. Perhaps, Kjorn thought, beholding the long plain, he'd had other plans in mind.

If he is, after all, prince of the Vanir and plans to make his claim once again, where does he plan for that to leave me?

Only finding Shard would tell.

Nilsine ordered her scouts to fan out and find lions so that they might announce Kjorn properly.

His thoughts lost in the Silver Isles and Shard—he still couldn't truly imagine his wingbrother as a prince—Kjorn jumped to discover Fraenir standing next to him.

"What should I do, sire?"

He seemed to delight in calling Kjorn by a title, as if he'd craved leadership and now had something on which to focus the high energies of his youth. Kjorn managed not to sigh. "Pick a group, and search for lions with them. Keep your head down and be respectful."

Disappointment flashed in Fraenir's face but Kjorn didn't budge. The young gryfon needed to learn discipline and rank, not act as Kjorn's personal errand pigeon.

"What about *her?*" Fraenir asked of Nilsine, who strode toward them, ears constantly ticking back and forth, on high alert in the high grass and smoky air.

"Your Highness," she said to Kjorn, and he wondered that she seemed to be genuine, and began to wonder more why she'd volunteered to help. She didn't acknowledge Fraenir. "With your leave, I'll have you search with me. The lions will have gone to ground until nightfall, but my scouts have the scent of a pronghorn herd where the lions might go to hunt."

"Lead on," Kjorn said, following her. Over his shoulder he said, "Fraenir, you have your orders."

The younger gryfon huffed, fluffed his wings, then called to a group of the departing scouts to wait for him.

Beside Kjorn, Nilsine's cool countenance broke and she scoffed. "You shouldn't waste your time. He's exile stock, born and bred. A thief with no discipline, no honor. I warn you, he will betray you in the end, maybe not directly, but through cowardice or some other thievish—"

"I appreciate your concern," Kjorn said, lifting his head high to catch the scents on the wind. "But I'll handle him."

They waded through waving, golden grass, and as the sun dipped, so did the warmth of the day. Kjorn felt a chill, but it was nothing compared to winter in the Silver Isles.

"Will you tell me something?" Kjorn asked. "I didn't wish to ask back at the Vanheim Shore and seem too ignorant, but I thought you might indulge me."

"I might," Nilsine answered blandly.

"What did the priestess mean when she spoke of the Four Winds?"

Nilsine loosed a soft breath. "Not a belief the Aesir recognize anymore? It is the oldest of traditions. Before gryfons knew Tyr and Tor, they knew only the earth, wind, sea and sky. The Four Winds—Star, Night, Sun and Dawn...they all have their own purpose, their own messages."

"I see." He considered the four directions. "And what wind does your priestess think is blowing now?"

Nilsine squinted, ears twitching. "Before we left this morning she told me that the air is still."

"What does that mean?"

"That means no one knows what will happen."

Kjorn's tail twitched but he maintained a neutral expression. His father had little patience with prophecy, and he was beginning to understand why. But he couldn't dismiss their beliefs. "Well then. Perhaps we shall stir the winds with our own wings."

She looked amused at that. "Perhaps. We could do with a change."

"What kind of change?"

Nilsine dipped her head, sniffing at an imprint in the grass. "All I know is why I patrol our borders. The exiles, rogues, and poachers run amok throughout the plains, the Dawn Reach, and the Outlands surrounding the Dawn Spire. They have no order, though if I had to pick a leader among them, it would be Rok." Her expression soured, and Kjorn kept his opinions to himself. "The families of the Reach remain at the Dawn Spire. The Aesir clans of the Ostral Shores have left the Dawn Spire and keep their own borders. Obviously, the Vanhar have left. Some families, refusing to serve the new king and unable to go home without his support for fear of the wyrms, live in exile, but scattered."

"The Ostral Shores..." Kjorn wracked his memory of why the name was familiar, but his father had spoken so little of their home-land. "Caj," he blurted, and Nilsine watched him, bemused. "I just recalled—my father met his wingbrother at the Ostral Shores. Caj, son-of-Cai."

"Then you may have allies starward of the Dawn Spire, if you can make it there in one piece. Perhaps they know of your friend."

"They well might. Caj is Shard's nest-father."

"They might also be enemies," she added bluntly. "We don't know how their feelings might fly toward your family now."

"I appreciate your honesty," Kjorn said dryly. Nilsine merely inclined her head. Kjorn considered the fractured land and gryfon clans, and the great enemy that threatened them at night. He won-dered, almost idly, what might have happened if Per hadn't fled, and if this land was his birthright, still.

But he did flee.

The sun was dying, wind and dim purple light washed the First Plains. Kjorn still shuddered instinctively at being out in the open at night. Since he was a kit his father had forbidden flying at night, and now that Kjorn knew there was a great, real enemy in the Winderost which hunted at night, he began to understand why. A cry went up, and Nilsine perked her ears. "They've found lions! Come."

She bounded forward and Kjorn followed at pace. Grass scratched at his face and whipped his eyes until he mastered a rolling lope, his head tilted back above the stems.

Gryfon shouts and lion snarls cracked the evening, and dread swarmed Kjorn's chest at the sound of a skirmish.

When he saw the combatants, his temper flashed.

"Fraenir!" he shouted, bounding toward the fight. "You fool!"

Nilsine tried to snag Kjorn's tail to keep him from entering the fray, but he had to. The younger gryfon fought two larger, young male lions and would surely lose. Kjorn took them in with a glance, their size that nearly matched an average gryfon, golden, muscular feline forms and short, bristly dark manes flying in the fight—saw an opening, and slammed into his target, shouting, "We're here in peace!"

"You've broken the borders," rumbled the young lion Kjorn had knocked to the ground. He whipped to his feet and prowled in a cautious circle as he took in Kjorn's size, and Kjorn did not pursue. He stood still, wings folded, tense in case the lion leaped again, but didn't advance. Vanhar surrounded them and the lions drew back. Nilsine's warriors dragged Fraenir back from his opponent and that lion stalked away, prowling back and forth behind the one who spoke to Kjorn.

"A gross trespass of our agreements with the Vanhar. Or are you poachers?"

"I am no poacher." Nilsine trotted up next to Kjorn. "You should know me. Nilsine, daughter-of-Nels, of the Vanhar. And by your scent I guess you to be Ajali, brother to Ajia the Swiftest."

He bared his long yellow fangs. "And this?" His ears flicked forward toward Kjorn. Fraenir limped up behind Kjorn, looking sullen, and Kjorn gave him a brief, sharp look before turning to the lion.

"I am—"

"Kjorn," said a liquid, female voice from the grass. They all turned, and the male lions made way for six lionesses who rose from the grass. The wind shifted and Kjorn caught their scent at last, and the sight of them was surprising, not the least because of their abrupt appearance.

Like the wolves of the Star Isle, they wore feathers knotted into the fur of their necks. Kjorn took that as a hopeful sign, because the feathers had obviously belonged to gryfons. The leading lioness, long and muscled, had a pale, tawny coat. She inclined her head to Kjorn, and the feathers that ringed her neck stood a little like an eagle's. It was then he saw that knotted near the base of the display of feathers were also broken talons and tiny bones.

His sense of hope cooled.

"Kjorn," she repeated, as if familiar. "The long awaited heir of Kajar." Her golden eyes found Nilsine, in the last dim light of day. "You were right to bring him to us, daughter of the Vanhar. He is the last of three—three who we knew would follow the starfire to our land."

"Three?" Kjorn asked, mantling belatedly when he saw that Nilsine bowed to the lioness. "Of whom else do you speak?"

"First, a dragon, bearing hope." Her gleaming eyes searched them all, and Kjorn held his breath. "Second, the Summer King, bearing truth. And you. The third and last."

And what do I bear? Kjorn wanted to ask, but kept silent for another moment. She seemed to be measuring him, and he stood as still as he could as darkness fell.

"Wise Ajia," Nilsine murmured. "We come seeking only help. Kjorn has come to find his wingbrother, Shard, of the Silver Isles."

"We know Rashard, the Summer King."

Kjorn's heart quickened and he stepped forward, then when Nilsine made a negative grunt, backed up again respectfully. "You've met with him? Is he well? I wish to find him and reconcile. Can you tell me what's become of him? I would owe you a great debt."

Ajia tilted her head and Kjorn gave the feathers another furtive glance, searching for any gray, or a talon of pale color. He was relieved not to see any.

"We know him. He met with us, spoke and listened. He listened and spoke with a heart of earth, like a lion, like a true son of Tor. He walked with us to behold the enemy."

"The enemy," Kjorn said quietly. "I believe I had a vision of them. Great beasts with wings like storms, all dark, and greedy and violent."

"Yes, that is their nature. This vision of yours, in it, did you fight them?"

With a sideways glance at Nilsine he said, "I rose victorious from their darkness and chaos."

Ajia watched him for a long moment as final night enclosed them. Not one other lion spoke or moved, and Kjorn understood that she was a leader among them. Not even between gryfons had he seen such perfect stillness and obedience.

"You have returned, son-of-Sverin, at the height of your strength and power, knowing the truth of your family's flight from this, your homeland, only to find your wingbrother?"

"That is my intention, yes." It was a simple question, yet Kjorn felt he was being challenged.

Ajia looked at Nilsine, whose passive expression, as far as Kjorn could tell in the new dark and starlight, did not change.

After another stretch of silence Kjorn could bear the scrutiny no longer. "With all respect, yes. I have no other aims here. You said you'd met with my wingbrother. You know Shard. Do you know what's become of him?"

Ajia glanced to the lioness beside her, who lowered her head and lay back her ears. Ajia returned her gaze to Kjorn. "We know him, and consider him a friend. But we do not know you. Why should we tell you what we know?"

"Wise Ajia," Nilsine began, and Kjorn stepped in front of her, knowing it would appear aggressive, but he felt some aggression was needed, some show of strength. Ajia tilted her head back to study him.

Kjorn spoke to her alone. "I am Shard's closest friend since kithood. We had a falling out. We mistrusted and lied and did poorly by each other, and I hope to find him and make amends."

As if she hadn't even heard him, the lioness spoke thoughtfully. "Shard hoped to understand the great enemy that stalks the

Winderost, and perhaps help us rid our lands of them. Do you mean to help him with this?"

Taken aback, Kjorn considered his answer, and stood as tall as he was able. With some satisfaction he noticed two of the younger, male lions draw back. "If he wishes for my help, I will do it. If the Winderost wishes my help, I will give it."

"Bold words. You have never seen the enemy."

He turned his ears back. "I would face them. I had a vision and was victorious. If Shard wishes to fight them, I will fight and die beside him if needed. I must find him first, of course." He hoped that was a strong enough hint.

Ajia studied him, then looked at Nilsine, whose expression remained guarded, though she slanted an ear Kjorn's way, as if surprised by his words.

"Why should we trust your words? You could be an enemy of Shard. He fled a troubled land, seeking truth."

"Why should I trust *you*?" Kjorn growled, growing weary of riddles and unanswered questions. "I walked respectfully into your lands and sought you out before searching, hunting—why, scarcely before we even bent the grass with our feet. Tell me, those feathers on your neck, are those signs of friendship, or battles won?"

Ajia tilted her head and Nilsine sucked a sharp breath, but Kjorn stood firm. Starlight sparkled through the haze above, and after a moment, Ajia threw back her head and roared with laughter. Then she trotted forward, bowing her head so the feathers stood in intimidating display like a mane, though her eyes lifted to remain locked on Kjorn's.

"Perhaps they are both. Tell me, isn't winning a difficult friendship sometimes like a battle won?"

Kjorn opened his beak, and when he had no answer, she laughed again and circled away, speaking over her shoulder. "Come, walk with us. You will hunt with us on the next egg moon, and if you do well under the bright eye of Tor, perhaps we will tell you what we know of the Summer King."

"I don't have time to—"

"Don't refuse her," Nilsine hissed, stepping abreast of him again. "It would be a great insult. You would make an enemy."

"I thought I already had," Kjorn muttered, watching Ajia walk away, looking fully confident he would follow.

"Oh no," Nilsine murmured, as the lions gathered around Ajia and she led a trail through the grass. "An invitation to hunt is a wonderful honor."

"It sounded more like a test to me."

"Come," Nilsine said impatiently. "Don't risk their good mood by dallying."

"Good mood?" Kjorn mused. "I would hate to see her in a bad mood."

Nilsine snapped her beak, and at last Kjorn fell in, following the lions deeper into the grassy plain. Ajia had challenged him. If she considered friendship a battle won, then this was a battle he didn't intend to lose.

16
HALVDEN'S LESSON

S HEETS OF SHARP, BLACK, VOLCANIC scree cascaded down the slope
toward Halvden, with Caj riding down the largest rock. He knew
he wouldn't have been able to stalk down the hill without upsetting the
loose rocks, nor make the long jump for the element of surprise. So
in the dimming light he used the slope and the rocks to his advantage.

Flaring his good wing to steer somewhat, Caj relished the look of
shock on Halvden's face before the first rocks struck him, threatening
to bury the green warrior under black, razor edges.

Halvden dragged away from the small avalanche and beat his
wings hard, trying to escape. Caj judged the distance and leaped,
flinging his entire weight against Halvden's hindquarters and slam-
ming the younger gryfon to the ground.

"You're *dead!*" Halvden shrieked, scrabbling away as the wave of
rocks skittered toward them.

"No, guess again." Caj reared up to his hind legs and forced
Halvden down, rolling him with hard shoves away from the last of the
sliding rocks.

"You're a ghost!" Halvden loosed a strangled noise, gained his feet and turned tail, kicking up dust and pebbles in Caj's face with both hind paws.

Caj ducked his head to shield his eyes even as he leaped forward, swiping blindly for Halvden's hind legs. "No such thing," he growled.

"Stay back!" Halvden sprang away and whirled, flaring his wings.

Caj crouched, tail whipping.

Slowly Halvden's eyes narrowed, his expression growing clear as he realized Caj was real, alive, and coming for him. Caj had vowed never to underestimate him again, so before Halvden could gather his thoughts, Caj lunged.

They clashed, fell together, and fought like witless mountain cats, Halvden's movements powerful, but wild and desperate, Caj's calculated and cold. He gave no quarter. Every swipe of his talons to Halvden's flesh and wings felt like redemption for the foolishness of his entire winter. Green feathers littered the black rock.

They whipped around the steaming fissures and across the broken, treacherous ground. When the ground evened out again, Halvden reared to his hind legs and Caj rose to meet him—they locked and yanked each other to the ground. Caj hit first and warm pain coiled up his broken wing as they rolled. He heard the mud casing crack. Halvden wrestled him across the ground, and the mud cast crumbled away with each twist of their bodies.

Growing weary and short of breath from the poor air, Caj knew he had to win the fight soon. Halvden could wear him down first if Caj allowed it. He would not. Halvden had no armor, he was still bewildered, and alone. It was time to end the fight.

Feigning worse pain from his broken wing, Caj broke away, fell back and twisted as if preparing to flee, leaving Halvden a false opening. The young gryfon should have known better. That time, Halvden lunged forward in attempt to knock him over.

Caj whipped about to meet the charge, sat up on his hindquarters, snaked his forelegs around Halvden's chest, and drove his own shoulders forward against the impact as the big gryfon slammed into him. Halvden snarled, caught, beak snapping, seeking an opening.

Caj thrust forward, driving them both up to stand on their hind legs, toppled Halvden off balance and slammed him backward. Halvden's back and wings smashed against the ground, and Caj pinned him there, crushing him into the rock. He pressed his talons deep under his green feathers, against the young gryfon's throat.

For a moment he reveled in Halvden's realization that he'd lost, in the perfect look of shock and defeat flashing in his eyes.

"Are you going to kill me?"

There was still no humility in Halvden's voice, no regret, no apology. He pressed harder and Halvden shut his eyes, taking a gurgling breath.

After a moment Caj muttered, "Do you think I want to face Kenna if I kill you?"

Halvden's eyes snapped open, again bewildered, as if he didn't know whether to laugh or curse. "Are you mocking me? What do you want from me?"

He knows, Caj realized. *He knows he chose poorly and acted foolishly, and that he must pay a price for his choices.* But still, like his father, Halvden couldn't let go of his arrogance.

"Admit you were wrong."

"No."

A deep, warning snarl curled in Caj's throat. "You weasely, mud-covered vulture. Admit you were wrong!"

"*No.*" Halvden dragged a breath against Caj's talons. "I did as any of you. I did what I thought was right. I served Sverin. I—"

"You did what you could to seize the most power, you bullied, divided, and endangered the pride, and you tried to murder me."

"The strong endure," Halvden rasped.

"Your father was strong," Caj growled.

Around them, three plumes of poisonous steam shot up, hissing. The drizzle deepened to freezing rain. They continued their stare-down, Halvden's beak open in a pant. Caj remained frozen, pressing. Not again. He would not falter and lose to Halvden again.

"You could be great," Caj said. "You could be everything you dream of being, everything your father wanted but could never be—if you will only let go of this insufferable pride."

Halvden struggled, but Caj held him locked to the rock at every joint.

"What do you want?" Halvden whispered at last. His muscles sagged under Caj and he broke eye contact, staring beyond Caj at the black rock of Pebble's Throw.

Loosening his talons a little, Caj said, "First, you're going to tell me what happened to Sverin, and where he is."

Halvden looked back at him with an incredulous glower. "And then?"

"And then," Caj took a breath, calming at last, "you're going to admit you were wrong, beg forgiveness, and apologize."

"Apologize," Halvden scoffed, "to whom?"

"Everyone."

17

THE SUNLAND

THE ICE FLOE ROCKED AND smacked against something hard, jarring Shard awake and nearly tipping him back into the water. He stared up at a towering cliff of ice.

His first sight of the Sunland was nothing but a rock-hard, white and azure wall stretching for leagues to either side. Forcing his stiff muscles to move, Shard gripped his ice floe with quivering claws and peered up again, then around. Land was near, indeed, as the dragons had promised, but not in the way he'd envisioned. At his back, icy ocean lapped on for leagues, for the moment, calm.

Fool, he thought, grabbing at the wall of ice to drag himself along it and find some friendlier place to crawl onto land. After two days floating—or it might've been three, he wasn't sure—he still seethed over the whales and the dragons taking Hikaru without him.

I should've shouted. I should have gone with them. My wings weren't broken, what's the matter with me? He briefly forgot he'd been almost dead from drowning, tossed about by whales, frozen, and losing blood. Still, he felt he could've tried harder. *Idiot twice-over, what would Stigr say?*

He paused, talons digging against the ice floe as it rocked and bumped the ice wall. He'd had a vision of gryfons and wolves he'd known who were dead.

Einarr...

Shard shook himself. There was no way to know if it was real. He'd had raven dreams before, and found them untrue.

He opened his wings, and aside from mild twinges, found them whole and ready. Crouching back, however, sent flashing heat up one hind leg and he barked in pain. Twisting his head, he examined the limb, and when he beheld the strips of torn flesh from the whale's teeth, the ooze of blood, and the bone itself, split and angled, his stomach curled. The ice, at least had kept the bleeding low, and the salt water cleaned it. He still *had* the leg, at the very least, could work through the pain and perhaps mend it, even if he moved with a limp from then on.

Shard drew a deep breath. One step at a time. He'd had enough of floating, enough of the sea, which was usually his ally and provider. He gave the ice floe a friendly pat in thanks for bearing him, leaned on his good hind leg and launched himself into the cold, clear sky. The bobbing motion of flight drummed a steady, nauseating ache through his broken leg, and he could only try to block it from his mind. Anything he tried to do would hurt, so he had to do the sensible thing, which was to fly away before he fell in the water, or whales attacked again and the situation grew worse.

The air along the ice wall shifted unpredictably before falling dead, and Shard worked cold, stiff wings to soar over the top, where he found a strong headwind and worked into it to rise. He stroked up as far as he could bear to go.

The sweeping landscape rolled and crested into hills and mountains and back into long plains much like the Sun Isle of home, except all of it shone white, white, white. Shard shook his head, eyes dazzled, and peered around in search of sign of any kind of forest or grass.

The land swept back from him in all directions, enormous and white. Upon that second inspection, he saw the dark edges of rock in the far mountains, and long patches of dirt along the nightward shoreline. Far at the end of his vision along that coast, the wall broke into arches, towers and slides of ice, translucent white and blue.

Distant splashes and high-pitched calls drew his attention to his own shoreline.

For a moment, having felt entirely alone in the world, he breathed in relief, and looked to the water. Life thrived. Gulls nattered in the distance. Larger splashes told him of seals, and he thought he spied the starkly black and white snowrock birds that he'd only ever seen once, on the starward most coast of the Star Isle.

With no better ideas, but relieved to find life, Shard angled inland and flew a course that matched the one he and Hikaru had taken over the sea, parallel to the back of the constellation of Midragur. He couldn't see it in the day of course, but he knew its path across the sky as well as a vein in his own wings.

For a time, flying, he felt at peace.

Evening fell shockingly swift around him.

He'd thought he was airborne for perhaps only a sunmark, then realized the sun was setting. He remembered the short days of winter in the Silver Isles, but during his time in the Winderost, he'd grown used to longer stretches of daylight. Now the whole landscape glowed dull silver in the weak sun. Shard flapped high again and studied his choices. Weariness crept up from the ache in his leg and washed his entire body as the sky darkened. Plains, mountains, coast. He chose the mountains, where he might find shelter from the night wind.

A whisper trickled through his mind.

"What?" Shard shook his head, looking around for a bird, or an earth creature below, but saw nothing. The whisper nudged again, like wind, no words that he could make out, but calling. Something felt distantly familiar about it.

"Who are you?" he whispered. The dark mountains, patched with snow, ringed a small bowl of a valley. Recognition darted through his mind. Shard dipped lower toward the pass that entered the valley, and then the whispering seemed not in his mind, but ahead.

The sun departed. Stars glowed to life and pulsed in the huge sky. A cold wind swept up and stroked Shard's wings. Adjusting his flight path to it sent a jolt through his injured leg and he ground his beak to stifle a snarl of pain, peering up to see that he now flew perpendicular to Midragur. *No matter, I'll get back on course tomorrow.*

The mountains stood silent, gleaming white and abyssal black under the impossible stars. Shard dove into the pass, soaring over a frozen river toward the valley he'd seen. The whisper itched now, as if in his left ear. Shard growled and turned, flared to a halt and landed on a ledge that overlooked the pass and the little valley. He caught his breath, listening, and stared.

The wind rushed through the pass, squeezed in by the walls of mountain, and Shard flicked his ear toward the sound of water. Perhaps the river wasn't entirely frozen. The whisper had faded and Shard's heart thumped in fear that he'd lost it, that it wasn't just his lonely, tired mind, that it was something he was supposed to heed.

He stood on the cliff, breathing in the wet scent of snow, the mineral smell of the mountain and somewhere underneath, frozen earth. Closing his eyes, his listened, as closely as he'd listened when he was first learning to speak the language of the earth and the birds. Wind flitted through the mountains, combed and played with his feathers. Shard leaned again onto his good leg, shutting out the pain of the other.

A wavering, distant noise chimed, one that felt more in his mind than in his ears. He flicked his ears, breathing softly. Like the notes of a choir of many birds, the noise pulsed, wavered, folded over itself and faded only to resume again. It was not the whisper Shard had heard. The whisper, he thought deeply, had faded in the face of the new sound. He opened his eyes, and sucked a sharp breath.

The Wings of Tor unfolded all across the sky, ribboning sheets of violent green, magenta, and blue light, ever shifting. Shard had seen the lights in the Silver Isles, but never as he saw them now.

The chiming, weird notes pulsed from the light. The very voice of the sky, of Tor, of a world Shard glimpsed only in dreams, sang through his skin. Cramped on his little ledge, he still managed a trembling bow.

Guide me, he pleaded.

The wind flitted around him and he remembered the dream he'd had before. The white star in the little valley. The circle of stones. He looked up at the majestic lights, then down to the valley. Though the first whisper had faded, he knew it had called him to the valley, and that it could be the one from his dream.

With a slow, building thrill in his heart, Shard plunged from the ledge and soared through the pass, exalting under the lights of Tor. When he neared the center of the valley, the orientation of the mountains and the pale gleam of snow all looked familiar. It was as in his dream. He stooped to land, and heard a small voice cry out.

"Hello?" Shard called in reply, gingerly setting down in the snow without putting weight on his broken leg. "Hello? I've come!"

The night was not dark. Between the stars and the great shifting lights, Shard saw everything in a bright twilight. From above and in the odd light, the circle of stones had looked like odd pockets in the snow, but indeed they were there, Shard had landed right in their center. Again a voice cried out, this time in glee.

"Hello! You've come! She dreamed you would!"

Shard turned, folding his wings and hobbling, to see a snow fox plunging toward him from outside the circle of stones. He thought of the white star in his dream, and how the dragon Amaratsu had taught him that sometimes, a dream thing meant another thing.

The white fox before him, Shard decided, was the star from his dream, and was the guidance he had asked for.

"I'm Shard," he said, dipping his head. "It's good to see you." And as strange as it all felt, it was good to see the fox, to hear another voice, to see a face happy to see him. "Who dreamed I would come?"

"Nest-mother." The fox padded forward and sniffed Shard all over by way of introducing himself, discovered the broken leg with a little yip, and returned to face Shard in front again. "But you're injured."

"Yes. Can you help? Who is your nest-mother?" Shard had never heard of a fox using that term. It was a gryfon word, for a parent who hadn't birthed a kit, but raised it as her own if something happened to the birth mother. "And, what is your name?"

"I am Iluq." He perked his ears, his black, narrow eyes glittering. "Come, Shard, Mother will help you with your leg, and she'll be very pleased to see you, very happy indeed."

"Why is that?"

Mischief stole over the fox's face. "You'll see. Come. We will have food and maybe songs."

Tingling relief threatened to make him collapse. "Yes, I would like that very much."

Iluq laughed and trotted a circle around him, his wide, flat paws not breaking the crust of snow. "Come with me. You can fly above if it's easier. We must go to the mountain."

"I'll fly," Shard said, following the point of Iluq's nose to see that he indicated the *far* wall of mountains. It would take two marks for him to hobble there. Much swifter if he flew and Iluq ran.

The lights wavered into pure, summer green as they traveled to the mountain. Shard wondered, with tingling anticipation, who the fox's nest-mother might be, and then he remembered the milky eyes from another dream, eagle eyes.

Gryfon eyes? Shard would've thought it impossible, but he was learning to use that word carefully.

He followed Iluq's darting form across the valley until they reached the foot of the mountains, where Shard landed. There he had to walk, for Iluq led him up a narrow trail that cut into the mountain, and he would've been unable to follow by wing. Shard continually slipped and tripped on the snow, biting back curses he'd learned from Stigr, until at last they reached a crack in the mountainside.

"Home!" Iluq announced.

Shard's first instinct would've been to carefully smell the entrance and be wary of danger or a trap, but he only stared at the familiar, orange light that glowed from deep within the cave.

"Iluq," he said hesitantly, "is that..."

"Oh yes," gushed the fox, "it is *fire*! Mother and I keep it alive. Mother learned from the dragons how to make it, but we must feed constantly, because it's so difficult for her to make, now, and I cannot make it at all."

"Oh," Shard breathed, and they stepped inside. The scent of wood smoke sent his mind reeling back to the Winderost, the bonfires, and, with a warm thrill, the memory of the gryfess Brynja.

For a moment he closed his eyes, for with the smell of wood smoke came the memory of her scent. He savored his last good memory of her, her eyes bright as he showed her a sky brimming with stars, her voice warm as she confessed to admiring him. With determination he pictured her standing at his side on the Copper Cliff, as queen of the Silver Isles, and tried not to think of all the reasons why that part couldn't be.

He didn't know what became of her after he fled, Nameless, from the Dawn Spire.

"Shard?" Iluq nosed a talon.

Shard shook his head. "Lead on."

They walked into the stone cave, and the warmth overwhelmed him. The thick smoke overpowered any scent of animal, and so he had to wait for any hint about Mother until Iluq led him from the tunnel into a cozy chamber. It was roundish, with a crackling fire in the center and an enormous stack of wood along one wall. Two wooden poles stood upright like bare trees near the wood stack, with smaller poles rising between them in rungs, bound at the meeting points with sinew. On those rungs hung drying, smoked fish. Shard tilted his head, studying the clever frame, and Iluq slipped past him toward the fire.

Little bones littered the edges of the cave, some fish, some hare, some bird, and some larger, perhaps seal. They looked ancient and dusty, as if larger game hadn't been brought to the cave in a very long time.

One pile of bones in the corner beyond the fire looked to be a wolf or some other larger creature, but Shard couldn't identify them through the smoke, and then, something else caught his attention.

A ring of wood hung on the rock wall behind the pile of bones, a long sapling branch warped into a circle, holding together a strange web that looked woven of thin animal sinew. Bits of shell dangled from it, and several long feathers, some gryfon, one enormous one that Shard recognized from his first dream of the fox. The work was too clever for fox paws. Maybe dragon, raven or, perhaps…

"Welcome."

A voice drifted, like the smoke, to Shard's ears, though it was so faint he could've dreamed it, like the noises from Tor's Wings, or the whisper at the head of the valley. Startled, he blinked, peering through the smoke. The whisper. It was the same, only it had become words. She had called to him. Shard stepped fully into the cave and sideways, out of the stream of smoke that followed the tunnel out. Peering across the fire, he saw the milky, blind eagle eyes from his dream.

He almost fell back, so surprised to see her sitting across the fire from him. Distracted by the fish, the fire and the bones and the strange false web on the wall, he hadn't even noticed her, and realized too that she blended perfectly with the color of the cave around her. Now, he tried not to stare. Never had he seen a creature so ancient, so thin that her feathers, which no longer held their hue, seemed only draped over her skeletal frame.

Foolish words came out despite himself. "You're a gryfon."

A dry, wispy chuckle. "Welcome, Summer King. My, how you shine. Like sunlight."

Iluq padded around the fire and settled next to the ancient gryfess, looking pleased with himself.

The gryfess seemed oddly still—but then, Shard thought, it probably took every bit of strength she had just to keep breathing.

"Tell me about yourself, Summer King. Your name. Your land. What brings gryfons back to the Sunland." She shivered. Iluq perked his ears, leaped to the woodpile and snatched up a few sticks in his teeth to deposit them into the fire.

Shard took a careful seat at the fire, favoring his injured leg. He would have to set it later. Hopefully they would let him use a few of their gathered sticks and perhaps, if there was no clay to be had, some sinew to bind the sticks to his leg. "I'm Rashard, son-of-Baldr. I'll tell you everything. But first, please tell me about you. This…I don't even know what to ask. Who are you? Why are you here?"

A soft, dusty wind shuddered through the cave, somehow, making the fire dance and their shadows flicker to life. "I am Groa, daughter-of-Urd." She took a breath. The names sounded old, like something from a legend. "I flew here seeking treasure, seeking adventure. I followed a starfire." Shard bit back a sound of disbelief. The ghostly creature looked ready to disintegrate. There was no conceivable way she'd flown, following the same starfire he had.

Unless she *hadn't* followed the same...

He guarded his voice. "I, too, followed a starfire. How did you..." He didn't want to insult her, and stopped.

Amusement crinkled the corners of her blind eyes. "You don't understand. I didn't follow the same starfire as you, this autumn past."

Shard watched her face, his amazement and understanding growing. Wind whispered and flittered through the cave and Shard tried to determine where it was coming from, then shifted closer to the fire. "Others have told me that it only flew once before."

Groa fixed her blind eyes on him steadily as if, through the fire, she truly saw him. "Yes. I flew when last the starfire soared. I flew with the first band of gryfons to come here and meet the dragons."

A quiver encompassed Shard's entire body. "You mean..."

"Yes." The fire shivered as Shard met her unseeing gaze. "I flew with Kajar."

18

STIRRING THE WIND

THE WARM, RED, MEAT SCENT of pronghorn floated to the spot where Kjorn crouched in the grass. Flanked by Nilsine and the lioness Ajia, he waited, grateful he had some practice hunting on land in the Silver Isles.

As Ajia wished, they had waited for the egg moon, bright and nearly full. They had waited, as Ajia wished, for an infuriating three days. All the while, Nilsine assured Kjorn that even the Vanhar were rarely invited to hunt with the lions. He didn't want to make an enemy of someone who claimed to be a friend of Shard's and might know his whereabouts, so Kjorn accepted their hospitality and waited. Now at last, the hunt.

"The herd," Ajia said, her voice a warm purr. "The herd grazes under the moon, and now the dark is high. The herd grazes under the moon, and one knows its time is nigh."

The other lionesses echoed her, and they fell into a hunting chant.

Ajia's voice woke something in Kjorn's heart and muscles, a thrill along his back that made him not want to fly, but to leap and sprint along the ground.

"The eye of Tor watches, her light guides us on."

"The breath of Tor whispers, we follow her song."

Only he, Nilsine, and the other female Vanhar with them had been allowed on the hunt. The male lions did not hunt with them, and Fraenir and the male Vanhar remained behind as well. Beside Kjorn, even Nilsine seemed caught up in the chant, and just as she began to hum along, the lionesses fell silent. It was time to close in, time for quiet.

Without a word Ajia crept forward, and Kjorn blinked as she disappeared in the grass. Ever shifting to remain downwind, he crept forward to remain within earshot of the lions. He could see a little in the moonlight, but not like the lions, who saw, he knew, as if it were day. The pronghorns wouldn't see them at all, but would hear or smell if they made a wrong move, possibly spot movement under the moon if they emerged from the grass.

Remembering all he'd learned of ground-hunting from Thyra, Kjorn stalked forward, placing his talons carefully, lifting his beak to smell through the hazy air. He spotted the herd, outlined in white moonlight. Several lookouts stood poised at the edge, and when they lowered their heads to crop a quick bite of grass, other heads raised, ears turning, ever alert.

A quiver slipped through Kjorn, a silent knowing. Tuned to the lionesses, he sensed and saw them fanning out. Ajia had chosen a target.

Kjorn saw it. An aged male with a crooked hind leg, a lookout at the far end of the herd. He and the Vanhar followed wordless cues from the lionesses and took up stations to flank the pronghorn.

Nilsine had told him they would not fly, that they were to hunt as lions. Another quiver trailed down his spine, some voiceless understanding that all the lionesses were in place. A liquid movement caught his eye, and he met Ajia's glowing stare through the grass.

The great honor of running down and killing the pronghorn was to be Kjorn's.

Under the piercing light of the moon, feeling suddenly as if perhaps the goddess Tor *did* watch his hunt with interest, Kjorn slipped forward. His breath tightened. He resisted the urge to hold it and breathed deeply and silently. Something larger seemed to poise on this hunt and his performance, and he meant to show well.

The old pronghorn's head flew up. Kjorn froze. The pronghorn's ears wagged back and forth. The wind shifted, bringing the scent of haze and meat, and Kjorn bellied forward. The pronghorn's head turned, and he bleated a warning.

"Mudding…" Kjorn swore. The herd broke into a springing run in all directions. Kjorn locked on his prey, bounding fast and dodging panicked pronghorn who leaped around him.

One sprang over Kjorn, caught a hoof on Kjorn's wing and went sprawling. Kjorn nearly turned to take that beast instead, but an electric bolt of pride shot through him. No. He would take the one the lions had chosen.

The old pronghorn had frozen rather than run, perhaps thinking Kjorn would lose him in the chaos. The lionesses hadn't moved from their stations. Kjorn bolted forward again, bowling through pronghorn like an avalanche, knocking aside any who crossed him. The old one spotted him and broke into a sprint.

Hunt thrill shot down Kjorn's chest and he surged to take chase. The pronghorn was fast, but Kjorn ate ground with huge, long leaps—wings closed—and the elder hoof beast tired fast.

With a chaos of bleating and leaping animals and the sudden blur of the lionesses and Vanhar falling in on all sides, Kjorn shoved into a final jump and crashed into his prey. He dug his talons into the hindquarters and yanked to one side, bringing down the beast and rolling with him to avoid a cloven hoof to the head.

Throwing his body on top of the pronghorn, Kjorn went for his throat. A splash of moonlight caught the creature's eye. For a moment it glowed silver, meeting Kjorn's eyes with terror, and knowing.

Flustered, Kjorn hesitated only a moment to stammer, "You ran well."

The pronghorn closed his eye, and offered his throat.

Warm voices rolled behind Kjorn as blood and life spilled over his beak.

"The herd grazes under the moon,
and now the dark is high.
The herd grazes under the moon,
and one knows his time is nigh.
The eye of Tor watches, her light guides us on.
The breath of Tor whispers, we follow her song.
One goes now to the Sunlit Land
But his Voice in the wind sings on."

Kjorn wiped his beak in the grass, and stepped back from the carcass. He mantled as Ajia slunk forward. "For you, my lady."

She dipped her head, rustling the feathers braided there. "You did well."

"Not to offend, but this task was not hard. I don't see the point of making me wait here for days, only to kill an old, simple hoof beast."

He distinctly heard Nilsine sigh, and the Vanhar huntress emerged with the others from the grass.

"It was not the task itself," Ajia said, "but how you carried it out." When Kjorn said nothing, she confirmed, "You have proven yourself humble, and honorable. Let us feast."

After eating, they walked toward a grove of stunted trees, their shadows stretching long under the low moon.

Ajia walked beside Kjorn. "The last we knew of Shard, he brought the enemy down on the Dawn Spire, and fled starward. After that we cannot say."

"Starward." Kjorn looked that direction, then to Nilsine.

She murmured, "The eagles dwell there. The Voldsom Narrows are a great network of canyons, starward, and bordering the Outlands. If Shard isn't still there, perhaps the eagles will know of him. The Vanhar have no quarrel with them, but neither have we any special friendship."

Kjorn wondered if he would have to perform a task for the eagles as well, but bit the thought back. "Then, starward we go. Thank you," he said to Ajia, stifling frustration that after all that, he'd gained so little information. But he stopped walking and mantled low as if to a queen.

"Be wary," murmured Ajia, lifting her nose toward the sky. "You have returned to a land that is cursed by the curse of your forefathers. You must tread and fly very lightly here."

Kjorn sensed a threat. "Tell me what you mean by that."

A low rumble emanated from the chests of all the lions, as if they warned off some greater danger, as if they guarded against the very curse of which she spoke. Ajia shook her head, rattling the talons and feathers. "Until the return of the first Red King, there were no wyrms who terrorized the night. Your ancestor drew them here."

"If that is true, then it may be my destiny to help rid the land of them. But first I must find my wingbrother."

"It won't be so easy," Nilsine said, and Kjorn looked at her through the dark. "Fighting the wyrms. Their very presence breeds fear and panic. No one flies at night anymore, for it draws their hateful eyes. I've never met a gryfon who has seen them and not forgotten his name."

"I have," Ajia murmured, and when they looked at her, she dipped her head to Kjorn. "Your wingbrother. Rashard. The Summer King. Perhaps if you stand together, you will stand a chance." She flicked her ears, and looked upwards again as Kjorn enjoyed a flush of pride at knowing that Shard had stood his ground against this supposedly unbeatable enemy. Ajia's low voice drew him back to the moment. "The Horn of Midragur is broken and breathes fire. This, too, is a sign, though only more time will tell."

Having proven himself, and sensing a moment when he could ask a question, Kjorn spoke slowly. "The dragon," he said, wanting desperately to understand her and fearing she wouldn't speak in any plainer terms, "when we first arrived, you spoke of a dragon who bore hope, and the Summer King, Shard, who brought truth. You said you knew that three of us would come, and I was the third. What do I bring?"

"You don't know what you've brought?"

Feeling hollow, thinking of the gold that he'd brought and lost, Kjorn lifted his wings. "I...brought nothing."

"That is right. You bring nothing." The breath seemed to drain from the group, and Kjorn narrowed his eyes. *Does she mean to make me look like a fool?* Ajia's eyes glinted in the moonlight. "You brought nothing, but with your wings you will stir the still air, with your wings you will raise the Sunwind."

Kjorn glanced around, discomfited by the sudden, worried expressions of the Vanhar. That she used his own words about stirring the winds also unnerved him. She couldn't have known he'd said that— unless she'd been listening, spying, unseen in the grass that day, and said it on purpose. Somehow he doubted that was what happened.

Hesitantly, he asked sideways of Nilsine, "You told me of the Sunwind, but not what it means to you."

"Change," she murmured, eyes locked on Ajia. "Sacrifice, and violent change." She turned to Kjorn with a new, cautious, measuring look in her eyes. "Kjorn, the Sunwind is the wind of war."

For a moment every gaze was on him, and the air smelled thickly of ash, and though he had come to the Winderost with peace in his heart, he felt as if a secret purpose even he hadn't known had just been laid bare under the white, silent moon.

19

GROA OF THE VANHAR

"KAJAR?" SHARD LURCHED TO HIS feet, wincing at the pain that shot up his hind leg, and the fire rippled with the wind of his movement. "That's not possible!"

Iluq whined, nose wrinkling in a worried expression.

Shard settled slowly, embarrassed at his outburst before the old, dignified gryfess. "Forgive me. But how are you still alive?"

"Iluq keeps me young," Groa said with a laugh. "My Voice in the wing sings on."

Shard glanced over his shoulder, back the way he'd come, but thought better of it. To think that she'd flown with Kajar, followed the first starfire, wasn't any stranger than anything else he had seen since the last wild spring when he'd first met Catori and learned of the Summer King.

"I see," he said, still mulling it over. A still, small flame of under-standing flicked to life in his mind. He remembered Amaratsu's tale of the dragons. He remembered her telling of a feast the great emperor gave for his gryfon guests, but one gryfess didn't trust him, and fled, never to be heard from again.

He watched Groa quietly.

"Here now," said the ancient gryfess. "Let us tend to that leg. Legend says the Summer King will be a healer as well as a leader…are you a healer?"

A spark popped and the fire sent up a plume of smoke. The little cave and Groa herself seemed to waver before Shard's eyes. He'd underestimated his weariness. What she said had to be true. He could think of no reason she would lie to him, or why else she would be there, alone, and so ancient, in the land of the dragons. Slowly, with surety, he began to believe that she was that last gryfess from Amaratsu's tale, that she alone had escaped the curse of Kajar and his band.

Realizing she'd asked a question, Shard attempted to gather his thoughts again and form an answer. "I learned a bit of healing from my nest-mother. Yes."

"Ah." She sighed deeply and the fire glowed hotter. "The vala are never wrong."

"Vala?"

"Prophets of the Vanhar. Enough now." She tapped talons on the stone floor and it sounded like brittle bones. "Iluq, help Shard fetch strong, supple twigs from our supply for a splint. Shard, if you need sinew for the binding you may pull it from the dream net." She tilted her head back to indicate the strange, round web over her head.

"Oh. No," Shard said, eyeing the intricate pattern of woven sinews. "No, I can use mud to pack and hold it and the torn flesh, until I reach the dragons. They should be able to help me if I need to redo it."

Groa turned her ears toward him, then laughed, and laughed, and the sound was oddly strong and true for such an aged creature. "Dragons? Help a gryfon? No, my young friend, better to stay here.

Better to stay and learn the ways of dream catching, as befits a seer and a healer such as the Summer King. Are you a seer?"

"Sometimes." Shard watched Iluq, who pawed diligently through the pile of kindling for good splint material. "I don't have much control over it, though."

"Many do not. But I learned much from Iluq, here, and the windward-most dwelling ravens of the Sunland, about dreams. With a net such as mine, you may see almost anything, any time you wish."

"Were you trying to find me? Is that why I saw Iluq? He appeared to me as a white star."

"You saw Iluq because you are the Summer King and your dreams guide you where you should go. Later, I saw you because I wished to. Yes, I was trying to find you."

"Why?"

She made a low, strange noise that Shard recognized after a moment was a purring chuckle. "Because you seek the truth, and I possess it. I can tell you what you need to know about the dragons of the Sunland."

Shard leaned forward. "I would like to hear that. And you can teach me about this dream catching? How to see things in my dreams on purpose?" Shard wasn't even sure if his own father had been able to do that. He'd never asked Stigr, and regret speared him.

"See," Groa confirmed, "and speak to others so they hear."

Shard marveled, and he almost stood again. A dancing pain shot up his leg. "It would be an amazing gift. Let me set this leg, and we'll talk more."

"Yes," said Groa simply. "Iluq will help you."

That said, Iluq brought his selection of strong pine sticks to Shard. First would be to set the bones straight. Because Iluq had no way to grip and Shard suspected Groa didn't possess the strength to do it right on the first try, he had to do it himself. Gingerly, he wrapped his talons around the broken ends of the bone, sucked a breath, and with a yank, a twist, and a bright, stunning pain, his leg was straight again.

"Iluq," Shard gasped, every muscle trembling. "I need mud. And, the skin must be set back over the muscle." Tenderly, the little fox helped Shard to correct the torn flesh and muscle, cleaned by salt water but still ripped. A trickle of water ran down a sliver in the rock in the back of the cave, and Iluq clawed enough mud to pack around the splints and the damaged skin, as Sigrun had taught Shard. That done, Shard stretched out, with his throbbing leg toward the fire, hoping the mud dried hard enough to hold it in place.

When that was finished at last, Iluq brought him smoked fish. With food in his belly he could think clearly, and he hoped Groa would indeed be able to remember all and tell him of Kajar, and the dragons.

"Lady Groa, I would like very much to hear what you know of dragons, and to learn dream catching from you. But how long might it take? I must find the dragons, find my nest-son and be sure he's well."

Her delicate ears flicked back. "The dragons will not help you as I can help you, but because you already posses the power to see in your dreams, I could teach you in perhaps two nights. Perhaps one, if your strength holds out."

"One night?" He ground down and swallowed the last of his fish. "If you can do that, then I would be grateful."

"Then I will teach you, even as I tell you my tale of Kajar. I will show you in a dream, the way you may learn to show others images in dreams, if you possess the knack." Her milky eyes narrowed in concentration, though she stared just beyond Shard in the wrong direction to be looking at him. "First, tell me what you know of Kajar and what you think you know of the dragons."

So Shard told all he knew, which was very little, ending with, ". . . then the emperor of the dragons issued them a challenge to choose friendship or more power and riches, and Kajar said he needed to think it over. But when a friendly dragon went to find Kajar, he and the other gryfons betrayed and killed her. Then they gathered what treasures the dragons had given them and left the Sunland." Shard yawned, sleepy in the warmth, and Iluq curled up at his flank as if they were old friends.

Groa didn't say anything, and so Shard continued, watching her expression. "One gryfess didn't face the emperor dragon's challenge. She thought it was a trap. She fled, and no one knew what became of her." Shard lifted his head, raising his voice. "It's true, isn't it? And you're her."

"Yes," she said at last. "I was the gryfess who fled the dragon emperor, I who never returned home, I who avoided the bright curse of Kajar and his followers. And what became of them, do you know?"

Feeling hesitant, Shard told the end of the story as he knew it. "Their descendants were forced to leave the Winderost when the wyrms—Voiceless, Nameless cousins of the dragons, invaded."

"Invaded," Groa echoed. "And why, I wonder?"

"I've wondered the same thing," Shard confessed. "I was told that they were jealous of the Sunland dragon's love for the gryfons, of their esteem, jealous that they were given treasures and it drove them to anger and hatred."

Groa scoffed. "And where did you hear this story?"

Again, Shard hesitated, sensing that Groa grew more frustrated, or angry, at the account, though he didn't know why. "A dragon," he said. "A Sunland dragon. A friend. She saved my life and in return I hatched her son."

"It's such a simple tale," Groa said disdainfully. "Almost like a kit's story, don't you think?" She seemed to weave before him and Shard wondered if he was succumbing to the heat of the fire. "So simple. Passed down for a hundred dragon generations. They lead such short lives. And you don't think some parts might have changed in the telling? You heard this story one hundred times removed from a dragon who was not there."

Shard hadn't considered that, when first he'd met Amaratsu, but now he did, and wondered. Groa lifted herself up and Shard felt like he should rush to her side and assist, but he was so weary. The pain in his leg had finally eased a little with the stability of the splint, the warm fire crackled and he only stared as she opened drab wings to frame the dream net above her head.

"I will tell you the true account, and you may judge after. Let yourself grow tired, young prince. Let yourself succumb to sleep, and listen to me. I will see you in a dream, and you will see me, as you have once before. Listen and dream as I tell you all as I remember it. I, Groa of the Vanhar, I who was there."

Shard's gaze trailed up her ancient feathers and then along the spiral web of the dream net until he felt caught, the hot fire and his weariness overcame him. The whisper of Groa's voice that had drawn him to the valley drew him into the dream she wove for him. Together they followed a familiar starfire to a Sunland day that had dawned a hundred years before Shard was born.

20

A NEW TALE

"I FLEW WITH KAJAR TO REPRESENT the Vanhar on the glorious flight windward, the flight that followed the starfire." In the dream, Shard saw everything as if he and Groa flew side by side. As if she called up ghosts, gryfons and dragons appeared and moved before them to show Shard the tale.

"The beginning was, perhaps, much as the dragon told you. We met the dragons when we came to the Sunland and, yes, we were all taken with each other. You've seen how majestic, how impressive, how powerful the dragons are. Of course Kajar, who was young and had an eye for strength and opportunity, was captivated by them."

"As the dragon told you, we settled there for some time, learning of fire—though they never told us how to make it, only feed it. We saw them turn raw metals into liquid fire and back into metals again. They possessed great stores of jewels which, with their talons, they could cut into any shape they like."

"The dragon kit I'm helping," Shard said, and his voice sounded far away to his own ears. "His claws can dig through stone."

Groa's blind eyes seemed to flicker. "Yes. And much more when he is grown. I saw dragon claws cut diamond."

She laughed at the memory and as she laughed, her age faded and he saw a young, fit huntress the shape and size of a Vanir.

"The hardest stone imaginable, you know, a relic from the First Age, and precious to dragons. Their most prized gems were the ones of the brightest colors, the ones that reflected their beautiful scales—their scales, which change to at least four miraculous hues through the course of their lifetime. A new skin for each season. They used metal and stone to create adornments which flattered their scales, and it was Kajar who asked if they could make armor. Intrigued, they forged gauntlets, collars, and helms to—"

"Helms?"

"To protect the head. Crafted specially for a gryfon's face. Did Kajar not take any of those home?"

"No," Shard said. "Or I've never seen them. Maybe they were already so burdened it would've been too heavy to take over the sea."

"Perhaps. It would make sense." They hovered effortlessly in the half light of the dream place she had created, a Sunland from long ago. She swept her talons through the air, sculpting a shape from the wind, and held out to Shard a headpiece of gleaming bronze. It was shaped to fit over a gryfon head, contoured around the ears and eyes and with a clasp under the chin easy for talons to manage. Shard studied the vision, intrigued, and then Groa flicked her talons open, and it disintegrated. "Oh, Shard, you should have seen Kajar in the full armor they cast for him. Glorious, young prince. It was glorious, though cumbersome to fly in. There would be no enemy who could defeat him in that dragon armor."

"The wyrms of the Winderost—"

"If you will listen quietly," Groa said with all the patience of a mother, "I will tell all I remember, and then you may ask your questions at the end, if I haven't answered them."

Shard dipped his head in apology, and in the dream she could see the gesture. "Pardon me."

Groa continued, and though Shard smelled smoke, he saw only her vision. Enormous dragons soared through his vision. As she wove the dream he also watched what she did, and thought he understood how she led him from one image to the next.

"They would not teach us how to make fire. It was then I began to suspect they weren't as enlightened and flawless as we first thought." The half light of the dream darkened to a hazy red with her change in mood, like sunset just before a storm, and Shard shuddered.

"And worse, something changed in us at the sight of sparkling gems and moonlight shining on gold. The treasures also began to seep into the minds and hearts of many of Kajar's warriors, and they competed with each other to see who could charm the more elaborate or bejeweled bit of gold or silver or armor from the dragons. Oh, the dragons found us amusing. We would host games and contests of skill to show off, to impress them."

Shard saw fighting arenas nestled in the valleys of vast, snowy mountains. The arenas, built to accommodate dragons sparring, filled with competing gryfons.

"These games grew fiercer and more dangerous with each passing turn of the sun until, at last, the unthinkable happened. A gryfon, in the midst of mock-battle, lost himself in the fight, blinded by the prospect of winning, of treasure, deafened by the encouraging roars of the dragons. He killed his own wingbrother."

Shard closed his eyes against the sight—against Groa's vivid memory of the battle. Almost afraid to know, he asked, "Who?"

Groa stared below. "The murderer was Kajar. And his wingbrother, his closest sworn ally and friend, was my brother. To kill one's own wingbrother—unthinkable. That was the first blood to stain Kajar's name."

Eyes narrowed, his heart cold, Shard looked toward the arenas. "What happened then?"

"All grieved after the death of my brother," Groa said at length. "The dragons felt terrible—or acted so—that their encouragement had led to the accident. They made us more gifts. More *things*," she said, her voice sharpening, "as if metal and stones could replace my brother. They burned his body, the highest honor of their kind. But our hearts were turning cold. I longed for home. Kajar, I could tell, longed for home, for his family.

"Our band was splitting into those who sympathized with him and those who desired revenge, though on Kajar himself or the dragons no one could decide. There was so much anger and fear. It had been nearly a year at that point, mind you. I should have been there for him, Shard, but I never spoke to him again. I know what it is to become Nameless in the hunt, to forget yourself in a fight, but I never thought it would happen to Kajar. Not his noble bloodline, the blood of the very first kings to ever rise out of the dust of the Winderost.

"Kajar began asking more questions. Where did all the gold come from? For we'd kept exploring and found no tunnels or the mines of which the dragons spoke. He demanded to know where the riches came from, why the dragons were so powerful, why they led such brief lives. Why wouldn't they teach us how to make fire? Oh, they didn't like the questions. They thought he was being greedy."

"He was curious," Shard said softly, more to himself then her. Amaratsu's story was much simpler, more misguided, or, as Groa had said, kit-like in its portrayal of the events. For a moment the vision of the Sunland faded, and he saw only mist, and her voice in his mind. "I would have been curious too, after that."

"Yes. Anyone would have been. Certainly a prince like Kajar. I don't know what they say of him in the Winderost now, Shard, but I wish you could have known him as I did."

Shard thought of Kjorn, and was able to imagine what Kajar might have been like. "I do too."

Groa seemed to gather herself, re-appearing as her young self in the dream and flinging her wings out. The vision of the Sunland and the dragons and gryfons unfurled before Shard again.

"Kajar, disgusted with himself and with the dragons, disillusioned, made preparations to leave." Groa's voice swelled with a distant passion, and for the last part of the tale she looked and sounded young again, as if it had only happened the day before. "The dragon emperor was displeased. Perhaps he feared we would try to take revenge later, or would spread tales of the sad events through our homeland." A mountainous dragon whose scales shimmered like pearl flashed before Shard's eyes.

"He invited Kajar and all his warriors to a feast, and Kajar agreed, mostly to make sure his band was well-fortified for the flight home, and to make as peaceful an end possible.

"The dragons laid out every extravagant manner of food you could imagine, Shard. Fish from the deepest sea, seabird eggs boiled in water using fire, mussels, seal, great carcasses of snow bear and penguin and reindeer." Shard saw the feast, and through Groa's memory, smelled it too. "Much of it they roasted using fire, but we never cared for the taste of it. It appeared to be a gesture of honor and friendship.

"Kajar knew better. We knew better. We ate politely, made conversation, spoke of our homeland while not exactly saying which direction it was. Near the end of feast, the emperor rose, and, looming enormous over the rest of the gathering, asked Kajar's forgiveness. It was then that he told us from whence all the jewels and metal ore had come.

"He spoke of other dragons in a green land in the far, far, Nightward Sea, a land rich with metals and jewels. He spoke of those dragons, but called them wyrms, more like beasts than Named allies, who toiled happily in exchange for shining things. All the Sunland dragons had to do was promise them ornaments, and they dug in their mines, took orders, submitted to discipline. A reward here and there, for the wyrms are much longer lived than any other being, with an ancient memory.

"Do they also battle for your entertainment? Kajar asked him. I nearly choked, Shard, while Kajar continued. Do you dangle pretty pieces of metal at them rather than teach them the ways of honor, friendship, the light of Tyr, and use their own greed against them? Why do they toil for you, if not out of ignorance or fear? For Kajar could see the dragons had no love for those nightward wyrms, no respect, only contempt.

"All they care for in the world is gold, the emperor responded. Will you be like them? Or will you accept our true friendship?"

A dark sense of foreboding and revelation sat heavily over Shard's heart, and he gazed, rapt at the scene Groa painted for him. But it wavered and faded before him. Then he remembered that part in Amaratsu's version of the tale. "That's when you left. You knew it was some kind of test."

"I admit, Shard, I was a coward then. I could feel the tension gathering like a thunderstorm. I claimed the cooked meat made me ill and fled the gathering. I left the dragon's grounds and waited outside the limit of their territory, where I could see if the rest of my companions made flight, and join them home.

"But instead of a great host of gryfons flying, after a time I saw them walking out of the dragon's territory, toward where I hid in the foothills beyond the mountains where the dragons nest. A single dragon joined them. I knew her. She'd only just hatched the summer before we arrived, and had lived her whole short life knowing gryfons—and she was besot with Kajar from the moment we'd arrived, whether as a brother or in some other way I never knew. They came close to me, but I didn't trust the dragon, and I stayed hidden in a cluster of rocks, eavesdropping.

"She told Kajar she'd never met the wyrms but that she felt as Kajar did, that there had to be another way of mining their gems, or a more equal partnership. She knew the emperor took advantage of the wyrms' hunger for gold and thought it was wrong. She admired Kajar, and feared for him, for standing up to the emperor. And it was there, in front of all his gathered warriors, and I who wouldn't come out of hiding, that this now old and withered dragoness told Kajar that she loved him, and that she had a gift for him, a true gift.

"Help me die, she asked of him. I am old, she said, and I don't want to live in this land without you. I hurt, and I cannot bear the greed of my brothers and sisters any more.

"Kajar said she could fly with them and she only laughed and answered that she was too old, that she would fall in the ocean and die there.

" 'I give you the gift of my love,' she told Kajar, and the others. 'I am summerborn, and my element is fire. With my death and the fire of my blood you will see yourselves as I see you. The world will see you as I see you and your descendants for all time will bear the strength and beauty of the Sunland in their blood. But be warned, with a dragon's blessing, everything that you are will be more so. If you are strong, you will be stronger. If you are arrogant, you will be more so, and if you are fearful and dishonest, you may lose yourself and your very name. If you are kind and honorable, there will be no creature alive to match you, and the blessing on you will serve as something to aspire to, or as a warning against arrogance and greed.

" 'Take the gifts my kin and I made for you, to remember us by, but remember they are not us, they are not our friendship or our time together. Only remembrances, only rocks and metal. Kajar,' she begged him them, 'now let me die.'

"I looked away, Shard. I knew Kajar would do as she asked. I heard great gasps from the rest of the warriors and I looked back, expecting to see them covered in dragon blood—but oh…I cannot tell you how it looked. Her body had burned into shining red flames like fire, but so much brighter, and washed Kajar and the others in that fire. Then it faded, and they stood there with her ashes and the snow. They looked radiant, like cut jewels. The colors that had once been natural were now impossible hues. Kajar himself, once ruddy like a Winderost hawk, now blazed the red of a dying fire.

"I'm sure the rest of the tale is much as your friend Amaratsu said. I fled after that, fearing for Kajar and the others, fearing for myself. I couldn't bear to go home without my brother, without the blessing of the dragon on my feathers and in my blood. I have been here ever since, learning of the other creatures here, of dream catching, of fire…and at last, at long last, I heard a bit of silver in the wind. I heard a song of summer, and I sought you."

As the dream images melted into a vague, starry twilight around them, Shard tried to gather his scattering awe. He had no words.

Groa laughed softly. "Shall I teach you dream catching and weaving? Then you may seek visions of your own, or send dreams to others, to any who dream."

"I watched you," Shard murmured. "I think I understand."

They stood on a familiar cliff, and the thick scent of seawater and pine drew a loose breath from Shard's throat. The Silver Isles.

Groa shimmered before him. "Is this your home?"

"Yes." As she had done, he opened his wings, and felt in that place that he could gather and send his thoughts and his heart ever outward for all the dreaming world to hear. From his wingtips burst an apparition of Stigr, and the black gryfon wisped in front of them like smoke before fading.

"Well done," Groa murmured. Her voice sounded old again, breathless, and he noticed that she was blind again in the dream. It was now *his* dream. "Again."

Through her eyes he saw the dream net, and understood at once how the spirals echoed in the waking world—the winds and star light and the darkness of night tilted and turned in patterns repeated by leaves, shells, unfurling wings and beating hearts. He saw how he could soar along a strand and find a friend's dream, and weave an image for them.

So Shard did it again, folding together the salt wind, the stars and earth to show Groa all the things that he loved. He showed her the pride, his birth mother Ragna, his nest-sister, Thyra, now a queen. Stern Caj and practical, caring Sigrun. For her he wove wolves rushing through the dark forest, and Aodh the graying caribou king, and the laughing ravens, Hugin and Munin. He showed her Brynja, the huntress's wings broad and ruddy as fire in the dream light, and Groa laughed in delight to his desires displayed.

"I thought you might have the knack."

"You see why I have to go," Shard said, and drew forward all his memories of Kjorn, and his new and dear memories with Hikaru. "You see why I have to *try*."

"I do," Groa said. "And I wish you all luck and the blessings of each wind. But I urge you to be wary about the dragons. They are not all that they seem. There will be one dragon among them who keeps separate the truth and the lies. A storyteller, I can't recall…"

"Do you know that dragon's name?"

"In my time it was a dragoness called Umeko, and she was my friend. She gave me a silver chain. But she had a title too, I can't...I can't recall. I'm sorry."

"I will find a dragon to tell me the truth. Thank you." They stood on a dream of the Copper Cliff, near the King's Rocks. "Thank you for all of this."

Groa seemed bright, and he realized he could see the sea and the sky behind her, through her. She was waking, leaving his dream. "I have told you all I can, and I grow weary."

A sound made him aware of his body, of the cave, the smell of smoke. He was waking, too. For a moment he strained to remain there, to find Catori or his mother or a raven and tell them he was well.

"It is morning, young prince, and time to fly."

Groa seemed to speak in his heart, not his ears. "Shard. I have two last gifts for you, Shard."

Shard curled tighter on himself, eyes closed. Bitter wind gusted beyond the warm cave.

"Shard," she whispered, and he made a soft sound of acknowledgement, unable to open his eyes, still trying to see her in the dream. He was so weary, the story was almost too much to take in, and his leg ached from too long in one position.

"Come over to me, Rashard. I have two gifts for you. The first is a set of fire stones. A raven stole them from the dragons for me. You need only strike them together to make a spark, and if you have dry tinder ready, you will have fire. The second is the only dragon treasure that I bothered to keep."

Her words overlapped the very last dregs of his dream, she seemed to call him from across the waves.

"Shard. Shard, come over to me."

Come over to me.

Shard.

Shard jerked awake. As he opened his eyes, the dream still felt more real, for a moment, than the cave. Dull silvery light touched the entrance, and the last warmth was seeping out into the rock. The cave was empty.

The fire was dead.

Trembling, Shard pushed himself to his feet, favoring his leg. "Groa?" He peered around. She could not have left without him hearing. Really, she couldn't have left without crawling over him. "Iluq? Groa!"

He spun around. *She was only just here, just speaking to me!*

After shaking himself hard enough to jolt his injured leg, Shard limped around to the other side of the fire ring, and stopped, looking closely.

There lay the bones he couldn't identify before, from behind the smoke and fire. There, where the ancient, blind, impossible gryfess had sat weaving her dream tale, lay the bones he'd thought were wolf bones. But as Shard looked closer he saw that the dusty skeleton had the unmistakable skull of a gryfon, and two tucked sequences of bones had once been wings, now coated by dust and the decay of ancient feathers just barely preserved in the cold.

21
THE QUEENS' DECREE

THE WIDE BUT LOW-CEILINGED DEN where Ragna dwelled, alone, faced the starward sea and boasted a view of the Star Isle. A respectably sized cave for a small gryfon family, or one queen, it was now filled to cramping with Caj, Sigrun, Ragna herself, Thyra, Halvden and his mate Kenna, and her wingsister, Astri.

Caj watched the Widow Queen. After the first bustle of outrage at Halvden's return, the chaos of Aesir, Vanir and half-bloods alike demanding Halvden pay for his crimes, the Vanir queen had ushered them away for private council.

Unlike Sverin, Ragna preferred to deal with large matters privately, not loudly before the pride.

It was Thyra, however, who allowed Astri and Kenna to be present.

Caj, Sigrun, Astri, and Kenna sat ringing the back of the den like an audience, while Halvden stood before Ragna and Thyra, who blocked the exit and were outlined in sunlight. They'd let him sleep through the night in a guarded, empty den.

164

"Halvden, son-of-Hallr," Ragna said quietly. "You stand ready to admit your crimes and atone?"

Halvden looked at her, then turned and addressed Thyra. "I do, my lady."

Beside Caj, Sigrun tensed at the affront to Ragna. He nudged her with a wing, trusting their daughter to handle the situation.

"You will show respect," Thyra said, "to the regent of the Sun Isle."

"*You* are my queen," Halvden said, voice low. "If Sverin is restored to his senses, he will be my king. If not, then when Kjorn returns, I will bow to him alone, and atone for my crimes to him."

Caj had to admire that he held his tail still, didn't show his agitation. Young Astri, star-white but brighter than Ragna in the way of a half-blood Aesir, let out a muffled, whimpering snarl. Kenna tapped her beak in warning.

Ragna remained unruffled, cool and still as marble. She turned her head to face Thyra as well. "What will you then, my lady?" Her voice sounded too amused at the idea that Halvden thought he had any choice in his punishment at all, or who he would respect, and not.

"Halvden, as usual, you spew bold and arrogant words," Thyra said coldly. Even though her belly bulged, she stood tall and fair in the dim afternoon light, and Caj could have fluffed with pride. "My father led me to believe that you were willing to show humility, that you were ready to ask forgiveness. Of all the warriors in this pride, it is his forgiveness you should seek. You tried to murder him. You lied. You covered your lies with further, cowardly *lying*, and when Kjorn himself returned and presented himself to Sverin, you tried to discredit him. Him, the very prince you now claim to wish to serve. Tell me why we should allow you to live, much less to atone for these unforgiveable crimes?"

Kenna made a quiet noise and Caj glanced to her, unable to tell if the violet huntress approved of, or feared, Thyra's questioning.

With a quick, seeking glance at Caj, Halvden shifted, his gaze flickering with the first sign of doubt. Then, to the surprise of all, he mantled low.

"For the sake of my unborn kit. For your own sense of honor." There was a long, cold silence, thick with gathering anger. Head bowed, Halvden lifted only his fierce golden eyes to Ragna, and to Caj's surprise, addressed the Widow Queen again. "Now you may prove that you're a better and more merciful queen than Sverin was king, that the Vanir are all you say they are."

"Let it never be said you aren't clever," Ragna murmured, and Caj had to agree. He exchanged a dark look with Sigrun, and feared he may have been soft and foolish in sparing Halvden's life.

The green warrior bowed his head again. Ragna and Thyra looked to Kenna, and Ragna spoke. "You chose Halvden as your true mate this summer last. Tell me, do you still desire him, after all that has happened? He begs for his life in the name of his unborn kit. Do you wish for him to be father to your young, if he changes as he promises?"

Kenna's beak opened slightly, perhaps stunned to be asked such questions. Her gaze rested on Halvden and for the first time, he appeared hesitant. But he did lift his eyes and in that look, Caj saw with some reassurance that he was at the mercy of at least one gryfess there. When Kenna hesitated to answer, Caj saw in Halvden's flattened ears and widened eyes that he loved her, that he actually felt regret, that he was afraid. And, it seemed, so did Kenna.

"I do," she said, low but clear, for hers was not a whispering nature. "I hope he will atone for everything and make himself better for the pride and for his family."

Thyra nodded. "Then he will have his chance—"

"No!" Astri rose, having endured all she could. Sigrun stood with her, making a soothing sound, and Caj saw that she feared for the young gryfess. "No, how could you? It was he who goaded Sverin, he who tried to kill Caj! He faked Kjorn's death, he bullied my mate! He is wicked, my queens, I beg you, he must *die*."

Caj stood, seeing that Astri was ready to leap and murder Halvden herself. Her white wings raised like gleaming sheets of ice, beak opened in a pant, her eyes pinpointed in disbelief and feral panic. "You cannot let him get away with this."

"Calm yourself," Sigrun said, her own expression guarded. "Think of your kit."

"I am! I am thinking of my kit, and my mate whose blood is not just on Sverin's talons, but on *his!*"

She leaped. Caj barreled between her and Halvden even as Kenna caught the smaller gryfess around the chest to restrain her.

"I didn't kill Einarr!" Halvden shouted, his temper and pride at last unleashed.

"You as good as did," Astri cried. "You wretch. My queen," she begged first of Thyra, then Ragna, both of whom remained where they were, fearing perhaps that Halvden would take the chance to flee the cave. "Please, you cannot let his crimes go unpunished. He doesn't deserve your mercy."

"Enough now," Ragna said quietly. "This will not do. We have all been injured. We have all suffered loss. He will not go unpunished. Contain yourself."

"Astri," Thyra murmured. "My friend. We have hunted together, shared injury. Laughed, and wept. We chose our mates on the same Daynight. You must trust in me now, and remember that shedding more blood will not bring Einarr back."

Astri crumpled in Kenna's grip. Her wings fell to her sides, Kenna loosened her hold, and Astri sat back, touching gentle talons to her belly.

"Tyr watches you," she whispered to Halvden. "You may say pretty things to appease those here, but there is one who knows your true heart and you will atone in the end—here, or in the Sunlit Land."

Halvden laid back his ears, but wisely said nothing.

"Wingsister," Kenna murmured.

"No." Astri broke away, stumbling on her own wing before folding it, and brushed by Ragna, who allowed her to pass. "No. I'm not. Not anymore. You severed that vow by choosing *him.*"

"If it were Einarr," Kenna began, and Caj thought she couldn't have chosen a poorer comparison, "wouldn't you choose him?"

Astri paused in the entrance, looking like a snowflake in the low light. "I am," she breathed, and left with a whimper, climbing out of sight.

"Sigrun," Caj began, but his mate knew her work well, and was already following.

"With your leave," she murmured to both queens.

"Take care of her, Mother," Thyra said quietly.

"I will." Sigrun turned a wicked glare to Halvden, who actually looked struck by Astri's pain. "You. If you have it in your greedy, conniving heart to speak an honest word or do one genuine thing for another, now is the time to begin. Then, maybe, you will see forgiveness."

After giving Caj a measuring look, as if to gauge his intelligence for letting Halvden live, she left.

"I should go too," Kenna said, and walked close to Halvden. "She's right. Now is the time to begin."

Halvden met her gaze, then lowered his head.

Kenna search his face, laid her ears back in a warning look, and left the cave to help tend Astri.

Caj stood. "If you're done with my presence, my ladies, I must resume my search."

"Your search," Ragna said thoughtfully. She drew herself up, watching him. "Caj, it's taking too long. It's becoming a wolf hunt." Ever since Sverin's obsession with hunting wolves that winter, "wolf hunt" was a phrase the Vanir used for any pursuit that could be deemed mad or fruitless.

Caj fought against a growl.

Ragna lifted her wings in warning. "I know you fear it will harm your efforts but I must insist on sending warriors. Halvden can tell them where Sverin is sheltering, and they will restrain him until you arrive and can try to restore him to his senses. This is what we should have done from the start. In honor of you and of Sigrun, I didn't act when she told me of your search. I must act now."

Caj kept silent until he had something to say. The decision was not brash—he could see she meant no harm or disrespect. On the surface the idea sounded sensible, but he could think of nothing more foolish than to send more gryfons into Sverin's path.

"Father," Thyra said quietly, and he looked at her, feeling betrayed to see that she agreed. "You see the sense of it. It will take you too long, and when you reach him, you'll be alone."

"I must be alone," Caj said, looking between them. Halvden watched, looking relieved that the focus was off him for a moment. "He will attack any other. I won't risk that."

"And if he attacks you?" Thyra asked, and her gaze fell on his broken wing. "You couldn't possibly hope to overcome him."

"I'm the *only* one who could hope to overcome him, daughter." Caj managed to keep the growl from his voice. He dipped his head. "My ladies. You must allow me to continue. You must leave him to me."

"In your condition," Ragna said, "you could not best him."

Caj could tell she hadn't meant it to insult him, but it pierced his pride nonetheless, and for a moment it was all he could do to restrain his temper.

"He bested *me*."

They all looked at Halvden.

"In his condition," he clarified when Ragna and Thyra only stared at him, and he nodded to indicate Caj's wing. "I'm not Sverin, but still, he bested me. Forgive me for interrupting, but I have seen Sverin most recently. Caj is the only one who can hope to make him see reason. He'll feel threatened by anyone else, he'll…" He looked between the two gryfesses and a keen look came into his eyes. "Ah, but you don't mean for Sverin to return alive, do you?"

"Don't goad him," Ragna warned, and Caj realized it was exactly was Halvden was trying to do.

Thyra stepped forward, answering Caj's quiet growl. "Father, he's wrong. Of course we do want him alive. If it's possible."

"If it's possible," Caj echoed flatly.

Thyra watched him warily, and behind her, Ragna remained quiet, deferring. "Father, Sverin threatened me with exile and death even knowing I carry Kjorn's kit. He killed Einarr, who tried to serve loyally until it became clear that Sverin was mad. Before he left me, Kjorn was resigned to let us do what we needed to do if his father could not be contained nor brought to see reason."

"Do you have any idea what will happen?" Caj looked between both queens. "He could kill anyone you send. Do you want more weeping gryfesses to tend to? More injuries, more death?"

"Not even Sverin could best a number of young, healthy warriors," Ragna murmured.

"He's not Sverin anymore," Halvden said. "My *lady*. He's not a king, not an Aesir even. He's Nameless." He looked to Thyra. "He's a wild, starving beast, desperate to survive. He has no sense of honor. He won't spare them for the sake of their families." He looked at Caj. "Or they'll kill *him*. Something has driven him mad, and mad he remains."

"Be silent," Ragna snapped, showing a temper at last. Caj agreed, though he recalled earlier that winter during the Long Night, when Ragna hinted she knew something about Sverin that Caj himself didn't, some guilt. Something enough, perhaps, to drive a king mad. Ragna shook her head. "It's no business of yours, now."

"But it is." Halvden inclined his head when she fixed her cool green eyes upon him. "He is my king. More than that, I swore a wing-brother vow. Though he wasn't in his right mind, I was, and I will be true to it."

Surprised, Caj appraised Halvden's expression and found it genuine.

"Very well," Ragna said. "Then you may help by leading our chosen warriors to him. And restrain him, by any means necessary, until Caj can arrive."

"If I could suggest, instead, that I serve Caj. My greatest crime was against him, and it's to him I wish to make amends."

Halvden looked sidelong at Caj, and both Thyra and Ragna looked momentarily bewildered by the suggestion.

"Father?" Thyra asked. "It's your decision."

"Oh," Caj said, tail twitching, "if Halvden wishes to make amends with me, I will have work enough for him."

"Then let it be so," Ragna said. "Thyra and I will choose warriors. Halvden, tell them where you know of Sverin last sheltering. They will find and restrain him, then fetch you to him so you can attempt to restore him. Does this satisfy all?" She looked from Thyra to Caj, and Caj could only incline his head. Any other argument would be fruitless.

"Let it be so," Thyra said.

"Thank you, my lady," Halvden murmured graciously, and Caj watched him with growing suspicion.

"Go make your preparations, and Thyra and I will choose warriors to seek out Sverin."

"They what?" Sigrun looked dismayed, later in their den when Caj told her. She packed new mud around his wing. "I shouldn't have left you. I could have convinced Ragna—"

"No, they were set. But at least I'll have Halvden," he said blandly.

"Halvden." Sigrun nearly spat the name. "Watch your back."

"He knows I can best him. What's more, I think he genuinely wishes, at least, to prove himself to Kenna. How is Astri?"

"Well enough." The short answer suggested he shouldn't pursue the matter. Sigrun continued muttering as she combed gentle talons through the feathers of his wing, followed by a cool pack of fast-drying mud. "Do try not to break this one."

"I will."

She sighed, frustrated, but her soft touched eased Caj's heart. "All this business with two queens, it does nothing to serve the pride. Everything feels split, disjointed."

"It will be well again, when the princes return."

That thought quieted them both for a moment. Then, at the same time they asked each other, "What will you do—"

". . . when Shard returns," Sigrun said.

". . . when Kjorn returns," Caj said.

They both paused, then broke out in long, rueful, weary laughter. Very quietly Sigrun said, "I cannot see Shard exiling anyone, but if it's to be so, then I will go where you are, my mate. If the Aesir return to the windward land, you will have a daughter, her mate and kit and your lost kin there—"

"I have a son here, too." He stretched out a foreleg, flexing his talons against the rock floor. "Or maybe that remains to be seen, if he'll even allow Aesir in the Silver Isles."

Sigrun's voice grew tight. "Caj…"

"It's a possibility we must consider." He didn't meet her eyes.

"I will go where you are," she said again, firmly, and finished rebuilding the cast. "There. That's as well as I can make it. I suppose you won't wait until it's dry to set out."

"I can't. I must try to keep up with Ragna and Thyra's warriors, though they'll be flying. Halvden's already told them where he knew Sverin to be nesting. I can only hope he doesn't kill any of them or fly again before I arrive."

"Be safe," Sigrun whispered, touching her beak just behind his ear. Caj tucked his head against hers for a moment, then a rush of wings drew them up.

"Ready?" Halvden asked, not entering, but beating his wings hard to hover just outside the den.

"Show respect," Sigrun snipped, and Halvden landed, folding his wings.

"I'm ready." Caj stood.

"Take care of…each other," Sigrun said, tightly acknowledging Halvden. He inclined his head and Sigrun looked back to Caj. "I will do what I can to help you from here. Don't stray from your path."

Caj tilted his head curiously, wondering what she could do from there, but she looked past them toward the entryway and flicked one ear back, indicating she didn't wish to elaborate. He stepped forward to touch his beak just behind her ear. "I'll see you soon."

"You'd better," she murmured. He chuckled, and followed Halvden from the den.

They walked in silence from the nesting cliffs, and Caj felt eyes on them, pride members watching their departure. They walked nightward, which he found odd, but Halvden had sworn to help him. Gradually, a half mark later, when Caj noticed they were out of sight of the nesting cliffs, Halvden turned starward to follow the Nightrun River.

"We must move quickly," Caj reminded him, alert for betrayal and wary of Halvden's meandering course. "We must try to find Sverin before Ragna's warriors do. For all her talk of only restraining him, I fear what will happen if they find him first."

"Oh that won't be a problem."

Caj stopped walking. They stood under the spindly cover of birch trees, and heard but didn't yet see the river. "You lied to them."

Halvden looked up at the naked, grasping trees. "Ragna's warriors are heading to the nightward shore as we speak, to search those cliffs there. Far away from the last place I saw Sverin." He met Caj's gaze squarely. "My debt is not to those warriors, but you. And I will take you, alone, to Sverin. We both understand that's best."

Caj stared at him, and finally collected himself. It was not his first choice to lie, but the deed was done and he was not above taking advantage of it. "Then lead on."

Halvden nodded once, and turned to lead the way upriver, toward the White Mountains.

22

MOUNTAINS OF THE SEA

S HARD BACKED AWAY, TAIL LASHING.

He swallowed hard. It felt as if he swallowed his own heart.

His hind paw pressed on something sharp. Lifting his foot, Shard peered back, then edged to the side. There, by the fire, lay a small skeleton, and the grinning skull of a fox.

Shard fought to keep his breath calm.

Two gifts, Groa had said. *Come over to me.*

Gulping down his horror and the slow, eerie cold of understanding, Shard crept back to the gryfon skeleton.

Grasped within the cracked talons was a pouch of rabbit skin tied shut by two long cords of leather. Inside, Shard found two oddly straight stones. Or not stones exactly. One was metal, the other flint.

Fire stones. He looped it over his head by the leather cords for safekeeping.

"What else?" he murmured. *The only treasure I kept.* At first he saw nothing, then when he shifted and faint light shone through the entrance, it caught on a thin, tarnished silver chain that still hung around the skeleton's neck. There was nothing else, no jewel, no thick and gaudy pendant, just a simple, silver chain. If she wanted him to have it so badly, Shard thought, he should take it.

Drawing a breath and murmuring a respectful thank you, he drew the long chain carefully through the neck bones, examined it in the dim light, then slipped it over his head with the pouch. It promptly disappeared beneath his long winter feathers. He'd never been honored with any dragon crafted treasures before, and he found that it didn't make him feel much different.

Shard rested his talons briefly on the brow of the skull, wishing her well in the Sunlit Land. He wondered with no small dismay if part of being a Summer King meant that the dead would be speaking to him often, now.

"Oh," said a voice from the entrance, and Shard turned, lifting his wings. Iluq stood there, outlined by the dim and rising light. "You're awake! I'm sorry I let the fire die."

Shard didn't know if he'd moved in a dream for the entire night, a dream woven by a long-dead gryfess, but certainly he was awake now. "Iluq…"

"I know," the little spirit said, and Shard tried to catch a scent, realizing, then, that he'd never smelled either of them, and had thought it was only because of the smoke. "You want to go."

"You should go, too." Shard drew a deep breath. "You should go on, to the Sunlit Land."

"I promised my nest-mother I would wait for you. I promised I would guide you here."

"Thank you for everything," Shard said, wondering how long the fox had waited. "For the fish, and the warmth and the splint. Do you know how I can find the dragons?"

Iluq bared his teeth. "Oh yes." As the dawn light grew, it shone through him until all Shard saw was a beam of sunlight on stone, but he clearly heard Iluq laugh and say, "Follow Midragur."

The great Wings of Tor spread above Shard as he soared across the Sunland night. After flying all day, the light died and waves of green and trembling pink rippled across the sky. Through them he followed the clustered line of stars of Midragur.

After Groa's story he worried for Hikaru, and feared that he'd taught the young dragon a false tale, one that showed gryfons in a poor light.

But what was I to do? He thought, talons flexing. *Amaratsu was the only link I had....*

To know that Kajar had been more honorable, had spoken out against the Sunland dragons using the wyrms to dig their gems, made Shard glad. It would be a good thing to tell Kjorn. A good thing, a tiny part of him thought, to tell Sverin, if the violent Red King would even hear him.

Perhaps I could send him a dream, Shard thought with a chuckle, then sobered, considering it more seriously. But he would not send the king lies. He understood now how Munin had once created false images to trick him. He hadn't dreamed of the Silver Isles since fleeing the Horn of Midragur, and realized it was because he feared what he might see.

The vision he'd had of Einarr during the whale attack unnerved him. In his heart, he knew that his friend was dead, which meant things were still unwell in the Silver Isles. If he could help to resolve the situation in the Winderost, he could return swiftly home and restore order. That would mean facing the wyrms again.

The Sunland dragons have their claws in this too and they must help.

Surely the next generation would see reason, would see that perhaps it was only they who stood a chance of speaking sense to the wyrms, of perhaps restoring their hearts and minds.

I wonder, Shard thought with distant hope, *if even now Hikaru has managed to convince them.*

Flat, icy air forced him to focus on his flight and work hard for lift. The muscles in his wings and chest ached. A dull throbbing pulsed up from his broken leg and eventually pounded through his skull. The landscape below glowed as if under a false, colorful sun and he soared high over rolling hills of snow, plains, and black rock.

At last, as dawn whispered in the sky, he saw a hard coastline of ice cliffs plunging into the sea. Inland, the cliffs surged into a jagged jaw of dark mountains, their snow swept peaks so high he couldn't see over the top of them, and Shard flew over their foothills.

The constellation of Midragur dove down beyond the mountains, looking as if it plunged into their heart.

Talons tucked up under his downy chest feathers, wings straight out to soar, Shard peered forward, looking for any sign of the mountain range's inhabitants.

Sign of them was obvious, and startling.

Uniform, precise shapes formed the face of the mountain and as Shard flew closer, he realized they were ornate pillars and arches carved into the faces of stone. Only dragon claws could have done the work.

Spilling air from his wings, Shard dipped lower, coming upon the mountains at mid-level as he sought an entry. The foot of the mountains looked as any do—rough hills of rock, ice, snow and straggling trees—but about halfway up, long balconies were carved into the sheerest section of the faces, supported by towering columns, and each appeared to lead into a hall carved into the mountain. The dragons had shaped roofs over each balcony, pointed at the top and sweeping down like the bows of a pine tree.

Just as Shard spied what looked like a main entryway, a flash of unnatural blue caught his eye.

A dragon.

Amazement glowed through him. He'd almost expected not to see them, that Amaratsu was a dream, that Hikaru was a dream.

But he watched as a fully grown dragon of the Sunland slithered out of one of the stone tunnels and whipped out pearlescent, feathered wings, undulating through the air toward Shard in quick, graceful movements. Its scales glittered rich blue, reminding Shard of the sky at midnight.

"Greetings, great one!" Shard called, attempting a mid-air bow. "I am—"

A rush of wind bowled him forward and he kicked out a hind leg, flaring to a hard stop as another dragon, this one flame-orange, shot overhead from behind him.

Shard flapped back, trying to take in their size and majesty. The blue was smaller than the orange, but still enormous. Every scale gleamed like polished sapphire, and gold jewelry glittered from its ears, branching silver horns and nimble fore claws. A long silver mane flickered like flame around its face and in a stiffer ridge down its back.

He tried again to greet them. "I am Shard, the son of Baldr, prince of the Silver Isles! I seek Hikaru, and…"

"You will come with us," boomed the blue dragon Shard could only assume was a sentry.

"This way," said the orange dragoness—Shard knew once she spoke that she was female—and every bit of her also dripped with gold and adornments of polished stone.

"Thank you."

They fell in on either side of him, dwarfing Shard as a gryfon dwarfed a hare. "Is Hikaru here, and safe? I know some of your number recovered him from the sea—"

"You will come with us," said the orange again, her voice like crackling flame, "and be silent."

Feeling small, Shard closed his beak and stared down the length of both dragons, trying to determine how many gryfons would be able to stand along their backs. Muscled, enormous serpents, they glided straight alongside Shard as gracefully as eels in water. Shard thought of how different the wyrms of the Winderost were, with their thicker bodies more like enormous boar than reptiles, though had had long necks and tails. Their broad wings were bat-like and veined, not feathered, their heads horned and square, their colors dull, earthy. The wyrms had their own kind of majesty, but they were nothing like the winged serpents of the Sunland.

He noticed the orange dragoness returning his curious stare, and he flicked his ears forward in a friendly gesture. She looked away. Disheartened, Shard looked toward the mountain again. Up close, the stone pillars and sweeping roofs spread dizzyingly high and wide around him. Of course, it was built to a scale that would be comfortable to dragons.

The dragons dipped under Shard to fly ahead, leading the way across one large, main balcony of stone. Shard had to bob and glide in swift, falcon-like swoops to keep up. Upon entering the mountain, darkness swallowed up the sunlight and huge torches mounted on the pillars lit their way. The floor was so distant, Shard couldn't see it in the dark, for they flew into the middle of the mountain. It reminded him immediately of the Horn of Midragur, and he saw where tunnels on different levels led from outside, and all into the main, hollow expanse.

Far, far away, the distant, twinkling of torches told him the entire mountain was carved and hollowed into dragon dwellings.

Whispers of wind and the *shushing* rush of wings that sent the torches dancing told him of other dragons, but he didn't have time to look around and see all of them.

His escorts soared across the great, central cavern and Shard followed, trying to take in as much as he could and remember which way they'd come. Looking up, he saw that little daylight leaked in from outside, but the cavern was so vast the light was swallowed up without brightening the interior, and firelight alone lit the dark hall.

He'd never seen anything like it before.

"Are those dens?" he asked the dragoness, pointing toward archways carved into various tiers of the cavern, and forgetting that he was supposed to remain silent.

The orange flicked a look to him, then the blue dragon, who rumbled an answer. "Some. Some are exits. Or workshops. Some are treasure rooms."

"It won't matter to you," said the orange.

"Oh, but it does," Shard said. "I think it's incredible. I want to learn all I can about you."

They exchanged another look. "You don't understand," the dragoness began, but the blue male interrupted her.

"Be silent now. We are already getting too much attention."

"Are we?" Shard looked around and behind them. Then he saw the blue was correct. Silent, curious eyes glittered in the firelight from

all levels, dragons peering out from behind various pillars, from archways and even crawling in from outside.

A thrill shivered through Shard's chest. "Hello!"

The blue dragon snapped his jaws in warning.

"Sorry," Shard mumbled. "But I'm so honored and excited to
meet you. I never dreamed your home would be like this." He paused.
"I *would* like to know where we're going."

"To the empress," answered the blue. "She will know what to do
with you."

At that, his twinge of misgiving deepened. Recalling both versions
of Kajar's venture in the Sunland, he realized that the dragons might
not be pleased to see him at all, despite his having helped Hikaru.
Amaratsu had spoken of them as closing themselves off, disheartened
at the greed and shallowness of others.

*But if Groa's version of the story is true, then they might very well see me
as a threat, or worse, an outright enemy.*

Shard folded his talons together and followed his escorts in silence,
taking in the lay of the hollow mountain and trying to make out the
rest of the dragons who watched them in the dark. If Hikaru was
among them, Shard could not see him, and he didn't come forward.

After a flight across the mountain cavern, they reached the far
side, where only torches lit the stone halls. The blue dragon turned
up and slipped under an archway that led into a longer tunnel lined
with torches. The orange followed, and instructed Shard to fly just
beneath her. He thought the tunnel must be cramped for them, but he
could've fit a whole hunting party of gryfons side by side and as many
above and below him. The floor below them was polished smooth by
ages of dragon feet walking, and the ceiling fanged with stalactites.

Ahead, the torches ended, and a strange, blue light took their
place, an eerie, cool glow around the next bend in the tunnel.

Nervous, Shard held his breath as they banked and flew around a
long curve.

They emerged into a cavern of ice, and Shard gasped with delight.

The faraway sun reached faintly through a mountain of ice to
the new cavern, smaller but similar in structure to the first stone hall.

Archways and pillars and polished tunnels glowed—translucent white at the top and deepening to turquoise and blue toward the bottom. Fresh, frosty air filled Shard's senses and he fought the urge to shoot ahead of his escorts and dive and play in the strange, magical place.

The ice columns boasted intricate reliefs of dragons and foreign, decorative patterns. Shard imagined the stone pillars of the first cave also had such carvings, but he hadn't been close enough to see them in the dimmer light.

Upon entering the hall of ice, the dragons turned and glided down, and down to the floor, so far below that Shard's ears crackled as they descended. They must've been flying near the top of the mountain.

"Land," instructed the blue dragon, touching down himself. The flame dragon landed beside him, and Shard between them. He tilted his head back to see the open stretch of ice and air above, as tall as a mountain. The scale of the place nearly sent him reeling, and made him feel the size of a cricket in a gryfon den.

Jewel-toned dragon heads poked out of various archways and around pillars, either new observers or having followed them from the first cavern. The blue and orange ignored them and walked across the oblong ice floor toward the far end. Shard followed, staring ahead, placing his feet gingerly so as not to slip on the slick ground. His broken leg presented a challenge, forcing him to hobble slowly, with as much dignity as he could muster.

The great, towering wall of ice at the far end of the cavern was carved into massive reliefs of dragons, eagles and other creatures in a precise pattern that Shard recognized, after a moment, as the layout of the constellations. Twined above all was the great form of a dragon, arching over every beast like a massive rainbow. Midragur.

Shard, with the sentries now at his back, walked down the hall of ice, breathing the dry, cold air, and staring.

At the far end of the hall, framed by pillars and a sweeping roof, was a giant dais of hard packed, crystalline snow and ice.

On that dais, coiled in layer upon layer of radiant golden scales, waited a dragoness who could only be the empress. Shard couldn't tell where her scales ended and her gold adornments began. Colorful jewels glimmered on each of her five toes, her horns, in rings that pierced her soft deer-like ears, and even in delicate chains and bands on the end of her tail. Parts of her silken, white mane flared free, and in other places, was braided into tight plaits, woven here and there with more jewels, bright feathers and polished gold. A large, liquid red cabochon ruby the size of Shard's head winked and shone from a collar at her throat.

The blue dragon nudged Shard with a talon and he realized he was staring like a witless magpie. He mantled as low as he ever had, beak tapping the frozen floor, wingtips pressed to the ice. Beside him, both sentries did the same.

"Rise." Her voice slipped through the cavern, deep and rich.

Shard stood, leaving his wings open if only to feel slightly larger. "I'm so honored to be in your presence, my lady. I am Rashard, son-of-Baldr, prince of the Silver Isles in the Starland Sea."

"Welcome, Rashard, to the dragon dwelling of Ryujan, the Mountains of the Sea." An almost imperceptible twitch of her claws sent Shard's sentries away. They slipped around themselves, long bodies leaving and re-coiling near an entrance there on the ground level, though they never turned their faces fully from the empress. Shard looked back to the golden dragoness before him.

"I am Empress Ai, the Radiant. The two-thousand-and-tenth daughter of the First Emperor of Ryujan. Ruler of the Sunland and all the Windward Sea."

Shard bowed again.

"You are he," the empress began incredulously, "who Amaratsu's son calls the Shard of Sun?"

"I am." Shard could imagine her thoughts. *Shard of Sun indeed, with my dull gray feathers? I must be nothing to them, unimpressive. What will Hikaru think of me now, too, now that he's seen his own kind?*

As if reading his thoughts, the empress asked, "Why does he call you this?"

Shard felt the burning of her eyes, all their eyes, all their listening ears. He was the first gryfon they had seen in a hundred years. *No, he* thought. *The first gryfon any of them had seen.* They would've all been born within the last year.

To them, everything he did would be what gryfons did. Everything he said, everything he was, would be the very definition of gryfon, to them.

He inclined his head, mustering more respect. "He calls me that, because Amaratsu called me that." Shard put every ounce of strength in his voice that he could, despite growing apprehension. "She said I was like a shard of sunlight in the darkness of the cave where we met. Please, is Hikaru well? We encountered blackfish, in the sea, and he—"

"He is well." The empress shifted, leaning back against her own coils and toying with a long chain that sparkled with at least one thousand cut diamonds. "It is good you thought to bring him home. If that is your business, you may leave with our blessing. My sentries will show you out, and the best way back across the sea."

Shard tapped his beak closed for a moment, speechless. "Thank you. But that isn't the only reason I've come. And I would like to see Hikaru, to speak to him."

Her ears flicked, and her black, slit pupils contracted. "What other reason could you possibly have for coming here? We have nothing for you. And you, I'm quite certain, have nothing for us. You must go. Hikaru, you must know, is quite happy here. Seeing you again will only confuse what he is learning now."

Shard met her suspicious look with narrowed eyes. "Will it? What is he learning now, exactly, my lady?"

With a soft rumble, the empress unfolded layer upon layer of shining coils, opened her long swan wings and loomed above Shard with a huge, piercing stare. "Our ways."

Though anger began to heat his skin, it would not do to show her disrespect, or temper. "Please, you must let me speak to him. We're friends. And I have come for other reasons. I think you can help me." In trying to sum up all of the reasons he'd come, it was all Shard could say. No wings rustled, not one spying dragon moved. The vast, frigid hall of ice felt like sudden, crushing weight.

"We have nothing for you," she repeated. "And as for Hikaru, he is better off not—"

"*Shard!*" A joyous shout cracked through the ice cavern.

Before the empress could react, Shard found himself knocked to the ice floor in a roiling tumble of polished black scales, feathers and gentle claws.

"Hikaru!" He laughed, dizzy with relief even as pain shot up his leg.

"I told them you'd come, I knew you would find me! I knew you were all right!" Hikaru butted his head against Shard's and then coiled around him, and Shard stared up at the dragonet who had grown to nearly four times Shard's size during their separation, not even including the length of his neck and tail.

"Careful, Hikaru, my leg is broken. Of course I found you." He freed his forelegs from Hikaru's coil and swiveled to see the empress, who regarded Hikaru with the patience of a gryfess watching a fledge chase grasshoppers.

"Forgive me, Ai-hime, Radiant and Gracious One." Hikaru bowed his head to the empress and splayed his wings, still hugging Shard in his coils. "I didn't know if my wingbrother was still alive, and here he is, and well. Forgive me for bursting into your hall."

"It is to be expected," the empress said, watching them with an indulgent look, "from the young."

Whispers and mutters broke out through the dragons who peered at them from the various levels and archways, speculating in un-amused tones. Shard's belly tightened and he pressed his talons to Hikaru's scales to remind himself why he was there. The empress twitched her soft ears and the hall fell silent again.

"Rashard of the Silver Isles, we understand you have come to see Hikaru. But we have no other interest in affairs outside our mountains, and we can be of no help to you. You may shelter with us, and heal, as long as Hikaru takes responsibility for you. You will not wander alone in our tunnels, nor hunt in our waters or surrounding lands without supervision. You will not seek out our treasure rooms or forges. You will not pester any dragon who does not seek your company. You are here for Hikaru's sake and because of my good will and in honor of Hikaru's father and Amaratsu. Do you understand?"

Shard, taken aback, began to speak a protest, but Hikaru squeezed him gently, and his liquid-gold eyes hooded with warning.

"Yes," Shard said slowly, turning back to the empress. "Yes, my lady. As you wish."

"I will look after him," Hikaru said, and the nearly adult depth of his voice, so serious in tone, sent a shiver through Shard. "Thank you for your generosity, Radiant One." Dipping his head low, he murmured to Shard, "Come with me. Please stay silent. I'll explain everything."

Shard inclined his head deeply, to show Hikaru he'd heard, to hide a new wash of frustration, and to show respect to the empress. Hikaru uncoiled from Shard and they bowed again, and Shard followed Hikaru's lead when he backed toward the ground-level exit, not turning his face from the empress. He ground his beak, wanting to ask when he could see her again, speak his piece and ask for assistance. But the young dragon promised him an explanation.

As they neared the exit, Shard's feathers prickled with unease. He took a final, quick look up and around and realized, with a growing chill, that it was not curiosity with which most of the dragons regarded him. He met the stare of one young, gleaming red male, and was easily able to read the expression on his face, but it was not curiosity. It was not even anger, and as Shard looked around he saw that every dragon wore the same expression.

Every dragon who watched him leave with Hikaru was watching with disgust.

23

ALLIES OLD AND NEW

"VANHAR TO ME!" NILSINE SHOUTED over the wind. "Keep alert!" Kjorn flew at her right, forming a wedge with four other gryfons and Nilsine, on point as they soared high and toward the vast network of canyons they called the Voldsom Narrows. They'd left the lions of the First Plains a day after Kjorn's hunting trial, with a promise of friendship should they ever need shelter, and the blessing to cross their lands if needed, again.

Ajia promised to mind her dreams and the winds for sign of Shard, and Kjorn thanked her, though he wasn't sure what that was worth.

I will raise the Sunwind, indeed.

Flexing his wings, Kjorn snorted. His father would've rejected such nonsense, and Kjorn did the same. Aesir made their own destiny. He had no intention of bringing war to the Winderost, only of finding Shard, reconciling, and returning to the Silver Isles and Thyra before spring, before his kit was born.

"Keep alert," Nilsine said again, and Kjorn realized he'd drifted out of the formation. He flapped twice, steering back into the wedge. Nilsine looked ahead again with an expression of approval.

A thick haze of smoke clung to the rim of every canyon wall and they had to rise high to see over it. Great jagged mazes of golden and red rock split into deep crevices and splintered off from one main artery, at the bottom of which ran a silver slip of river.

*The Serpent River Pack...*Kjorn recalled the painted wolf Mayka and wondered if this had been his home, then refocused as Nilsine called orders. He peered forward through the haze, amazed that the smoke from the Horn had drifted so far windward. The wall of haze blocked any view of the horizon, the distant Dawn Spire that Nilsine told him lay a day's flight dawnward, or the lands they'd crossed to reach the Voldsom over the last days.

"Eagles!" reported one of Nilsine's warriors.

Kjorn snapped to attention, and admired the scout's good eye. He saw a smudge of movement through the haze, then it clarified into an entire flight of eagles, formed in a swan wedge similar to their own. Quickly Kjorn sized them up. A third the size of a gryfon, they had broad wings and colors ranging from golden brown to ruddy and spotted cream on the juveniles.

"That doesn't look like a greeting party," Kjorn said to Nilsine.

"Don't be so quick to seek battle," she answered, though Kjorn saw clearly that the leading eagles' expressions were narrow, fierce and hostile, and they began to break into smaller formations he was sure meant imminent attack.

"Hark!" Nilsine called to them. "Eagles of the Voldsom, we are of the Vanhar, and we—"

An eagle dropped from nowhere and landed on her back with a battle scream. The other gryfons fell away in surprise, realizing at the same time that the eagles out front had been a diversion, and now they were under attack from above and from the sides.

Kjorn lunged through the air and swiped at the eagle attacking Nilsine.

"We come peacefully!" he snarled, just as two others shot at them from the sides. All around, the sentries fell under attack, and Kjorn saw that they fell on the gryfons in threes, making up for size with numbers and angles.

"Pair up!" he shouted to the gryfons, still wrestling with the eagle on Nilsine's back as she worked to stay aloft and Kjorn tried not to beat her with his wings. "One above, one below at angles!"

He didn't know if they heard, but it was the only way to prevent the eagle's three-pronged attacks of one from above and two from the sides.

What felt like a boulder slammed into him and knocked him into Nilsine, crushing the eagle between them. The bird shrieked and wriggled free, rasping taunts as he dove away. Kjorn, locked between two struggling gryfons, realized the new gryfon who'd knocked into them was *attacking him*, not fleeing attack from the eagles nor trying to help him.

More rogues? He thought wildly, *rogue gryfons, allied with the eagles?*

"Desist," he growled. He grabbed his opponent's foreleg and a scruff of russet feathers and wrenched back, dragging them both away from Nilsine. A huntress's battle scream rang in his ears.

"These are no longer Dawn Spire hunting grounds," declared the female, a stocky, sturdy gryfess, and snapped at his face. Kjorn shoved her away, trying to see her face clearly.

"We aren't from the Dawn Spire. We've come from the Vanheim Shore, and I from the Silver Isles, we—"

"Silver Isles?" his attacker relaxed for half a breath.

"Prideless wretch!" shouted Nilsine, having doubled back. She grabbed the rogue gryfess and they tumbled away from Kjorn in a knot of beating wings and slashing talons.

An eagle smacked into Kjorn from below, scrabbling at his belly, and he flipped down, grabbing for the smaller bird's wings. Another landed on his back and a beak sliced at his ears, seeking his eyes. He grasped the first and managed to fling it away, kicking with a hind leg for good measure. Another two eagles shot in at him from the sides. All around gryfons shrieked, the haze stirred by thrashing wings, and eagles zipping in to attack from all sides.

Weighted by his attackers, Kjorn sank, desperate to dislodge the eagles before they delivered serious injury or drove him into the river, but he couldn't lift his head, or the eagle on top would have his eyes.

"Get off of him!" shouted a young male voice, and someone tore the eagle from Kjorn's back. Freed of that threat, Kjorn twisted and grabbed the first eagle foot he found, yanked, and flung it and the bird it belonged to away.

"Fraenir," Kjorn panted as the young rogue dipped lower. "Thank you."

"My pleasure," he chirped, seeming thrilled with the fight.

"Where is Nilsine?" Kjorn circled, taking in the scene, and realized that the eagles were falling back. He didn't think it was because the Vanhar had overpowered them. Someone called them off. A female voice. The gryfess who'd attacked him.

"Fall back! Brightwing eagles fall back, these are not from the Dawn Spire!" The russet gryfess soared above the scene, calling them off. "Fall back, these are allies! Hildr, call them off!"

To Kjorn's surprise, a female eagle broke from the scattered group and called in shrieking tones. At first, Kjorn heard only witless bird sounds, then he listened more closely , as he'd learned to listen to the wolves of the Silver Isles and the lions of the First Plains, and understood that she called orders, and the others answered with respect. Grateful, Kjorn watched warily as the gryfess winged back toward him.

Nilsine flew up through the haze and joined her, face lit with triumph. "Kjorn!" She quickened pace to reach him first, and Fraenir circled protectively. "You're all right?"

"I am. And you?" When she nodded, Kjorn motioned around. "What's all this?"

"A misunderstanding. I think we have friends here after all."

"Oh," breathed the strange gryfess as she caught up, meeting them in the air. "You are him. You are…"

"Kjorn," he said. "Son-of-Sverin."

"Yes," she said, and made an awkward midair bow. "I see now. Forgive us. There's been so much…but you have friends here. We've been waiting, and Shard said—"

"Shard?" Hope flared that maybe his search was coming to an end. "I'm seeking him. Is he here? We came to speak with the eagles. You're a friend of Shard's?"

"Oh, yes." She gazed at him as if she'd awakened to find either that a long nightmare had ended, or a great dream come to life. "But forgive me, I haven't introduced myself."

"Yes, please," Kjorn said.

"I'm Brynja," she said breathlessly. "Brynja, daughter-of-Mar."

"I see the blood of the Red Kings in you." Brynja flew on Kjorn's right, and he on Nilsine's right, as the eagles led them to their nesting grounds. Fraenir glided just behind them, and Kjorn was certain he eavesdropped, but didn't see the harm in it. Brynja watched Kjorn thoughtfully. "Though you favor your mother. Shard spoke of you."

"I hope it wasn't all bad."

She chuckled and shook her head. To hear another voice speak Shard's name at last warmed Kjorn's heart like the sun. It made his wingbrother feel closer, and alive. For months he'd thought Shard was dead.

Brynja tucked her talons up into the paler feathers of her chest, her gaze set forward in determination. "Though thin in blood, we are cousins, by your distant kin and mine. I'll help you however I can."

"I'm grateful for your friendship." They followed the eagles lower, dipping into the largest of the broken canyons, flying in columns over the winding river below. "Can you tell me what's passed? What happened while Shard was here, and where he's gone? There's so much I don't know."

Brynja told him her account of Shard and his uncle's time at the Winderost, their integration and success within the pride—until the wyrms attacked the Dawn Spire. Kjorn's cautious hope that he might see his wingbrother soon quickly faded.

"Stigr fell," Brynja said quietly. "Cut down, a wing severed. King Orn and his warriors would've imprisoned or killed Shard for accidently leading the wyrms to the Dawn Spire, so we told him to flee." She looked over at Kjorn, and the worn lines around her eyes and her angled ears told him of distressing memories. "I saw his face at the end of the fight, when he flew toward the Outlands. I don't know if he knew himself, knew us, or even where he meant to go."

"Nameless," Kjorn said, feeling raw.

"Ashamed." She tilted her wings as the columns of eagles and gryfons turned a bend in the canyon and slipped lower. The haze thickened within the canyon walls, and Kjorn trusted the eagles to know where they were going. "Grief-stricken. I don't know what became of him. Then, after a fortnight, the Horn erupted and…Well, the only good thing I can say is that we haven't see the enemy since that day, nor heard them hunting in the night."

"The enemy?"

"The wyrms."

"And your other allies you spoke of? Your aunt Valdis, Asvander? What of Shard's uncle, does he live too?"

For a moment she closed her eyes, wind ruffling the feathers of her neck. "I don't know. Orn turned on all of us and we scattered. If Valdis didn't remain with Stigr, she probably would've gone to the Dawn Reach to find her estranged kin. She told me to flee just as Shard did. Asvander's family reside at the Ostral Shores and if he wasn't captured as a traitor then he may have gone there. I'm ashamed that I fled but what could I do? They would've imprisoned or killed us, and I thought…" She sighed, ears laying flat. "I thought there was hope Shard would find whatever he was seeking, or that he would find you and return. And I intended to be ready either way."

A little ember of hope glowed again within him. "And are you?"

She looked sidelong at him, a new spark in the golden eyes that reminded him of his father. "For anything, my lord. My wingsister, my huntresses, and the others who feared Orn would suspect them of treason followed me, and they await good news. Now I have it."

"If I can help you, I will."

"As will we."

Kjorn looked over at Nilsine and she merely inclined her head, though she'd been listening with interest.

After another few moments, they reached the eagle's nesting cliffs. Brynja bid the eagles farewell there and led Kjorn, Nilsine and the

Vanhar band down to the canyon floor, where a series of larger caves and dens riddled the rock face. The scent reminded Kjorn of Mayka, the painted wolf, and it was oddly comforting if only by its familiarity.

"You can sleep in the dens here," Brynja said as she landed. "The painted wolves who used to dwell here have disappeared. Maybe the wyrms' blatant attack on the Dawn Spire frightened them or they drove the wolves out, but whatever the reason, they're gone, and their dens are comfortable enough if you don't mind the smell. The eagle Hildr who leads this clan knows Shard as well, and has allowed us to remain for now." She lifted her wings, looking amused. "Strange days make for strange allies."

"Strange allies to you," Nilsine said as she settled her wings. "The Vanhar have always been friendly with all creatures of the Winderost."

Brynja seemed to take a deep breath, her gaze darting from Kjorn to Nilsine, then Fraenir, whose eyes brightened at the prospect of an impending fight. But Brynja inclined her head.

"Perhaps, someday, we of the Dawn Spire will enjoy the same friendships."

"Perhaps," Nilsine said, tail flicking. "Where may my band rest?"

"These dens are unclaimed. My huntresses are farther down."

"Thank you." Nilsine looked to Kjorn, offering a half mantle, a quick courtesy. "With your leave."

"Go, thank you. We'll meet at dawn, speak with the eagles and make a plan."

Nilsine dipped her head, gave Brynja one last, measuring look, and called her warriors off to find resting places before night fell.

"Go with them," Kjorn instructed Fraenir, who looked disappointed, but trotted away. After a moment, Brynja chuckled, and walked toward the riverbank. Kjorn followed her to the water. "What's funny?"

"Now I know why my aunt calls the Vanhar 'stuffy.'"

"The Vanhar have been a great help to me."

Brynja waded into a slow pool, close to the bank, and dipped herself, ruffling to remove dust and flecks of blood from the brief fight.

"I meant no disrespect. I'll do whatever I can to help you find Shard, and as long as *you* trust my intentions, I'm not worried about Nilsine."

"You were good friends with Shard?"

She gave him a sharp look, and he thought he detected a flush of pink about her nares, but perhaps it was the cold water. "Yes."

"Then I trust your intentions." He waded into the water and closed his eyes a moment before following suit to wash himself clean of blood, dust and the haze and ash. Evening gathered quickly in the canyon, between the smoky air and the sun dipping below the rim, and with it came a cold wind that reminded them it was still winter.

After a moment, Brynja spoke again, her gaze traveling along the canyon wall. "I can't believe you're here, really. Shard spoke so little of his homeland it seemed imaginary, because we had to keep up the pretense that he and his uncle were Outlanders. So the king wouldn't think they had come to roust him." She paused, studying Kjorn's face. "What is it?"

"Just—something Shard said. Anyway it's good to know he has friends such as you."

"What did he say about me?"

She shook her head. "Not as much as he could've. He said that you were wingbrothers, and I respect Shard, so that says enough. Though you are much taller than I thought."

Kjorn laughed. "My father's side, I suppose."

"The mighty line of Kajar," she said quietly. "I thought the stories exaggerated. But I see not."

Kjorn shifted, feeling as if she expected something from him.

But she looked away, and Kjorn didn't push her. "I wonder if you could tell me more about the Silver Isles, about yourself, and Shard?" When she looked back to him there was curious hunger in her gaze, and at once he began to understand her a little better, and what Shard might mean to her.

"I would be glad to."

They waded from the water and shook themselves before stretching out on the bank. Brynja dug a talon into the sand. "Begin wherever you remember."

"You're in luck," Kjorn murmured, watching the swirls and eddies of the river. "For all of my life is tied up with his. I was newborn when my grandfather led our pride from the Winderost. My mother carried me, in her talons, across the sea." He tilted his head and closed his eyes. "They conquered the pride there. And when I was still a squalling kit, my father's wingbrother, Caj, took the only other living kit in the pride, and they placed him in the nest beside me, to comfort me. They raised us together." He opened his eyes, looking toward the sky. "They raised us as brothers."

Darkness closed on the canyon as he told Brynja of his life and Shard's, and with darkness came a reminder of winter cold and a light layer of frost. Stars pierced feebly through the gloom of haze just as Kjorn reached the tale of he and Shard's initiation hunt.

"And then, Shard began calling ridiculous insults, goading him to attack—"

A hollow, discordant roar cracked through the night.

Kjorn startled to his feet and flared, staring around, while Brynja leaped up beside him.

A second roar, metallic and grating, bounded along the canyon rim, so thunderous it reverberated in Kjorn's chest and the ground under their feet. Kjorn could see nothing, smell nothing, the canyon was a cold, murky void.

He looked at Brynja, feeling breathless as a hollow, witless fear squirmed in him at the noise.

"We must get under cover," she said. "Now."

Kjorn didn't argue. They bounded toward the canyon wall. Just as they ducked into the safety of a cave, a rush of wind from massive wings whistled above the canyon and a sour, reptilian scent drenched the air, blotting out the fresh smell of the river.

Kjorn murmured, "The enemy?"

"Yes." Brynja's voice was tight with contained horror. "They've returned."

24

DWELLING OF ICE AND STONE

A S THEY LEFT THE ICE cavern, Hikaru gusted a breath in relief. "Oh Shard, there is so much to tell you, to show you!"

"Hikaru—"

"I know, you're injured." He looped around Shard and snaked his head under Shard's belly, and with a quick, rolling bump, had landed Shard neatly across his shoulders. "First I'm taking you to the healer, for your leg. Tell me all that happened since the blackfish attacked us." He sucked in a breath and paused, one forefoot lifted, and twisted his neck to look at Shard fully.

"And forgive me. If I had listened to you, we wouldn't have gotten in the fight. And you wouldn't have been hurt. And we wouldn't have been separated." He flicked his ears forward, tilting his head to see Shard's leg more closely. Then he hung his head. "Forgive me, brother."

Shard settled himself more comfortably and drew a tight breath against the ache in his leg. "It's all right now. I learned some very important things in the time we were separated, and I have a feeling you did too. I'll tell you my tale first."

"On the way to the healer," Hikaru confirmed, and turned forward again.

Riding Hikaru felt awkward at first, then comfortable, and Shard told of his journey and tried to keep track of the tunnels and halls of ice and stone. After a while he gave up, and trusted that Hikaru would take him where he needed to go.

Feeling watched, he lowered his voice when he re-told Groa's tale, certain for the moment that Hikaru was the only dragon interested in hearing it, possibly the only one who would believe him. Spreading it around, Shard sensed, could be more dangerous than he'd realized.

"That is good," Hikaru said, thoughtfully, his body undulating in warm, rolling movements that lulled Shard to calmness. "Though I don't like the way the emperor treated Kajar. We should tell the empress now, tell everyone, so that they know." His voice quieted with worry. "Shard, they don't like gryfons, here. They only know the story my mother told you, and they don't understand that you're not greedy and foolish and barbaric as the old story says."

"I see," Shard said. "Maybe we can change their minds. But let us bide our time a little." They passed through a broad tunnel laced with trickles of silver. The constant torchlight, flickering with the movement Hikaru brought to the tunnel, turned the silver to life with dancing light. It seemed the only fit dwelling for the magnificent dragons that Shard could imagine. "Only while we seek out the dragon that Groa spoke of. Then, when we have more information, and perhaps another dragon who knows the truth, we'll approach the empress again."

"Yes. That would be wise."

He walked on, turning down another silver gilt corridor. In that place the silver was carved into visions of dragons performing various tasks, Shard realized, that had to do with healing. After a moment

Hikaru murmured, "I will ask Natsumi if she knows of this dragon who keeps separate the truth and lies."

Shard perked his ears. "Natsumi?"

In the firelight, he detected a flush at the end of Hikaru's velvet nose. "She's a new friend. She tried to help you when the warriors in training were out at sea. That's who found us—warrior class dragons of my year and their masters, learning to fly during storms, learning to fly out at sea." He fluffed his wing feathers around Shard. "I told them you were the greatest flier ever, dragon or gryfon, that you had battled a powerful tyrant during a storm at sea."

Shard sensed a change of subject. He did recall a female voice after the whale attack. "And this Natsumi, is she—"

"Here we are!" Hikaru said brightly, and sat up so that Shard was forced to gently slide to the stone floor in front of a carved stone entryway. "You first," Shard said, eyeing the tall, tall archway. A reassuring scent of herbs wafted from the archway that reminded him of Sigrun's den.

"Of course," Hikaru murmured, and led the way inside.

"Well it was messy, very messy indeed." The healer coiled around Shard, an older dragoness the color of iron ore, with a bristly, short, white mane. Having broken away his makeshift cast and splint with an air of disdain, she gently examined Shard's leg while Hikaru curled in the corner, watching with his usual curiosity.

The healer lifted larger silver eyes to meet Shard's. If she was disgusted by him the way the other dragons were, she hid it behind a healer's practicality and appeared only to care about his injuries. "You set it yourself, you say?" She looked sideways at Hikaru, who tilted his head, listening.

Shard glanced between them. "I set it and held it with splint and mud," he said. "It was the best I could do at the time. It's mostly the flesh I'm worried about."

"Hmm. Hmmm." The dragoness glanced at Hikaru once again before prodding Shard's leg. He flinched and flattened his ears, stifling a hiss. "Forgive me for that. The bone looks to be in good order. The flesh, I'm afraid, will always tell the tale."

"A scar!" Hikaru exclaimed with relish, as if it was the best outcome possible. "A battle scar." He laid his head on his forepaws, his whiskers drooping on the ground, making him look forlorn that he hadn't won a scar, too.

Shard wasn't as thrilled with the idea of scarring, but was just glad to have his leg. *Though perhaps*, he thought with a fledge-like glimmer of hope, *such a scar would impress Brynja. Someday. When we see each other again.* The thought was enough to make him sit straighter. He *had* battled grown blackfish in the middle of the ocean, in a storm, and lived. He would enjoy telling Brynja the tale. As the healer examined the torn flesh, Shard imagined creating a warm fire to gather around, and watching Brynja's face as he told of his travels. And Asvander. He would tell the tales with Asvander present. And Kjorn. Someday, when he saw his wingbrother again, they would make amends, and he would love to see Kjorn's face when he spoke of all he'd done.

If only, he thought with sharp, lancing regret, *if only I could tell Stigr.*

The healer spoke after a moment, apparently unworried about scarring one way or the other. "I will sew the skin, and administer new splints and an ointment with soothing herbs to help the pain."

So saying, she uncoiled half her length from around Shard to reach for her store of herbs. Her den reminded Shard of Sigrun's, though many times larger, and she stored her herbs not open on rock ledges, but in clever wooden and silver bowls.

Hikaru sat up. "Dragon medicine is wonderful, Shard. They helped my wing, and there was hardly any pain. I don't want to see you in pain, and it will help you rest too."

"Thank you," Shard said to him, and to the dragoness.

She made an affirmative huff and leaned back over him, holding a bowl of herbs crushed and mixed into a paste. "This will help you sleep while I recast the leg and apply an ointment."

Shard sniffed the bowl. He had been raised by a healer. Pain was part of healing, and so was managing the pain to the best of one's ability, but he often didn't trust such treatments if over-used. Perhaps it was Caj who had instilled that—enduring pain took strength—and simple caution. He knew Sigrun possessed knowledge of powerful herbs that could dull pain, but he recognized only two out of nearly six different scents in the bowl of paste.

The healer met his curious gaze. "Normally you will eat it with food. But this will help you sleep more quickly."

She uncoiled from him entirely and set the bowl before him. He glanced to Hikaru, who nodded once in encouragement.

"All of it," the healer said. "Then, when you're drowsy, I will begin."

Shard's stomach growled as he tasted the herb paste. Sharp, bitter odors washed down his nostrils and the taste and texture left his tongue sticky. He ate obediently, with Hikaru creeping forward and the healer weaving before him like a serpent.

"What did you put in…" He thought the rest of the words, but didn't hear himself say them. Hikaru caught him in a strong embrace, and Shard trusted his dragon brother to hold him as he fell into sleep.

He thought he saw the dream net spiraling before him, and grasped at a strand.

The Sunland felt too far away for him to dream of his home, his family, or of the Winderost and his friends there. He drifted, instead, on icy ocean winds, feeling now and then a twist of pain in his leg. When he twitched, strong claws held him fast, and he dipped once more over the sea. Perhaps if he couldn't travel far enough on his own, he might travel farther with help.

He heard a daydream, an albatross alone at sea. So he swept along on the wings of an albatross for a time, though not the one he had once met and named Windwalker. When the albatross veered away from where Shard wished to go, he soared to a tern…to a gull…hopping through the threaded dreams of floating sea birds until he saw a jagged shore.

There he dove into the dreams of an eagle who hunted in the Winderost, and lately dreamed only of fire.

"Show me," Shard said in the dream, and the eagle said, "Since you are the Star Sent...."

Haze clouded the air, and the sour reek of smoldering ember and smoke. The Horn. The smoke from the fires of the Horn of Midragur. It clouded the Forest of Rains, the Winderost, the Dawn Spire.

Shard wondered if what he saw was only fearful thinking, or if this was a true vision. If it was true, then it was exactly what he wanted to see, though the awful smoke left a sour taint in his throat. He left the eagle and found one who could bear him farther, a magpie with clever and shifting dreams like a raven.

The magpie took him to a carcass where he hopped to a crow, and the crow took him high, high above the haze.

He met Munin there.

"Ah! You've found me, my prince. I didn't think any gryfon could outfly myself, the dream walker, the..."

"Show me my friends," Shard said firmly before Munin began talking too much, feeling the dizzy tug of his body, hearing concern in Hikaru's voice beyond the dream.

"Ah, yes..."

Munin snagged him in spindly claws and bore him with unnatural swiftness across the plains, past the Dawn Spire, which Shard missed in a blink, the broken canyons of the Voldsom, another sweeping plain full of rocks, and spun him about to show him a golden gryfon, huddled in the dark, alone. He'd lost control of the dream. He didn't know if Munin showed him something false or true, and he heard Hikaru, trying to wake him.

"Kjorn," Shard breathed, grasping at the dream. *"Is he truly in the Winderost?"*

Munin laughed, tossing other dreams to Shard with his beak, and he fought against them like a spider web, unable to sort the true from the false.

Caj, pinned to the ground by a mad and Nameless red gryfon.

White Ragna, a fierce, terrifying expression of vengeance on her face.

Wyrms, hunting along a canyon. White wings flared before his eyes and he thought of Amaratsu, then the white owl. She tried to say something to him but he couldn't hear. Then there was only fire, fire, fire—

Freezing water doused his face and he woke with a gasp.

"We must fly!" he shrieked. "I…" He blinked when Hikaru whipped away from him in surprise, eyes wide. "Hikaru. I was dreaming. What happened?"

"You didn't wake up," Hikaru said, his eyes slitted with what Shard thought was worry, then when the young dragon's gaze shifted to the healer, realized it was suspicion.

The healer peered at Shard, nonplussed. "Perhaps the dose of sleep was too strong, for one of your size."

"It seems so," Shard said, and looked down at his leg, now bound properly with strong splints of wood and, he noted, fine, metal wire. Fine threads of sinew tied the torn flesh together. A pale paste was smoothed over all, and he felt a pleasant, cool tingling in his skin. "I'm not a dragon, after all. Thank you. This feels wonderful."

"Eat a bit of this with every meal, to help with the pain and to quicken the pace of the healing." The dragoness handed him another bowl of the paste. "Be sure you don't eat too much."

Hikaru took the bowl from Shard, showing his teeth in amusement when he saw Shard's look of distaste. "I'll make sure. Thank you, healer." He bowed his head, and Shard did the same. "Come, Shard, I'll show you my den. And I'll tell you all I've learned here, and then we'll see the forges, and the arenas where the other warrior class learn—"

"First, you will let him sleep." The healer slipped away from the entryway to let them pass, and Shard thought he read distress in the scaled lines around her eyes, but it was hard to discern reptilian emotion. "He'll need rest, Hikaru. Lots of rest."

"Yes, of course. Come with me, Shard."

That time, the healer assisted Shard with climbing onto Hikaru's back, and as they walked, Shard worked to find things to remember about the stone halls through which they passed while also listening to Hikaru's story.

"They said I was lucky my wing wasn't broken." They passed back through the halls of silver that led to the healer's dens and into the first, massive cavern Shard had entered with the sentries. "And they fixed all the scrapes and cuts with ointments and now it's as if I was never hurt. I don't even have a scar." His voice rang a bit with disappointment.

Though Shard suspected it would've been faster to fly, Hikaru remained on the ground level, twining around the pillars and flicking them with the end of his tail in a seemingly unconscious habit. Shard tried to ignored the stares and the occasional hiss from other dragons walking or passing overhead.

"They gave me the den that was my mother and father's, and told me that because of my mother, I am of the warrior class."

"Class?" Shard asked, staring up, and up, at the mountain cavern and the torches lining the stone pillars. Winking jewels adorned some of the carved reliefs, forming eyes, or suns, or stars, in the images on the pillars.

"Yes. What we are destined to do. My mother's ancestors follow the warrior way, my father was crafts class. Those who work with the gold and treasures. But I wanted to be a warrior," he turned to look at Shard, "like you."

Shard ruffled, unable to help feeling pleased that despite the wonder of Hikaru's home and the magnificence of the dragons there, Hikaru still wanted to be like him. "Tell me about this warrior way."

"Oh, the warriors are very honorable, like you—like gryfons."

Shard flicked his tail thoughtfully, pleased that Hikaru thought that, but also knowing it could be folly. "Hikaru, honor is individual to everyone. I'm glad you think of gryfons that way, but remember that there are wicked gryfons and good ones, just as there are wicked dragons and good ones. And probably wicked blackfish, and good ones."

Hikaru huffed. "I'll believe a good blackfish when I see it."

"Why don't you tell me about the warrior dragons?" Shard had genuine interest in them. If they were honorable and their purpose was war, then he may find the help he needed after all. Not to destroy the wyrms of the Winderost, but, perhaps, at least have a show of strength so they would consider listening.

So Hikaru, still walking along the ground of the seemingly endless mountain floor, told him of the warrior way.

"There are eight virtues. I've had to catch up, since the others of my year have been learning since autumn, when Natsumi hatched. So far I've studied justice, courage, and mercy."

"Those sound like good things," Shard said quietly. "I think it's wonderful you've found your place." *Wonderful, and terrifying. What if he wants to stay?* "Tell me what the dragons think of justice."

As Hikaru spoke, Shard leaned out to study the pillars, and realized they were created in sets, in lines that led to and framed specific exits from the mountain hall. Each line of pillars had a series of images carved into it that told of a way of life. One showed dragons forging and creating. One, he recognized as the healers again, and noted that it led back the way they'd come, toward the healers' hall. Another showed dragons dueling, great battles and victories, and Shard realized Hikaru followed this line of pillars through the mountain toward an archway at the far end. Perhaps once he learned of the different dragon occupations, he could find the one of which Groa had spoken.

"…so justice is the wisdom to decide," Hikaru said after some dragon history of the warrior class, "to use reason without wavering. It is the bones beneath the warrior skin." He paused mid-step to swipe his claws through the air. "It's the ability to strike when it is right to strike. And to die when it is right to die."

Shard thought first that Caj and Stigr would get along well with the warrior dragons, and then he thought of Amaratsu, who had carefully chosen the moment she would die.

"You have a mighty legacy," he said quietly.

"Yes," Hikaru said, raising his head to a high angle.

"And what of courage? Your second virtue? What do dragons consider courageous?"

Hikaru slipped around a pillar, touching his claws to an image of a dragon rising through what looked like flames to face an encroaching storm cloud. "Courage," he recited, "is doing what is right."

"Yes," Shard said, and could think of no truer definition. "That does often take courage."

"I know," Hikaru said, and bared his teeth at a dragon of his year who stared for too long.

Despite the dragons who halted their business to stare at Shard, eyes narrowing, or claws lifting to clutch protectively at their gems, he listened quietly as Hikaru told him more of the Sunland dragon virtues of justice, courage, and mercy.

25

THE RED SCOURGE

THE WHITE MOUNTAINS OF THE Sun Isle soared up in ragged grandeur from low, forested foothills and sweeping plains. Several narrow passes made it easier for gryfons to fly through if they wished, but Caj's broken wing forced them to take the long way, on foot through the deepest and widest of the narrow canyons. Flying, it took only a sunmark to reach the mountains.

Walking, it turned out, took days, alternating in long lopes, a steady trot, and more walking. Now and then Halvden flew ahead to scout, though it was with silent, odd, mixed relief that both of them realized that the only true danger they might face was Sverin himself.

"You might've been better off serving your punishment with the pride," Caj observed at the end of the second day as they took shelter in the lee of a great hump of rock and snow. The peaks of the mountains glittered white under the rising moon, and the night promised to remain clear and cold. The rock cut the worst of the wind and Caj sat, hoping to press on later in the night after a rest.

"I think I'm better off with you," Halvden said. "I owe you a debt, and the queen bears me ill will."

"Which one?"

"Both."

Caj huffed a sigh. "When the warriors sent after Sverin discover your ruse, you'll have explaining to do."

"I trust you'll help with that," Halvden said, "Since you're taking advantage of my ruse."

Caj flattened one ear, and had to nod once. They'd seen no sign of the gryfons chosen to hunt down and restrain Sverin, so either they still searched diligently where Halvden had sent them, or they'd returned to the queens to tell them of the deception.

"I could fly on," Halvden said, changing the subject, pacing away from the rock and perking his ears toward the mountains. "If you're anxious about time I could scout ahead, and see if he's even still where I last saw him."

"You could," Caj said, watching him carefully.

Halvden looked over his shoulder and flattened his ears. "You think I mean to flee."

"Now why would I?"

Green feathers prickled up along Halvden's back and he opened his wings. "I won't run again. I'm not a coward, I won't betray the pride. I made a mistake, and I'll admit it. Are you pleased now?"

"Not especially. My wing is still broken, and that was your doing. You finally confessing it doesn't change that. If you think it isn't too dangerous for you to fly ahead and seek Sverin, or run into Ragna's warriors and have them think you're fleeing or worse..." Caj lifted his wing in a shrug. "By all means. Go. Otherwise, rest here and follow my orders as you promised to do."

Halvden looked again toward the mountains, then walked to Caj and sat beside him, sharing warmth. Caj lay down in the snow, regretting their scant shelter, but there was nothing for it. Grudgingly, he appreciated Halvden's warmth at his back as the younger gryfon settled.

Just as Caj slipped toward sleep, Halvden's voice pulled him back. "Did you mean what you said before, when we fought, when you said I could be great? Or were you trying to distract me?"

Caj lifted his head, and weighed his words. "I did mean it. But a great warrior has no need to announce his greatness, nor especially, the need to use it against those weaker. It's your heart, Halvden, that should be strongest. Not your talons, and not your pride."

For a moment it was quiet, and wind whistled against the rock. Stars glittered fiercely in the moonlit sky, and Caj found his gaze resting on the cluster the wolves called the First Pack.

"My father said the heart is like any other vital organ," Halvden ventured. "To leave it open is to risk death. Pride and strength, he said, are a warrior's greatest shield."

"Well," Caj said. "You've heard my opinion."

It was all Caj could say. *For how can I argue with a warrior's dead father? Hallr's death speaks for itself.*

Halvden didn't say anything else.

A low, deep howl sang across the snow. Caj perked his ears, recognizing it, and blinked as Halvden surged to all fours, wings opening. "Wolves!"

"Don't fret. This is a friend." Caj stood, and called out Tocho's name. The wolf bounded into sight under the moon, raced a circle around their stone shelter and then tossed a hare at Caj's feet.

"I found you at last, my friend! Who is this with you? I thought you would at least rest a few days with your pride, but no, they told me…" Tocho stopped and the moonlight picked out the edge of his hackles rising when he looked more closely at Halvden. He sniffed the air and Caj heard a low, thrumming sound he realized was a growl. He hadn't heard a wolf growl in some time. "What is your name?" he demanded of Halvden.

Halvden lifted his head high. "Halvden, son-of—"

"*Hallr,*" Tocho snarled, and leaped with a roar, his jaws bared wide.

"Oh, no you don't—" Caj charged between them and shoved Tocho back with his good wing. "Not here. Not now. Hallr's attack on you is already avenged."

Tocho showed Caj his shining teeth. "Halvden would've helped! If not for Shard—"

"I stopped," Halvden snapped. "Stopped, instead of attacking, you mud-covered—"

"You chased. You would've attacked!"

"Mudding fool, your pelt should be lining my nest—"

Tocho darted around Caj, growling and snapping his fangs. Instead of retreating, Halvden lunged to meet him. Caj ramped to his hind legs and twisted, lashing out with his talons and his one good wing. He caught Halvden's face, swiping a quick cut near his eye, and raked Tocho's cheek just before flinging up his wing to again shove the wolf away.

"This ends now!" Caj fell to all fours again as wolf and gryfon fell back from him, shocked.

"My eye!" Halvden swiped at the cuts, wiping away blood.

"I missed your eye," Caj snarled, "on purpose. Next time I will not. I've dealt worse to misbehaving fledges. I'm better off alone than dealing with this. You will put your enmity aside, as I have, or leave me to my task alone."

Halvden sank down and pressed the side of his head to the snow, still gasping at the pain and then the sight of dark blood staining the moonlit snow. Tocho did likewise, burying his head briefly under the snow before shaking briskly. Both wounds were shallow, as Caj had meant them to be. Warnings.

For a moment they were silent under the stars. Tocho stood slowly and shook himself again. He lowered his head deeply to Caj.

"Forgive me, my friend. But just like your wing, mine is a wound that has not yet healed. I will not run with the son of Hallr."

Before either gryfon could answer, Tocho turned about and padded away. Caj watched until he couldn't make out the wolf's form against all the other odd shapes in the dark. Halvden made no noise.

Halvden, Caj thought. *See what other trouble your arrogance has wrought.* Tocho could have been a great help to them. Caj picked up the rabbit the wolf had left and split it down the middle, tossing one half to Halvden.

"Eat. And don't tell me you won't eat the food a wolf brought."

Halvden seemed to swallow an argument, and the rabbit swiftly after that.

Caj ate in silence, with deliberate slowness, and felt he had a responsibility to instruct Halvden somehow on what he should have done, but he grew weary of it. A grown gryfon should know better on his own. Caj tossed the last bit of rabbit fur away and curled up again by the stone.

"I apologize." Halvden's voice was stiff as the cold wind. Caj twitched an ear his way. "I'm sorry," he said more loudly, and, Caj thought, more honestly, "that my actions caused trouble for you."

Caj waited for Halvden to add an argument about Tocho's behavior, but he did not, and Caj flicked his tail. "I accept. Now get some rest. We'll travel again at middlemark of the moon."

After a moment, Halvden lay down, and with the extra warmth beside him, Caj slept a little. A part of him hoped that Tocho might too realize he could've acted better and they would hear him return, but no wolf howl broke the night, no crunch of paws in snow. They rose again at midnight and traveled on without him.

Another half day of walking, keeping mostly along the more shel-tered banks of the Nightrun, and Halvden and Caj stared up at the peaks of the pass the river had cut through the mountains in the First Age. Rock and stubborn pines showed here and there but otherwise, snow coated the land and the mountains, making distance difficult to judge.

"It's strange to be on the ground so much," Halvden said, in a hollow tone.

Caj heard fear and said casually, "You can always fly if you want to."

The green warrior's ears slipped back and he strode forward, head held proudly.

The river widened, leaving them only a thin trail on which to travel the pass. Halvden remained on point, testing the treacherous, snow-covered banks for steady footing before he would let Caj proceed.

Quiet, grateful but alert, Caj let Halvden lead and earn back his sense of pride through honest work. Walking tested him. Caj could feel it. The river, half frozen but roaring where it wasn't, splashed and licked at their heels like a hungry animal whenever their narrow path took them too close to the water. The empty, open air above, though tricky with shifting winds from the canyon, constantly drew Halvden's eyes, and Caj noted his wistful looks.

Caj paused as Halvden once again signaled a stop by fanning his tail, creeping ahead like a stalking mountain cat, pressing his talons firmly to the snow.

"If you want to fly—"

"I don't want to fly," Halvden snapped, swiveling to glare at Caj. "Let me do this." He looked forward again. "I promised to help you. I can do this."

If I can do it, you can do it, is that it? Caj kept quiet and tried to wipe any pleasure from his expression any time Halvden looked back at him. *Maybe there's hope. Whether he's trying to prove something to me, or to himself...Maybe there's hope.*

"It's fragile here." Halvden tapped his talons against the bank. "We might try climbing a bit or..." He scanned the area but there was no "or." Sheer, frozen rock face on one side, the river on the other, and their narrow trail. "This way," he said.

"Halvden, if it's not sturdy ground we'll go back and find another way."

"It's sturdy enough. Stay close to the cliff, that's all."

Caj shifted his feet, then stepped forward after Halvden. The young warrior wouldn't be so desperate to prove himself that he risked his own skin—someone else, perhaps, but not his own, not while he was leading. They hugged the cliff face and sure enough, the ground held, though Caj suspected they walked on ice, not earth, and his ears flicked back and forth at every creak under his feet, and every splash of water.

"You say Sverin's made a den on the far side of the pass?"

"Yes. Across a valley ringed by forest." Halvden squinted ahead, still patting every few steps to listen for cracking or to feel soft ground.

"Of course, when I fled from him at last, at the end, I was flying. I would say another day walking in this direction will see us there."

"And he was…"

Halvden didn't look back at him. "He was lost. I did try. You must believe that I tried, that I was loyal, as loyal as a wingbrother could be, but he would have killed me. We fought at last, and the fighting made it worse. He wasn't angry, he was just—possessed by survival. I fled. And then I couldn't return to the pride, so…"

"And now here you are," Caj reminded him. "And serving your queen," he didn't specify which one, "and repaying your debt to me."

When Halvden glanced back, Caj was grateful to see that his usual smug expression was gradually fading to one of determination and focus. "Yes. Look, the trail widens ahead—"

A warped, feral scream shattered through the canyon.

For a moment, the blood seemed to go out of Caj's head, then he came to himself with a growl, and looked up to see a stain of scarlet in the sky. His heart crammed into his throat and he ramped high, reaching talons outward.

"Sverin! My brother—"

"Don't!" Halvden crouched, pressing to the rock face.

The exiled king's cry sounded again, this time deepening to a lion's roar, a warning. A threat to anyone invading his territory.

"Son of Per!" Caj shouted.

"It isn't him," Halvden hissed. "This isn't the way, you have to listen to me."

Sverin banked hard and wheeled once, scanned the area, focused on them, and chose his target. Caj.

"Oh yes, I dare you!" Caj called, falling back to all fours and bracing himself. "I could beat you in a spar with both wings tied—as a matter of fact…" Breathless, trying to make his tone light, to call Sverin back to himself, Caj refused to see the emptiness in the sharp gold eyes, the talons splayed, the powerful red warrior hurtling toward him, without recognition, at killing speed.

But it wasn't Sverin who struck him and sent him rolling. It was Halvden. Sverin smashed into the bank where Caj had stood before

Halvden shoved him out of the way, and a high-pitched crack resounded over the roar of the water. Caj gasped for a breath as Halvden whirled, flaring his wings as if to shield Caj from Sverin. For half a breath, Caj wished Ragna's warriors would find them and assist.

But Halvden said fighting made it worse.

Fighting...

"Step aside," Caj growled, dragging to his feet. Once again, his mud splint was ruined. There was no time to wonder if he would ever fly again, for Sverin stood before them at his full height, wings open, ears flat to his skull and eyes so empty he looked more like a crimson viper than a gryfon who had been a king.

"I won't," Halvden said. "Look at him. He'll kill you."

Sverin crouched, tail swiping across the snow, his gaze darting between them. His beak opened in a long hiss.

"He will not," Caj said, trying to shove around Halvden. "I know him. I trust him, and he's in there somewhere. Shame and fear have hidden his name. You said fighting makes it worse. Move."

Halvden didn't—partly because there was nowhere to go between the cliff and the river.

"My brother," Caj called. "My king. This is not you. Your heart is—"

The gryfon that was once the Red King lunged. Halvden fell back, smashing into Caj, and Sverin hit them like a boulder, beak snapping for Halvden's throat. They rolled, and with a sickening crack, the ice broke.

At the first touch of frigid water, Sverin shrieked and his great scarlet wings slapped at the river, then Halvden and Caj as he shoved out with brute power. He flapped up high, retreating deep into the canyon again.

Caj grabbed for the rocks of the bank, then saw that the current had swept Halvden out to the middle of the river. He swore, shoved from the bank and let the river rush him toward the green gryfon. It took only two breaths for the freezing water to slip under his feathers, to soak his oiled fur and squeeze the wind from his chest.

"Halv—" water splashed into his face and he gave up calling out. Halvden fought to swim, but churning swirls of water dragged him under again and again. Caj had not the skill of a Vanir for swimming, but he faired better than Halvden, and managed to struggle to Halvden's side. He grabbed the green scruff and dragged Halvden's head out of the water. The green warrior hacked and sputtered but his head lolled. The cold was overtaking him. Caj kicked his hind legs hard and used his good wing to help remain afloat, grateful the freezing water numbed any pain from his broken wing.

Deciding that the far bank had a broader shoreline and would be an easier swim, he kicked out that way. Downstream about fifty leaps, rocks kicked the river into a wrath of foaming rapids and spinning chunks of ice. Caj swam diagonally, as Sigrun had once taught him, trying to let the current assist him toward the shore.

Ahead, a long, thin dead birch stretched over the water, as if the tree or the mountain itself was offering help. Desperate, dragging Halvden along while trying to keep his own head above water, Caj strained toward the branches. Two more leaps and they would be swept past it.

His hind paw kicked the river bottom and sharp pain broke through the numbness—but Caj laughed madly. The bottom. He let his head dunk under, scrabbled both feet against the gravel and shoved his body toward the branch. He caught it in his talons and with his beak and clung hard, holding Halvden close by the scruff between his shoulders.

Now what.

The birch shifted at the weight of them and Caj's belly lurched. Beak clamped around the branch, he reached out with his talons and pulled them farther in, alternating beak then talons. His foreleg strained against Halvden's weight and he shook the younger gryfon, trying to rouse him, but he must've gotten a chest full of water.

The birch shifted again, loosening, and Caj groaned against the bark, clawing forward.

A blur of animal movement caught his eye, and his gaze darted downstream. A wolf raced toward the birch tree.

Caj tried to shout Tocho's name but it came as a guttural gurgle around the birch. The wolf sprinted nimbly up the snow-covered bank, splashing through water where he needed to, but leaping out too quickly for the river to catch him. Caj's tree lurched, almost loose of the rocks. Caj felt the current grabbing at them.

Tocho burst forward and leaped the last distance, skidding through rocks and snow like a goose coming in to land. He lunged up and pounced the birch trunk, wedging it firmly back between the rocks.

With the tree once again anchored, Caj was able to drag himself and Halvden out. Tocho helped him bring Halvden onto the shore, and when they rolled him to his side and Caj slapped him between the wings, he gurgled up river water.

"I'm glad you're back," Caj muttered to the wolf, and they both curled around Halvden to warm him, and themselves.

"I had a feeling," Tocho murmured. "A bad feeling for you. And I realized you were right. I sought guidance from Tor, and under the moon, I understood and decided that if Halvden will put his judgments aside, so will I."

"We saw Sverin," Caj told him. "He's witless. He didn't know me, but I know I can reach him. If you two will stand with me, I know I can bring him around."

Halvden coughed, and Caj took that as confirmation.

A feather prickled and Caj bent his head to straighten it, then realized it was near broken, and he plucked it out with his beak. After pausing a moment to consider, he dropped it and pushed it to Tocho. The gold wolf perked his ears at the feather, then at Caj.

"It's for you," Caj said gruffly.

"I thought you didn't like it when wolves wore gryfon feath—"

"I didn't understand why, before. Now I do." Caj lifted his good wing and draped it over a shivering Halvden and Tocho, and felt renewed warmth in his own skin. "I'm...proud, to call you friend. I want everyone who sees you to know what you've done for me, to know that I owe you my life."

Tocho, not taking his eyes from Caj, bent his head to sniff the feather, then laid his head over it protectively and averted his eyes. "Thank you."

"Halvden." Caj nudged him. Halvden groaned. "Will you survive?"

"You could have let me drown," he stammered through cold, "and saved yourself."

"Well if you're talking, that's a good sign."

"No one would've known," Halvden snarled. "An accident. You could have, and the pride would've been rid of me."

"Don't be stupid." Caj gave him a firm shake to snap him out of it. "Tocho saved us both. I take it you don't mind his company now?"

Halvden shivered, and managed to lift his head. "Thank you," he mumbled to the snow, then looked sideways at the wolf. "I owe you a debt."

Tocho showed his teeth in a not-unfriendly expression. "Let us consider all our debts paid."

"We'll rest," Caj said, "warm up, hunt, and then we will finish this."

They all lifted their gazes to the canyon, and stared down the frozen pass in the direction Sverin had flown.

26

THE BRIGHTWING AERIE

THE AIR HUNG DAMP WITH melting frost as the first hazy sunlight broke over the edge of the canyon. Kjorn gathered with Nilsine, Brynja, and four eagles. Two leading females, and their favorite male consorts.

"This is all your fault," one of the males accused Kjorn.

Kjorn lifted his head. "How does that follow? I wasn't here when the wyrms left the region, and I only just arrived. I don't know them, they don't know of me."

"Your pride is cursed. I can see by your bright feathers you are part of the cursed family who fled—"

"That will be quite enough, Arn," said Hildr, the leading she-eagle Brynja had named on the first day. Kjorn had met her briefly, as they gathered near the river at first light. Grunna, a sleek auburn eagle Kjorn gauged to be of middle years, watched quietly, and her consort beside her.

"He draws them near," Arn said, edging in a last word, "I'm sure of it. We of the Brightwing should never have allowed gryfons to nest here."

Kjorn suppressed a low rumble in his chest.

Arn opened his beak and his feathers pricked up high, giving him the illusion of size. "Do you think I fear you, giant, lumbering—"

"Do you prefer wyrms nesting here?" Brynja asked with a touch of ice. "We're happy to go and leave you to them."

"As if you've done anything about them," Arn said. "Your kind brought the enemy to this land, and you flee when they become too dangerous."

"Arn." Hildr nipped his wing with her beak. "If you won't be silent, then leave." She dipped her head, eyeing Kjorn. "I allow these gryfess huntresses to remain because they showed respect and humility after being cast out of their home. I allow you to remain because you were a friend of Shard, who was the first gryfon I met to bother asking my name. So I'm curious about you, though you look like typical Dawn Spire ilk to me."

It had taken Kjorn a few moments, at first, to understand the eagles, for they spoke in slightly different tones. But as he'd learned to understand the wolves of the Silver Isles, he listened carefully.

Now, finally given a chance to speak, Kjorn lowered his head so he was not towering over the eagle, who stood on the ground and barely reached his chest. "I was raised in the Silver Isles, with Shard. Only recently have I begun to understand how arrogant my kind can be, and how much we might learn from others. I hope we can be friends, your aerie and my pride."

"I see no pride with you."

"In spirit," Kjorn said evenly, "friends of mine are allies of my pride."

She swiveled to peer at him with one eye, sizing him up, then looked to the older eagle, Grunna.

Grunna lifted one taloned foot and set it down firmly, as if testing the ground between them. "Words mean nothing. It is what you do. Time will tell. Do you have any intention of ousting the enemy that plagues us all? The enemy your forefathers drew here?"

"It has never been proven to me one way or another that these beasts came here because of my ancestors," Kjorn said. "I won't take responsibility for that. But Brynja tells me my wingbrother wished to help them see reason, or wished to help rid the Winderost of them if possible. If that's his wish, then I will help too, and perhaps make friends of the Brightwing aerie and renew my ties to the Dawn Spire as well."

Grunna considered him, then said again, "Time will tell."

Nilsine spoke, abruptly. "And if gryfons rose against the great enemy of us all, would eagles fly at *our* side?"

Kjorn and Brynja watched the Vanhar curiously. She nudged Kjorn covertly with a hind foot.

"*If* that happened," Hildr said, while her consort Arn made disgruntled noises, "we would consider it. Depending on the intelligence and courage of the gryfons involved."

"I believe we can all prove ourselves on those accounts," Nilsine said calmly, even as Brynja and Kjorn flattened their ears, feathers prickling with indignation.

"Then prove yourself," Hildr said. "Face the enemy."

"Gladly," Kjorn said.

Nilsine scoffed. "You said courage *and* intelligence. It's foolhardy to barge forward against the wyrms just to satisfy you."

"Who said anything about barging?" Kjorn stood. "I just want to get a look at them."

Brynja and Nilsine stared at him.

"Well?" Kjorn looked between them, and the eagles. "Didn't you say they sleep during the day? That they avoid the sun?"

"Yes," Nilsine said quietly.

Brynja stepped forward, tail lashing. "This is foolhardy. You said you were here to seek Shard. You must trust that it's a fool's mission to seek out the wyrms merely for a look, to satisfy your curiosity."

"Shard faced them," Kjorn said, meeting her stern face. "A lioness told me that Shard faced them, and the first time he saw them he didn't lose himself in fear. Do you think I can do less?"

"No one is questioning your bravery," Brynja said, and Kjorn noticed the light of admiration in her gaze at his mention of Shard's courage. "I question your timing. If you mean to help Shard, to help us in dealing with this enemy, the time will come. Let us continue the search, instead. He may have answers we don't know."

"He may be dead," Hildr said flatly. "We saw him not, after the attack on the Dawn Spire. I can't say that no small, gray gryfon wandered Nameless into the Outlands, but he is certainly not sheltering near the Voldsom. If I had to judge, I would call him reckless."

"You were just surprised," Brynja said, "by how well he flew and that he spoke to you."

Hildr fluffed and looked toward the sky, repeating only, "He may be dead."

"Thank you," Kjorn said tightly. "If so, then I will find where his body rests and bear it home."

"If not in a wyrm's belly," chuckled Arn. Hildr pecked at his neck but didn't send him away. Kjorn began to understand how strained gryfon-eagle relations were.

"Midragur breathes fire," Nilsine murmured, diffusing a few of the choice, heated remarks rising in Kjorn's head. "Could your Shard have something to do with that?"

"Shard? Set off a volcano?" Kjorn paced. "I suppose at the moment anything is possible. If I can go about raising Sunwinds, then why shouldn't he set off a volcano?"

"I mean," Nilsine said, "could he have gone to the Aslagard Mountains?"

That silenced them for a moment and Kjorn walked back and forth thoughtfully, restless. He was weary of hearing about the great, wrathful enemy which supposedly followed his great grandfather back from the dragon kingdom to wreak havoc. He was weary of having his mettle questioned by creatures his own father would consider lesser. Weary of being without his wingbrother who, he had to admit, knew him better than his own father after all.

Kjorn stopped walking, tail twitching, and saw that all gazes were on him.

I came here with one purpose.

"You're right," he said to Brynja. "I must stay on my course." He turned to Hildr and Grunna, and ignored Arn's smug look. The eagle probably thought him a coward, but Kjorn told himself he didn't care. "If it's within my power to help rid the land of these wyrms or strike a truce, I'll do so *after* we find Shard."

"I think that's wise," Grunna said softly. "If he passes this way or we hear of him, we will tell you." She studied Kjorn quietly. "If you remain here long enough, you will face the wyrms. And all who face them feel fear."

"I've felt fear," Kjorn said.

"Not like this," said Arn, challenging.

Grunna ignored him, focused on Kjorn. "The only trick is, to feel that fear, and face them anyway."

Kjorn studied her fierce, wise face, and dipped his head. "When I face them, I'll remember that."

Brynja spoke. "If I could make a suggestion?"

"Please," Kjorn said, turning to face her fully.

The ruddy gryfess stood, stretching her broad, flecked wings. "If Shard went as far as the Aslagard Mountains, for whatever reason, and then the Horn erupted, I think he would've fled like any other creature. Would he not have sought shelter with possible friends? Not at the Dawn Spire, but somewhere he might have allies who've heard of him or his family?"

Kjorn tilted his head at her. "You mean Caj's kin, at the Ostral Shores."

Brynja nodded. The eagles listened quietly and Nilsine examined her talons, looking thoughtful while Brynja continued. "It's most likely our friend, Asvander, would've gone there if he wasn't taken prisoner, and Shard knew he hailed from there, knew Caj's family was from there. Might he go there, seeking friends?"

"Are Dawn Spire gryfons not on poor terms with the Ostral Shores?" Nilsine asked.

Brynja shook her head. "Not my family. I'm...I was meant to be pledged to Asvander, to unite our families. They've split ties with the Dawn Spire, but we are exiled from there as well now, as far as King Orn is concerned. If nothing else, we may find at least one friend in Asvander, and he may know more of Shard than us." Her expression darkened, frustrated at being split from her strongest friends, Kjorn knew.

"The Ostral Shores then?" Kjorn glanced at Nilsine. "I'd like to avoid the Dawn Spire, for now."

The Vanhar remained seated, and contemplative. "I don't know the way. We could venture windward, pass back through the First Plains and the Vanheim Shore, up to the Dawn Reach and around."

It sounded like a bleakly long distance to Kjorn, to circle all the way back from where he'd first washed ashore.

"Faster to cut across," Hildr said, ruffling her feathers. "Across the unclaimed hills and plains twixt here and the Ostral Shores."

"We don't know what we might encounter," Kjorn murmured, thinking.

Brynja raised her head. "As far as you've come, it would be much faster to cut a straight path, as she says." She looked between him and Nilsine. "It's a solid two days of flying, but faster and less likely to meet rogues, or any gryfon from the Dawn Spire. Of course, we won't want to be airborne at night, with the wyrms out hunting."

"We?" Kjorn asked.

Brynja angled her head, ears perking. "I thought I was clear. I'm coming with you. I know the way. I know what routes the scouts of the Dawn Spire fly, and I told you I would help." She looked around at the eagles, then Nilsine, before her gaze settled on Kjorn again. "We've been waiting here for a sign, a call to action, or some sense of hope. You're it. You also seek Shard," her voice took on a new, challenging note, "and I have unfinished business with him."

Kjorn couldn't argue with her firm statement nor the bright determination in her eyes. "You said we shouldn't fly at night. Do the wyrms range that far from the Outlands?"

"Yes," Nilsine answered before Brynja could. "They eat prey beasts just as we do, but they will range, seek the scent of gryfon on the wind and hunt them down at night, kill them, and leave their flesh wasted in the dirt." Her voice remained quiet, her expression cool, but her red eyes sparked warning in Kjorn's heart. "The Vanhar learned this at great cost."

He dipped his head, thinking of his father's fear of the dark. "Then, we'll fly with the sun on our backs, and walk at night." He looked to the eagles, and mantled. "Thank you for sharing your canyons with us for the night. I hope to meet again, in better circumstances, and prove myself to you."

Hildr appraised him, having listened quietly to their plans. "I will look forward to that day."

"I thank you also," Brynja said. "My wingsister and the rest of my huntresses will leave with me. Your hospitality will never be forgotten."

"Nor your courtesy," said Hildr, not quite grudgingly. She lifted her wings, then hesitated, looking at Kjorn. "When you find Rashard, let him know he still has my respect, and, should he need it, my friendship."

Kjorn dipped his head. "I will."

With a final word of farewell, the eagles lifted from the ground, beating their wings against the haze to lift away into the canyon.

"A common enemy," Brynja said beside him, "can sometimes make the greatest allies."

"Or a common friend," Kjorn said, and her expression quirked in amusement. "I'm glad you're coming. I'm glad to have both of you," he looked to Nilsine, "and any you bring with you. This is further than I think you intended to go, and I'll understand if you don't come to the Ostral Shores."

"I'm at your service," she said, unblinking.

Kjorn nodded, trying not to look surprised, wondering at her motive. Brynja's was clear, though he'd just met her, but he wondered if perhaps the priestess of the Vanhar had suggested that Nilsine go with Kjorn...

To what end?

He looked at both of them. "Then we leave as soon as your bands are gathered."

27

A QUESTION OF HONOR

S UNLIGHT GLANCED WHITE AND GOLD off mountain peaks and the broad, flat valley where the young warrior dragons trained. Clear sky, pale with frost in the air, yawned above.

Shard wondered what Stigr would've thought of the dragon training grounds, and their method. They prized accuracy and form just as much as winning, if not more. Everything was precise and worked according to a certain order. The dragons kept the valley clear of the deepest snows to make room for their practices.

Ancient black boulders defined five sparring rings, arranged in a spiral and growing smaller with each succession, with the smallest ring at the center. The idea, Shard learned, was to keep the fight within the ring of stones. Breaking out of the line with wing, tail, or other limb, was equal to losing the spar.

Hikaru had explained that each circle represented a state of mastery, for as the circles grew smaller the fighting became more challenging. Very few dragons, he'd said, actually mastered the fifth circle, where it was scarcely possible for a fully grown dragon to move without breaking the circle.

No dragon but Hikaru had expressed an interest in sparring with Shard, and his first day out, when Shard had tried to join Hikaru in the largest circle, one of the masters of fighting had barred him.

"Not this day," was all she said, and didn't speak to him again. Rather than dishonor Hikaru by arguing, Shard contented himself with studying dragon fighting. Every day, Hikaru asked if Shard might participate, but every day, no matter who oversaw the training, the answer was, "Not this day."

So it went, too, when Shard asked anyone about speaking to the empress again. Hikaru was reluctant to pester his elders about it, and Shard assured him he didn't have to.

Days stretched into a fortnight, and Shard maintained his patience only in the interest of letting his leg heal. Now the bone had knit and the skin formed into smooth, firm scars with magical speed. He would have to learn more about their herbs, to tell Sigrun when he returned home.

Home. He stretched his leg in the cold, warming the taut muscles and relieved to be free of the splint.

He breathed slowly in the thin, icy air, watching Hikaru spar with a dragoness four months his senior and twice his size, her scales the same pale, shifting rainbow of color as the inner wall of an oyster shell.

Dragon-sized tiers were carved into the foothills of the cliffs and barren rock mountains, into the ice and snow. Shard sat on a low tier of rock nearest the sparring rings. The first three rings were filled with dragons fighting. Shard found it ironic that the older and more skilled they grew, the smaller their circle became. Perhaps that was the point. Other dragons lined the stone tiers, watching, preening, waiting their turn, while the master dragons walked or circled above, calling out corrections or admonishments.

"Kagu, tail out!" barked the hulking blue dragon Shard had met on the first day. He was a training master as well as sentinel, named

Isora. Immediately, Shard could think of nothing but Caj, patrolling among the fledges as they sparred.

Kagu, who Shard gauged to be five or six months old, with scales like yellow buttercups, stopped, landed, and bowed to his opponent. Then he slunk from the ring and back toward the sitting tiers.

Thinking of Caj, and home, made Shard restless. He looked anxiously back to Hikaru's spar, hoping one or the other of them would win quickly and they could resume their search for the dragon Groa had spoken of, a dragon who knew the truth. He reached up to tuck a talon into the silver chain, to reassure himself it had all happened. Once he had the truth, he could take it to the empress.

Hikaru hadn't been able to speak with his friend, Natsumi, since Shard's arrival. When Hikaru had sought out her parents, they'd forbidden her from being near Hikaru and Shard, and that was that.

It would be difficult to find anything the dragons wanted to hide, though, even another dragon. The Mountains of the Sea and the dragons' dwelling within was so vast Shard could easily see that a dragon could be kept away. Secrets could be kept away. And truths.

"Rashard of the Silver Isles."

Shard turned, then stood up and bowed his head, in the dragon manner, to Kagu. The yellow dragon didn't return the favor. "Kagu."

"Still spying, I see?" His large, serpent eyes looked nearly all gold, the pupils slitted against the brilliant day.

Though he was only a few months older than Hikaru, Shard had trouble thinking of him as nearly fully grown. In another three months the dragons would consider him a seasoned adult, so now, Shard thought of him as an initiate, nearly grown but a ways to go, a bit younger than Shard himself.

So Shard would treat him appropriately. "I'm learning," he corrected, and managed not to flick his tail. A steady, soft wind filtered around the valley, and the brush of it felt good against his leg, for the scars still felt warm. "I love to watch how all of you fly, and fight."

"I'm sure you do." Kagu raised his head, looking toward the largest fighting ring where Hikaru spiraled in the air around his opponent, seeking an opening. "Hikaru has suffered from lack of training, both of his body and his mind. That will be fixed."

Shard ignored the barb. If he'd known anything of dragon ways, he would've taught Hikaru. "Why do you train to fight, if Sunlanders remain sheltered, away from war?"

Kagu's head whipped back to glare at him, then he drew himself together, with fine discipline. "It is a waste of our gifts not to train."

Shard had wondered, more than once, if he might be able to interest the younger generation in the rest of the world. "Have you ever seen real battle?"

"Are you questioning my honor?"

Shard lifted his wings. "No, I'm asking if you've ever seen a real battle."

"Our spars are real enough." He reared his head back, sitting up to his full height. Half the size of an adult, he still towered over Shard.

"What have you fought for? Your honor? An insult? I've fought battles," Shard said quietly. "Battles for real things. Protecting my home and family. I've fought and killed wyrms your size in the Winderost." He didn't mean for it to sound like a threat, but it must have, for Kagu's ears flattened against his head.

"Those are lies," he said, then laughed pointedly. "It's not possible."

Shard narrowed his eyes. "Courtesy," he reminded, for that was another of the warrior virtues Hikaru was learning.

"I won't be courteous to a liar. To a spy. What's the point of your questions?"

"What I'm asking you," Shard said quietly, "is if you've ever fought when it *mattered*."

Kagu bared his teeth, shuddering at the implied insult. Instead of attacking, however, he sat up to his full height and opened his pale wings. "Training master!" he bellowed over the training field. Shard flinched as the spars ceased and blue Isora, circling above, glided nearer. "How long will this be allowed to continue?" Kagu gestured to Shard. "He continues to spy and learn our ways. What other reason than to bring honorless, dangerous thieves like himself here once again?"

"I am trying to learn your ways," Shard said, "out of respect and curiosity. Spy? No. Never. I have no reason."

From the corner of his eye Shard saw Hikaru leap from his ring and fly toward them, fury lighting his face. The black dragon landed hard between Kagu and Shard. Shard ambled back, his leg still stiff in the cold.

"Leave Shard alone," Hikaru growled. "He has ten times the honor and skill you ever will."

Shard eyed the big yellow dragon warily, wishing Hikaru didn't believe in him quite so much.

"Stand back both of you." Isora remained aloft, circling, but his tone was sharp and warning. "Stop this snapping like hatchlings." Hikaru and Kagu glared at each other and backed a pace away, bowing to their training master. "You," Isora said to Shard. "You will leave. Every day you're here you disrupt our work and unsettle the younger dragons."

"They need to be unsettled," Shard said, and Hikaru lifted his wings in approval. It was dangerous, challenging the master in front of the others, but Shard was no fledge, no training dragon, no dragon at all. He could respect their ways, but he didn't plan to cower before them. "Why train to fight, if not for some purpose?"

"We are ready to defend. We are ready to keep our homes and families safe—"

"From gryfons?" Shard asked mildly, spreading his wings wide to remind them of his small size. "What threat—"

"You threaten our way of life by coming here, by spreading your lies, spying, who knows what schemes you have to—"

"You know nothing about me!" Shard shouted, since the dragon refused to land and speak on the ground.

"We know enough about your kind," he rumbled, and a dangerous murmur of agreement wove through the younger onlookers. "Our history tells us so."

Any plans Shard had to remain civil were dashed in the face of the dragon's willful ignorance and accusations. "You know nothing, except that in good faith I helped Hikaru to hatch safely and escape the wyrms who would've captured or killed him, or maybe even raised him—but raised him Nameless and wild and hateful. You know nothing but that I nearly died trying to bring him home, to *you*. You know only that I searched this wretched land to find him and make sure he was well, and that I sit here, sometimes, to try and learn more about you, and because I've been banned from wandering alone. So I stay close to Hikaru."

As Shard spoke his heart at last, Hikaru backed down further from Kagu, who stared, unblinking. Uncertainly, both young dragons looked at the training master.

"All this," rumbled the great, blue serpent, "we know you have done in order to further your own ends."

A hollow, burning heat filled Shard's chest, for a small part of that was true. Hikaru looked at him with huge eyes.

Shard shook his head. "I won't deny that I hoped Hikaru could help me here, help me to work with you and get to know you. But everything else, I did because I love him. Everything else, I did for my brother."

"Brother?" Kagu curled his lip to reveal startlingly long, white and pointed fangs. "That's ridiculous." He raised his voice. "It's obscene."

"It's not," Hikaru snarled. "Shard has been a better family to me than any of you. At least he is *trying* to be friends."

"Be silent," said Isora. "Your heart must be stronger. Right now, it shifts like water." His great, pearly wings beat a constant, cold wind on them. "And you, Kagu. You have too much fire. Learn to temper it."

Kagu's gaze darted from Isora to Shard, and he latched onto his opportunity of shared prejudice. "But how can I, Master Isora, in the face of this lying, bragging—"

"Bragging?" Shard demanded. The same restless, indignant energy that sent him after the starfire, that sent him to speak with the wyrms, that drew him to take Hikaru across the sea, kindled under his skin.

"He's not bragging," Hikaru said, bristling, now fully coiled around Shard to shield him even as he defended his strength. "He's done everything he said."

Every dragon in the fighting arenas, a dozen at least, had stopped to watch them.

"Enough," said Isora. "You will leave," he said to Shard.

Shard's tail lashed. "I've done nothing wrong."

"Your very presence disrupts our very short time to practice."

"My presence does nothing. His arrogance caused this." He lifted his beak to point to Kagu, and couldn't seem to stop the next words. "If he believes me to be a lying braggart, then let me prove myself. I challenge him to a spar."

To their credit, none of them laughed, except Hikaru, who exclaimed, "Ha!"

And as soon as he said it, Shard knew both that he couldn't take it back, and that it was the stupidest thing he'd done since drawing the wyrms to the Dawn Spire. In his brief days there he'd learned that dragon honor was like a vital organ. It spanned their mind, their spirit, their family, all the way to their ancestors since the First Age. He might as well have stabbed an icicle to Kagu's belly and expected to walk away with no consequence.

"I accept," the yellow dragon said gravely, showing all his teeth. "And let us fight in the fourth ring, since you claim to be a master."

"I never claimed that," Shard said. "But I'll fight wherever you like."

"Fifth ring," declared Isora.

Kagu's head jerked up, eyes bright with surprise, his soft nose flushing with pleasure. "You think I'm ready? But, he has a clear advantage in size—"

"*I* have an advantage in size?" Shard wondered. Standing, the yellow dragon was eight times the height of a gryfon. From nose to tail Shard could've stood twenty gryfons along his length.

"The spar isn't to blood," Hikaru reminded him. "It's form, precision. You have only to drive or throw him from the ring."

"Ah, good," Shard said. "I'll just throw him from the ring."

Kagu bared his teeth wider. "This will be a pleasure."

Master Isora spiraled high and his voice rang like iron striking iron across the training valley. "Kagu's honor has been questioned by the intruder, Rashard." No one dared to laugh, as Shard had been laughed at in the Dawn Spire for challenging their First Sentinel, Asvander. The mood here was much more dignified, more serious, curiosity reigned and the training dragons gathered in the tiers to watch. "They will settle this matter now, in the ring of Sky."

28

HUNTERS HUNTED

REGRET AND CURIOSITY BURNED THROUGH Kjorn for not having taken the chance to see the great wyrms, but he knew it would've been a fool's errand, and put him further behind in his search for Shard.

A day of flying saw them to a long sweeping plain, studded with uneven hills. As the sun sank, so did Brynja and Nilsine's motivation to keep airborne.

They'd risen above the haze and as the sky darkened and stars twinkled, they dove in a loose formation toward the ground. Kjorn liked to think they would've been able to see the great lake from that height, if there were no smoke and ash clouding the air, but such as it was it could have been days and days away.

"Look there," said Brynja, gliding in neatly on his left, and pointing roughly dawnward. "You can barely make out where the hills turn into the Dawn Spire territory. You can't quite see the Spire itself, but…"

"I see." Kjorn tilted his head, staring hard until his eyes smarted against the smoke, and in the dimming light, made out the small, ghostly outline of rock towers on the horizon.

231

"Do you remember any of it? My father says you were just weeks old when Per and his allies left the Winderost."

"I don't," Kjorn murmured, then raised his voice over the wind of their flight. "Some scents bring a rough familiarity. But that's all."

"Did you ever think you would return?"

"No." Kjorn shifted his wings as the wind picked up, catching scents as they descended. "My father and his father's story was that we'd left with honor to conquer new lands, and we did. The Silver Isles was my home. It always has been."

Brynja twined her talons, watching him thoughtfully. She seemed about to say something else, then extended a foreleg to point down. "We could shelter in those hills. No creature claims this part of the land that I know of."

"Very well." Kjorn called to Nilsine and together they all glided in to land. The low, bumpy rises gave little shelter from the cooling, constant wind, and only stunted grass grew. The haze, turning gray with evening, covered most scents, though Kjorn thought it caught a faint, old trace of pronghorn.

"Too late for hunting now," Brynja said, trotting up to him as she tucked her wings.

"From the air," he agreed, and looked over as Nilsine approached. "Though we might hunt as lions do. I could use a meal."

A rare look of approval shone on Nilsine's face, and Brynja dipped her head, chagrined. "Yes, we could do that."

They gathered the gryfon band, now a hearty two dozen in all.

"We should split up," said Dagny, Brynja's wingsister. The younger, quick gryfess nearly disappeared in the near-dark, with her richly sable brown feathers, but she spoke clear and bright. "Range in at least three directions, since we don't know the land, and converge again if anyone scents prey."

Brynja and Nilsine nodded at this plan, and Kjorn deferred to the huntresses' wisdom.

"We can use bird calls," Brynja said. "Raise a call if you find prey. It will be less conspicuous to them and to anything else." She didn't say wyrms, but they all thought it.

Kjorn looked at her. "Shard used bird calls, in the Silver Isles."

Her ears flicked back, self-aware, and she nodded once. "He worked with the huntresses here. It works well."

"I know a blue jay call," Kjorn said.

"I learned a magpie," Dagny said, excited for the hunt.

"I, a red hawk," Brynja said, and they looked to Nilsine.

"I suppose a gull would be conspicuous, this far inland." Brynja looked uncertain and Nilsine tossed her head. "Honestly." With that they realized she was joking, they laughed, and she dipped her head, seeming more comfortable. "I can make the sound of prairie owl."

"What shall I do?" Fraenir, sitting too close to Kjorn and quivering with the excitement of all his strange new adventures, seemed to Kjorn to be too excitable just then to go hunting.

Kjorn flicked his tail, and paced to the top of the small hill. "Fraenir, I want you to stay here, to relay calls—"

"*Stay?*" He flared his wings. "But we're only hunting! We're so far from the wyrms, from any danger. Why am I being punished?"

"Punished?" Kjorn shook his head. "I need you to stay here. We don't know these hills. If anyone gets lost, they can't fly to find this spot again for fear of attracting wyrms. You're the center point. I'm not punishing you, I'm asking you to do this task, to serve me as you wished to."

Fraenir's ears flattened. The other gryfons remained silent, and Kjorn noted a touch of smugness on Nilsine's face. "But I'm a good hunter. I hunted with Rok."

"No one doubts you," Kjorn said evenly, resisting the urge to snap and simply order him. Fraenir served him out of some sense of whimsy, not true duty, and Kjorn had to remember he was not a prince here. He remembered the times Caj and his own father had calmly explained their reasons for asking him to do things, rather than just snapping orders. He walked down the hill to stand tall in front of Fraenir, who stepped back. "This is what I ask of you. If you cannot do *this*, tell me what larger task I should entrust to you?"

Chilly wind buffeted around them, raising an eerie, whistling song from the stunted grass and dead, dry flowers. Fraenir huffed. "What bird sound shall I make?"

Kjorn fluffed in a shrug. "A crow."

That done, Brynja and Nilsine divided their bands into four groups, and Kjorn went with Brynja, since he had hunted at night and he didn't know if she had.

She climbed the low hill and looked down at the groups. Kjorn could barely see her now in the murky evening. "Range," Brynja said. "If you catch a scent, call twice. If you become lost, call three times. Fraenir, if you hear a thrice call, respond. No one is to fly. No one."

The wind picked up and they set out.

Cold laced Kjorn's bones. It wasn't the wet, snowy cold of the Silver Isles, but a dry and constant wedge against his skin and his chest. The smoky air blotted out the scent of prey. Walking seemed to take ages, careful smelling, trotting along hoof trails only to watch them scatter and then fade. They found old scat here and there, but that was all. Kjorn was ready to call the hunt and sleep a little hungry when they came across the day-old scent of a painted wolf, and tracks.

"Odd," Brynja remarked, setting her talons into a paw print to confirm its size. It had been nearly a full mark of wandering after half dead trails. Kjorn discerned gray moonlight filtering down through the haze. "I didn't think there was a painted wolf pack in this area."

"I wonder if—"

A crow croaked faintly in the dark.

Both stood silent. Brynja's huntresses gathered close, ears perked, and they all heard the crow again. Then a third time. A fourth time, louder and more like a gryfon.

"Come," Brynja said, "That's—"

The fifth crow call broke into an eagle's piercing scream, then Fraenir's frantic voice, distantly shrieking in panic.

Then, nothing.

The singing wind brought them a faint, sour scent.

Brynja and Kjorn looked at each other, and without speaking, their hunting band broke into a sprint, running hard back to the hills.

29

THE RING OF SKY

I SORA MADE HIS FORMAL ANNOUNCEMENT to the young trainees, and Kagu left them to lope down to the fighting rings.

Shard looked at Hikaru. "I thought you said the rings were named after the elements. The first four are earth, wind, fire, water?"

"Yes," said Hikaru uncertainly.

"What is sky?"

Hikaru uncoiled from him, ears flattening back into his mane. "I...I don't know. I haven't learned yet."

"Well, it can't matter," Shard said, though surely it did. "It's just about the size, isn't it? It's harder because it's smaller?"

"Oh, no," Hikaru said, and they turned to walk down from the sitting tiers toward the flat stretch of the valley and the fighting rings. "It's much more. Each ring has a principle to learn. In the ring of earth, we learn to stand strong and defend. Wind, to move quickly, to evade. Fire teaches us to be aggressive and to attack. Water, to flow around, to use our opponent's energy against them."

Shard considered that, and studied the massive, spiraling rings. The snow in the ring of sky was untouched by fighting, but combed

235

by dragon claws into a uniform, spiraling design that echoed the great spiral of the rest of the rings. In the sunlight, for half a breath, Shard saw Groa's dream net, then a shell, a fern leaf, a great spiraling wing of stars.

Shard blinked hard, looking back to Hikaru. "So each ring has a technique. But you don't know what it takes to win in the ring of sky?"

Hikaru shook his head. "No. I'm sorry, brother. But you'll be fine." He bared his teeth. "You're a master."

Shard wished he felt the same. As custom dictated, Shard followed Kagu through each ring, showing a moment of respect. The ground was a mix of mud and snow, churned by dragon claws. He considered what Hikaru said. Defend, evade, attack, flow.

I'll bet Stigr would've known what the last principle was.

Kagu stepped into the fifth ring, his claws breaking the perfect design in the snow. A look of bliss overtook the young dragon's face. Shard supposed it was a high honor, to be deemed fit for the ring of the masters, even if his opponent was a gryfon.

That must mean it's a high honor for me, too.

Shard entered the ring. While Kagu reveled in the ring itself, Shard tested the ground with a couple soft pats. The snow within was groomed, smooth-packed but not frozen to ice, soft enough to grip with hind claws and talons for decent footing.

Shard drew a breath, staring up at the dazzling yellow length of his opponent, for the first time truly appreciating the long muscles under his scales, the narrow wings, perfect for precision flying, the articulate, nimble forepaws, perfect for snatching one small gryfon and tossing him from the ring.

They bowed to each other.

I've seen him fight, but he's never seen me. So I do have that advantage. The challenge would come in remaining aware of the ring, and Shard made a quick note of the diameter. Only five leaps. Worse for Kagu than him, but still a small space to fight a dragon.

"Begin," commanded Isora, and the only sound, for half a heart-beat, was wind in the valley.

Kagu whipped forward, head and horns down as if to simply butt Shard from the ring. Shard swallowed his first impulse, mind racing to the rings.

Defend.

He held his ground for two heartbeats, then leaped hard, flapping fast for height. *Evade.*

Circling tightly in the ring, Shard hoped Kagu would simply barrel out by mistake, but the yellow dragon was no fledgling. Whipping around the very instant Shard leaped, Kagu circled the inner perimeter of the ring, eyeing Shard with a new spark.

Attack.

Shard took the dragon's moment of curiosity and turned down, plummeting toward the shining target of Kagu's eyes. Kagu stood his ground, offering his face. Shard ground his beak, forcing himself to hold the dive. Surely Kagu would dodge. Surely…when Shard was within striking distance, the dragon flung his jaws wide open.

With a yelp of surprise Shard threw himself to the side. Kagu caught him in the crook of his foreleg and surged up to throw him from the ring.

Flow.

Rather than try to fight free, Shard let the dragon toss him toward the border of stones. Head over tail, he flared upside down and halted short of the line, shut his wings and dropped to the ground, throwing himself onto his own back. Gasping once, he rolled as Kagu darted forward again, and scrambled directly under the yellow dragon's belly, trying to dizzy him.

Kagu circled about, swiping for Shard's tail.

With a surge of hope Shard quickly noted his advantages. If not speed, then size, in this ring at least. Kagu might lose track of him for brief seconds, or the stone border. If not strength, then strategy. Kagu had spars, Shard had fought battles, and had studied their fighting for days. With what Hikaru told him, he recognized each movement as Kagu used it.

As they circled, snapped, and tried to drive or outsmart each other from the ring, Shard's mind spun with the sequence, and he realized

Kagu met each of his attacks with a principle of the elements. *Defend, evade. Attack. Defend. Attack, flow, defend.*

Ever aware of the stones at their heels, they grew more distracted by trying not to cross out of the ring than by trying to attack.

Unable to outwit each other on the ground, and with a low buzzing growing in his ears and an ache in his leg, Shard shoved from the earth into the air. Kagu followed. Shard realized the buzzing was a churring murmur among the dragons, the rustle of wings, audible tension.

They flew narrowly, twining around each other with swipes and shoves, Shard almost feeling choreographed as they matched movement to movement.

Spirals of yellow dazzled before Shard's eyes as he looped through Kagu's coils, trying to fool him into flying outside the now invisible but still real barrier of the fighting ring. They were allowed to fight in the air, but crossing beyond the stones still meant losing. Distracted, neither of them brought strong attacks, and Shard's flight suffered from constantly checking down for the position of the stones.

Defend. Evade. Attack. Flow.

Defend, evade, he looped under Kagu, leading him on an artful twist upwards. They pursued, looped, twisted, swiped, neither winning, both failing.

Defend, evade, attack, flow…what comes after flow? What great technique does a master have to fight with that I don't?

Shard flapped higher, eyeing the ring below them as it seemed to shrink. *How have I won my greatest battles?* He thought of Sverin, of fighting in the storm, of plunging into the sea. He thought of fighting the wyrm. He thought of Stigr at his side, mad with laughter, remembered how he'd dived straight at the ground, straight, unwavering, certain that he could lead the wyrm to its death but stop his own dive in time.

Certain.

*Defend, evade, attack flow…*he thought of the ring of stones. They'd flown, fought, circled. Shard realize now that he *felt* how far he could go to one side or the other. Without looking now, Shard *knew* the parameters of the circle around him. He knew. With certainty, he knew.

Shard flapped hard, and high, and Kagu chased.

Defend, evade, attack, flow.

Shard gasped into the cold, frost gathering on his face, chest tightening around dry, thin wind. He turned to face Kagu as the dragon leveled with him. The yellow dragon spiraled, flared—and glanced down to check his position.

Shard swept in toward his face, talons splayed. Kagu flapped back, once, and braced for Shard's attack.

But Isora's voice pierced the wind from far below.

"Kagu! You've broken the ring. The spar is won."

The yellow dragon sucked in a breath, his serpent eyes white-ringed and furious. "How?" His breath sounded short. "How did you know, without looking?"

"I just knew," Shard said. Kagu shook his head, unsatisfied. "And I *trusted* that I knew," Shard added quietly.

Kagu gazed at him, eyes deadly pale, as if he might ask ten more questions—or attack. Then, mute, he turned to glide down. Shard followed, slowly spilling air and taking deep breaths.

When they landed on the ground outside of the rings, Kagu turned and bowed to Shard. Then he lifted his head to the see the training masters and the other dragons who flocked down to stare and to confirm that, indeed, a gryfon had just beaten one of their own, in their own highest ring.

"Thank you for the spar," Kagu said, surprising Shard with a quiet, respectful tone. "You have proven your skill and perhaps I've learned something today."

"From a *master*," Hikaru said, drawing forward to coil around Shard. Kagu eyed him sidelong, and dipped his head again, the long muscle in his jaw flexed, biting back comment.

"Enough," said Master Isora. "Well enough. Back to your spars. Hikaru, you are dismissed for the day, for your impudence. Go to the warrior shrine and reflect upon your disobedience, and how you might have better honored your mother's memory." Hikaru bowed and Isora looked to Kagu. "Kagu, you will groom the snow in the ring of sky."

Kagu's gaze flickered, his ears flattened, and Shard assumed this was the loser's chore. "Yes, Master," he murmured, dipping his head low. Isora stepped away to answer the eager questions of the younger dragons.

Kagu's claws whipped out to grab Shard's foreleg, though his head was still bowed, wings hunched to hide his movements from Isora. Shard hissed, ears flattening.

Kagu's eyes burned molten. "I will not forget this humiliation."

"Release me," Shard growled, shaking his head once to warn Hikaru from interfering.

"You may fly well, but I will show everyone what you really are. I will show everyone that gryfons, like Kajar, are not to be trusted." His gaze snapped to the side when Hikaru hissed, low. "And you, winter-born, stay away from me. I don't need your ill luck."

He backed away suddenly, as Isora's shadow fell over them. "Now, Kagu. To your task."

"Yes, Master." He bowed low and slithered back to the ring of sky.

Isora watched him go, then looked at Shard. "You did spar honorably, and you proved your skill. The empress did not command that you couldn't be here, but left it to our judgment. You may watch our practices and learn more. "

"Thank you," Shard said, bowing deeply to him and draping his wings in a mantle. Then he straightened. "But I don't think I need to."

30

A FEARFUL LEGACY

THOUGH KJORN AND BRYNJA HAD resisted the urge to fly, the rest of their band had not. Kjorn heard Dagny shouting from above even as Nilsine barreled toward them from the opposite direction. The Vanhar, at least, had remained land bound as instructed. All had heard Fraenir's frantic cries, all returned.

"Wyrms!" Dagny shouted. "I smell—"

"Get down," Brynja commanded, running hard at Kjorn's left, their small band behind her. "Land, now!"

A rush of unnatural wind struck them along with the scent of old meat and sour flesh. Kjorn fell rolling and realized Brynja had struck him from the side, shoving him from the path of a massive tail. The wyrm tail ended in a spade that struck the ground and gouged a trench before the wyrm flapped higher.

"Fraenir!" Kjorn shouted, regaining his feet and staring upward. "Where are you? Everyone, to me!"

"Be still," Brynja panted, trotting up to him. The wyrms had flown impossibly fast to have caught them there. Or not all had returned to the Outlands, Kjorn realized, feeling foolish. They might be scattered everywhere. They could be anywhere, anywhere, hunting and waiting for gryfons.

Gradually, he better understood the terror they'd wrought.

Brynja shouldered him into the shadow of a hill, though he was certain the beasts saw in the dark, if that's when they hunted. The rest of their two dozen gryfons gathered toward Brynja's soft, urgent jay calls.

The wyrms circled, wing beats flattening the grass, roars soaring through Kjorn's bones and sending the rest of the group pressing together with soft whimpers.

Kjorn sank to his belly in the low grass and crawled forward, ignoring Nilsine's hissing to return, and peered up. Though the night laid dark on them, and the haze diffused any moonlight, he discerned the wyrm's shape, and that there were only two.

Kjorn sucked a sharp breath, and held it, grasping to his courage.

Their leathery wings stretched taut to the wind, membranes dull and dark and blotting out the stars. Their heads were nearly as large as Kjorn's entire body, with wide, wedged jaws, sprouting thick crests of horns around their faces and down the long necks. Limbs as thick as tree trunks hung down, bearing thick, curving claws, and the great heads swerved back and forth as they gusted great breaths in and out, smelling. Kjorn eyed the sharp, spade end of their tails.

His heart twisted into his throat, his ears twitched back. Their size could crush him. They could kill him with a blow. One claw could take his head. The tail could sever, the horrible roar deafen, and the hide looked thick enough to repel the sharpest talon, should he be stupid enough to fight.

Everything about them overpowered his natural senses and told the deepest, animal part of him to flee.

Kjorn forced himself to remain where he was. They were only flesh, blood and bone like him.

The vision he'd had in the underground pool rose before him and for a moment he closed his eyes. The vision, brought by the wolf seer and a raven. He saw the dark, shadow versions of the wyrms crowding around him, saw Tyr's light spread from his own wings, letting him rise above them.

With slow, beating surety, Kjorn knew it was not the wyrms he was meant to overcome, after all, but his own fear. It could be done. He knew it, because Shard had done it.

He stood, not meaning to fly or attack, but only prove that he could, in their terrible presence, still be himself. To know that he could stand, as Shard had stood, and face them.

He knew now what terror haunted his own father's nightmares, and he refused to inherit it.

Breathing slowly, he found that their scent could wash over him without instilling mindless terror, that he could stare hard at them without succumbing to mindlessness. Their size, their witless, savage rolling snarls plucked at the Nameless instinct in him, but he refused to give in.

Instead, he narrowed his eyes, watching their roving, circling flight, and saw that they drew gradually away. Brynja hissed at him to lie back down, but Kjorn remained still. He knew the wyrms saw him, and threatened him by gaping their jaws and roaring.

He stood still, and after a moment, was able to speak.

"They aren't attacking," he observed, and saying it out loud, was able to breathe normally again.

Brynja crept out beside him, still flat in the grass, and Nilsine joined her. Behind them, the rest of the group pressed to the hillside, watching.

"Threatening," Brynja whispered in agreement, and Kjorn heard her swallow hard; her voice had cracked. "But not attacking. They're leaving."

Nilsine edged up on Kjorn's other side, also staying low. "We scented a herd, just before Fraenir started his caterwauling. A pronghorn herd. Perhaps they mean to keep us from it."

"If they want the herd," Kjorn murmured, "then we need only remain here, still." He had to force the words out, for it sounded like cowardice. "And they'll continue away."

"I don't understand," Brynja growled. "I don't understand why they attacked so willfully at the Dawn Spire, as if they had a grudge, and now...I know they saw us. They tried to kill you. They see you even now."

"Perhaps these are different," Kjorn said. "Perhaps they weren't part of the attack, and they're only acting as witless beasts about their prey."

"Doubtful," Brynja said.

"Do you count them all as a single creature?" Nilsine asked, her voice cutting. "Not all gryfons act the same, why should all these?"

"They all hate gryfons," Brynja insisted.

"How do you know?"

"Why don't you go speak to them," Brynja offered, "and see how you fare? You said yourself they sought out gryfons who fly at night."

"Enough," Kjorn murmured, gaze still following the strange, roving flight of the wyrms. And indeed, they were drawing further away, downwind, in the direction Nilsine and her hunters had returned from. "There, see. They've gone. No one take flight. We remain here, without hunting."

"And Fraenir?" Nilsine asked.

Kjorn shook his head.

They rested through the night, posting a watch, and resumed a search for Fraenir in the daylight. They found no blood, no shed feathers, no sign of a fight or that he'd been injured or seen battle at all.

"He's gone," Kjorn confirmed after wasting a sunmark searching and calling.

"Fled," Nilsine said. "As I told you he would."

Kjorn couldn't meet her gaze. He had so wanted to be right about the eager young rogue, to give him a chance. "He was alone when the wyrms came. None of us could say we wouldn't have done the same."

Nilsine only shook her head. "And now?"

Kjorn looked starward. "Press on."

31

THE RAVEN'S GAME

THE SIDE OF THE RIVERBANK where Caj, Tocho and Halvden hunted was wider than the opposite shore where they'd first entered the pass, and they traveled at a good pace after their encounter with Sverin. Tocho and Halvden managed to cooperate well enough to hunt down a red deer within the canyon, and they ate well the first night, enough to keep them going through the day.

Caj told Tocho of the warriors Ragna and Thyra had sent out.

"I imagine they're onto us by now," Halvden said.

Caj checked the sky, heavy with trundling clouds. "But they won't know where to look."

Tocho flattened one ear. "It was easy for me to find you. There has been no fresh snow, so I followed your tracks. If I'd known, I would have covered them."

"You didn't know," Caj said, to mollify the young wolf as he grew distressed.

"There, look." Halvden paused mid-step, jutting his beak forward. "We're almost to the valley. Walking, it will take at least another day to cross it. Perhaps slower still, since the snows are deep." He looked at Caj. "Though if Sverin goes out hunting, you might meet him sooner."

Caj looked toward the valley. From there he could see it was long and narrow, as if carved by the claw of Tyr, bare of trees in the center but bordered on all sides.

In silence, they walked, the opening of the pass beckoning, silent and cold under clouds. Caj's muscles slowly tightened and he moved his gaze and ears continually from the sky to the rock cliffs towering above, to the shadowy line of trees on either side of the valley.

At any moment he expected to see Sverin's bright wings against the leaden sky, to hear again that awful, mindless shrieking.

Tocho whined at the gathering tension, and Caj shook himself of imaginary fears.

They all halted at the sound of a gryfon call.

Tocho went still, quivering and lifting his muzzle to the gray sky. "No scent of other gryfons."

Halvden's ears flicked to and fro and Caj stilled, searching the sky just above the river. He saw no sign of Sverin or other movement but for a pair of ravens, mucking about over the water. Tocho eyed the ravens, nose twitching.

"Ragna's warriors?" Halvden asked, sounding unconvinced.

Caj shook his head. "If it is, they're distant, or not well. Their calls sound strained."

"I think it's them," Tocho said, thrusting his nose toward the ravens.

Caj looked over, perking his ears. "What reason would they have?"

"Or it is gryfons, giving bird calls," Halvden said. "You know, the idea Shard gave us last summer…" He trailed off, ears laying back. Caj hid his own expression by looking away. "Is it true that Shard is coming back?"

"He will if he can," Caj said, turning to face the narrow deer trail, a neat line of packed snow along the riverbank that led them deeper into the canyon. They were almost to the valley—he could see it opening out ahead, ringed with pines. "Anyway, let's get under cover in case they are on our trail. You'll have questions to answer for lying, and I'll have to convince them to stay well back. I don't think either of us will do very well."

Thankfully, Halvden offered no further questions or opinions on Shard, or the pursuit of Ragna's warriors.

As they trotted forward Tocho murmured to Halvden, "Shard will return. He is the rightful prince of the Sun Isle, and the Summer King."

"Summer King," Halvden snorted. "Vanir nonsense."

"You should think carefully what you'll say when he returns," Caj said quietly. "He will be your king."

"Sverin is my king."

Caj sighed, and turned away. He didn't know if Sverin, even returning to his senses, would ever be anyone's king again.

"Oh, look there." Tocho sprang to one side before standing straight and still, his long nose pointed up the canyon. Caj and Halvden stopped, looking up. At first he only saw clouds, then discerned three gryfons in a wedge formation, flying high. By their movement, Caj guessed they hadn't seen them yet. Halvden loose a reverberating growl. Tocho whined. "I'm sorry, Caj. The wind was wrong, I didn't smell—"

"No fault of yours," Caj rumbled, edging under the scant cover of overhanging rock and hoping it would be enough. "Get to the trees, now."

"You get to the trees," Halvden said, and before Caj could stop him, the younger warrior turned tail and sprang away, leaping thrice and then into the air, to wing fast back the way they'd come.

"Coward," Tocho said.

"No," Caj said. "See, he's going toward them." Quietly, Caj cursed.

Tocho turned, perking his ears. It was true. Halvden soared up high, shouting, and the wedge of gryfons paused and banked to see him. All of them turned with a chorus of furious yells when they realized it was Halvden, and dove.

As the trio fell lower, Caj recognized orange Vald, a full blood Aesir and friend of Halvden's, an older Vanir named Ingmer, and a female half-blood, nicknamed Rowan for her deep brown feathers edged with red. Strong warriors all, a good mix to represent both queens, Caj thought, and for a moment, he was transfixed by Halvden's brazenness and stupidity.

"Come!" Tocho urged. "He's giving you a chance to get to the valley. You know where Sverin nests, you can still reach him first, come."

"I thought the queens sent five," he muttered, more to himself than Tocho, and searched the strip of sky above the canyon again.

Tocho padded a circle around him, snuffling at the ground, though his gaze was locked on the sky. "Perhaps they're still lost, or ranging behind. Come, my friend. Don't waste Halvden's diversion."

Caj wavered. Halvden would suffer punishment for helping him and for lying about Sverin's location. After a moment, he knew he had to press forward. Halvden risked himself to give Caj a chance, and he wouldn't waste it. Trusting Thyra's orders, Ragna, and the discipline of a Vanir warrior and two who had trained under Caj himself, he turned and loped, hugging to the rock face, toward the valley and the cover of trees. Halvden would suffer punishment—but not death.

And honestly he could use a little more punishment, Caj thought.

A cacophony of shouts and snarls filled the canyon and Caj nearly stumbled in surprise. He stopped and stared up and around, searching for the source.

Tocho burst into laughter at the seemingly invisible voices, sprinting ahead, then circling back and sniffing, ears turning about.

"Oh, look, what games? What it this? Caj, it's ravens!"

Again, the small, strange gryfon cries scattered around the canyon. Glancing back showed that Ragna's warriors had broken their formation and pursuit of Halvden to circle and look around. Caj pressed to the rock, holding still in the wet shadow of the towering cliff face.

Halvden taunted the warriors from down near the river, landing on the bank and flashing his emerald wings against the backdrop of rock and snow. "All right, you've caught me! Follow and I'll take you to Sverin's den!"

A laughing raven echoed him, the black bird spiraling down in flashy loops from above, and calling out in gryfon tones.

Noticing the ravens, Halvden mockingly called, "Which way?" to which the ravens responded gleefully with, "This way!" as they split in five separate directions.

Caj slanted one ear forward, and the other back. He heard Vald shouting curses at the birds, and got the feeling that the ravens had been pestering the gryfon warriors for their entire hunt.

But why?

He knew he should run, but for a moment he stood mesmerized, wondering why ravens would care about distracting the warriors, would care about helping him at all.

Soon the air filled with them. Ravens swooped and circled above the canyon, calling first in their own guttural voices, then, with laughing *caws* they each loosed a perfect, seemingly faraway mimic of a grown gryfon male. One had even nearly perfected Severin's own, deep-chested snarl.

Then Caj remembered Sigrun's promise to help.

Sigrun, daughter-of-Hrafn. Hrafn, another name for Raven. In all their years together, Sigrun had avoided doing anything to make Caj uncomfortable or remind anyone overtly that her father had been a powerful, Vanir healer with mysterious ties to the nature of the isles— or that she herself possessed those same ties.

Did she call these ravens forward to help me? To trick Ragna's warriors?

"No this way!" cried a cackling female raven. "He shelters in rocks past the river of night."

"He cowers from darkness and flies only in light."

"He listens to none, and by none is heard—"

"The Red War King is nothing but a *bird.*"

Even though they taunted Ragna's warriors, not him, Caj felt locked to ground as the raven jeers began to heat his temper. Tocho brushed against him, reassuring. Caj grunted acknowledgement, staring at the storm of ravens.

Knowing that Sigrun would stand against her own wingsister to help him stoked the determination in his chest. She believed in him. She believed that Severin could be restored and she had done what she could to help him.

Their calls echoed on. "*I* have seen him, I have seen the Red King! He flies and shelters round and round and I have watched him up wander uphill—"

"—and down!"

"Silence, tricksters," shouted the Vanir, Ingmer. "We've had enough of you."

The ravens laughed on and on and scattered, still calling, mimicking gryfon growls and shrieks.

"Let's *go*," Tocho pleaded, and thrust his cold nose under Caj's neck feathers to his skin.

"*Ah!*" Coming to his senses with a quick, breathless laugh, Caj butted his head against the wolf, feeling an affection and gratitude he would've never thought possible. He realized the other reason he'd hesitated, and met the wolf's amber eyes.

"No. I will go on alone. Help Halvden distract them, and don't let him do anything too foolish. It's Sverin they want, not him, and certainly not you." Tocho looked ready to argue. "Now go. I won't let you face Sverin or come close. You've done enough, Tocho, for ten wolves, and I hope it brings you the esteem you desire."

Tocho studied him, ears perked, and appeared to resist the urge to lick Caj's face in deference, which Caj appreciated.

"I wish you luck my friend. Good hunting to you."

"Thank you. Fair winds."

They parted, Tocho breaking into a run back down the canyon, Caj slinking quickly along the rock face.

As Caj had hoped, the ravens soon clotted the air so thickly the warriors were forced back, higher, and away, and raw, laughing calls bounded through the mountain pass. Tocho's howl joined Halvden's voice, calling out to the warriors. Caj kept running, cold air cutting his chest, his broken wing aching. *No matter. Soon this will end, one way or another.*

After a few moments of breathless running along the river, the pass broke open, the mountains widening out at last. The river wound off and grew wider, cutting an icy trail down the middle. The walls of the mountains sloped into gentle sweeps of snowy fields, the foothills darkened by snow-covered evergreens.

Caj waded through snow, out of the pass and directly along the foothills to the tree line. He would've preferred to cut across the valley to the far side, but realized that not only was the snow neck-deep, but any of Ragna's warriors would've spotted him easily from the air, if they ever made it past the ravens and Halvden.

With one last glance over his wing, he plunged under the cover of trees. Under the pine boughs, the untouched snow came only to his belly, and he slogged through the woods.

The valley beside him was silent, empty of bird, game, or rival predators. Only wind moved, rushing around in hurried gusts, now and then raising funnels of dry, sparkling snow.

Caj set his gaze toward the far end of the valley, showing through the trees. At last, as he had intended from the outset, he went on to meet the mad king, to meet his wingbrother, alone.

32

AT THE SHRINE

O VER THE COURSE OF AN Age, the dragons had hollowed the mountain range they called Ryujan, or the Mountains of the Sea, and their dwellings, workrooms, tunnels and intricate architecture of ice and stone stretched for an area larger than the Silver Isles. Everything was molded to their size and comfort, and Shard always felt tiny when he followed Hikaru through the vast caverns, tunnels, or between mountains.

Now they flew to the warrior shrine, for Hikaru to do his reflection, and then Shard planned to search for Groa's dragon. He slipped talons under his feathers to touch the fire stones, to make sure they hadn't fallen off during the spar.

Thanks to Hikaru, he understood their use, and how he would make fire. The once bright pyres of the Dawn Spire had been doused during the battle with the wyrms, and Shard planned to relight them when he returned, as a sign of his friendship, and other reasons.

First he pictured Kjorn's face. Then he imagined, with relish, what Brynja's reaction might be to see him wield and *create* fire, not just feed a skyfire spark, as the Dawn Spire gryfons had done. Brynja loved fire.

She had thrilled to see him fly with torches, expertly lighting pyres without putting them out, without singing his wings, and had taught her to do the same.

He remembered foolishly thinking that such a display would be enough to win her. To ask her to leave her obligations and ties. To have her break a promise, to become his queen—for truly, that's what he asked of her—to leave her birthplace and family and begin a family of her own far from home, all for him.

Shard took a deep breath. It was much to ask. It was too much to ask of anyone, and he didn't know if love was enough to offer her. Rubbing a talon over the rabbit skin pouch and the stones within, Shard wondered what, if anything, would be enough.

One wing stroke, then another.

One foot in front of the other.

Stigr's advice calmed his agitated thoughts.

It was still a distant thing, and many other obstacles stood in the path between them, no matter what way he looked at it. Shard tucked his talons together and laid his ears back, fiddling with the silver chain Groa had given him.

He and Hikaru winged in silence across the long, main mountain cavern, the quickest shortcut to the next mountain. Shard ignored the dragons who stared at them—still, though it had been weeks, and caught the scent of smoke and hot metal from one female who whipped by overhead, her claws overflowing with long golden chains.

With a shudder, he recalled the forges—a network of caverns and tunnels so hot and moist Shard was surprised there was any snow left in the Sunland.

Glimpses inside the stone caves showed him fire—fire and gold so hot it flowed like water, and the scent of hot metal and warm dragon flesh clotted the air. Smoke seeped out through cracks in the mountains but still clouded the forges, and any dragon who spoke to them had a voice rough with the months they'd spent breathing it.

Still, the dragons seemed content in the miserable conditions, doing their work. Shard had marveled how they, like the warrior dragons and the healers, performed each task, no matter how small, with careful, ceremonial attention.

Hikaru had shown him on the third day there, despite the empress's warning. They'd been ordered away from the forges, but Hikaru saw no punishment from it, and Shard doubted anyone told the empress. Shard noticed how reluctant dragons were to truly punish their young, at least one as young as Hikaru.

Or perhaps it was something else. Perhaps it *was* Hikaru.

And you, winterborn, stay away from me.

He is winterborn, Amaratsu had said. *Already a difficult fate.*

"Shard, there!"

They burst from the exit in the main cavern and fresh cold wind brightened Shard's thoughts as the sun glared down on them. He followed Hikaru's pointing claw to behold the azure sea, stretching away and away beyond the mountain peaks. Shard breathed deeply, smelling mostly snow, but a whiff of salt air. It tempered his longing for home, and his determination to finish his business with the dragons as soon as possible.

From there they winged to a smaller, icy peak Shard had never entered.

They landed in the center of the mail cavern, and Hikaru led the way. "Each way of life has a shrine," he explained, for Shard. "The warriors, the crafters and healers and so on. And the highest, of course, to Tyr and Tor and Midragur, is beyond the valley in another mountain."

"Midragur is a god, here?"

"No, not like that exactly. Midragur is...the First."

"The first dragon?"

"Yes. But we call him Ryu, the first son of Tyr and Tor."

Shard looked around, wondering if the wyrms considered Midragur the First dragon also. If they thought of him all. If they *thought* at all. He hoped the dragon Groa had spoken of would know much more about them. His quest to find out about the Aesir had rewarded him greatly and let him better understand Sverin, Kjorn and the others. Shard was certain if he could learn more about the wyrms he could understand and either befriend, or know how to fight them.

The small, quiet mountain was mostly empty of dragons and immediately Shard felt calm, beholding the quiet patterns carved into the pillars of the main cavern. Natural tunnels and carved openings let in long shafts of sunlight from above, shining in great rough circles on the floor. Shard felt, oddly, the same as he did when wandering the deepest forest of the Star Isle.

Hikaru led him to an archway that bore an image of a Sunland dragon rampant, which Shard recognized now as the warrior dragons' emblem.

"We must be quiet, in the shrine," Hikaru said, though Shard had guessed, and they both bowed to the dragon image above the arch, and entered the passageway.

After walking for a moment Shard realized there had been no torches in the main cavern, only the shafts of sun, and none lining the tunnel where they walked. Instead, a familiar, pale light glowed from up ahead.

They emerged into an ice cavern much smaller than the empress's throne room, but on a dragon scale nonetheless. Life-sized reliefs of battling dragons blazed on the curving wall. Now Shard recognized each principle of a dragon defending, evading, attacking, and flowing like water. He looked for a dragon to represent the principle of sky, but saw none. At the far end a raised dais was littered with herbs, smooth stones, carved gems, and other offerings, all overseen by an eternally glaring dragon carved from the stone and ice above the dais.

Shard would have marveled at the detail and light of the cold shrine, but as they stepped inside, they saw they were not alone.

A dragoness sat coiled to one side of the shrine, head bowed in meditation. Smaller horns told Shard she was female, only a couple of months Hikaru's senior, leanly muscled under scales the delicate hue of an apple blossom.

Hikaru sucked in a breath, his wings lifted, and the dragoness raised her head at the commotion.

Warm breath misted in front of her silver eyes as she exhaled in surprise. "Hikaru?"

Shard ventured, "Is this—"

"Natsumi!" Hikaru cried, shattering the reverence of the shrine and barreling forward, only to slip, slide on the ice and crash into her in a fit of laughter and flaring wings. As Shard tread more carefully forward on the ice floor and watched the two young dragons dissolve into the chatter of catching up, he thought this happy bit of serendipity was a much better way for Hikaru to spend his time than reflecting on his "disobedience," as Isora had instructed.

"...and this is Shard," Hikaru said as Shard approached. "Of course." Perhaps realizing the introduction of the only gryfon in the Sunland was unnecessary, Hikaru slanted one ear, looking chagrined.

"I'm honored to meet a friend of Hikaru's, Natsumi." Shard bowed, and she bowed her delicate head in return.

"And I'm honored to meet you at last, Shard of Sun, of the Silver Isles." Her voice sounded like wind in autumn leaves, bright, crisp and intelligent. "I hoped I would meet you before you left us."

Shard found her to be uniquely beautiful, and in response to her beauty and courtesy, sorrow clutched him. She would die so young. No wonder Hikaru was so thrilled to see her, so unbridled in his joy. They had so little time. Shard looked from Natsumi to Hikaru, and wondered how much more wondrous and beautiful they must seem to each other.

But more than that, Shard at last heard genuine respect and curiosity, was proud to know Hikaru chose his friends well.

Hikaru broke back in, his reason for coming to the shrine happily forgotten. "Natsumi, I'm so happy to see you, and I've missed you, but, and I'm sorry to be blunt, but we need your help."

By her bright, admiring gaze, Shard thought the young dragoness didn't mind. "Of course I'll help you if I can."

"Didn't your parents forbid you from..." Shard trailed off when she turned a serene look to him.

"I'm certain you have enough to worry about, without including me in your cares." Her nose crinkled in amusement. "I benefit from being the youngest of three. My parents might indulge me one more bit of disobedience. Tell me, Hikaru, what I can do."

Hikaru sat back on his haunches, coiling his tail around his own feet. "Shard is looking for a dragon who a spirit told him would tell the truth. A storyteller. Do you know who that would be?"

"Hm." Not questioning that Shard had spoken to a spirit, Natsumi re-coiled herself with such neatness and precision it looked like a dance movement, and thought.

Hikaru waited, and Shard shifted on the ice.

Sunlight filtered into the ice cavern and Shard glanced to the shrine, thinking he might make a tribute to the warrior dragon, for Stigr, when Natsumi spoke again.

"Yes, I think it must be the chronicler."

33

THE SERPENT RIVER PACK

R OLLING HILLS DOTTED WITH DWARFISH trees and tough, scraggly undergrowth varied little as they flew. Brynja and Nilsine each assigned one of their own to scout ahead and behind for wyrm sign, and to watch for possible scouts from the Dawn Spire or the Ostral Shores. If the attack on the Dawn Spire had been as horrific as Brynja said, Kjorn couldn't imagine any gryfon venturing far from their home, but they scouted all the same.

Low haze still clung and a soft rain did nothing to lighten the mood or pretty the landscape, only leaving the ground slimy with ashy mud when they rested.

The weather slowed their progress and they knew they wouldn't reach the lake until the following morning.

Once again, they landed at near-dark, though that time they were sluggish, wet and hungry. If it were not for the wyrms, Kjorn would've gladly pressed on to the great lake during the night. A chill wind gusted and their only shelter was a mere stand of hawthorn saplings, scarcely wide enough to shelter five gryfons, much less over twenty.

"Almost there," Dagny said, sounding too cheerful. "By tomorrow we'll sup with the Lakelanders and perhaps see Asvander again." A bright note warmed her voice, and Kjorn wondered at it.

"A fine thing," Nilsine said. "I will be glad to see water again, and eat fish."

"Shall we hunt?" Kjorn asked them, generally.

Brynja ruffled her feathers, looking around skeptically. Before she offered an answer, the wind shifted, and they all caught a scent at the same time. Painted wolf.

"I'll meet them," Kjorn said, stretching and re-folding his wings. "I have dealings with wolves in the Silver Isles."

Brynja remained back, and at Kjorn's word, so did Nilsine, though the Vanhar claimed to be friendly with all creatures of the Winderost. Fewer gryfons would look less threatening, in his mind.

Kjorn left the stand of trees and walked to the crest of a low hill, smelling the area and looking around.

A female wolf appeared first, at the top of an adjacent hill. Her face was painted in a black mask, whorls of white and brown streaking her sides as if wind had blown on her colors while they were still wet.

"Hail!" called Kjorn. "We mean to pass through these hills peacefully, and hunt only if you allow it. We thought no one claimed this land, but we honor yours."

A big male crested the hill beside her, perked rounded ears at the sight of Kjorn, bared his fangs, and barreled down the hill. Kjorn kept his high ground, but the wolf lumbered forward.

Brynja and Nilsine raced towards him even as Kjorn leaped into the air to avoid a fight, and the rest of the painted pack rushed over the hill behind the female, howling and snapping their jaws.

"Stop!" Kjorn shouted. The big male turned, jaws wide to warn Brynja and Nilsine away, and the gryfesses circled warily.

Kjorn landed hard, between them, as the rest of the pack swarmed in. Most of the pack milled behind their leader, but before anyone could move, another male rushed forward and barreled into Kjorn.

A familiar scent came with him and Kjorn, his limbs tangled with the wolf's, found his face not bitten, but vigorously sniffed, before the wolf leaped away again.

"Mayka," Kjorn grunted in surprise, and relief, shoving to his feet again. "You've traveled far."

"As have you, Shard's friend." The painted wolf circled back, watching Kjorn with a mouth full of gleaming teeth. "And I have found my pack, who left the Voldsom when the Horn of Midragur breathed fire." He ducked his head as the bigger male stepped forward, ears flicking with interest. "Please, my leader, a word. Please meet Kjorn, of the Silver Isles, who was a friend to Shard, who was friend to your sister, Nitara."

"Greetings," said the big wolf, glancing from Mayka to Kjorn, wary.

Relieved, Kjorn felt he should offer some respect, and mantled.

Mayka looked pleased at the gesture, offered to his leader. "Kjorn, this is Ilesh, leader of the Serpent River Pack. Please, my leader, these are allies. Let them be welcome here."

Ilesh regarded Kjorn, then looked to Nilsine. "You are of the Vanhar?"

She dipped her head. "I am. We have only respect and honor for the painted hunters of the Winderost."

The wolf shook himself of drizzle as his pack milled around him. "Then you may pass through these lands that we now claim."

"Shall they hunt with us?" Mayka suggested, nosing his leader's shoulder. Ilesh showed him one fang, and Mayka chuckled and tucked his tail, padding away.

"You may," said Ilesh, "because I know that your friend Shard was with my sister when she was killed, and tried to avenge her. You may hunt with us, only if you do not fly. This attracts our great enemy."

"We won't," Kjorn said, impressed with this account of his wingbrother, and grateful for the path of friendship Shard had left in his wake through this land.

"Then, come. We have scented a herd of wild pigs this way. With your strength we may very well feast tonight."

With no more ceremony he turned, head low, and loped back over the hill.

Kjorn looked at Brynja and Nilsine, hesitant, but hungry.

"I like wild pig," Dagny called from the shelter of the trees, and that decided it. Somewhat bewildered by their change in fortune, the gryfons gathered themselves up and fell in behind Brynja, Nilsine and Kjorn.

As they picked up their pace and moved as one large, wolf and gryfon pack, Mayka trotted in next to Kjorn. "Now, tell me what has befallen you, and what became of my rogue friends since the Vanhar came and took all of you away, and where you mean to go, and if you found Shard, after all."

In brief, Kjorn told him all that had passed. "Thank you for stepping in, back there. For your friendship, and help."

"I'm happy to help a friend of Shard."

"You speak of Shard highly. What did he do, that you honor him so?"

Mayka opened his mouth in a happy pant, thinking, then watched Kjorn seriously. "You heard Ilesh. First, Shard spoke to us. Honored us. And, he did what no one has yet done." In the muddy light of the moon, Mayka's eyes were like black, haunted pools. "He faced the enemy, offered them honor and friendship, and when they bellowed their mindless hate, he did not run."

Kjorn, proud to called Shard his wingbrother in that moment, shuddered at the memory of wyrms. He'd stood tall himself, but not spoken or challenged them. "Let's hope, when the time comes, we can all do the same."

"I ran, when first the wyrms roared, and I lost my name for too long." He showed Kjorn his teeth. "When the time comes, I will not run again."

34

Secrets in Fire and Gold

"I T WILL HAVE TO BE at night," Natsumi said. "And alone."
They sat near the fire in Hikaru's den, picking at the last of a pile of fish Hikaru had caught. The dragon dens were tidier than gryfon dens on the whole, carved to almost perfect roundness, with smooth, flat floors of stone. A hearth on one wall heated the den to summer warmth, and three torches that ringed the walls shed bobbing light. Carved channels in the stone guided the smoke out of the den, where it could vent naturally in the massive cavern outside.

"He isn't supposed to wander alone," Hikaru said after a moment.

"Nor am I supposed to talk with you," Natsumi said mildly, her pale scales taking on a mesmerizing, amber hue in the firelight.

"I'll be less noticeable alone," Shard said, picking up on her thought. "And Hikaru, you won't get in trouble by showing me dragon secrets."

Hikaru tilted his head down stubbornly. "But the empress will find out anyway, when you go to tell her what you find."

Shard considered the fire. "Yes, but it's different. I'll have the information I need, and hopefully she'll listen to that rather than focus on my trespassing."

"She'll have to listen," Hikaru agreed, running talons down his belly scales in his old, nervous habit.

"I can tell you the way." Natsumi sat up a little in her coil and stretched her wings.

"Why haven't I met this chronicler?" Hikaru asked, glancing toward the entryway as if he expected someone to be spying. One ear flicked to the side. Shard flicked his ears, but heard nothing.

"We usually only go in our second season," Natsumi said reassuringly, averting her gaze. "After you shed your first scales."

Hikaru dipped his head down near Shard. "Oh, Shard, it's so exciting! I didn't tell you about our shedding. For each new season, we become new, we have new scales, and new strength."

Shard nodded. "It sounds wondrous." He would've compared it to gryfon molting, but he was sure it was nothing like.

"I will have new scales by the Halflight, when winter turns to spring. Kagu says I will always have black, though, because I am winterborn."

"Kagu doesn't know anything," Natsumi said, a growl in her delicate voice. "And even if you do, what does it matter? I like your scales."

"My uncle had black feathers," Shard said quietly. "All his life. He was very handsome."

That soothed Hikaru and he considered his scales in the firelight, while Shard looked to Natsumi. "Can you tell me something about the elements?"

"Of course, Shard." She sat up attentively, ears perked forward.

"Isora said something to Kagu about having too much fire, and everyone says that to be winterborn is ill luck. Why? What does it mean?"

"Oh." Natsumi looked at Hikaru, her gaze shadowed. Then she sat back, neck arching, and explained. "It is unfortunate because winterborn are ruled by their element. Hikaru knows this now. The winterborn tend to have very difficult lives."

"Everyone says that," Hikaru said darkly, "but no one will tell me why, as if I should already know."

Shard tossed fish bones into the fire. They popped and crackled and sent up a delicious, oily aroma into the den. "Amaratsu said the same thing. Why do you believe that, Natsumi?"

"Because of how water rules them." She didn't quite look at Hikaru. "We really don't have to talk about it. I want to hear about where you came from, the wyrms, and all of it. When night falls, I will tell you the way to the chronicler."

Hikaru coiled near the fire and began to clean his claws. "But I would like to hear about water, and being winterborn. I still don't know much about the elements."

Natsumi looked between them, and stretched her wings in a graceful motion of surrender. "Each season has an element. Springborn take elements of the earth, being steadfast and grounded. Summerborn are like fire, aggressive and dominant." She fluffed her wings. "I am autumnborn, wind-ruled, and my mother says that means I like change, and adventure. That is true enough." Looking to Hikaru, she finished apologetically. "Winterborn are..."

"Ruled by water," Shard said, following the progression.

Natsumi nodded.

"But water isn't bad," Hikaru said. "Isora taught that water is one of the strongest elements."

"They are all strong," Natsumi said quickly. "But water is *difficult*. To be born in the dark winter of the year, and to die then, is to be ruled by water, which means you are ruled by your heart."

Hikaru chuckled, nudging Shard with a wing tip. "That's not so awful."

Natsumi stroked her own flight feathers, looking uncomfortable. "It isn't awful—that is, it doesn't mean *you're* awful. It's just difficult. The heart doesn't always want easy things. To be ruled by the heart is to be terribly vulnerable. That's what my father says. But he was springborn."

That made Hikaru look thoughtful, and he glanced to Shard, who considered the many times his heart had been split, and he'd had to decide between two equally important things.

"I see," Shard said, then butted Hikaru's flank. "Well I think you're strong, Hikaru, and you have a strong heart. I think it will rule you well."

"I do too," Natsumi said softly, gazing at him. Hikaru dipped his head, though his brow ridge furrowed down, ears back in contemplation.

For a moment they all looked at the fire, as if seeing their own hearts as displayed by the elements. In dragon estimation, nearly all gryfons were springborn, so should be ruled by the earth. Shard found that ironic, as much as most gryfons valued the sky, and seemed to forget the earth.

"Well now," Natsumi said, drawing them out. "Let me tell you the way. Soon it will be dark, and most resting, and you're so small you should pass unnoticed, if you go the way I tell you."

"But don't take too long," Hikaru warned, eyes glowing with firelight, "Or I'll come find you."

True to Natsumi's word, Shard found the caverns and passageways quiet and deserted. He was so small and plain of feather, he blended with the mountain, and any dragons passing high above him took no notice. He avoided the torchlight the best he could, and followed Natsumi's directions, guided by the carvings over each archway and along the walls of the tunnels.

He knew he'd passed under one mountain into another, caught a whiff of the forges, and then ducked away into another tunnel. He would've liked to fly, but it might have gained attention.

Once or twice he thought he heard a whisper of wings behind him, or saw the flash of another's shadow along the wall. Every time he paused to look, he was alone. He hoped it was just nerves.

At last he found himself in a long, wide tunnel, where sparse torchlight reflected off winding veins of gold in the rock. Natsumi had said he would be close when he came to the halls of gold.

Wishing only that Hikaru was with him, but knowing the necessity of going alone, Shard picked up to a lope through the glimmering tunnel.

Following a bend, the passage opened before him into a shining display of gold and silver.

Shard stopped short, staring up, staring around, beak open.

It was the most massive hall he'd seen thus far, larger than the main cavern he'd first entered. Larger than the Dawn Spire, large enough, Shard thought with a dizzy thrill, to fit around the White Mountains from the Sun Isle. It yawned so long and wide that the torches winking from the far end seemed to be distant, golden stars.

Reverently, Shard stepped forward, realizing he could see as well as if it were daylight, not night, underground in a mountain.

He quickly understood why.

Torches bounced warm light around the endless hall where the wide pillars were not mere stone or ice, but sheathed in hammered gold. They stretched all the way up to the ceiling far away, and depicted scenes of dragon lore.

Distracted by the shining pillars, Shard walked a few more steps in, only to look behind him and see that hundreds and hundreds of dens were carved into the walls, ringing the cavern in neat tiers, level upon level.

He peeked over to see the inside of a den on his level, and his skin prickled to see that the walls were entirely lined with translucent, honey-colored amber. Raw stones of all colors piled within the room, waiting to be polished or cut.

Feeling distinctly like a trespasser, Shard backed away quickly and looked around again, realizing that every room must be stacked with precious gems and treasure.

He turned his attention back to the pillars. Slowly he realized these were not simply art or fancy, but tales with clear beginnings, middles and endings.

Dragon history.

Growing excited, he followed a story that ran its course in images across the bases of several pillars. A dragon emerged from a wild sea and encircled the earth like Midragur. The same dragon raised mountains from the sea, which, on the golden pillar, were inlaid with pearl that looked like snow, so Shard knew it was the Sunland and the Mountains of the Sea.

The sun and moon rose and set on the Ages across the pillars and Shard saw war, peace, famine and abundance. He saw the Sunlanders learning how to bend gold and jewels into their crafts, saw them swimming, fishing, flying.

"Like gryfons," he murmured, touching a talon to the gold. "Dragons dwell in earth and sky."

Eagerly, Shard wound around the pillars, seeking the Tale of the Red Kings.

"You enjoy history, I see."

Shard yelped and sprang into the air, whirling about and flapping two leaps high.

The withered voice, female, came from above him. "I thought the empress expressly forbid you from entering the treasure rooms." Shard spotted her, peering out of a den four tiers off the ground level—an enormous, aged dragoness with scales the same soft hue of a fading aster.

For a moment Shard couldn't respond, for he saw that she sat coiled in a den lined, like the one in amber, with nothing but panels of polished emerald. Firelight glowing off the precious stone wall cast green warmth around her and the den like a summer day in the woods. The dragoness, sitting comfortably in the den and with a sheet of thin, hammered gold before her, watched him curiously as he stared. "But then I suppose it is a gryfon's nature to ignore such a command?"

Shard heard irony in her voice, not condemnation, but he tread carefully as he re-gathered his voice. "I think gryfons are very misunderstood here."

"I'm sure you do."

"I'm Shard," he said, flying up to her level. "Son-of-Baldr." Dwarfed by dragon treasure and the dragoness herself, he felt he should add more. "Prince of the Silver Isles in the Starland Sea."

"Yes. I've heard. You may land, there." She pointed to a ledge just outside where she lounged. "It wearies me to watch you hover so."

Shard touched down on the rock, taking another look around the gleaming den, then mantled to her. Her soft, shifting gray-violet scales had lost their shine, but light brightened her eyes and her mane and whiskers seemed to drift about in their own invisible breeze. He was sure he stood before a springborn dragon, one near the end of her life, a strange mix of ancient knowledge, swift growth and naïve wisdom.

Taking a breath when he beheld her more closely Shard blurted, "You're beautiful."

She chuckled, taken aback. "Oh? Among my kind, I am considered plain. I would return the compliment but I don't know how your looks fare, among gryfons." She seemed pleased, embarrassed that she was pleased, and she carefully set her sheet of gold aside to make room for Shard. Glancing at it furtively, Shard saw she'd been in the middle of tracing out images. He wondered if he was in any of them.

"I fear I'm also considered plain," he confessed, and the scales around her eyes crinkled. "I hope you don't find me disrespectful. Everything seems wondrous here." He settled his wings. "Are you the chronicler?"

"Yes. I am Sora's daughter, Ume."

Shard mantled again, bowing low. "Honorable Ume. A spirit told me of a dragon who keeps separate the truth from lies, who keeps the stories. She gave me this token, from a dragon who was once her friend, long ago." He lifted the silver chain and she bent her head to examine it. "She said you might be able to help me."

Her eyes widened. "Yes, I know this work. These links are signature of my family. To what spirit did you speak?"

"I'll tell you everything," Shard murmured. She smelled of earth and warm dragon flesh, mineral and sharp. He had a feeling she didn't often leave this vast cavern. "I have so many questions for you."

"And I you." She leaned forward, sniffing the air about him, then backed away into the emerald cave to give him more space. "You've stirred the winds of Ryujan with your arrival, no doubt about that. And I hear something in your voice I haven't heard since I hatched." She looked beyond him, to the long, endless hall of history and treasure. Then her large eyes settled on Shard's face. "I didn't think I would know it when I did, but I do. Amaratsu heard it, and followed it, and now I know it too."

"What do you hear?"

She closed her eyes, ears lifting. "I hear the summer. I hear life and truth and hope. I hear the Silver Wind."

35

THE CHRONICLER

U ME LED SHARD THROUGH THE golden pillars, explaining their history as she went, and pointing out details of particular interest within the shimmering reliefs.

Shard had told her his tale, and she appeared unsurprised by any of it. "Why are all the other dragons repulsed by gryfons, without even knowing me?"

"Ah, well it has to do with Kajar," she said dryly, looking away toward a distant end of the cavern. "And the Great Betrayal."

"I've heard two versions of that story," Shard reminded her, searching her face, but her eyes had grown distant. Boldly, with respect, he touched his talons to her forefoot to draw her attention back.

She swiveled her head with a flash of surprise, then lowered her head to regard him closely. "Yes. You may have."

Shard stepped back, tail flicking. "If the chronicler keeps separate the truth from the lies, I would like very much to hear your version, and if it's different, why it's been hidden all these years."

"How I wish young Hikaru had come with you."

"Me too. But we couldn't risk it. His friend Natsumi is convinced we would all suffer great punishment if he was caught showing these things to me."

"Great punishment," she echoed thoughtfully. "How much greater could the empress punish us? How much greater than to be trapped here for our short lives, repeating our same lies to ourselves again and again, the moment we hatch? Telling our tales until they seem to us true, and are only a way to hide from the rest of the world?"

Shard looked from the golden pillars to her, and dipped his head low. "I hope to help you change that. Hikaru does. Amaratsu did."

"I know." She sighed, and resumed walking in sinuous undulation through the pillars. "I hope to learn from your brave example. Come with me, Rashard of the Silver Isles. I know you have particular questions, but first I must show you something."

Without warning she bounded forward twice and jumped up, pale wings beating the still, warm air to fly high where the pillars were not yet covered in metal.

Shard spiraled up with her, and she showed him to a golden panel that covered only half of one of the pillars. Shard circled around it, taking in the images.

"Why, that's Amaratsu flying to the Winderost, Hikaru, and..." He paused, staring at an image in gold. "Is that...?"

"Yes," Ume murmured.

"A gryfon?" Shard flew closer to examine the relief of a small gryfon in gold, the wingtips edged with silver.

"Yes. The first gryfon in our halls since the time of Kajar." She watched him, her eyes seeming to flicker with fire as the torches dodged and danced with their wing beats.

"What's that in the background. Wind? Fire?" Shard flapped forward, studying the swirls and slashes around the gryfon's wings, and realizing they looked familiar.

"That is *sky*."

"Sky," Shard breathed, recalling the combed swirls of snow within the fifth ring, and seeing that Ume's marks were the same.

"Yes. The highest, the lowest, the first and last, all in one."

"I learned a little of it, with Hikaru, in the warrior rings."

"I know. All that happens in Ryujan makes its way to me."

"What does it mean? Hikaru couldn't tell me, and I won against Kagu but I still don't understand."

Ume seemed to hover without effort, but Shard had to bank and circle slowly, watching her as she explained. "You learned, perhaps, only of the four elements born in the First Age. Sky has *always* been, will always be, like the Silver Wind, is between us, around us." She stretched her claws upward, then swept her foreleg around in a graceful movement.

"A great crafter may wield sky as he works with gold to create art. A warrior may fall into sky when she does battle. Or a master of flight." She dipped her head to Shard. "It carries our songs to those who listen. It is not the *wind* that carries your dreams, it is *sky*. You were springborn, prince of the Silver Isles, which keeps you grounded. But I think your true element is not earth, but sky, for you seem not to seek the easiest path like water, nor to forge brashly ahead like fire, or to remain still, like earth—but to seek the path between them all. That is the way of sky."

Shard remembered the feeling he touched when he flew high, or when he dove fast and trusted that the sea would catch him, when he'd trusted himself within the fifth ring. "I don't think I'm worthy of that element."

"Oh," said Ume. "But you must be."

"Why?"

"Because for us to move into a new Age, we must be more than we are, and we must be shown. One must—"

"Fly higher," Shard whispered. "I know the song. Did you make this panel?"

"I did." She gazed fondly at her work. "This will be my legacy, which all chroniclers will preserve until we are no more, until the end of Ages when great Ryu, whom you call Midragur, uncoils and the egg of the earth hatches, and the end of the world returns us all to sky."

Shard took a slow, hard breath. "And this gryfon is me?"

"That is my hope."

"There's nothing after," Shard said, winging up higher.

"Of course not," she murmured, watching him. "For we have only reached now."

Shard circled once more around the column, then glided down to land. Ume followed, settling in tidy coils upon the ground.

"Our time is short," Shard said quietly. "I hope that I can fulfill all you want, but I need help. I need to know the truth about the Red Kings, and I need to know all you know about the wyrms and why they are in the Winderost."

"Ah." Her gaze shadowed. "They are woven together. "

"I thought as much. What do you know of the wyrms? "

Ume's gaze traveled along the pillars. "They are an ancient race, with an ancient memory. A relic of the First Age. They seem ever Voiceless, but they do have names—or at least, ways of knowing and addressing themselves. They may never speak, but we must not treat them lesser because of this. Oh, if only the others would listen as you do."

She uncoiled and slid past Shard to gaze out into the massive cavern and the tier upon tier of precious rooms adorned in jewel and metal. "They understand us, or did once, but they do not speak the way we do. They live to be very old."

"My uncle taught me that whales are the oldest living creatures in the earth or sea."

With a kind, pointed look Ume said, "I doubt your uncle knew of the wyrms."

"No…I suppose he didn't really know much about them." Something tight caught in Shard's throat when he thought of Stigr, and he forced himself to focus on his questions. "You say they have names. How do you know, if they can't speak?"

"They are in the histories. But their names are not like our names. They are…sounds. When we met them, we turned their sounds into proper names. They responded, it seemed, and they appeared honored. So we know they can understand. But they don't speak. The last named wyrm was called *rhydda*."

It sounded like a growl. When Shard repeated it, it felt natural at the back of his throat. "Rhydda." The name, for some reason, made him think of stone, and of Brynja. "Does it mean red?"

"Yes. So you see, there is something in us which recognizes them. So just as creatures of the earth may speak to birds of the air and sea dwellers beneath the waves, we can talk to them. But they, perhaps, are not ready to speak. Who knows if they will ever be. They age as slowly as we Sunlanders do quickly. Like the earth, they are slow to move, to learn, to act, and, apparently, to forgive."

"Forgive what?" Shard asked, stepping closer. Ume looked deeper in the cavern, toward the age of Bronze and Stone. "Ume? Amaratsu said they like nothing but treasures and hoarding and that when Sunland dragons tried to enlighten them, they turned away. Is that true?"

"We know only what is told in our tales, and on the pillars here. How can we truly know, if we were not there? How can we know their hearts, if we have never faced them?"

He felt she was keeping something from him, and sought around the edges of her words. "I've faced them." Shard looked toward the entryway, feeling strangely watched. "And I fear what she said might be true, though I would still like to find out why."

"It might be." Ume, too, glanced toward the entrance, but it was still. "But, perhaps, we all have our own truth too. Since the Second Age it has been the duty of the Chronicler to remember that we can only ever understand the past through the stories that are left for the future. Those stories are the truth as the storytellers saw it. That is why one must rise higher…"

"And see farther," Shard said quietly. "I know the song. I've tried to see farther, to learn why the Aesir acted as they did. I learned they fled the wyrms. And now, I'm trying to learn why the wyrms are in the Winderost, and whether Kajar was honorable, or a murderer and a thief as Amaratsu said. That has led me here."

Ume bowed her head a moment, then collected herself. "For those answers, we turn to the Tale of the Red Kings. Come with me."

They walked through the pillars which felt to Shard like a towering forest of gold, and he blinked to realize, after a few moments of walking, that they now walked in pillars of silver. The light changed with the metal, the forest of silver more ghostly and pale with the torch fire, like icicles lit by sunrise.

Shard looked up, and up, cramping his neck to realize he couldn't see the ceiling of the mountain chamber. "Why the change to silver?"

"We mark our cycles thus," Ume said, stopping to wind herself around one silver pillar in particular. "Though we repeat our origin story at the bottom of each new set of pillars. Right now, we are in the Age of Gold. You see thus, farther back, Silver, Bronze, Iron, Stone."

Shard narrowed his gaze, staring hard toward the back of the cavern, and marveled to think how much better dragon eyesight must be than his. He could vaguely discern a shift in color where the metal wrapping on the pillars changed, but far away, wherever the Age of Stone began, was too dark for him to see.

"What happens when you run out of room in this mountain?" Shard asked, and the question made Ume laugh with surprise.

"We will start again. A new mountain. A new age. Look here, now."

Shard looked, and saw a continuation, in silver, of the beginning of the world, but in this Age the stories were more detailed, and wound up a single column in distinct rows, rather than stretching across multiple pillars.

Shard told himself he was ready, ready to hear the truth, good or bad, about Kajar and the dragons, and what it would mean for Kjorn, Sverin, and the other Aesir.

Just as Ume turned to another row of silver columns, Shard heard a shout from the entryway.

"Shard!"

He whirled. "Hikaru? What are you doing?"

The young dragon hopped into the air and whipped between the columns to the Age of Silver to land beside Shard. "You were taking too long . Oh…" His eyes grew huge as he took in his surroundings. "Oh, it's so beautiful. Shard, isn't it amazing? Much more beautiful that I thought. I wonder why do we wait until our second season? Oh, greetings, Honorable Chronicler," he added, mantling to Ume, whose eyes squinted in amusement and fondness. "I was worried. We had to come."

"We?" Shard looked, dismayed, to see Natsumi following on foot, more dignified in her approach.

"Forgive me," she said when she reached them. "I couldn't stop him."

"Natsumi," Ume said, looking just as pleased at their arrival as if her own kin had come to visit. "How lovely you've grown."

"Mistress Ume." She bowed, lifting her pale wings. "Forgive the intrusion."

"How I wish more young dragons would intrude," Ume said. "You've come just in time." When she noted Shard's expression she said, "They're already here, you know. They might as well hear along with you."

Shard eyed Hikaru with a stern glare, but it had no effect.

"Yes, we might as well hear. Are you going to tell the truth?" Hikaru demanded, and Ume's loud laugh leaped around the silver columns.

"As well as I can."

Despite his worry, Shard was pleased that Hikaru and Natsumi would see the tale alongside him. No matter what, they would see it together, and no dragon could say that Shard was lying to Hikaru, whatever the truth turned out to be.

"You have joined us just in time," Ume said again, her voice carrying the note of an instructor, "for me to reveal the truth to Rashard about the tale of Kajar."

"Oh good," Hikaru said with relish.

As they wound through the pillars, Ume explained to Hikaru everything she'd told Shard about the pillars and the history.

Which was why, when they were still well within rows of silver columns, Hikaru looked indignant when Ume stopped before a pillar of gold.

"This one doesn't match."

"Because it is the Tale of the Red Kings," Natsumi said, touching Hikaru's wing. "It's important, it must stand out."

Hikaru began reading the column, and his expression narrowed to concern. "Shard, this looks just as my mother told you."

Ume nodded. "The arrival of Kajar, as it is told to every young dragon today, as it was told to Amaratsu, as she told it to you, Shard."

Shard, his hopes shrinking with each step around the golden tale, saw that the chronicler of Kajar's time had recorded the details faithfully, and it was as Amaratsu had first told him. The gryfons were turned by the treasure into witless, fighting beasts, mad with greed. Kajar betrayed a dragon, and killed her.

After all that had happened, after speaking with Groa's spirit, Shard could barely believe it.

He *didn't* believe it.

He looked around. The golden tale was standing in the middle of a host of silver columns, in the Age of Silver. It didn't make sense.

Unless…

He looked to Ume with growing understanding, and she rose slowly to her full height, three times as tall as both the young dragons and towering like one of the pillars over Shard.

"Natsumi, you were told, as all young ones are told, that this tale is in gold, and all others in silver, because it must stand out. And perhaps we chroniclers feared for ourselves too greatly, and would not stand up to the emperors throughout the ages. But I am near the end of my life. I have nothing left to fear. And you were right, Shard. It is the duty of the chronicler to keep separate the truth," she set a claw against the highest golden panel she could reach, "from the *lies.*"

In one fluid movement she slashed through the gold and they saw it was only thin, delicate gilt, not as thick as the panels in the Age of Gold. It fell away like peeled birch bark and underneath, in aged silver, glittered a completely different tale.

36

THE OSTRAL SHORE

T HEY BID FAREWELL TO THE painted wolves at dawn.

"Good hunting to you," Kjorn said to Ilesh, bowing his head.

"It has been interesting." The painted wolf tilted his head. "Meeting gryfons so willing to befriend and hunt with us."

"Perhaps we'll meet again," Kjorn said.

"I would not be opposed," Ilesh said. "Brynja, of the Dawn Spire, and Nilsine, of the Vanhar, you are also considered friends of the Serpent River Pack. You, and those who fly with you. Fair winds, as you say."

"Good hunting to you," said Nilsine.

"When you see Shard again," Mayka said, slipping forward from the pack, "tell him I remember his courage."

"I will," Kjorn murmured, and hoped that would be soon.

As the gryfons turned and took to the air, wolf howls followed them aloft, a warbling song on the chilly dawn wind.

"Impressive," Nilsine said to Kjorn, soaring up to his level, "how you've befriended the creatures you've met so far."

"It was needful," Kjorn said, turning his gaze starward.

"It was impressive," Nilsine said. "The Vanhar will be glad to know that not all Aesir are as arrogant and closed minded as we thought them to be."

Kjorn glanced at her sidelong. "Thank you?"

She dipped her head, expression quirking. He realized her joke, and laughed, and Brynja flapped up ahead to lead them to the Ostral Shore.

"Hail! Hover and state your business!"

The gryfon sentry called from a good twenty wing strokes away.

They flared, wings beating in the smoky air.

From where they flew, Kjorn could see the great, mud-red lake that gryfons of the Dawn Spire called the Ostral Shores, but that was all. Deep, smoky haze hung low, obscuring the rest of the landscape, and Kjorn marveled to think that the fire and ash of Midragur still fell. With a chill, he looked starward to the mountains he couldn't see through the smoke, and he wondered about the wyrms. And Shard.

"State your business in the Ostral Shores, Outlanders!"

"We're no Outlanders," Kjorn called, though they all looked a mess after hunting, eating, and sleeping in the mud with Mayka's pack of painted wolves. Still the encounter and the time spent had been worth strengthening their friendship, he thought.

"We are Kjorn, son-of-Sverin, Brynja, daughter-of-Mar and her huntresses, once of the Dawn Spire, and Nilsine daughter-of-Nels, and her warriors of the Vanheim Shore."

The sentry, flanked by two others, glided forward, looking them over skeptically. "What's your business here?"

In the distance, Kjorn made out another patrol of three gryfons, winging toward them in the haze. They must look threatening, their ragged band of two score warriors and huntresses.

"We seek Asvander," Brynja called, circling slightly below Kjorn, for it was difficult to maintain a hover just for conversation. "We're friends, allies."

"Friends also to Caj, who is the son of Cai, once of the Ostral Shore," Kjorn added, feeling it couldn't hurt, especially if Asvander was still estranged from his family as Brynja had hinted. "Is his name known here?"

The sentry's eyes widened and he looked them over again. Before he could speak though, a strong male voice boomed from the haze, and they all looked to the newly arrived sentries.

"His name is known, and he has friends. And so do you."

Below Kjorn, Brynja laughed breathlessly as the head of the new wedge of sentries emerged from the haze, long, broad wings sending the smoke swirling away.

"Asvander!" Only it was not Brynja, but Dagny who whipped forward from the hunting band to collide with the big gryfon and send them both toppling down through the air.

"I thought Brynja was his betrothed," Nilsine murmured, winging up beside Kjorn.

Brynja looked more amused than jealous at the display, which strengthened Kjorn's suspicions.

"I have a feeling her heart is elsewhere," he said quietly, but was glad enough to have a friendly welcome. "But it looks as though Asvander won't suffer for it."

The sentries made room for Asvander as he and Dagny recovered and flew back up to join Kjorn, Brynja and Nilsine.

"Greetings, honored friend," Kjorn said.

Asvander took his measure, and his gaze flickered. Kjorn had a feeling the big warrior rarely saw a gryfon larger than he was, but Kjorn had him by a head and was a bit broader besides.

"Did I hear correctly, the son of *Sverin?* Grandson of Per?" Asvander looked from Brynja, expression softening, back to Kjorn, as if calculating. "Did Shard bring us a new king, after all?"

"Asvander," Brynja said quickly when Kjorn made a surprised noise, "we have much to discuss, and much to tell if the Lakelanders will offer us shelter."

"Of course we will." Asvander chuckled, his gaze roving over their assorted band, and banked to lead to the way to the lake.

"So I've been here," Asvander said quietly. "I fled just as you did, Brynja, and my family accepted me back after hearing of the wyrm's attack on the Dawn Spire."

They rested at the edge of the great, red lake, and watched Nilsine and her Vanhar band swoop and dive over the water in the morning light.

Brynja nodded. "And do you know if Shard—"

"There's been no word," Asvander said, and Kjorn pushed himself up to pace along the damp, pebbly sand. "No word at all of Shard. I believe Valdis lives, but she wouldn't leave Stigr's body. He was in a bad way—the blood, the wing. I don't know if Orn let the healers treat him, or not." He watched Kjorn. "I sent out scouts to the Dawn Reach to see if Valdis perhaps went there, if she was not taken prisoner for treason, but I haven't heard back."

Brynja sighed in frustration, gazing out over the lake. "I should have gone to the Reach myself, but I thought Shard would come back from the Outlands, so I stayed…"

"You did the right thing," Dagny said. "The only thing we knew to do at the time. And now, we've met Kjorn! What better outcome?" The brown gryfess sat closest to Asvander, Kjorn noted, and he wondered exactly how strong Brynja's betrothal to Asvander remained, now that they were all exiles from the king who'd arranged it.

"She's right, Brynja." Asvander extended a wing to lay against Brynja's back. "And I expect the scouts back any day with word. I expect they might even bring more scattered exiles. I hear Orn was on a spree of exiling and threatening executions, though most escaped his wrath."

"Most?" Brynja asked, and Dagny left Asvander's side to nuzzle her wingsister.

"It will all be well in the end. We have strong friends," Dagny murmured. "Strong families. And I believe that Shard will find us again, and I believe that he had a plan."

"Should we travel to the Reach ourselves?" Brynja asked, with a glance to Kjorn.

Before he could answer, Asvander stood, with a sharp grunt of negation.

"No. You've only just arrived, and look at the state of all of you. Rest here. Be patient. We must stay together, now that we've found each other again." His gaze traveled from the Vanhar over the lake to Dagny, Brynja and Kjorn. "Do you agree? Now is not the time to scatter again on the wind. Stay here. Eat well, be safe. We'll know more soon."

Kjorn stretched. "I hate to wait, but I believe you're right. And while we wait," he said, looking from Brynja to Asvander with narrowing eyes, "I'd like to hear more about this new king Shard promised you."

Brynja's gaze darted away, and Asvander's booming laugh rolled across the water.

37

WINGBROTHERS

S NOW DRIFTED DOWN AS CAJ crept toward the slash in the rock
face that he knew was a cave. A cave where, if Halvden was
right, Sverin still sheltered. The mountain rose up sharply from the
clustering boulders and the hump of rock cliff, the Nightrun river
flowed sluggishly two leaps away, and Caj imagined the whole area
would flood with the spring runoff. The steep mountain face cut the
wind and terraces of overhanging rock created an area of shelter in
front of the cave where the snow rose only ankle deep.

Good ground to defend, Caj thought admiringly, then less cheerfully,
Good ground for a fight.

He paused, ears flicking forward as wind whispered on the rock
and, more distantly, rushed through the pine boughs.

His plan was simple. Without other gryfons to make Sverin feel
threatened, Caj would not offer a fight, but speak reasonably, calmly,
until Sverin came to himself again. He wouldn't engage, but defend,
retreat, and keep talking until Sverin came to.

Deer bones and frozen clumps of fur littered a wide swath around the cave in the manner of a wild thing, messy and uncaring. The memory of Sverin's blank, dead stare made Caj shudder.

He had never seen a gryfon so far gone, so fully witless and lost. There had to be something that drove him to that other than grief. During the Long Night, Ragna had hinted there was something that had passed which Caj knew nothing about, some secret that haunted Sverin not with fear or anger, but with guilt.

If only Sverin would trust him.

Trust me, he thought, bellying forward like a mountain cat, his every movement muffled by snow, ears perked and every sense taut. Snow curtained the entrance to the cave with white and deadened any sound.

It wouldn't do to surprise him. So Caj, a safe three leaps from the entrance where the snow became less deep, stood tall, shook the snow from his body and called out.

"Son of Per! Sverin, my wingbrother. Father of Kjorn. Come out and face me."

Wind sent the falling snow into swirls and Caj ducked his face against it, stepping forward into the scant shelter of the rock, though not near enough to the cave to appear threatening.

He checked over his shoulder, wary that Ragna's warriors might finally have gotten the true location out of Halvden, but the valley lay empty and white. Too, he checked that the Red King was not stalking him from behind or above.

It had taken him a full day and a half to travel the length of the valley and he'd meant to watch the cave entrance to confirm Sverin's presence, but fallen asleep, dead to the world, until a raven woke him. So he wasn't sure if Sverin was even in the cave.

"I'll own my part," he said. "I haven't been the wingbrother I should have. I lied to you and I withdrew, and I confess that and ask forgiveness. Sverin," he called, "let's make amends. Let us be the friends and wingbrothers we once were. The two fledges who spread our wings on the lake shore—"

A low, warning hiss cut him off.

Caj forced himself to remain still, his tail low, his wings closed. He had to remind himself it was a good thing Sverin was in the cave, but he had never fully realized the fear a gryfon of such size and might could instill, for Sverin had always been Caj's trusted friend.

Is this how the young half-bloods felt? How Shard felt?

"I hear you. Now hear me. Hear my voice, and remember your own." Snow coated his wings. Another quick hiss, then a rumbling growl. Caj detected movement within the dull black of the cave and he lowered his voice further, as if soothing a witless thing, or a nestling.

"I'm not here to fight, and I will trust you not to. I trust you, Sverin, as I haven't allowed myself to since we conquered these isles."

He'd had enough time to ponder the problems between them on his long hunt, and he poured it out to Sverin, speaking as he hadn't for years. "Your father's stubbornness, our own fears, this strange land, and torn loyalties made us fearful of even each other, of being honest with each other. But no more."

The movement took form, stalking forward. Wind gusted and pelted the red gryfon with snow as he emerged, less aggressive than cautious and curious, like a wild cat, his ears twitching at Caj's voice.

Caj stood perfectly still, not advancing, not retreating. "Sverin." In vain he searched for a sign of recognition, of comprehension. In all his years he'd seen nothing as terrifying as the blank stare which greeted him. "Brother. Tell me what haunts you. Trust me, as I couldn't, but should have, trusted you with the truth about Shard."

Sverin's gold eyes held on him, empty, watching. Fearful, Caj realized. As fearful as a wild thing.

"Tell me now," Caj said softly, "what Ragna knows, but that you could not tell me before." At those words, something kindled in Sverin's gaze. Catching a careful breath, Caj forced himself not to step forward. "Whatever it is, my king, my friend, I am your servant. I am your wingbrother. We'll fly this wind together."

He fought not to raise his voice, to plead, to fly forward and pound Sverin's head until he came to recognition.

"You know me. Stop hiding in fear. I thought you'd be glad to see me. Halvden told you I was dead, but that was a lie. You see me here, whole and alive."

He clung to the fact that Sverin did not advance, did not attack, rather seemed attentive to the careful, low timbre of his voice. So he kept talking.

"Oh, Sverin, I've been thinking for days what to say to you, to make you remember yourself. Do you remember, our third summer as wingbrothers, when your father forbade us from returning to the Ostral Shores to watch the mating flights? He said the celebration was too wild, but I think he feared you and Elena would wing off together without another word. Too young, too feckless," he parroted Per's rough words, the memory fresh and alive from their time as initiates. Something flickered in Sverin's face at the mimic of his father's voice.

"So…" Caj edged a step closer and Sverin bent his head low, ears flat. Caj stopped, but did not retreat. "You don't frighten me. You remember the story. You drenched poor old Ringvul in chokecherry juice to dye him red, fruit that you'd made *me* smash, and swore him to silence. My talons and his feathers were stained for a fortnight. You commanded him to your sentry post at sunset, and he looked red enough to fool your father for as long as it took us to sneak away— and off we went. Do you remember?" Caj murmured, and when he slipped another two, slow steps forward, Sverin didn't move or growl. "Do you remember Elena, sunrise by the lake? She told me once, that was the very moment she knew she would be your mate. Not because you were a prince, not because she thought you were handsome, strong, or brave, but because you dyed a poor old sentry red and disobeyed your father so you could have an adventure together."

Sverin advanced one step, then another, out of the shadow of the rock, watching Caj. Caj was within leaping distance, and he held his ground there. "Have you ever told Kjorn that story?"

The light in the valley did not change, but a warmth seemed to come to Sverin's face, as if the sun touched his eyes, as if Tyr awakened the knowing part of him.

Then a warrior cry cracked the frozen air.

Two half-blood Vanir, whom Caj hadn't seen blended with the rock and snow, lunged out and dove at Severin.

"For Einarr!"

"For the Queen!"

The light winked out of Severin's eyes and his ears laid flat to his skull.

They'd waited there, waited for Severin to be distracted and emerge fully from the cave. Caj knew them. His own students, young, vigorous, honorable. Stupid.

Severin snarled. Even through his fury, Caj thought he discerned words.

"A trap?"

The Red King ramped up to meet their dive, hissing shrilly with fury.

"No!" Caj broke out of his shock and surged forward. "Andor, Tollak, fall back!"

For half a breath he and Severin stood side by side, flared wings eclipsing.

Tollak, lean, mottled gray and falcon-faced, banked hard, surprised by Caj and Severin's mixed ferocity. Andor, heavier and near black in color, swerved, but came around to redouble and aim for Severin.

"Leave him!" Caj screamed, voice cracking, with frustration. "You fools!"

He flared his good wing defensively, trying to block Severin from Andor as he swooped down.

"Leave him!" He realized he could no longer command in Severin's name, or on any of his own rankings. Severin crouched to meet the diving warrior, for a moment seeming oblivious to Caj. Caj could not let them engage, but couldn't ignore Severin to beat them off himself.

Instead he turned, ramming into Severin's side. His only element was surprise and Severin staggered from it and fell, sprawling, sliding on the icy rocks into a deep, wet embankment of snow.

Andor cursed and circled tightly. Thankfully, younger Tollak flapped up higher, watching, looking toward the pass as if he expected reinforcement. Caj hoped he didn't, and looked up at Andor.

"Leave him, I beg you—in—in the name of the Summer King, in Tor's name," he checked behind him to see Sverin recovering, shaking snow from his wings, and flared as if he could block him from Andor's sight. "Don't fight. Leave him to me."

Perhaps the surprise of Caj calling on both the goddess the Aesir never recognized and the Summer King he didn't believe in was as good as a strike. The dark warrior dropped to the ground a leap from Caj, staring uncertainly. "The queens ordered—"

"I know. I beg you leave him to me." Caj fell again to all fours, and had only the sight of Andor's eyes widening to warn him that Sverin's focus had changed. He spun and threw up his talons in time to lock with Sverin and shoved, rolling through the snow.

"Stay back," he shouted when he sensed the young warrior darting forward. "*Stay away.*" Talons clenched against Sverin's, Caj managed only to twist and avoid crushing his broken wing again as Sverin shoved him down.

Sucking in cold breaths of air and desperately kicking in attempt to dislodge his massive wingbrother, Caj uselessly recalled Halvden's warning that fighting made it worse.

But now there was no other way.

Sunlight gleamed through breaking clouds, littering the snow with brilliant patches of white. Sverin yanked his talons free of Caj's grasp and swiped for his face. Caj caught Sverin's wrist joint in his beak and resisted the battle urge to crunch down and break bone, fearing it would only worsen his fury.

Tyr, Tyr, make me strong.

When Sverin tugged, Caj released, and grasped for the leg again with his talons.

"I didn't come to fight," he grunted, slapping talons against Sverin's chest to keep him from snapping at his throat.

Yet I do...I do fight. I fear.

For ten years he had feared. Sverin had feared. They had not trusted each other, and it had broken them both.

Sverin reared up to slash talons at Caj's throat and rather than defend, Caj wrenched over to his belly, shoved to all fours and blundered away through the deep snow.

Sverin plunged after him, then launched into the sky, wings slapping gouges into the snow.

"That's just like you!" Caj shouted, relieved that Sverin circled him, apparently forgetting about the younger warriors who stared from the rocks. "Knowing I have a disadvantage and using it! You miserable cheat."

Caj dragged forward through snow as deep as his chest, challenging, drawing Sverin away from the den, out into the valley. Perhaps he should've drawn him to the tree line but it might help him catch sight of the young warriors again, and if he flew at them, Caj couldn't stop him.

"You know you can't best me in a grapple, so you'll fly and dive, is that it?" Caj gasped, finding the deep snow almost a greater challenge than the fight. But it would hamper Sverin too, and give Caj some cushion.

The baiting worked. If he didn't understand the words, he understood the tone, and with a fierce cry, Sverin dove. Caj whirled about to meet him, ramping high. Out of instinct he thrust open both wings—and barked in pain at the hot, snapping sensation that lanced up his injured bones.

Sverin smashed into him and Caj's scream rang into the sky, bounding off the rock and mountainside.

"Stop," he panted, delirious with pain and sudden despair.

If only they hadn't intervened. If only...if.

"Sverin, you must stop—I know you don't want to kill me—"

Sverin pressed, his razor beak gaping wide, his eyes locked on Caj's neck.

"You know me," he grunted as Sverin rocked down on him like a bear trying to disable a threat. Caj, flat on his back, talons locked on Sverin's forelegs, managed a hard breath, and laughed as blood stung his own eye. "There, brother, first blood. You win. Are you happy? You won't kill me, I know it."

Sun lanced across them between the racing clouds, sun and stinging, gusting snow. Throbbing pain in his wing seem to weaken his grip and he tightened his talons, shoving against Sverin, giving him a shake.

"It's me," he growled. *'Me.* Trust me. We must trust as we once did. I know your true heart. I know you to be honorable, merciful—"

Sverin shrieked and Caj winced as it rang in his ears.

Still holding Sverin back with the last of his strength, he gazed through a bright fog at the lashing beak, at the blood-red feathers in the scattered sunlight.

Fighting makes it worse. Fighting.

Fighting.

Blood pounded the warning through his ears, his own racing heart.

With the whirling delirium of pain and the certainty of death suddenly striking each other in his mind, Caj realized with bright clarity what he had to do. The only thing left he *could* do.

"You must trust me," Caj growled again to the mad creature who could be the end of him, "as I trust you."

With a shuddering breath, he loosened his grip, and Sverin leaned into his weight, eyes glassy with a killing light.

"I submit," Caj rumbled, locking eyes. "My brother. My king."

With final resolve he let his grip fall slack. He let fall his wings, his limbs, and relaxed against the ground. He turned his face toward the blinding, sunlit snow, and offered Sverin his throat.

Red lashed in the corner of his eye, Sverin's face swooping in. Talons pressed against his chest, pinning. Caj didn't wince as the beak squeezed tight against his neck.

All he saw was white, winking with glittering motes of gold, and he thought his death had been swift and painless. He waited to see his father.

Wind sifted against his flight feathers.

No dead came to greet him, no shining warriors of Tyr, and he realized he was cold.

. . . As cold as if he still laid there, aching, crushed into the snow under the weight of an enormous opponent.

His wing throbbed with pain. The brightness in his eyes was sunlight on snow. The dim, distant shapes he saw were mountains and trees, the very mountains and trees of the Sun Isle.

Sverin's weight was real, and the red gryfon had not killed him.

Caj didn't move. Still Tollak and Andor hung back, staring and uncertain, mercifully still, and the first sound to break the silence did not come from them.

"Caj."

His voice, raw from animal screaming, rough and guttural from many turns of the moon without use, sounded like the purest birdsong to Caj.

Warily Caj shifted, turning his face again and blinking back the sunbursts from his eyes. "Sverin."

"Yes." Still he hesitated, pinning, measuring his options with a lost, exhausted expression on his face.

Lost and exhausted, but present, aware, and knowing. Caj had been right. His near sacrifice had worked to awaken Sverin to himself.

"You're alive," the Red King croaked.

"I am, Sverin. I am."

"Why did you come here?" With a sort of calm horror Sverin appeared to realize that he'd almost killed his own wingbrother.

"To find you," Caj said firmly. With a heavy, slow weariness that alarmed him, Sverin climbed back, letting Caj rise to all fours again. "To speak to you."

"Halvden told me you were dead." His eyes narrowed.

Caj spoke quickly. "It's past, my brother. He's made amends, and I have. And I'm..." He found himself without words, suddenly dizzy, as if the entire journey caught up to him in that moment. "I am so glad to see you."

Sverin made a rough noise, and cast a sideways look to the half-blood warriors waiting, now looking completely unsure what to do. "The Widow Queen sends her regards, I see."

"Thyra too," Caj said. Sverin, thinking perhaps of the last time he'd seen Caj's daughter, when he'd tried to exile her from the pride, lowered his head.

"Andor," Caj called over his shoulder. "Tollak. I have him. Go find Ingmer and the others, and tell them."

They hesitated, and Caj lifted one wing with a growl.

Years of training and obeying under Caj appeared to overcome them, especially now that Sverin ceased to attack, and they moved quickly.

Sverin eyed them as they flapped hard overhead, toward the pass at the far end of the valley.

"Sverin," Caj murmured.

The red gryfon looked back to him, seeming ten years older and at the end of his strength. "You should have left me here. You should have let me die wild, and Nameless, as I deserve."

Not since they were fledglings had Caj seen Sverin express self-pity, and he rustled his wing feathers in disapproval. "That's not what you deserve. And you *will* face your fate with honor and courage. Did you hear all of what I said, before we fought?"

"I did." Sverin rustled against the cold wind and turned toward the shelter of the rocks. Caj followed him, wading through the trail he'd blazed earlier in the snow. "You're sorry you lied. You're sorry about Shard." He stepped into the shallow snow near the cave, and turned again to face Caj. "Why did you lie to me?"

Caj had had time to think about that, too. "I wasn't afraid of you, but Per."

"You took Shard as your nest-son. I would have protected you both."

Heat closed Caj's throat for a moment. "I know that now. I didn't then, and when Per died, it seemed too late."

"You should have known." Recovered to his senses, Sverin's gold eyes pierced him hard, knowing, aware. "I never trusted the Vanir, but I did trust you. Though of course, now..." he trailed off and looked pointedly at Caj, and they both thought of Shard, now prince of the Vanir, surely planning on returning and claiming his Isle.

"While we're speaking of lies," Caj said evenly, keeping his temper only because he was happy to argue with words all day rather than with beak and claw, "what have you kept from me?"

"It doesn't matter now."

"It's over, Sverin," Caj said quietly. "During the Long Night, when we could all see you slipping from us, Ragna told me something." At the sudden, guarded expression on Sverin's face, Caj knew he was close to something important. "Sverin, it's done. It's over. Ragna rules as regent, Thyra waits for Kjorn—"

"Waits for Kjorn?" he asked sharply, ears perking. "Where has he gone?"

Caj sat, carefully folding his wing. "Home. To the Winderost."

"No," Sverin whispered, looking stunned.

"There's nothing you can do," Caj said firmly. "He's gone to find Shard, and he'll return or he won't. Your line is secure, in Thyra."

"I always hated your lack of tact," Sverin said, ears laying back. With the same expression he said, "And admired your honesty."

Feeling struck, Caj merely shook his head. "Now, I'll tell you all you like about what's happened since you left, after you answer my question. What secrets do you hold from me, still? What passed between you and Ragna? What secret does she know that you could not tell me? Tell me what drove you to this, what split the trust between us. I've owned my lies."

Sverin looked at him, and a quick, burning gratitude flashed across his features so quickly Caj almost mistook it for sadness. "I know I owe you that. I will tell you everything, though most of it you know. My failure as a king, as a father. But you don't know where my failure began."

"You didn't fail as a father..." Caj fell quiet at another hard look.

"And I will not tell you here," Sverin said, raising his head as sunlight reached over the valley and fell across his broad, red chest. "I will go with you," he said, gazing across the snow field, "you and the others, as their prisoner, if that is necessary." He looked to Caj. "And I will confess everything, for I have committed worse crimes than you know, and I must confess it all, before the pride, before you, Sigrun, Thyra, and Ragna."

"Sverin..."

Sverin's gaze grew distant and shadowed. "And I must ask her forgiveness, though I fear it's too late. My fear of you and Kjorn learning the truth—both of our coming here, and what came after—was so great that it drove all else from my mind, Caj. I wore my broken honor like a shield. But after all I've done to you, to Shard, to the pride, my offense to her was greatest of all, and it has lasted these ten long years. I can bear it no more, and surely she can't either."

"Who?" Caj asked, frustrated that he wouldn't be plain, but relieved that he would no longer fight. "Whose forgiveness must you ask before we can leave this behind us?"

The weary golden eyes met Caj's glare. "Ragna." His voice was quiet. Broken. "White Ragna, who has more courage than ever I had, and made me a promise I never deserved."

38

A SILVER TALE

THE TRUTH WAS WROUGHT IN silver before their eyes.
And it was as Groa had told him.

"I knew it!" Hikaru said shrilly. "I knew that all those terrible things about gryfons couldn't be true." He slipped around Shard in a protective coil, as Natsumi, wide-eyed, peered at the new account.

Ume bobbed her great head. "The emperor of that time didn't like being portrayed honestly, and commanded that the chronicler disguise the tale. So Umeko did, but it has passed from one of us to the next to remember, to know, that the truth was beneath." She looked at Shard, ears perked. "And to wait until the right time to reveal it."

Shard did note that the tale in silver was a bit more equal between Amaratsu's and Groa's stories. He noticed a bit more fault on the part of the gryfons than in Groa's tale—more greed, more boasting, but the tragic ending was the same, with Kajar falsely accused of murdering a dragon and he and his band driven out with some of the treasures they'd been given. Neither side fully villainous, neither side fully wrong.

295

Shard thought of the Aesir and the Vanir, his divided family in the Silver Isles.

"See there," Ume said to Natsumi as the younger dragoness read the tale, tracing intricate lines drawn into the background. "That is to show the elements at play—here is fire, and air, a volatile mix that ended in great sadness."

Shard spotted a figure unlike any other. "There," he said, opening his wings with excitement, "is that a wyrm, there?" He patted Hikaru's coil and climbed out, peering up to see the higher panel.

"Yes," Ume said. "You see here, after the Aesir left the Sunland, when we closed ourselves away."

Shard followed the intricate reliefs in silver, marveling at the detail of the wyrms, the thick horns, the deadly tail. "It looks like a wyrm came to the Sunland?"

"That was Rhydda," Ume murmured, touching a claw to the wyrm, flying over plains of pearl. "The last named wyrm. A year after Kajar left."

"And then?" Shard asked. "Why did she come? What became of her?"

Ume rose higher, touching the silver panel as she opened her mouth to explain—then her ears laid back and she looked quickly toward the entrance.

"There!" shouted a new voice.

Hikaru and Natsumi's heads whipped up, and Shard slipped around Hikaru, ears lifting.

Kagu charged into the far entryway, yellow scales blazing in the torch light, bouncing dazzling reflection off the golden pillars.

"I told you I saw them leading the intruder here!"

Blue Isora and two more fully grown sentries wound their way into the cavern behind him.

"I told you!" boomed Kagu.

A rolling growl began to build itself in Hikaru's chest. Shard felt it thrumming against his whole body.

"Hikaru don't," Ume murmured. "Be still. Natsumi, be still. Show restraint and your youth may earn you some lenience."

"You've been spying!" Hikaru burst out anyway, quivering with rage. Natsumi laid a forepaw on his wing, but he remained crouched and tense.

"Take the gryfon," said one of the sentries, a sinuous jade female with a mane of lustrous gold. The other was flame orange, the same Shard had met on the first day.

Ume rose to her full height, spanning her wings as if to embrace them all. "Welcome, honored dragons of the warrior way. What may I do for you? Family histories, perhaps?" She bobbed her head once, watching them with hooded eyes.

Kagu snorted, and cobalt Isora silenced him with a look. He shrank back, but met Shard and Hikaru's glare with a smug, fanged grin.

"Chronicler," said the jade sentinel, dipping her head, though her gaze was hard. "You have much to answer for. The gryfon was not to see our treasures or our histories."

"I cannot feel bound by an arbitrary rule," Ume said. "We've had no rules about gryfons until the day Rashard entered our halls, and now rules come only by the empress's whim. Tell me, how does your own upbringing console you to blindly following an unjust—"

"Be silent," snapped the jade, her teeth gleaming in the torchlight. She reared up, but was still a head shorter than Ume. "I am loyal to the empress until my end."

"Show them," Hikaru cried, stretching up to point to the pillar. "Show them the truth, about Kajar, about the emperor—"

"Be still, hatchling," Isora rumbled, and true to his new training, Hikaru huddled down, edging closer to Shard.

"Enough." The jade dragon snapped her jaws. Her golden gaze traveled from Hikaru and Shard, back up to Ume. "You will all answer to the empress."

The hall of ice glowed liquid amber in the light of only a few torches, held by careful young sentries who stood well away from the walls or supporting columns.

Isora tossed Shard on the ground in front of the empress's great ice throne. He tumbled, scrambled to his feet and slipped, only for Hikaru to whip forward and catch him in gentle claws. He helped Shard stand upright while the golden dragoness watched in cold, beautiful silence. She'd been given word, apparently, and risen for the occasion, but Shard suspected she'd been asleep, for her mane looked wild, as if wind-tossed, and she wore no jewels but for the great collar of gold and ruby. She looked more mortal than the first time he'd seen her. Shard felt braver, but someone spoke before he could.

"Radiant One," said Ume, walking sedately forward with Natsumi at her side. "Wise, just, and benevolent Ai." She bowed deeply, her nose nearly touching the floor. "It is my honor to stand in your presence. I hope you will see it in your great heart to allow me to explain."

"Explain," Empress Ai said, with the barest flick of her tail, "quickly."

Hikaru tugged Shard back and they stood side by side with Ume.

Ume paused only a moment to note that other dragons had risen at the commotion of them all being escorted through the mountain to the throne room. They had a silent, but large audience gathering.

"Radiant Empress, I would have hoped that the next generation would be more welcoming to the first outsider our land has seen in so many—"

"I said quickly," Ai said. "Don't waste your breath on flattery or sentiment."

Ume bowed her head, but Shard stepped forward.

"I'll explain, because it's all my doing."

"*You* will be silent," growled the empress, and the light from the torches bobbed as the younger dragons holding them edged away.

"I won't be silent," Shard said. "I've been silent before, and always with regret. You will listen to what I say, then do as you will."

"Shard," Hikaru murmured, but Shard only dipped his head to the young dragon before stepping forward.

He bowed, mantling to the empress, who looked surprised enough to hear him out. "I came here to seek and offer friendship, to ask your help in resolving a mortal feud between wyrms and gryfon kind that I know now began in the time of Kajar."

Her mane, though long and thick, seemed to stand higher, and it made her look feral and fierce, but she didn't interrupt him yet.

Shard inclined his head. "I assume you are much wiser and more knowledgeable than your forebears, so of course I don't hold you at fault for the problems between Kajar and the emperor of that time. As I expect that none of you would hold me at fault," he glanced around as motion caught his eye, and saw that their audience had tripled, "for the deeds of gryfons nearly one hundred years dead."

"I won't bear your insults," Ai said, her voice now a steady, thrumming growl.

"He hasn't insulted you," Ume said, "nor anyone. If you will only come with me, come to the hall of histories, I will show you the truth, as I should have shown you in your second season."

"The truth," said Ai, "as the chronicler of Kajar put it down? Umeko, so beguiled by gryfons that she slandered her own kind? No. I will not believe it."

"You have never seen it. There is no slander but truth, only truth. Fault on both sides, redemption, acts of selfishness *and* love."

"You should have asked my permission," Ai said to Shard, turning from Ume.

"I would have," Shard growled, "if only I'd been allowed to see you."

"None of this is necessary. We know the ways of the world beyond our pure mountains and waters."

"Do you?" Shard asked softly. "I don't think you do, and I don't think your mountains are so pure."

"The world *is* terrible," Hikaru said, loudly, more to the dragons around them than to the empress. "But it's even more *wonderful*. I know, I have seen it."

Ai rose, the breath of the movement setting the torches flickering and casting translucent shadow dragons on every wall. She raised her voice, addressing all those who now stared from every level. "We want no part of it. You have corrupted one of our own. You will not take honest responsibility for the greedy actions of your kind, and I will not trouble myself with affairs that no long matter to us. These wyrms in the Winderost, they're not my concern."

"I think they are your concern. There were never wyrms in the Winderost before the time of Kajar, not until he returned from the Sunland. They won't hear me. I don't know what they want. *You* might be able to get through to them."

"At this, Amaratsu failed."

Shard's tail lashed, he raised his wings. "We must try again! What of your honor? What of a warrior's responsibility? What of compassion, justice, mercy?"

She bared her teeth, paused and collected herself, rearing back to a more dignified pose. "I will not hear dragon teachings growled into my face by an uncivilized beast from a backwards, broken land."

Shard felt as if his feathers had caught fire, so hot was he with amazement and rage. "You're not even listening!"

"Great Empress, Ai-hime." Natsumi's autumn wind voice whispered delicately. "Please, hear him. On behalf of us, the new born, on behalf of Amaratsu, who was his friend—"

"Friend?" Empress Ai turned with liquid grace and lowered her head to address Natsumi. "Or victim? How do we know he didn't assist in her death and hatch Hikaru only to find his way here? Natsumi, you're too young to—"

"*You're all young*," Shard shouted, losing hold of his anger. He whirled, slipping a little on the ice, to behold the dragons staring from the higher tiers. "I've lived ten years. I should be a wizened elder by your reckoning, but you treat me like a witless beast, a kit, or spy. I know more of the world than any one of you ever will, if you stay on this wind."

The torches fluttered. Shadows shifted.

Shard turned back to Empress Ai. "I have no interest in your rocks and metal. I care for Hikaru. I care for my pride. I need your *help*, and all you care about is peace, quiet, and gold."

"I will hear no more of this. Your assumptions and insults are too much to bear." Ai planted her forepaws on the ice, head rearing back. "Honored Chronicler Ume, you will be punished for indulging this behavior in the young ones, and for enabling the gryfon's acts of spying and attempts at thievery."

"My radiant empress," Ume began, but Ai laid back her ears, warning her to silence.

"I will not be accused of ignorance, so you will show me to this tale you claim is the true account of the Red Kings."

"Good," said Hikaru. "Then you—"

"Be silent, winterborn. You've been indulged too far, and not to your betterment." Ai raised her great swan wings, looking aflame in the torchlight. "Isora, you will take the gryfon away from here, and see that he cannot return. We may educate ourselves in our own time, without arrogant interference."

"No," Hikaru said. "You can't! Shard hasn't done anything wrong—"

"Be still." The jade dragoness who had come upon them in the hall of histories slithered forward to contain Hikaru. "Be silent now, young warrior. We must be better in your discipline." Hikaru was not fast enough to keep her from snaking him in her coils, and closing her claws around his snout.

Isora came at Shard in the same moment, and before Shard could twitch a feather, the dragon grabbed him, rolled him up in careful azure talons and surged into the air, bearing Shard as easily as a gryfon would its nestling.

"Shard!" Hikaru shouted, twisting his head free of the jade dragon's grasp. The orange sentinel fell in to help restrain him, and the empress called in others to contain Ume and Natsumi if needed. "Stop!" Hikaru called, then his cries were muffled again.

Shard managed to shout, "I'm all right, Hikaru—"

But Isora had flown out of the ice cavern, winging through the halls and tunnels with the speed of a serpent whipping through the grass. At least the dragon was careful to hold Shard tightly without piercing his skin, and so Shard held as still as he could to avoid the appearance of struggling. It would do no good anyway. By the time he craned his neck to see where they were he was lost, utterly lost in the inner mountains.

He tried to track where they were going but was only able to note the change when they flew into the halls of ice. The air felt cold and still on his face.

They flew through long tunnels, through one expanse of open night air between mountain peaks that lasted a blink and smelled of seawater, and dove again into a rougher, unrefined series of rock and ice caves.

Through the dull dark and phantom moonlight that suffused through the ice into the caves, Shard saw a glimmering, subterranean lake.

"Breathe," Isora warned, and Shard sucked a sharp breath in the same instant the giant dragon plunged underwater.

Pure ice seemed to grasp Shard's feathers, his muscles, his eyes, and he was grateful for the warmth of the dragon's paws wrapped around him.

The dragon wound and twisted under the water, swimming fast. Through blurred bubbles and stinging eyes, Shard made out dark, underwater passageways and dead-ends. Just when Shard's chest burned for a breath, Isora lunged out of the water.

There, he dumped Shard on the ground. Shard shook himself quickly, getting his bearings. He stood in a cramped, dark cave of ice, with a pool of slushy water before him just wide enough for Isora's head to emerge. He bobbed there, checking the walls to make sure Shard had no other exits but the water. Satisfied, he looked to Shard.

"You'll stay here."

Shard eyed the water, and Isora set his claws on the ice around the pool.

"I don't recommend trying to swim out. It's a labyrinth. You'll freeze or drown before you find the right tunnel out."

"How long will I be here?"

"I don't know." Isora watched him, and Shard seized on the fact that he hadn't yet abandoned him.

"You've seen me more than the others have, Master Isora. You've seen me with Hikaru. You've seen me fly and spar, surely you don't think everything you've learned about my kind is true? Or that you can judge all of us based on a single event involving a few gryfons, that isn't even remembered truthfully?"

Isora's rumble vibrated the water into ripples around him. "I will not disobey my empress." He sank lower in the water.

"Wait!" Shard jumped forward, poised at the edge of the pool. "What will happen to Hikaru and the others? You must know that Natsumi didn't do anything wrong, nor Ume. If you must, put all the blame on me, but not them."

"I will let it be known you said this."

"Thank you. What will the empress do?"

The blue dragon paused, his claws tightening on the ice ledge around the pool. "Hopefully," he said, "she will only forget about you."

With that, the blue dragon plunged below, leaving Shard alone in the small, icy prison.

39

EXILES OF THE REACH

F OR SEVERAL DAYS THEY RESTED at the Ostral Shore.
Though *rested* was not quite the right word.

Kjorn ramped to his full height and slashed talons at Asvander's flank, scoring just deep enough to draw blood.

The Lakelander swore, whipping around to see that he'd lost, for they fought to first blood. A crowd of fledges cheered, or hissed if they'd hoped for Asvander to win, but all were well entertained. A cloudy evening brought gloom on the lake, and Kjorn smelled rain.

"That's the *third time*," Dagny grumbled, shoving past Kjorn before he could move out of her path. "Isn't that enough?"

"He's the one who wishes to spar," Kjorn said, unable to contain his pride at winning. Again. "Ask him."

The Lakelanders were a sturdy, hearty pride of gryfons whose focus and point of honor was their skill in fighting. In general tall with a long reach, or stocky with big muscle, they ranged in colors from seabird grays to more dusty, hawk-like hues. Their clear lines stretched back to the Second Age, and during his stay, Kjorn had listened more than once to old timers' tales of their own fights and great

304

battles of their ancestors, told in such detail they might've been there themselves.

"I will figure out how in all winds you do it," Asvander said, glaring at the spot of blood on his flank.

"I had a good teacher," Kjorn said, and raised his voice to add, "a warrior once from the Ostral Shore."

Older males and females called their approval, and a gaggle of younger initiates crowded forward to interrogate Asvander and Kjorn on how he'd won, if they could spar, and what technique Kjorn was using.

"Give him a rest," Asvander said. "I'm sure he'll be happy to humiliate all of you in due time."

Kjorn chuckled. "Perhaps in the morning. It's growing dark."

A chorus of groans answered him, but before Asvander or Kjorn could offer one more lesson or spar, they heard Brynja shouting.

"Kjorn!" the red gryfess bounded toward the cleared sloped where the fledges trained. "Asvander, Dagny, oh—the scouts have returned."

"They've brought word?" Asvander asked.

Brynja stopped beside Kjorn, breathless, almost laughing. "They've brought more than word. Come!"

Asvander looked at Dagny, then Kjorn. Dagny was the first to hop forward, and they followed Brynja toward the lake.

A crowd of Lakelanders had gathered at the dawnward shore, the farthest border of their territory in that direction. Asvander had to shout and shoulder his way through, driving a trail for Brynja, Kjorn and Dagny to follow. From the excited chatter, Kjorn gathered that a large number of Aesir, exiled from the Dawn Spire, had arrived with the returning scouts.

"Why did they take so long?" Asvander demanded. "I sent scouts a whole moon ago, and the Reach is less than three days' flight."

His question was answered not by a particular gryfon, but as word spread through the throng that, for some reason, they had walked the entire way.

Loud talk, laughter, and old acquaintances calling each other's names overwhelmed Kjorn until at last they broke through the crowd to behold the newcomers.

"Valdis," Brynja cried. "Kjorn, I see my aunt, come and meet her!" She sprang from Kjorn's side, shouting. "Oh, Valdis!"

Kjorn turned, watching her greet an older gryfess of similar bearing and color. His hope burned. Perhaps Shard had not gone to the Outlands. Perhaps he'd gone to the Dawn Reach and would be here even now.

He strained up, searching the sea of gryfon faces in the fading light, seeking gray feathers and green eyes.

"So," snarled a gruff voice. "You're Kjorn. Son of Sverin."

Surprised, Kjorn turned, looking for whomever had addressed him. "I am."

"You're the famous, just, kind, golden prince Shard nearly killed himself in loyalty to."

In the growing dark, an older gryfon separated from the throng, coming forward through the shadow only to reveal feathers black as shadow.

Kjorn couldn't speak as he found himself sized up, and the gryfon snorted, ruffled, and smoothed his feathers again. "I thought you'd be taller."

"I know you," Kjorn said quietly. "You're..." he found himself staring, speechless, into the gryfon's single, moss-green eye.

"You know me. Now, you tell me where, in all great blazes, is my *nephew?*"

40

ENDLESS NIGHT

WHEN ENOUGH LIGHT GLOWED UNDER the water so that Shard knew morning had come, he made his first attempt at escape.

Filling his chest with air, he dove into the freezing pool. At first it shocked him where his feathers were thin, and he kept moving, stroking his wings like fins, peering through the sullen blue. He'd thought a clear source of daylight would make it easy to find his way out, but now from under the water he saw multiple tunnels equally aglow with promising turquoise water.

After surfacing for a breath, he dove again, trusting the thick down under his feathers for at least three chances before he went completely numb.

He followed one tunnel, keeping track of the pool behind him. Pale blue brightened to white. Diffused rays of sunlight lanced down through the water up ahead.

Shard swam fast in a wake of bubbles, only to strike a wall of clear ice. He slashed and kicked against it, then, throat tight, whirled and swam back to his pool. To his prison. After warming up, he would try again.

The light shifted to late day as he made more attempts, rested, then leaped circles around the pool to warm his muscles again. When the water became dull he knew it to be evening, or a gathering storm, and he knew it would be wisest to rest.

He settled as far from the cold water as possible, scrunching himself against the cold rock that formed his prison, and worked very hard not to panic.

He closed his eyes, feeling that the rock was shrinking in around him.

The ice creaked and groaned. Scrabbling up, Shard stared around, ears flicking. Slowly he realized it was an echo, that the ice shifted or expanded or tightened elsewhere, but was not about to crack beneath him.

Settling again, he gazed at the darkening pool of water.

When he at last closed his eyes, the world seemed to lurch and the rock at his back tighten in, holding him fast so that he couldn't fly or even move. Then it all tipped upside down and he stood on the rock with a roof of ice and water gushing on him from the pool, and he was drowning, crushed under chunks of ice.

Shard jerked awake. He squeezed his talons against the rocks around him.

The cavern was still. The ice was hard under him, the rock hadn't moved.

Somewhere, water dripped.

"It's not real," he said quietly, to the rock. He'd never been trapped in a place so small, with no hope of leaving. He shut his eyes, and thought of the sky.

That only made it worse, knowing that he might never see it again. Knowing that the empress might well forget him so that he died there, knowing that he couldn't swim out, knowing that Hikaru might be punished or worse, forget about Shard as he grew up. Sunland dragons would never rejoin the world. The Winderost would remain prey to the wyrms, he wouldn't be able to help, and his own pride at home would only know that he left them, and was lost.

He would never see his family. He would never see Brynja, never get a second chance. He would never see Kjorn again.

He would die there...if he didn't do something.

In the very last dregs of gray light left, Shard rolled to his feet and dived back into the pool.

He knew three directions that led to dead ends, and only two choices remained. A wide, open expanse that went on and on into abysmal, icy darkness, and a dragon-sized tunnel that was not quite midnight blue.

Shard surfaced once more, taking a huge breath, and chose the tunnel.

As he swam, he yanked tiny feathers from his own shoulder and set them to float against the ice over his head, leaving a little trail behind him.

The light brightened, rich blue and silver. Moonlight. He heard a dull, pounding roar that was the ocean, rocking under the swollen moon. He kicked, pumped his wings, swam hard through the water as the cold slipped squeezing talons around him. He knew he'd emerged from the caves into another, wider cavern, or perhaps the open sea ice.

Below him yawned a fathomless, featureless blue.

He didn't look down again.

A slow, threatening burn heated his chest. He released a huff of bubbles and turned slowly, looking for an opening.

Is this the lake where Isora entered? It wouldn't have frozen over so quickly...and there was no moonlight this bright...

He'd chosen the wrong way.

Forcing himself to stay calm, Shard searched for an opening. He didn't have the breath to return to his prison.

I will die here.

I will die...

I will NOT die—

Wasting breath with a furious, terrified shriek, Shard whirled in a twist of silver bubbles, kicking hard and squinting.

A circle of light drew his desperate eye, two leaps away. He struggled for it, his limbs beginning to lock and jerk from the cold. The water shifted, rippling in the little circle ahead. Moving, splashing. An opening.

Shard thrust his head out, sucking down hard, painful, breaths. He wasn't sure he would even have the strength to drag himself from the water. Then he realized with hot, crawling dread that he hadn't found an escape, but only a bubble in the ice, a little pocket of air, perhaps a snow bear's old hunting hole that had frozen over.

Treading water, he breathed.

The liquid ice seeped under his feathers, trailing silky cold across his skin. He'd been there too long. The ice seemed to penetrate and close around his hindquarters so that his steady kicks became weak and loose.

Shard gulped air, shutting his eyes.

Go back. Go back. One more breath, then back.

Back where?

A violent tremble overtook his muscles and he slipped under water, then shoved himself back up, panting for a breath.

"Go back," he rasped to himself, turning sluggishly. Rippling shivers overcame him and his beak slapped the water, then his muscles calmed. "Go back…"

He kicked, shivering, wings sliding slower and slower until he wasn't sure if he was moving them or floating.

He would dive soon. *One more breath.*

One more breath.

His shivers faded.

At once he felt warm, and he was floating comfortably on warm water.

Then on warm air.

"The world is in danger, son-of-Baldr."

Shard flew under the moon with a snowy white owl. "My friend," he cried, but there was no joy in her. "Tell me what to do, where to go. Everything I've done has failed."

She had guided him before.

"You must not fail. A longer winter than you know threatens all creatures. The wyrms of the Winderost have begun to feed on fear, and so they will spread it as far as they can. Fly high, my prince, to see."

A strange, hot wind swelled under their wings, lifting them beyond the Sunland and the world. That high, he saw the black rim of a forever night sky touching the blue of day, saw that the world curved softly like a robin's egg.

The owl circled him, drawing his eye.

"If they spread their terror further, all will be Nameless with it. You are borne high by the Silver Wind. Look beyond, look at things as they were before, as they may be again."

He saw a great battle of Nameless beasts, the First creatures who came from the Sunlit Land beyond the Dawnward Sea who, entering the dark, broke into points of light that creatures of the world called stars. They fought like savage, witless animals, like creatures who had no love or knowledge of Tyr and Tor.

The stars wheeled and swelled in front of him and became great gryfons, wolves, boar, mountain cats and caribou and bizarre beasts from other lands whose names Shard didn't know.

It was not honor or courage that drove them, but fear. Nameless, empty fear such as Shard had only felt staring into the baleful eyes of the wyrms of the Winderost.

"Fly high, Shard," whispered the owl, bright as starlight, and her voice sounded like all the voices he loved. Then she winked out like an ember, and he was alone.

He fell, gliding fast over the world, and grasped for the spiraling dream net. There he snagged his talons around the dream of a red wolf who slept beneath a distant, deep, snow-covered forest.

"Catori," he called with relief, with joy, with sudden, immeasurable sorrow. A part of him felt there was some reason he might never see her again.

"My prince!" She bounded forward and then her happy expression darkened. *"My friend, where are you? I search for you on the wind, and there comes no word, no dream, no song, nothing at all."*

"I've failed you, Catori. I've failed all of you. It wasn't meant to be me. Hikaru, the dragon, or Kjorn…"

He had trouble speaking, breathing, and felt that something choked him. He tried to wade toward her in the snow and had to swim, to kick and glide as if he were in water.

"Hikaru may be a Summer King to his mother," Catori said, her fur blazing like flame against the snow, "Kjorn may be king to the pride in the Winderost." She was in front of him, and Shard strained for her familiar scent. "But you are Summer King to us, son-of-Baldr. You must fly higher. And you must come home."

"I'm not strong enough. I failed—I'm dying, Catori—"

She leaped, fangs bared and snarling, and bowled him over as easily as if he were a kit. Shard gasped, thrashing, lost his grasp on the dream net. The wolf became enormous, and he the size of a wolf pup. She clamped jaws on the looser skin between his wings and shook him, and the moon glowed huge in the sky.

A voice like Catori's, but not like hers, boomed around him. "You answered the call, son of the Vanir. You are meant to right the wrongs. They will call you the Summer King, and this will be your song."

"I can't!" Shard screamed into the dream light that was swiftly dissolving to chaotic snow and stars. Catori was gone, and in her place stood a tall, golden-eyed wolf whose pitch black coat glittered with stars, and who smelled of the hot ozone after skyfire struck the air. "I'm weak! I failed!"

"You must not fail," the wolf snarled, and flung Shard away. Her long, piercing howl split the stars.

Fear closed Shard's throat, and lack of breath swept him with dizziness. Cold locked his muscles. He fell. He fell fast, screaming eagle's terror into the endless night above the world.

Air, ice and water roiled around him. Shard seemed to land in a waterfall of ice, falling upward.

The howl of the black wolf warped into a different cry, desperate, angry cries splitting the air around him.

Then he realized he wasn't falling, but that something was pulling him up out of the water. Sweet, icy breath swept into him and he came fully awake to a very real crashing of breaking ice and surging sea. Strong claws grasped him, tugging him away from the hole in the ice. Wings beat the air around him, he was rolling, rolling from the water, held fast to a warm, scaled body.

Shard fell limp as Hikaru's scent filled his nose.

"Please be alive," Hikaru moaned, shaking his head hard to send water flying from his mane. "Oh please, Shard—"

"Al-ive," Shard croaked, coughing, seizing into hard breaths as Hikaru scooped him closer.

"I found you," the dragon breathed, shoving up to fly from the sea ice, carrying Shard almost as easily as Isora had done.

Shard let his head loll, and pressed to Hikaru's scales as the dragon bore him toward the mountains.

Hikaru clutched Shard close to his chest, which felt as warm as a fire. "I have you, my brother. I have you."

41

HIKARU'S CHOICE

"I SORA TOLD ME WHERE TO find you." Hikaru and Shard rested on a ledge overlooking the sea, a good distance from Ryujan. "I think he took pity on us both."

Shard flicked his ears, nodding once, still coming back to his senses.

Hikaru tightened his coils. "When I realized you'd swam down the wrong way, trying to escape, I thought I would find you dead. But I saw your feathers and followed…"

He took a trembling breath, and bumped Shard gently with his nose. Shard ran his talons through the silver mane on Hikaru's back, trying to calm the dragon, and himself. The warmth from Hikaru's scales helped to soothe his frayed nerves and trembling muscles. His body felt achy, light, as if no amount of fish or red meat could fill him again.

A part of him curled in that icy cave still, a small, cold piece of him that would never escape that prison, would always try to panic at a space that was too small.

Shard's stomach was not so panicky, and snarled.

Hikaru laughed, ears perking, and shifted. "I'll get you some fish."

"No." Shard grabbed for his foreleg. "No. Just—stay with me, Hikaru. Stay and rest." He twitched his ears, and drew a breath of the wide, starry night. "What happened after they took me away?"

Hikaru shook his head in disgust. "The empress was merciful, at least, because we are young. Natsumi was sent to her family. I'm to remain in my den. She thinks I'm still there." He showed his teeth, then gusted a sigh. "Isora told me that Empress Ai did go with Ume to see the pillar and the Tale of the Red Kings, but still denies the truth of it. They've been lying to themselves too long."

Shard shook his head slowly, and closed his eyes, listening to the wind against the snowy plains, and the wash of the sea. For a moment, he pretended they were in the Silver Isles, and all was peaceful.

Hikaru glared out at the sea. "I suppose I should consider myself fortunate that she didn't have me killed or exiled to the white waste, and that no one else was exiled or…" His ears twitched and a spasm of irritation tightened his whole body around Shard for a moment. "She said we had been misguided. I don't understand, Shard, how she can say those things, when the truth was plain in silver on the wall. A dragon who was *there* left it for everyone to remember, but they don't want to."

Shard shook himself, ruffling his feathers. "I don't understand either. I suppose Sverin and Per did the same thing, retelling history, making themselves out to be conquerors. But we don't know what else is in her mind."

"How can you only say that? Aren't you angry?"

"Of course," Shard said quietly. "But I've also seen what anger without intent of justice can do. Your empress won't hear me, but I know the truth about Kajar now, and I know a little more about the wyrms. I can tell Kjorn that his great grandfather was honorable, and courageous. I can help him to reclaim his own birthright, do what needs to be done for my pride, and then…"

"You're going to face them again," Hikaru said. "You're going to face the wyrms."

"I have to try." The owl's vision circled around him like a vulture. He crawled from Hikaru's coils, his muscles warming and anxious to stretch. "I tried to talk to the wyrms in a way that I understand. It's time to approach them in a way that they understand."

Hikaru perked his ears as he unfurled his full, lengthy body. "How?"

At that, Shard ground his beak. The stark, terrifying nightmare of Nameless beasts and endless night weighed on his heart. "I don't know yet."

Hikaru loosed a breathy laugh. "I admire you."

Shard flashed him a grateful look. "I admire you. You saved my life, Hikaru."

"You would have escaped."

"No." Shard met his eyes. "I would have died. Without you, I would have died."

"So would I," Hikaru whispered, and bent his head forward. Shard leaned in, and pressed his brow to Hikaru's broad, delicate face.

Accepting his close moment of near death, Shard backed away with sudden vigor, tail lashing. "You mentioned fish?"

Hikaru laughed, drawing up, but didn't open his wings.

"Race you." Shard leaped, shooting free of Hikaru's coils and risking cramps by flinging himself from the mountain face and throwing open his wings. The harsh wind battered against him and he gasped, laughed, made a full, sweeping turn in the night air to clear his head before winging back to Hikaru, who waited, bunched on a ledge outside the tunnel.

Shard hovered, and the dragon joined him in flying out to sea, though Hikaru insisted that Shard let him do the fishing. Shard did, gratefully, and watched, realizing how quick and graceful the young dragon had become—both in body and in heart.

Hikaru caught two wriggling herring, and Shard joined him back on the mountain ledge, where Shard consumed both fish, to Hikaru's satisfaction.

"Thank you," Shard said, flicking scales from his talons.

Hikaru bent his head and gently touched his nose to Shard's brow. "Of course, my wingbrother. Of course. I wish I could do more. I wish the empress would help you."

"You've done enough. Don't risk yourself for my sake again. I can only hope that now that the seed has been planted, curiosity will grow. Perhaps one day…" Shard huffed, shook himself, and looked around in attempt to gain his bearing. "But now, Hikaru, we must fly this very night. Too much pulls me away, and I can't risk being captured again. For your sake, or mine."

"No," Hikaru said hesitantly, "I know you can't."

A strange note touched his voice, and Shard studied his face, and his eyes, with dawning sadness.

"But you're not coming with me, are you."

Hikaru lowered himself to his belly, forelegs on the ground, like a mountain cat, so that he was more at Shard's level. "No."

The relief Shard felt at his escape tightened back to anxiety. "Why, Hikaru? There's nothing for you here. The dragons don't care about the truth, and if you make another mistake, who knows what the empress will do?"

"I know. But you're wrong—there is something for me here. Many things. Some of us do care about the truth, Shard, and I must find those who do and we must stand together and rejoin the rest of the world. That is what my mother wanted. That's why she left the Sunland, and why she left me with you."

Shard swallowed against his dry, tightening throat. "I had so many more things to teach you."

"You taught me the most important things first." Hikaru huffed a cloudy silver breath and laid his head on the ground near Shard. It was nearly as large as Shard's whole body. "I thought I would fly beside you always. But I think Mother knew this would happen. That we would become brothers and through that, my heart would be stronger, that I would need a good heart because I am winterborn."

"You have one of the strongest hearts I know," Shard said softly. "I hope you *will* let it guide you. I only wish you would come with me. You can always return here."

"Maybe, or not. Journeying out into the world isn't quite safe, either. I learned that the hardest way." He winced, perhaps thinking of the whales. "Besides, now gryfons are in everyone's thoughts. They've seen you, the young are curious, and I might have a chance at opening their minds." He showed his teeth in attempt at an amused expression.

Shard couldn't laugh, and Hikaru sobered. The wind tickled them, icy and unsympathetic, the stars piercing like eyes above.

"Shard, do you remember when you told me that we always think we know what we'll do, but then when we really face a decision, it's not as easy as we thought?"

"I remember," Shard murmured.

Hikaru closed his eyes. "This moment is like that for me. One of the warrior virtues is loyalty. I must be loyal, and help my kin here if I can. I was disappointed to find out what they think of you, to know that they wouldn't help us. But now I understand that they needed *my* help. They shouldn't be secluded or ignorant any longer. Shard, I owe you a great debt for all you did for me—"

"No you don't," he said sharply. "You owe me nothing, do you understand?"

"I understand." Hikaru tilted his head. He looked as if he might speak, but his large, liquid gold eyes only studied Shard thoughtfully, gently, as if to memorize him.

Shard watched him in return, his gaze traveling each black scale in the moonlight, the wispy mane and growing silver horns, the black wings. His thoughts drifted to Amaratsu and his promise, to the other dragons, the help they could have been, the help Hikaru could have been.

Then, simply, he knew with a hollowing pang how much he would miss Hikaru's bright laughter and the dragon's presence at his side.

He knew, with hard certainty, that Hikaru's short life meant this would likely be the last time they saw each other.

But he couldn't linger any more. The stars in the black sky reminded him of the black wolf in his chaotic dreams. Cold wind brushed against the rock and snow and with it, her words.

You are the Summer King, and this will be your song.

He stepped forward and rested his talons on Hikaru's scaled brow. "Fair winds, little brother."

Hikaru shut his eyes and whispered, "Fair winds."

They stood there a moment, then Hikaru raised his head, his expression clearing as he turned to the sky. "I've learned the stars you can follow from here to take you to the Silver Isles, if you wish."

The Silver Isles. He could go home.

"Do you know the stars," Shard asked quietly, "that would lead me back to the Winderost?"

42

THE RED KING'S SORROW

TWILIGHT FELL AS THE PRIDE gathered on the Copper Cliff. Days after their final confrontation, Caj, Sverin and the rest of the warriors returned to the nesting cliffs. Sverin had refused to fly since Caj could not, and so the whole procession, including now Halvden, Tocho, and Ragna's five warriors, had walked all the way from the White Mountains back to the pride, arriving near sunset on the fifth day.

At Sverin's request, Ragna gathered the entire pride. Grudgingly, Caj thought it a sign not only of her honorable nature, but her sense of security, that she allowed his request and didn't simply imprison him. She did not require the old to attend, or those gryfesses with kit who felt too weary or ill—but all of them came anyway. All of them wished to hear what the fallen king could possibly have to say.

Ragna stood on top of the King's Rocks, dove-white against the clear dome of delicate blue sky.

For so many years Per and Sverin had stood there. Caj watched Ragna quietly, for she had said nothing about Sverin's fate. There had been no time. Now the red gryfon sat behind her, awaiting his turn to speak and flanked by two large, fully grown Aesir who would not look directly at him.

Caj sat with Sigrun on a lower ledge of the King's Rocks, not as Sverin's honored wingbrother now, but as Thyra's honored father. The father of the queen. The noble warrior who had captured, restored, and returned the Mad Red King.

Rather than watch the pride gather and read the expressions of revulsion and fear, Caj sought out Thyra, who stood the same level with Ragna but well back, letting the Vanir queen rule this moment. Sensing his look, Thyra glanced at Caj and lifted her beak reassuringly.

Caj inclined his head to her, and looked back to the Widow Queen.

When all appeared settled in the snow, Ragna spread her pale wings. "Sons and daughters of Tyr, of Tor, mixed blood of Aesir and Vanir, conquerors who are now mates, family…friends. We gather as one pride, healing, to hear the confession of one who would have divided and ruined us."

Caj eyed Sverin, but the fallen king's expression remained distant, neither angry nor arguing.

Ragna addressed the pride, telling of Caj's bold initiative to find and bring Sverin to his senses, and to justice, telling of Halvden's redemptive actions and the warriors who sought out Sverin, in the end. All watched her, rapt, her voice like balm after long years of the aggressive Red King.

All the while, Caj watched Sverin, desperately seeking some reaction, some hint of what he might say. He looked better than when Caj had found him, preened and eyes alert, as if finally aware of everyone and everything around him, a prisoner of war.

"Come forth, son of Per," Ragna said. Her voice carried across the frozen field. Every ear perked. Caj shifted, and Sigrun made a low, reassuring noise beside him. "You are here to answer for your crimes against the Vanir, the wolves of the Star Isle, every other creature of the Silver Isles bullied and abused under your and your father's reign. Come forth, and speak, as you wished to."

Sverin drew himself up, and with a sour pang of regret, Caj saw that he was truly defeated. The arrogance had drained from him, his once-proud stride dragged, limbs liquid and slow as if he walked to his death, not his confession.

Ragna swept back and stretched her wings as if to present him to the pride, and all drew a breath as the War King turned his back to them, and bowed before her. "This chance to speak is more than I deserved."

"Use it well," Ragna said, her voice now flat and neutral.

Caj's blood quickened more than before he'd faced Sverin in the valley, and he perked his ears.

Sverin turned to face the pride, as he had so many times before. His wings remained closed, his tail low, his ears slanted back as if to continue regarding Ragna, behind him. "I stand before you, defeated. I pass on my right to rule to my son, and to his mate." He lowered his head toward Thyra, who still would not look at him. His ears twitched, and he turned back as the older Aesir mumbled amongst themselves.

"Why did I not fight openly?" His tail lashed, showing some of his old aggression, but he didn't move otherwise. He struck a harsh, red outline against the sky, like an open wound. "Why did I not call out the enemies of my rule and deal with them honorably?" He paused, his voice checked, then he closed his eyes and tilted his head toward the sky, as if asking strength of Tyr. Caj fought the urge to leap up and stand at his side, to give Sverin whatever strength he needed. But he remained close to Sigrun. She also grew tense, for Ragna had kept secrets from her, too.

Caj had never seen Sverin hesitate before, and he almost wished he wouldn't confess—though certainly his rule failed at the end, some part of him was chilled to see the king brought so low.

After a moment Sverin lowered his gaze again to the assembled. "I should have, but I did not, because I was afraid—not of my foe, or of the Vanir king's son." He paused, corrected himself. "Rashard. Your prince. No, not because I was afraid to fight, but because I was afraid if I broke a certain promise, then my own worst secrets would be revealed. I was a coward, and a liar, and this brought suffering on the Vanir and on you, and your families, and ate away at me until I was no longer king, brother, or father to anyone."

Caj gazed at him in wonder and confusion, then around at the pride. Ears flicked. Glances exchanged, no one stirred otherwise or spoke.

"Two things I've kept in my heart, and they poisoned it slowly. The first concerns our coming here, of which the Aesir who flew with us know only half."

He looked to Caj. "We came here under the guise of conquering new lands, expanding the rule of the Aesir in the windward land. The Winderost." He said the name as if it tasted bitter. "But those who flew with us know that we left a great scourge behind us there. You know we left the enemies of Kajar to terrorize the land. Perhaps my father thought our leaving would draw them away."

He hesitated, his gaze now locked on Caj. "Perhaps he thought this, and his intentions were honorable. I can only hope, for it means my line isn't entirely ruled by cowardice." His beak remained parted, holding words, as he stared at Caj. Then he broke the stare, and gazed at the rocks. "But his true reason for leaving, was me."

A long, rasped breath led to his next words. "*I* begged my father that we might flee. I couldn't stand their horrible screams in the night. I couldn't stand knowing they haunted our borders. I could not fight them, and I couldn't bear the thought of my son growing up to the same nightmare. More than anything, I didn't want Kjorn to know the terror I had known."

He raised his voice, declaring his confession to the cold winter air, to Tyr's light, to the pride. "I was afraid. I was afraid, and I spent every moment of our reign here working to convince all of you, and my son, and myself, that I was a true king."

A light, frozen wind brushed their feathers up. Caj shuddered. Sverin would not look at him now, but his gaze settled on the middle distance of the White Mountains. No one moved. His voice grew hard.

"Ragna."

The Widow Queen, who had been watching the pride, turned her gaze to Sverin. He lowered his head.

"Please step forward."

Her ear flicked back. "You've said enough. This is unnecessary."

"No, they must know, they must understand that it was not greed or anger or arrogance that drove me mad."

"What more?" Caj breathed, so softly only Sigrun heard him, and she touched her beak gently to his ear. He'd known Sverin feared the great wyrms in the homeland. Everyone did. But never had he imagined that the reason they'd all left to conquer new lands was because Sverin had asked his father to flee.

Ragna and Sverin watched each other a moment longer, sharing some silent history Caj knew nothing about, then Ragna came forward, and Sverin retreated a step as if to present her. "All of you know that my mate died the first, bitter winter in the Silver Isles, drowned in the sea."

Low, disgusted grumbles washed through the pride, and Sverin snapped his beak to demand silence. It worked. His power still held the pride in thrall.

"For so many years I cast blame on the sea, on the winter, on the Vanir and then on Ragna herself." He watched Ragna's face, and it was like pale stone. "For so many years I did this, telling myself and the pride that the Vanir, that Ragna, had taunted and driven Elena to her death." The name of Sverin's dead mate, so long unspoken, struck like a bolt of skyfire. "I did this for so long that I began to believe it was true."

Ragna looked at Sverin, ears perked forward, and said nothing.

"But it was not the Vanir." Sverin's voice boomed and cracked, broken, over the pride. "It was not Ragna who pushed Elena past her limit and skill, it was not Ragna who demanded that Elena try to match the hunting skills of the Vanir, not Ragna who fought viciously with her because arrogance, hunger and terror of that first winter had driven all the Aesir nearly mad." He closed his eyes, as if unable to look at them and say the words at the same time. "It was me."

Sverin looked at Caj, and he began to understand at last the true horror of his wingbrother's confession.

"It was I who demanded that she try, that she prove herself equal to the conquered huntresses. *I* taunted her, I drove her out, and I watched when she fell, but I was too terrified to fly out and try to save her. And I watched as Ragna..." He straightened, lifted his wings, and forced out the last words. "...as Ragna, the only witness, calling for me to help, dove down to try and save my mate. But she couldn't do it alone, the water was too rough and freezing, and Elena drowned still calling my name."

No one breathed.

Caj could bring no expression to his face at first, no sympathy, no reaction at all. His stomach felt hot and hollow.

Sverin's ears laid back slowly, watching him for some reaction. Caj drew a breath, managed to raise his beak, lift his wings slightly to acknowledge him.

You will never fly alone, he thought, fiercely, hoping his wingbrother knew, hoping he saw it in Caj's face.

I promise you will not fly this wind alone.

Everything became clear. Everything washed over Caj in a blazing, fresh new light. Their flight from the Winderost, Sverin's stern rule, his unreasonable hatred for the Isles.

He had never hated the Islands, or the Vanir. He had hated himself.

Caj stood, slowly, not intending to go to him, but to show that he would not abandon him now, or ever again.

Sverin looked again beyond the pride, toward the mountains.

Before any other gryfon could close their beak or make a noise, Ragna took mercy on Sverin by speaking, for all could see that he had no more words. "We made a pact, that I would tell no one of what had happened, and Sverin would never allow me to be exiled from the pride."

No wonder she never seemed afraid of him, Caj thought, with a mix of bitterness and pity for them both. He wondered how much pain could have been avoided, if...*if.*

"It was wrong of me," Ragna said to all, though she watched Sverin, "to hold that terrible secret. Wrong of both of us, and it has brought nothing but ruin, guilt, and pain."

Sverin's wings closed slowly and he turned his face from the pride, who sat as frozen as rocks in the snow. "Forgive me," he said quietly to Ragna. "I beg your forgiveness."

"Since you ask it, I give it," Ragna said, though her voice remained cold. "For my own part, for I see how you suffer from our agreement still, I forgive you, for I agreed to silence as well. But for the rest..."

She raised her voice, and Caj watched her expression grow icy. "For your crimes against the Vanir, wrought by your own dishonorable acts of cowardice and lying, for the exiles you sent to die, the scorn you showed my own son and the Isles...for that, you will await judgment, and beg the new king for forgiveness yourself."

"The new king," Sverin murmured, staring at his own talons as if in a dream. "Shard."

"Shard," Ragna said. Her voice grew from ice to heat, and as she spoke, the pride realized that her forgiveness did not mean mercy or friendship. "*My son.* The son of Baldr and the rightful prince of the Silver Isles who once loved you, you who returned that love and loyalty with scorn, mistrust and fear. When he returns, he will decide your fate. Thyra has agreed to this. Your own son said we should do with you what we saw fit."

Speaking only to Sverin as if they were alone, and not in front of the entire pride, she finished.

"Until their return, I declare you a prisoner of war, charged with crimes against my pride and all the creatures of the Silver Isles. You will be imprisoned as we have been imprisoned these ten years."

Looking dazed as the pride thought on that change of fortune, it seemed Sverin could only bow his head. Older Aesir in the crowd began to shift, rustle as if preparing to speak, but Thyra raised her head, staring them down. Caj himself could not move, could not argue with the queen's statement nor sentence, grateful only that it was not a sentence of death.

Ragna called the names of four warriors loyal to her. "Take him to his nest. Bind his wings with the gold chains so precious to him, set a guard on him at all times, and let him await the return of the king."

"What will become of him?" Caj demanded, at last breaking his silence.

When Ragna's cool look switched to him, Sigrun stepped forward also, as if to shield him.

"Now?" Ragna watched Caj, he thought, with a mix of anger and pity. "Now that the truth is known, let him at last grieve his mate honestly, and face his failed rule. Let him hope that my son has mercy. Let him beg bright Tyr," she looked to Sverin, ears flat on her skull, "for the pity and mercy that he never gave."

43

END OF THE HUNT

"WOULD HE THINK TO COME here, Asvander?" Kjorn mused. "I don't know."

They'd gathered at the water's edge, under the moon. The earlier clouds had cleared without dropping rain or snow. They had no fires, but stars and moonlight and the brightness of happy news and finding living friends made the shore seem light. A low murmur from the rest of the Ostral pride, talking in their various dens and hollows, underscored their quiet conversation.

Kjorn paced, tail lashing. "Or if your scouts found him, would they know him, and think to bring him back here?"

Asvander lifted his wings, sitting with Dagny and Brynja. "The last we saw of him—"

"We know the last anyone saw of him," Stigr growled. "We don't need to hear it again."

"It's been a long search," Kjorn said, eyeing the black gryfon. "With challenges and heartache for all of us. We're just talking it through, trying to think of things we haven't yet."

"Pretty words." The black Vanir shifted, stretching out on his belly and leaning against Brynja's aunt, Valdis. She didn't intervene, but seemed content to watch Kjorn be challenged and to let them argue. "I heard your father was good with pretty words, too."

"I know you're afraid for Shard," Kjorn said evenly. "And I am too. Now is not the time to argue about it."

"Don't presume to know how I feel about anything," Stigr warned, "much less Shard."

"Do you know how hard I've been searching for him?" Kjorn demanded. "Do you think I care less than you?"

"I think you care about yourself. What's the worst outcome for you—that he's dead and you get to be king of both the Winderost and the Silver Isles?"

"He said nothing like that," Asvander broke in. "You surprise me, Stigr. Did your good judgment get severed with your wing?"

"Asvander," Brynja gasped, her gaze shifting to Stigr's mangled shoulder and the thick, raw scar there.

Kjorn laid his ears back. "I have no quarrel with you, Stigr."

"Don't you?" he asked shrewdly.

Kjorn did, once. It was Stigr who'd told Shard he was a prince, who had told him everything about being a Vanir. It was Stigr who had turned Shard against the Aesir. Against Kjorn.

"I've put it aside," Kjorn said, shortly. "Can't you, for Shard?"

"Everything I've done the last ten years was for Shard."

"He's my wingbrother," Kjorn growled.

Stigr stood slowly, and ignored when Valdis tapped her tail against his hind leg. "You don't know the meaning of the word."

"This isn't helping," Dagny said, stepping between them, her wings lifting. Her voice raised in pitch. "Can't we all take a moment to remember how we felt when we thought the rest of us were dead?"

Stigr's ears flattened, Valdis snorted, and Kjorn ground his beak.

Asvander paced around all of them, and stretched his wings. "She's right, you know."

"Dagny is right," Brynja agreed. She looked from Kjorn to Asvander, and Stigr. "We mustn't fight amongst ourselves. Shard hoped for peace between all of us. We can honor that, at least. And you mustn't give up hope, Kjorn."

When he remained silent, Brynja spread her wings, outlined in the hazy moonlight against the lapping waves of the lake. "You mustn't. Shard wanted more than anything to see you again and reconcile. He believed in you. You must believe in him."

"Brynja," Asvander began hesitantly. "You must be prepared to accept if—"

"He lives." She turned, her gaze hard and bright. She stepped back from them. "I know that he lives. He had so much to live *for*, and I…" Drawing a tight breath, she composed herself, folding her wings. "I believe that if he hasn't yet returned, it's because he had some purpose. Some greater purpose to attend to, some task, some reason not to return to us. He had larger designs than we might know."

The waves lapped, and wisps of fog gathered over the water.

"What task?" Asvander asked at last, gently. "What task could be more important than finding his friends again, his allies, his wing-brother? If he came to his senses, what could be more important?"

Kjorn stared across the lake, and saw no answer in the dark.

Stigr broke the silence, his voice low and gravelly. "I know of one thing."

44

SHARD'S BEACON

I T HAD BECOME TOO EASY to slip into Namelessness, to exist within his instincts and feel only the wind on his feathers and fur. He didn't count the days flying from the Sunland back to the Winderost, he slipped away from himself and became wind, became his feathers and his breath. After the dark, cold hole of his imprisonment, flying free and wild was a relief.

He landed on a rock cluster and fished there, eating his fill. Then he flew on, following the line of two stars above him, two stars that shone like the wingtips of a swan in flight under the moon.

Follow Sig's wingtips, echoed a soft memory, a voice he knew he loved. *They will guide you.*

One day, a new scent wafted to him under the constant wash of brine and fish.

Sage.

It brought many memories licking up like flames. Red rock. Hunting. Laughter. The face of a gryfess with keen, gold eyes and freckles of russet on the pale feathers of her face.

Bit by bit as the winter sea passed under him, he rebuilt the memory of his loved ones, his purpose, and his name.

By the time he saw, almost with surprise, the ragged, wind-night-ward coast of the Winderost, he knew again that he was Rashard, son-of-Baldr, and remembered all the reasons he'd returned.

Brynja. Kjorn. Stigr.

Anticipation kindled in his breast to think of Brynja, to see her again, to speak his heart again.

Stigr, he tucked in the same corner of his heart as his father.

Moving from sad thoughts, he pictured Kjorn, who was surely in the Winderost, if his own visions were true, and what they might accomplish together if they could reconcile.

Skirting along the coast, he kept a hard watch for any creature in the air or on the land. He scented and smelled no wyrms, no gryfons. Only gulls watched his lonely arrival.

He worked to recall the lay of the land as Brynja had told it to him nearly a season ago, and angled his flight accordingly. The landscape lay different from the coast where he'd first landed, different from the land he'd first flown over with Brynja and her huntresses.

Not planning on returning yet to the Dawn Spire without a plan or allies, he soared high over unfamiliar rolling hills, toward a different destination, and a task more important than his own reunions.

He turned inland, and starward, toward the Outlands.

A long lay of gray, cracked earth stretched beneath him. A half day's flight and the land changed after a range of gray, wolf-teeth mountains that showed little sign of life.

Shard saw no movement but for an occasional silent vulture. He hoped that meant the wyrms remained starward of the Voldsom Narrows, perhaps hoping to catch him and Hikaru coming from the Horn, or for other reasons he couldn't understand.

A great gash delved into the earth, neatly dividing the dead spread of earth from the rest of the Winderost. Shard remembered it. He remembered from when he'd flown, ashamed and Nameless, away from the Dawn Spire—wandering, lost and out of his head, he'd traveled a canyon. He soared low now, searching the landscape. He'd been witless, but he remembered flashes of the landscape. And he remembered gryfons.

A female gryfon and her son had met him, fought him away from their den. Then, she'd recognized him. She'd recognized him and called out to him in his father's name. Shard hadn't even known his own name, much less Baldr's, but he remembered now, and he knew what it meant.

There were Vanir in the Outlands of the Winderost.

"Hail!" He shouted to the empty, flat land. The sun hung high and warm on his back, though a chill winter wind still ruffed his feathers. "Vanir of the Silver Isles! If you shelter here, come forth! Vanir!"

He shouted himself raw, and no answer came. In the hottest part of the day—so odd, he reflected, to feel hot in winter, but such was the landscape—he landed in a shelter of rocks and collapsed. For a while he lay out of the heat, waiting for evening to cool the air and fiddling with the silver chain around his neck.

He'd thought that any gryfons there would come, curious at his voice, or the name of their homeland. But maybe they didn't recognize it, or maybe they were gone. Or dead. Or simply too far away. Maybe the gryfess had been a hallucination when he'd traveled near the Outlands. He touched the silver chain, and his talons bumped the pouch that held Groa's fire stones.

Or maybe, he thought, pushing himself back to all fours, *I'm going about it wrong.*

Despite the heat of the afternoon, he knew the night would grow chill. Perhaps instead of wearing himself down and flying for leagues and days across the Outlands searching, he could draw any exiled gryfons to *him* instead.

So, as the afternoon crawled toward evening, Shard hunted not for gryfons, but kindling.

It was well after dark before he'd gathered a large enough supply. He flared to land, dropping the last bit of kindling on his pile of brush and dead wood as tall as himself and twice as wide.

Ravenous again, thirsty, he planned to the light the blaze and find food and water, letting the fire attract the curiosity of the Outlanders in the night.

Shard sat in darkness, tail dusting back and forth in concentration. He wound a bit of dead grass into a little nest, as Hikaru had shown him. That nest, he tucked under a pyramid of grass and brittle twigs. Then he drew out the fire stones, and recalled with a soft chuckle how Hikaru had shown off and created sparks by merely swiping his own claws across rock.

For a moment, as a cool breeze flicked around him, Shard closed his eyes. He pushed hunger from his mind—and his fear that the fire would have the wrong effect, that it would not draw gryfons, but his enemy.

Still he had to try.

Thinking of dragon claws, he swiped the flint across the stone. The surprising rain of sparks made him drop both stones, but he laughed, ears perking. After collecting the firestones again, he sat on his haunches near his little tinder nest, and swiped again. Sparks flashed, lighting on the tinder. Pinpoint embers glowed.

Again he slashed the stones together, sparks showering like Tyr's bright breath from his own talons. Laughing, bristling with glee, Shard struck the stones again and again until at last the tinder caught, flickered to life, and burned. Carefully he nudged the tinder nest under the kindling under the fire caught and crawled, leaping high on the dry brush pile.

The heat forced him to back away and he did so laughing, eyes stinging from the smoke. Like a fledge, for a moment he was rushed with energy and he frolicked around the fire in leaps and rolls.

"The brave will call fire from stone," he breathed, recalling Hikaru's dragon rhyme. He skidded to a stop in the dust. "Ha! I did it, I…" He looked around, almost expecting to see others come out of the dark into his ring of light. It felt absurd that Stigr was not there, Catori and Kjorn and all those he loved were not there.

He was alone. There was no one to hear. No one to share the moment with him, see the miracle, behold the crackling beast he had created and tamed. In that heartbeat, he knew all he wanted was to go home, to see his family, assorted as they were, to have peace.

Shard forced himself to calm down, to remember that he must save his energy for hunting food, wood, and water. He tucked the stones back into the safety of the pouch and tugged it closed.

And then, he was not alone.

Turning once more toward the fire, he saw a gryfon face appear in the orange light, a feline form slinking forward from the dark. At first the other didn't look at Shard, only the waving fire, ears lifted. Shard stood very still, hoping to recognize the face, to see the female or her son who had called to him when he was Nameless, but it was not. He feared that the exiles would be lost and witless as he had been, but he saw immediately that the gryfon, an old male, was aware, knowing, Named.

He was not witless, but he was afraid. Wiry, too thin, and pale brown in coloring. Still, he looked like a Vanir.

"What is this?" whispered the old gryfon. "Tyr's flame…"

Shard straightened, lifting his wings in welcome. "A beacon."

The old gryfon's gaze darted to him and his eyes widened, scouring Shard with a look. As if no longer able to support his own weight, he sank to his belly on the dry ground. "So I have finally succumbed. Are you here to greet me, my king, who I watched fall into the sea, slain by Per the Red? Have I reached the Sunlit Land, at last?"

Shard's throat caught. "You're alive and well, and we're still in the Outlands of the Winderost. I'm not Baldr, but his son, Rashard. Tell me your name?"

"Frar, son-of-Eyvar. And if you are Baldr's son..." Understanding lightened his gaze, and he stood quickly, only to mantle low, but his hungry eyes locked on Shard's face. "My prince. You lived. You live. I never gave up hope. And you've come, you've come..." his voice broke and he lowered his head, shaking it slowly. "I knew..."

Shard walked to him, set talons on his wing and murmured for him to stand. "Yes, I've come." He met the old Vanir's eyes. "I've come to bring you home."

45

FAIRER WINDS

C AJ SAT ALONE ON A cliff overlooking the sea, staring out toward the windward quarter. Toward home.

It had been days since Sverin's confession, Ragna's sentence, and the former king's imprisonment. They would not allow Caj to stay all the time in the den with him—even Ragna's trust in him had limits, though Thyra had vouched for him. But he went to see the king every day, to assure Sverin that he would not abandon him, he wouldn't hold old faults against him.

The Red King remained quiet, but sane, and would sometimes even speak of Elena.

Perhaps, as Ragna had said, now that he could grieve openly and honestly about all that had passed, he could heal.

The pride continued to do their hunting, their fishing, for winter and hunger would not relent to give time for their shock and grief.

Caj couldn't have fooled himself into believing that all would be forgiven, all peaceful, that Sverin would wait idly by while they waited for Kjorn and Shard's return and that it wasn't needful to imprison him. Logically he knew Sverin must be imprisoned, but neither had he expected Ragna's vehemence.

Perhaps he should have.

Sigrun found him there, sitting at the edge of the cliff. The sea crashed on icy banks far below them, and great hunks of frozen sea ice jutted from the waves. Caj couldn't help but think of the milder, rainy winters of the Winderost.

"How do you fare, my mate?" Sigrun asked, landing beside him as evening fell.

"Well enough. I'll see Sverin when the hunters return with supper."

She nodded once, crisply, and both of them glanced in the direction of the red gryfon's den.

Sigrun folded her wings, her gaze distant. "What do you think will happen?"

He knew she meant in general. To the pride, to any of them, to their lost princes—whose return seemed as distant and fragile a promise as the spring.

"I don't know," Caj said quietly, opening his wing to invite her to his side. She ducked in against him, and Caj drew a deep breath. Gulls cried, and farther out, they saw Vanir, swooping over the waves in the last gray light.

"Shard won't be the only Vanir to return in spring," Sigrun reminded him, though after Sverin had first fled, she'd told him everything. Einarr's brother Dagr had flown to seek their exiled father and other lost Vanir, and Halvden's mother, Maja, had done the same. They'd been gone the long winter too, and would return in spring. The healer's gaze searched the far horizon. "I wonder what those who were exiled will think of us who stayed, and those Aesir who are now our friends."

"Some chose their exile," he reminded her quietly. "I know he did send many away, but some left rather than be ruled by Per."

"Did you think I forgot that?" Her tail twitched. "Or are you speaking of Stigr?"

"Of any of them," Caj said mildly, though she knew him too well. He had indeed been thinking of Stigr, who would've been Sigrun's mate but for the Conquering. Or not. He'd gathered that the Vanir warrior had never quite committed to mating, and in the meantime Sigrun had waited, and waited for him. He preened gently behind Sigrun's ears. "Whatever happens, I vow that we will face it together."

She swiveled to meet his eyes, hers soft, brown, and keen. "I vow that, too."

"And I will fight for you again, if needed. I will take his other eye."

She sighed, and lifted her talons to tap against his restored cast, as if to remind him that she was weary of his fighting. "Hear me. No matter what friends, what family, what lost Vanir return to this pride, you are my true mate. I will stand with you. You don't have to fight for me. You've won. I *choose* you, Caj, son-of-Cai."

Admonished, Caj dipped his head against her neck.

A scuffling drew their attention to the foot of the rocks, and Sigrun perked her ears to see Thyra, climbing up from the cliff trails to meet them. She looked as Caj knew he must often look, a strong facade of stone masking other fears.

"Mother, Father," she said quietly, gaze averted. "May I nest with you tonight? I'd rather not be alone anymore, until Kjorn returns."

In answer, Sigrun opened her wing. Still Thyra hesitated, though her posture was proud. "Father, about sending the sentries to hunt him, I hope you can—"

"It's done," Caj said to stop her, then more warmly, "my daughter."

With relief, Thyra stepped forward and stood next to them.

"How fares my grandson?" Caj asked, ears perking toward Thyra's round belly.

"Or grand*daughter*," Sigrun said.

Thyra laughed, seeming surprised, and nipped the air. "Feisty." Wryly she added, "He, or she, likes when I eat fish."

Caj grumbled as if the very idea of fish offended him, Sigrun fluffed between them, and despite all that had passed, they spoke only of the next day's fishing, how each pregnant gryfess fared, and the curious customs of the wolves who came and went on the Sun Isle now like extended members of the pride.

A scent filtered to them on the rising evening breeze.

"Speak of a creature and he appears," Caj murmured, turning to see Tocho loping toward them across the sweeping plain of snow.

"Caj, my friend! They told me where to find you." He trotted up and turned a quick circle, showing off a flash of blue in his neck fur. "A raven tied it for me. What do you think?"

"Very handsome," Caj said, and it did look dramatic, the cobalt feather against his pale gold fur. "Tocho, this is my family. Queen Thyra, and the pride's healer, Sigrun."

"Yes, I have heard of you both." Tocho dipped his head low, showing just the points of his teeth. "It's an honor."

"Thank you," Sigrun murmured, "for all you did to help Caj."

"Hear, hear," Thyra said. "The feather does look very handsome. You'll surely be the only wolf, ever, to sport a blue one."

"Ever?" Tocho looked hopeful, and Caj glanced sidelong at Thyra.

Thyra looked at him, her expression still one of deep admiration. "My father chooses his friends very carefully."

"But did it impress your lady?" Caj wondered, catching Thyra's gaze. She looked amused.

Tocho huffed. "I haven't seen her yet."

"When you see her, show confidence," Caj instructed, and felt Sigrun giving him a sideways look. "And dignity."

"Confidence." Tocho's ears flicked, and he lifted his tail. His nose quivered, and his ears flattened. "Oh..."

He turned just as Caj caught the same scent, another wolf on the wind, then appearing against the snow, using Tocho's trail. This was a she-wolf, long and lean and with fur like cedar bark, and sprinting toward them from the river.

"I fear why she's running," Sigrun said, ears laying back as she watched the wolf's swift approach.

"Some news," Caj said vaguely. He was distracted by the sight of her, certain by Tocho's sudden, low whine that this was the object of his affections. He had to admit to himself that she must be very striking, for a wolf.

"Queen Thyra!" she called, her voice a warm, low alto, "Hrafn's daughter, and Noble Caj. If only Ragna were here, I have such news!

Such tidings..." She slowed to a canter, then a trot. Caj noticed feathers braided into the shaggy fur of her neck, one pale gray, one rich black.

"Catori!" Tocho turned in another circle, then Caj could've sworn he heard the young wolf mutter, "dignity," to himself as he straightened and waved his tail in greeting.

"Tocho." She paused and they greeted each in wolf fashion, sniffing delicately. She seemed to take particular interest in the feather, looking from Caj to Tocho again, her ears flickering. "I see perhaps the rumors of your recent adventures are true?"

"All true," Tocho said, ears perked. One ear flicked back to Caj, and the gold wolf stepped forward, nosing behind Catori's ear. "I will tell you the tale of it, tonight, if you wish."

Catori shook her self and considered him, head tilted, as if they'd only just met. "I would like that."

Caj saw the quiver of happiness that took Tocho's body, saw him repress it and move back, stiff-legged. "Good. We'll hunt together, tell stories, and sing." He broke into a pant, Caj suspected to relieve his nerves, then calmed. "But you brought news. Forgive me."

She chuckled, taken aback, considered Tocho again, then bowed before the gryfons.

"Wait," Sigrun said, poised to fly. "I'll fetch Ragna first. If it's something she should hear?"

Catori pawed the snow, full of energy. "Yes, fetch the queen! I've dreamed, a vision that I trust to be true, and I have news." When she raised her head, her amber eyes glittered with joy. "At last, I have news of Shard."

46

THE LOST VANIR

THEY WORKED DEEP INTO THE night. Frar agreed to tend the fire while Shard flew to hunt food. A brief flight away, he found a thin trickle of a spring that tasted of mud and mineral, but it was good enough. Good that it was close, and it drew prey.

There, Shard waited, with the bonfire winking reassuringly in the distance, until a hare came to the stream to drink. Shard struck, but took that first meal to Frar. Then he went back again and again, hunting small game and taking it to the fire so that should more Vanir arrive, there would be food and welcome for them.

At last, he ate, after felling a starving greatbeast calf that had somehow lost its herd. Shard thanked it for its life but was almost glad to end its suffering. He ate his fill of the red meat, then dragged the rest to the fire, calling to Frar for help.

The old Vanir remained mostly silent, as if he couldn't believe how his fate had turned. Shard shared the sentiment and didn't invite conversation. His body was weary, but his heart alight. If Frar was the only Vanir he found, it would be enough to justify his journey.

But he was not.

When the moon hung nightward, a band of three gryfesses crept into the firelight, their gazes on the food, then on Shard. One was his mother's age, two of them perhaps a year older than Shard. By their size and bearing and color, he knew at least two of them were from the Silver Isles.

"Welcome." He stood, raising his wings.

"What is this?" asked the eldest female, whom Shard was certain was a Vanir. Frar confirmed it by coming around the fire to address her.

"Ketil," said the old gryfon, and she looked to him in surprise. "Yes, I still live." He lowered his voice, though it brimmed with mischief. "My old friend. Do you not know your own prince?"

The Vanir gryfess started, stepping fully into the light and looking Shard up and down again. With a soft sound, she mantled. "Rashard, so it is, little Rashard—my lord, I knew your mother. I knew Sigrun, too. I am Ketil, daughter-of-Var. This is my daughter, Keta, and Ilse, a huntress of the Winderost, though her family was exiled from the Dawn Spire." She nodded to the third gryfess, who looked indeed like an Aesir. Firmly, she said to Shard, "She is like another daughter to me."

"You're all welcome." Shard inclined his head. "I've come to gather you, to find all of you that I can. Others have flown nightward and starward from the Isles to find the other lost Vanir, and we will all return home."

Ketil's ears swiveled forward. "Does this mean the conquerors are overthrown?"

"The conquerors..." Shard chose his words carefully. "The tyranny of the Red Kings has ended. But their prince, Kjorn, is my wingbrother, and I hope we will have peace with them from now on. I'll tell you all that's passed, but please, eat now. Rest. We have much to do."

Ketil bowed to him again, as did Keta and Ilse.

He answered their questions, and told his tale. He told them even of Stigr, for Ketil and Frar had known him, and told them that Ragna was well, and Sigrun was mated to an Aesir and their daughter was Kjorn's queen.

He told them everything.

"Tell us how we may serve you," said Ketil after they'd eaten, her pale eyes taking in Shard's face, his wings, his whole body. In a motherly fashion, she seemed to disapprove of his state of health.

"You can hunt," Shard said. "Bring food. We'll need it if more come. Bring food, and find others."

They bowed to him, even the young Aesir, who didn't appear bothered by the differences between them, or that Shard was a prince she'd probably never heard of.

More came in the night.

It was like a dream. Shard's plan was working. For a long while he paced and searched the skies for signs of wyrms. Far off, he thought he heard roars, but they never came, so he might have dreamed them. He didn't leave to hunt again, for now that they had help, Frar had insisted Shard remain by the fire to greet the new arrivals, as their king.

Prince, he thought. *I've earned no kingdom yet.*

Yet as they came, they cried out in joy and disbelief to see him, and bowed, and pledged their loyalty. And he promised to take them home.

He told them all what had passed in the Silver Isles. He told the tale each time a new gryfon came, told them of his travels until his voice gave out, and was stunned at how many Vanir had lived, barely lived, there in the Outlands.

The more who came, the more went to search and spread the word, the more left to hunt. By the time dawn brushed the sky, they'd run out of tinder, and more than fifty gryfons slumbered around the dying embers of the fire.

Shard looked at them—very old Vanir like Frar, some his mother and uncle's age, and some younger who had been only kits during the Conquering. Kits like him, but whose parents carried them away from the conquered Isles in search of a new life.

There were males his age, and a few females, young and hopeful Vanir huntresses, who beheld him shyly. Shard had once thought there might be a Vanir female for him among the exiles, but when he met their gazes, he could think only of Brynja.

"These are as many as we could gather," Frar told him, speaking quietly so as not to wake those still resting. Shard had managed some fitful sleep and eaten plenty, but the night had wrung them out, all of them.

"There's someone missing," Shard said, searching each face. "We must stay longer. I met a gryfess here, and her son, when I wandered Nameless. Who else fled here?"

"I don't know. I didn't know there were this many." Frar watched him, one ear swiveling to track their little pride.

"A gryfess of middle years," Shard insisted, recalling her more clearly. "A son my age. They were here in the Outlands. I won't leave them. I won't leave any Vanir who still breathes."

"My king," Frar murmured, and dipped his head. "We will find her." He gestured with a wing. "Perhaps in the those fanged mountains—"

"Not the mountains. It was starward. Farther, almost to edge of the Outlands, starward of the Voldsom."

Frar flattened his ears uncertainly. "The wyrms are sheltering there. It's too dangerous."

"Then I'll go alone," Shard said.

"Please," Frar said. "We've just gotten you back. You can't leave us now. You must let others search."

"No," Shard said. "It must be me. I'll remember the way once I get closer, and I'll find their den."

"Please," Frar tried, one last time, stepping forward.

"Watch over them for me," Shard murmured. "Stoke the fire. Keep it burning. Any exile is welcome here—Vanir, Aesir, painted wolf, starving eagle. They are all welcome." He opened his wings. "Tell the Vanir where I've gone. And tell them I'll return."

Frar dipped his head, and when Shard looked back from a greater height, saw that the Vanir was still watching, and would watch, until they could no longer see him.

47

OATHS RENEWED

O N ASVANDER'S SUGGESTION AND STIGR'S insistence, Kjorn himself led a warrior party to the Outlands. By putting together all they knew of Shard's ultimate mission, they could only assume that he had gone there to track down any lost Vanir who, over the course of time, had ended up in the wasted fringes of the Winderost.

They didn't know what they would face there, but Asvander convinced the clans of the Ostral Shore to assist, for what glory there might be, for any warriors who faced the wyrms again.

Brynja and her huntresses, Dagny, Nilsine and the Vanhar and fifty assorted warriors of the Ostral Shore flew in a layered formation back over the hills.

With what Kjorn had seen of the wyrms, he felt better with nearly a hundred gryfons at his back. With what Brynja and Asvander had told him about the attack on the Dawn Spire, he knew it was not nearly enough.

Hopefully we won't see them at all, but hide in the night, fly in the day, find Shard and his Vanir and be gone.

"I wouldn't mind a few more talons," he'd said hopefully to Asvander just as they set out.

The Lakelander had shaken his head. "I wouldn't say that too loudly, or the ones you have will feel unwelcome. I truly wish I could do more, Kjorn, but these are all the volunteers I could muster."

"And well needed. I didn't mean any insult."

"Of course not," Asvander said. "Anyway, I agree with you."

But that had been the last word on the topic. They left the large pride at the Ostral Shore with what volunteers could be had from the young and eager, those who wished to see the wyrms, and some older, who felt a drifting sense of loyalty to Kjorn's bloodline, from the old days.

They settled for the first evening in the same spot he and the others had met with the painted wolves. No sooner had they landed than a shout went up from one of the sentries Kjorn had posted around the outskirts of their camp.

"Painted wolves?" Kjorn expected the warning to be about the pack, but there was no scent of Ilesh, Mayka or the others on the wind.

"No," the sentry called. "Gryfons, nightward."

Kjorn spotted them, a whole band of gryfons flying fast toward them.

"Ready up," Asvander ordered.

They formed a circle on the ground, faces up and out, every warrior crouched and ready to fly. Brynja fell into the formation by Kjorn, talons digging into the scrubby grass. Kjorn readied himself for a fight, then paused, peering at the approaching band of gryfons.

"Nilsine," he called uncertainly. The Vanhar was on the other side of the circle. "Isn't that—"

"Oh, we surrender, mighty warriors!" called a wry voice from the approaching band.

"Rok," Nilsine barked, half in recognition, half in surprise. "You devil, what's the meaning of this?"

"We've come to help!" called a younger, brighter voice. Behind the lanky rogue, but flapping fast to catch up, was Fraenir.

"Quiet, traitor," Rok ordered, in good humor.

Kjorn spied Frida, and at least twenty scruffy, ill-fed gryfons besides. He stood straight, watching as the band of rogues landed. Before Kjorn could speak, Nilsine broke their circle formation and trotted up to Rok, wings and feathers raised.

"You haven't had enough of poaching the Vanheim?" She demanded, in his face, and Kjorn tried not to be amused for she stood a head and a half shorter than him. "Now you bring your scoundrels to hunt this land? I doubt you can count on the Lakelanders to be more merciful than us."

"You're looking well, daughter-of-Nels," he said, smoothing his feathers from his flight. "For the romp you've all been having with His Highness, there, I mean. Pardon me, but I'm not here to speak to you and unless I'm mistaken, you have no say, here."

He inclined his head, and stepped past her to see Kjorn. "Your Highness. A pleasure to see you again, and drier this time."

Nilsine turned to keep watching him, half-crouched and ready to spring.

"What *is* the meaning of all this?" Kjorn strode forward with Asvander behind, and the rest of his band fanned out from a circle to form two lines, facing the rogues with admirable restraint.

"Friends of yours?" Asvander wondered.

"We'll see," Kjorn said shortly.

Before Rok could answer, Fraenir trotted forward, bowing to Kjorn. "I shouldn't have run, but I'd never seen the wyrms so close, and they surely would have killed me. I know I was a coward, but look, I've brought friends, and Rok, and he's a fine fighter, Kjorn…"

Kjorn glanced past Fraenir to Rok, who watched him with a gleaming look.

"My young friend is convinced," Rok said, more seriously, his look challenging, "that we might be of service, and for that, we might be pardoned of our crimes and taken back with open wing to the clans we've hailed from." He extended a wing to point to his rabble. "There are many more than these, believe me, but these are who I found on the way to you. And I promise you, all can fight."

Nilsine's response to this was a snort, and she paced away, studying the assorted gryfons who'd flown with Rok.

"Perhaps," Asvander said thoughtfully, while Kjorn remained quiet. "It has been done before. I have a little say at the Ostral Shore, and could speak for any who serve bravely."

"And I at the Vanheim," Nilsine said, her beak raised high, "though why I would speak for any of you—"

"Yet I have no power at the Dawn Spire," Kjorn said evenly, "and that is where your father was exiled from, isn't it, Rok?"

"Not yet," Fraenir said brightly. "But you will."

"Will I?"

Rok looked at the sky. "He's convinced you mean to return and take your—what did you call it, Frae? Rightful destiny? Kingdom? Something like that." He shook his head and watched Kjorn, expectantly.

Kjorn flicked an ear to Fraenir. The quiet question in his heart about his own destiny pulsed, like an ember, like a heartbeat. "Whatever gave you that idea? I've come here to find Shard."

"The signs," Fraenir insisted. "The starfire last autumn, the volcano, and then, what the lioness said about the Sunwind—"

"That's enough," Rok said. "Make of all that what you will. Anyway, if there is genuine honor to be had and glory won, we're here to serve."

At a loss, Kjorn appraised the rogues. Some watched him with ironic suspicion, like Rok, some with an empty sort of surrender, and some, like Frida and Fraenir, with true hope. He wondered how many more there might be, if these were only the swift bunch Rok had gathered before finding Kjorn again.

"I can't promise you anything," he said quietly.

Rok ruffled his feathers. "When I was captive, the Vanhar told me, with no small disdain, mind you, that you told them to let me keep this chain, when you might've had it back from me. Is that true?"

"It is."

Rok looked Kjorn over, perhaps gauging what sort of gryfon he'd been before he washed up on the shore of the Winderost.

Then he answered, quietly, for only Kjorn to hear. "Long ago, my father swore an oath to serve Per, but that duty was taken from him. From my family." His gaze slid to Fraenir. "And a naive young gryfon recently reminded me that keeping your oaths is a matter of honor, not gain. Though I can't imagine where he got the idea....he's right." The rogue inclined his head, but didn't lower his gaze from Kjorn's eyes. "So I will help you find your wingbrother. Then, after that, if I think you're worth serving, consider me your loyal subject."

Kjorn could say absolutely nothing. He couldn't help but glance at Nilsine, and though he could tell she seethed, she had no argument. She'd said Fraenir would turn against him or disappoint him, but already he proved her wrong, and quite.

Still, she managed her bite. "If Kjorn cannot restore you to the Dawn Spire," she said to Rok, "I suggest you find your new place not at the Vanheim, but the Ostral Shore, where they know less about you."

Rok's laugh was thunderous, and Nilsine laid her ears back. "I'm flattered that I bother you so much, my lady. Well, Your Highness," he said to Kjorn, and shifted, displaying the chain that Kjorn had left him, "what say you?"

He saw Nilsine give a slight shake of her head. Then he considered young Fraenir, the other rogue gryfons, young and old, with talons splayed and ready. He thought of when, seemingly so long ago, he'd told Fraenir his own definition of honor, and saw now that it had truly taken hold.

"I accept your fealty," he declared, formally, as he had seen Per do, and Sverin. "And will return that fealty with reward as I can, with protection, and loyalty." He raised his head and spread his golden wings wide, looking over the ragged band. "That goes for all of you."

Fraenir, nearly beside himself at the scant ceremony, bowed deeply. A few more bowed more cautiously, a few only murmured a wary response.

"Well enough," Rok said. "Now, where are we headed?"

The morning light remained dim enough that they saw the flicker of fire across the broadest part of the canyon that divided the Outlands from the Winderost.

"Kjorn," Nilsine said.

"I see it."

"It is gryfons," Brynja confirmed, swooping ahead. "A whole gathering of them, and they have fire." Her voice warmed with relish. She'd told Kjorn of the fires they used to burn, until the wyrm attack that had destroyed their pyres and doused them. They had no way to make new flames unless they were lucky and skyfire struck again.

Evidently, it had.

A gryfon flew up to meet them, halfway over the canyon.

"Hail!" Kjorn called, and introduced himself. "We seek Rashard, son-of-Baldr."

"He was here," called the female. Her gazed took in the war band warily. "And has gone."

Disappointment and wild, lancing frustration almost drove Kjorn to a fit right there in the sky, but he managed to contain himself and only mutter, "Of course he has. Where has he gone?"

She looked nervous. "Come and meet with us at the fire."

They did. Kjorn's band winged over the canyon that marked the border. Many nervous gazes peered down at the yawning, bleak canyon, as if wyrms might lunge up from the murky depth and devour them in a gulp.

Without incident, they all set foot on the dusty ground of the Outlands, standing around the fire of the exiled Vanir. Kjorn noted

also a few scruffy, bony, painted wolves, and ragged eagles. Bones of
prey animals lay scattered and stripped, and he smelled water, faintly.

Impressed with his wingbrother's strategy, Kjorn let the Vanir
gryfess lead him to the fire, which burned low but steady. Haunted,
hollow gryfon eyes stared at him from around the fire, and he knew
what they saw.

Aesir. Conqueror. Son of the Red Kings.

For the not first time that winter, Kjorn laid his ears back in uncertainty and shame. Then, he bowed his head to them.

"I seek my wingbrother, Shard, who is your rightful king. Who
among you leads while he's away? Who knows where he's gone?"

"Starward," said an old male. His wings hung wearily from his
sides, ribs sticking out against his dull pelt. "That's all I know."

"Not to face the wyrms? Alone?" *Not even Shard is that naive. He
tried once, and failed.*

"Seeking more Vanir," the old male growled. Tension flickered as
sure as the flame.

Kjorn kept his head low, and inclined it. "Of course, I understand.
But do you know—"

"I've told you all I know. Leave us. We want nothing more to do
with you."

"We've come to help Shard," entered Brynja's silver-smooth voice.
"To help *you*. He has made peace with the Aesir, and hopes to keep
ties between us. Let us help."

"Find our prince if you want to help." Ears flat to his head, the
old male didn't move nor soften.

The wind stirred the ashes of the fire and the ash on the ground,
and Kjorn took a deep breath of the thick air.

A hesitant, young male voice spoke up from the group. "You said
he went starward, seeking Vanir?" He looked at the old one, and his
voice rose, almost in accusation. "You didn't say that's why he'd gone!
You should've told me—"

"You've only just arrived," growled the old Vanir. "Settle down."

The young male stepped forward, a Vanir almost exactly Shard's age. "Frar, you don't understand! If he went starward seeking Vanir, he had be looking for *me*." He looked between the old one he'd called Frar, and Kjorn. "For me, and my mother. We're the only gryfons I know of who still nest starward of the Voldsom."

"But you came alone," said Frar.

He bowed his head. "I fled when the wyrms came back from the mountains, but Mother refused. She told me to get to safety, and insisted she wait." He looked around, perhaps fearing disapproval for leaving his mother alone. "She insisted. She thought he would come back if she waited..."

"Where is she now?" Kjorn asked, lifting his head. "Can you take us to where Shard might be?"

"It's wyrm territory. But I will show you." The young Vanir looked grim, and opened his wings.

"Wait," said Brynja, looking to Kjorn, then the bonfire, which gleamed reflected in her eyes. "I have an idea."

48

RHYDDA

S HARD REACHED THE STARWARD BORDER of the Outlands before dawn of the second day he'd flown from the Vanir and the bonfire.

When he'd heard the cracked screams of the wyrms in the night, he'd landed and ranged along the ground, wanting desperately to shout but knowing it would only draw them to him. Now in the deep hour before dawn, he trotted along the rim of the vast canyon that divided the Voldsom Narrows from the Outlands. He knew the canyon stretched deep into the earth and split off into the Narrows, but he saw little of it through the dark and the ash. That far starward, haze still blanketed the air, obscuring his vision and his sense of smell.

His hearing though, remained sharp. Guttural wyrm snarls and shrieks from high above and across the broad canyon warned him to remain low. When he found a pile of rocks, he ducked into its shadow and waited for the sun to rise and the wyrms to go to ground. His eyes stung from the haze, and exhaustion. The brief nap at midnight near the bonfire did little to help him. He stretched out on his belly, ears perked toward the yawning canyon before him, and waited.

Dim sunlight suffused the haze. The air glowed golden, then amber. Gradually the wyrms fell silent as they went to their nests. Shard rose, ears twitching back and forth, and crept to the cliff edge, his talons curled over the rocks before the face plunged down into the hazy deep.

Shard held his breath a moment, tail flicking as he squinted across the canyon, which was a good fifty leaps. The dim humps of rock and stunted trees looked passingly familiar. If that was where he'd wandered, Nameless, then he could find the old Vanir gryfess and her son again.

As surer rays of light beamed through the gloom, Shard leaped, gliding over the vast, dead canyon. Dust filled the air, joining the haze, and he sneezed, then resisted the urge to cough. The sound bounded down and through the canyon. His feathers prickled and he paused, hovering between cliffs, ears perked.

Nothing. Either the wyrms had not heard, or they avoided the morning light. Shard flew on across and landed.

He *knew* then that he'd been there before. The very shape of the trees looked familiar, and the layout of rocks. Head low like a wolf, searching for any scent or sign of life, he trotted on. That part of the Voldsom looked no better than the Outlands, with dry, baked earth all coated in dull ash, the grim haze, and no scent of water or life.

Ahead he saw a stack of boulders that he knew, and perked his ears before breaking into a sprint.

"Hail!" he called, trotting up to the boulders. "I've returned, Shard, son-of-Baldr." He circled around the den, wary, trying to catch a fresh scent. "You called to me. A moon or two ago, I came this way, lost." Shard stepped forward hesitantly, poking his head into the dark cave. ". . . Hello?"

Ash swirled in eddies around his talons. "Hello? I come peacefully…"

But there were no gryfons in the den.

Out hunting, he told himself. The wind shifted, bringing him the faint, distant scent of wyrm flesh and old blood. He shuddered, unsure if it was the blood of wyrm, pronghorn or gryfon. They couldn't be dead. He wouldn't be frightened off. The Vanir gryfess had called to him, and he owed it to her to bring them home again.

They'd gone hunting, and they would return.

He sat down to wait.

Afternoon stretched to evening. Shard shifted anxiously in the fading light, his energy sapped out into the dead land, the dry ground, the thick coat of ash everywhere, and a nagging sense of foreboding. He curled in the den for a time and rested, rousing again near evening. At last he could wait no more, and struck out in the direction of the strongest gryfon scent.

Catori and Stigr had taught him the best way to track on the ground, and he'd learned a little from Thyra, as well. Because of all the dangers flying in the Outlands posed, he thought the best course for any gryfon who lived there might be to hunt on foot. Sure enough he came upon a faint gryfon track in the ash, perked his ears, and trotted forward, head low as he followed the trail.

A few times he lost the footprints where wind had kicked up the dust and ash, but followed a faint scent and, here and there, a bit of down or tuft of fur caught on the brittle twigs in the ground. A gryfess had passed that way, hunting.

Maybe I should've waited for her at the den. What if, even now, she's returned?

The wiser, deep part of him knew that was wrong. The tiny, silver whisper in his heart knew that he would have waited forever. The part of him that the dragoness Ume would've called *sky* knew what he would find at the end of the trail. Still, stubbornly, he followed it as darkness closed a wing around him.

He coughed against the haze, and his steps slowed to a reluctant drag as the scent grew fresher, and it was not the proper scent of gryfon with a fresh kill.

In the last evening light, Shard rounded a tumble of rocks that stank of wyrm flesh, old blood, and rotting meat.

Deer bones littered the ground. The gryfess had hunted, indeed, but too far. Too close to the wyrm's nesting ground within the walls of the canyon.

Shard saw her.

For a moment he couldn't look, then, feeling it was his duty, he walked to her body. The rising night wind brushed up feathers from the still flesh, giving her the brief illusion of breath.

"I'm sorry," he whispered, smoothing the feathers back down over the wicked wound across her chest. He gently arranged her body into a dignified pose, wings outstretched, and knew she'd only died a day or so earlier. They hadn't fed on her. They'd killed her, taken the deer, leaving only its bones, and left her body in the ashes.

Shard spoke again, his voice pebbly and cracked. "I'm sorry that I didn't come, that I didn't hear you when you called my name."

His voice grew ragged and dangerously loud in his own ears.

"I'm sorry," he choked again, thinking of her empty den, of the wyrms entering the scrap of territory she'd called home. He imagined how she'd stood her ground. She'd stood her ground, waiting.

Waiting for him. Waiting for her king.

"No more," Shard pleaded, pressing his talons to her shoulder, and tilted his head to the hazy sky through which he saw no stars. "No more of this!"

A dry, wicked rumble trembled distantly in the air, from the canyon.

Shard whipped his head around, ears laying back.

"No more," he hissed, and lunged into the air. He had failed to be a prince, a king, for this gryfess once.

He would not fail again.

A shriek shattered the haze.

"Yes I'm here!" he shouted. "You'll fight an old, sick huntress and steal her kill? Well, she was one of mine, my pride! Now, fight me!"

Everything he'd plan to do, to try, to get through to them fell away in sick, righteous anger.

He heard them coming. Wings rushed the air. They'd heard. They'd heard his challenge from a league off and it would take them no time at all to reach him. Shard soared high, breaking the haze, letting the first starlight and the final glow of sunset declare his presence for all to see.

Below him, the haze swirled and, as if he stared through water, he saw shadows squirming as the wyrm horde gathered, rose, and burst from the haze. One, two, ten—he tried to count them all and failed.

Then he only saw one.

The bloodstained skin around her eye sparkled scarlet for half a breath in the last light, then the sun was gone and they all looked the same, dull color.

Shard made himself as huge as possible, flaring his wings wide with each stroke, bellowing with his dry, broken voice.

"You cannot ignore my words forever! Gryfon slayer, wrathful one, you will hear me and answer. Tell me why you're so full of hate!"

The wyrm's head ticked to one side. At first Shard thought she understood. Then he realized she'd caught sight of the silver around his neck.

"Or is this truly all you want?" He yanked the delicate chain from his neck and brandished it in the star light. "Are you only ignorant, greedy and jealous as the dragons believe?"

The wyrm's head flew up and she blared a roar.

"Is this what's so precious to you you've forgotten honor, and your name, and your voice? Well have it!"

Shard flung the silver chain away. Rage pumped hot through his wings and kept him strong, and he flapped higher, away from the larger horde. All the wyrms squealed with greed and threw themselves after the dainty chain as it fell. All but her.

"Or is it *this* you want?" Shard shouted, and tugged the firestones from their pouch. Keeping an iron grip, he struck them together. Sparks flared and died, tiny and useless.

The wyrm gnashed her teeth, almost seeming frustrated at her companions, squabbling over the tiny chain, below them. She turned with a shattering roar and dove upward at Shard, wing strokes hard and fast. For a heartbeat, Shard stared. She hadn't gone after the chain.

He knew he should dodge, or charge, or do something, but he only stared, mesmerized by her baleful eyes and jaws, slowly grinning wide. The meat stench on her breath snapped him from it.

Fumblingly he stowed the fire stones and whipped up higher, grasping to remember all he'd learned.

They are an ancient race....

A strange, warm light rose from somewhere. As if his sparks had set the haze alight, Shard saw an orange glow suffusing the shroud below them, a league off from where he'd flown and shouted his challenge.

....with an ancient memory.

Shard gasped for air and for clarity, darting up as jaws snapped near his tail. He banked and fell to one side and the wyrm tilted to follow.

Throwing himself around to face her, Shard beat his wings hard, hovering. "This cannot be all that you are!"

The wyrm flapped her massive wings, hunching up to his level and bearing her great fangs again. Sharp, snapping roars and squeals grated up from the greedy wyrms below, a storm of thrashing wings and wrestling reptilian bodies in the haze.

For a moment, their eyes met. With a sharp breath, Shard saw a familiar light there, one he'd seen during the battle of the Dawn Spire. First he'd thought it was like a serpent gaze, meant to snare and hold him. And he was held.

He gazed deep as their wings stirred the wind. Shard felt breathless, as if he could dive straight into her black, gleaming eyes, seeking that one point of light. For half a breath, he saw broad, rolling moors carpeted with reddish purple heather, and beyond that, constant, drizzling gray skies and hills brighter green than the emerald room of the chronicler.

A shriek from below yanked him from the vision, and he shook his head hard. Above him the stars blazed, the back of Midragur, the star dragon. Shard felt the dream net and thought, maybe, he could speak to her. He thought of the Copper Cliff, the nesting cliffs, the Sun Isle, laying the Silver Isles over the images of green hills and rain.

My home, he thought desperately, painting it for her as he had for Groa. If she saw his dream, or understood, she gave no indication. A low, hideous snarl began in her throat. Shard scrambled for all the chronicler had told him.

They live to be very old.

...the last named wyrm was called Rhydda.

Rhydda.

"Rhydda?" He barely realized they both still hung in the air, staring at each other, his shoulders cramped from hovering.

Her jaws closed, nostrils flaring with gusts of heavy breath.

A snapping howl from one of the fighting wyrms drew her gaze down and a growl curled again in her huge chest.

Shard flung out the name again like a weapon. "Rhydda!"

She sank down, tossing her horns with a snarl.

"Rhydda," Shard called again, extending his talons as if to implore her. "I name you! Are you the same? Have you lived, did you live, in the time of Kajar? Do you seek justice for some wrong?"

She didn't attack, didn't flee, didn't respond, but beat her broad, veined wings to hover again.

Risking all, Shard winged forward again, within striking distance, to see her eyes.

"*Rhydda.* Did you once fly to the Sunland..."

She'd stopped listening. Something else drew her gaze.

The glowing haze. Shard looked too.

The golden light grew beneath them like a second sunrise, too bright and orange to be a trick of the moon.

It looked like...

"Fire," Shard whispered, shocked, wondering if his sparks had caught on something below. But that was impossible. Foolish. He'd needed a tinder bundle and kindling to start one before.

The wyrm he'd named Rhydda hesitated, baleful gaze sliding between the growing wash of light and Shard, then to her band of wyrms who still fought over the chain like buzzards with a hare. The cacophony washed over them and the land like a thunderstorm.

Then she chose. She opened her jaws in a roar that felt as if it split Shard's bones, her wings stroking forward. Shard held fast to his strand of wind, opened his chest and screamed wordlessly in challenge, breaking into a lion's roar at the end.

His every feather stood on end. He stretched his talons wide as if to embrace her.

The wyrm closed, fanged jaws yawning wide, and her huge, bloody claws reached up toward him.

Shard scooped his wings, readying to dive.

Then, as if his roar had summoned the very flames and warriors of Tyr himself, the haze below them exploded upward in fire and gryfon screams.

49

THE BATTLE OF TORCHES

S HOCK BOLTED THROUGH SHARD AND he tucked a wing to roll away as Rhydda thundered past, jaws snapping hard enough to crunch stone. Shard circled tightly underneath her as she re-grouped, and he tried to make sense of the lashing smoke, confusion of wings, shouts, and fires everywhere.

Through the thrashing bodies, whirling flames and smoke, he realized with stupid glee that an entire war band of gryfons had appeared, bearing torches.

Among them, he heard a familiar voice calling commands.

Impossible hope leaped through him at that voice. Kjorn.

Fire flashed off of golden feathers. *"Kjorn!"*

A chorus of shouts and familiar voices answered him, and five gryfons shot higher skyward, two bearing torches.

"Brynja!" His own voice sounded high and coarse.

Briefly, he saw her—like a dream, he saw Brynja and Dagny, bearing torches and seeking him against the sky.

"I'm here!" he shouted, and sucked a breath as he plummeted down to meet them, Rhydda turning her huge body above them and readying to dive.

Then, Kjorn was before him.

Shard flared to hard stop and they stared at each other a moment, even as the murderous wyrm circled above them, checked only for a moment by the surprising sight of fire.

"I've been all over Tyr's creation to find you," shouted the big, gold prince over the roiling battle, "and where should I, but here in a pack of—"

"I'll make it up to you," Shard offered, breathless. "Later!"

Gryfons winged up to them with torches—Dagny, then he saw Asvander, and another, lanky brown gryfon he didn't know, wearing a thin gold chain.

"Is this him?"

"Yes!" laughed a familiar voice, and Shard flapped around to see Brynja, on his level. Brynja, bright with torchlight—flying with fire as he had taught her.

She met his eyes, and said, "Shard, just like the eagles."

Shard shook his head. "What—?"

"Now!" Asvander shouted, and he and Kjorn swung up higher into the sky. "Shard!"

Jolted, Shard joined them, with a last look at Brynja, but she was back to her task of drawing the wyrm's gaze with her fire. The brown male Shard didn't know swung off to one side, joined by two more gryfons. He saw a third triad winging toward them from the orange haze and the squirming, thunderous chaos below.

The wyrm Rhydda seemed to have lost track of Shard, and chose her new target—the flicking torches, Brynja and Dagny. Shard flew snug to Kjorn and Asvander. It was as if he'd never left either them, and none of them needed to speak. He understood what Brynja meant, and why she'd said it, with no time to explain.

Like the eagles.

Rhydda swooped down. Brynja and Dagny dove, their torches threatening to gutter out, the uncertain light drawing her furious attention.

By silent understanding, Kjorn, Asvander and Shard shot down after them, an arrow with Kjorn on point. Like the eagles of the Voldsom, they would attack above and from the sides, to bring down a much more massive foe.

Brynja and Dagny brought the wyrm up short by flaring to sudden stops and bearing the torches high, threatening her gaping jaws with fire. Rhydda flared with a hollow grunt, whipping her spade tail toward the gryfesses—but they scattered away.

Kjorn slammed down between her shoulders. Shard landed hard on her haunch, Asvander on a thrashing wing.

She wailed in rage, then a long, low bellow Shard suspected was to summon help.

Shard focused on digging his talons into her leathery hide, timing quick, hard shoves with Kjorn to push her down. They were one single, fighting mind. His body rocked with her hard, deep wing strokes. He felt her jerking with the impact of more gryfons, from the sides, from below. Like the eagles.

"Your idea?" he shouted at Kjorn, and the golden prince shrieked a laugh, wings flashing wide.

"I think Caj would be proud, don't you?"

Rhydda's head flailed at the end of her muscled neck, the thick, sharp horns seeking any target. Shard heard a scream, and knew a gryfon had fallen. Blood pounding, he dug in, shoving. Rhydda's spade tail curved, seeking targets but ruining her flight coordination. They fell, a knotted, writhing mess of gryfon and wyrm, leathery hide and claw and talon.

Haze and fire whirled around them.

They fell into the larger, squirming mass of battling wyrms and gryfons.

A smaller wyrm of near black coloring darted in, claws splayed toward Asvander. The Lakelander shoved off and away. The black wyrm ignored him, circling tightly to seek another target without harming the larger she-wyrm.

Kjorn roared a challenge, still dug into Rhydda's shoulders. He clamped his beak on her neck. The smaller wyrm's spade tail lashed toward him, but he didn't move. With a roar, Shard leaped, throwing his body against the non-lethal muscle near the spade.

"Fly, Kjorn!"

Looking stunned by his near-death, Kjorn disengaged and fell away, swearing.

The gryfons holding Rhydda peeled off as other wyrms thrashed away from their fights and closed in to save her.

Shard let the wyrm fling him off his tail, and rolled through the air, flaring only when he sensed enough room for his wings.

The wyrms screamed in renewed fury, and as Shard righted himself and glided fast, seeking Kjorn, he saw why. Through the fire he made out smaller, darting, winged shapes pelting toward the wyrm's heads, their faces, their eyes.

"Eagles!" Dagny's bright voice was unmistakable through the din. The unexpected assistance drove the gryfons to fight with fresh vigor, reform their triad attacks, and drive at the wyrms.

And the doubled assault was too much for the foe.

Shard saw Rhydda, clear of her attacks, bleeding but whole, flying up over the clash.

Her bone-rattling roar sliced through the fighting. The wyrms broke off. One by one, they broke from the knot of battle. And fled.

Younger warriors, hot with the energy of battle, sped after them.

"Stay!" roared Kjorn. "Don't pursue! Let them flee like cowards!"

She got away, Shard thought, trying to gain his breath and his thoughts. He had no time for his maddening frustration and disappointment. *She escaped my words, and she escaped vengeance.* But he had not imagined the vision in her eyes, the dream of that green land.

Maybe, yet, he could get through to her. But not that night.

A ragged cheer rose, lion roars, eagle screams. Voices shouted Shard's name, Kjorn's name, a dozen voices, then more, calling for their prince, and he didn't know which one they meant.

He landed hard on the ground, leaving his wings open, and at a loss. All around, gryfons stooped and landed, propping their torches against rocks, calling out for their friends. Eagles glided fast over the scene, seeking the wounded.

Still bewildered by the turn of events, Shard decided he would go where he was needed, to help the injured. He turned to follow the alarmed cry of an eagle.

"Shard," said Kjorn's voice behind him. Shard stopped, holding a breath. During the battle, it had felt like another vision, a dream. But when he turned around, Kjorn stood there in the orange half light of the torches, bloody, disheveled, and majestic, like something from a legend. A warrior prince. "Shard, come with me, my brother. You have a duty."

Shard gazed at him, with so much to say, but when Kjorn shoved back into the sky, Shard could only join him.

They flew high into the fire lit haze.

A torch bearer caught sight of them and followed, so all could see.

They flew until they could see all the war band scattered below. Shard saw Aesir, Vanir, ragged exiles and sleek, lean gryfons who reminded him of Vanir, but were not. He saw many of his own gathered pride, those healthy enough to fight. His heart beat a cautious rhythm of victory.

At Kjorn's first, triumphant roar, all halted and turned their faces upward.

When his roar died away, Kjorn looked at Shard.

"They need to see you," he urged. "Shard, they came for you. They need to see and hear you."

Every muscle in his body shook, but hungry, hardened, battle-shocked eyes stared at him. Shard shook his head, then gathered his breath, and echoed Kjorn's roar.

"Victory!" he shouted.

Kjorn laughed, and joined with his deep voice. "*Victory!*"

The cry took up. "Victory!"

"*Victory!*"

As the chant rose, Shard and Kjorn glided in a circle around the warriors, then landed in their rough center.

They stared at each other. Kjorn appeared taller than Shard remembered, brighter, and older. Shard wondered if he looked the same, and Kjorn answered the unspoken question.

"You grew, brother."

Looking at him, Shard thought of all that bonded them, and the lies and mistrust and divisions that had parted them. Now, they seemed a distant thing, the problems of two other gryfons who no longer existed. "And we are, still?"

In Kjorn's eyes Shard saw the hard winter, his flight, his trials in hunting him through the Winderost. He saw their own lies and revelations. He realized that Kjorn wanted forgiveness and friendship just as much as he did, and saw doubt that Shard would give it.

Kjorn stepped forward. "Always, Shard."

"You came all this way to find me?"

Kjorn gave a weak, broken laugh. "What else was I to do?"

Tilting his head, Shard extended his wing, and with a grateful look, Kjorn stretched his own to eclipse it.

Aesir believed important things best done under the light of Tyr. But they had the blazing light of fire around them, and the white light of Tor above, and the stars of Midragur.

"Wind under me when the air is still," Kjorn said. At first Shard thought he had raised his voice over the clamor, then realized all the others had fallen silent to watch them.

"Wind over me when I fly too high," Shard said, quietly, only for Kjorn.

Kjorn's wing pressed to his. "Brother by choice."

"Brother by vow."

Eyes locked, voices nearly breaking with disbelief, together they ended, "By my wings, you will never fly alone."

Shard let loose a breath he felt he'd held all winter. Kjorn laughed and swept his wing over Shard's head, running the feathers the wrong way. Someone raised a happy cry, and Shard thought it was Brynja. Then a new cheer began.

"Hail, Kjorn!" Firm voices of Aesir.

"Hail, Rashard!" Ragged, devoted Vanir.

"Victory!"

"Victory! Hail Kjorn! Hail Rashard!"

The cry swept them, thundered in rolling roars and eagle cries through the canyon, chased the fleeing wyrms, and pounded across the dead Outlands, their torches glowing like the light of dawn.

"VICTORY!"

50

A NEW WIND

THEY REMAINED ENCAMPED RIGHT WHERE they were, to tend the
wounded, to rest.

Before anything, Shard found and took the Vanir to his mother's
body. Together they sang the Song of Last Light. He offered to burn
her body in the way of the dragons, but the Vanir, named Toskil,
declined. He stood just taller than Shard, his feathers warm brown
and gray, with a paler, flecked face.

"This land was her home for ten years, as harsh as it was. She
raised me here." His gaze lifted up over his mother's body to the
dawnward horizon. "She would be glad to rest here. With my
father." He looked at Shard with a half glad, half puzzled expression. "You and I were born the same spring, my lord. We would
have grown up together." His ears flicked back, and he looked again
at his mother's body.

Shard watched him quietly. "We'll come to know each other now."

The Vanir dipped his head in acknowledgement.

Shard nodded, hesitated, then saw it best to leave him alone.

He found Kjorn first.

The gold prince was conferring with a huntress of the sleek, shore dwelling gryfons who called themselves Vanhar, but when he spotted Shard, he drew away.

Ears perked their way and whispers fluttered as they walked out to the edge of the fire light. They'd made bonfires to light the area, to warn against wyrms, and to warn them away.

Shard turned to Kjorn. Away from the fires the night was chilly, frost gathered on the rocks and his breath misted between them. A question nagged him, and he dug a talon against the hard ground.

"How did you do it? Asvander said the warriors always lose themselves in fear, that they've never been able to use a strategy before. But you did. It was amazing."

"We remembered ourselves," Kjorn said simply, his blue eyes near gold in the firelight, searching Shard's face.

"*How?*" Shard demanded. "They fell apart at the Dawn Spire."

"They were surprised at the Dawn Spire. And we were prepared." Kjorn's gaze grew shrewd. "And a wise old warrior suggested that before the battle, we all take a moment to think of what we love. And remembering what we love," he said quietly, his gaze hard on Shard's face, "we would not forget ourselves."

Shard nodded, almost wanting to laugh. So simple, and yet. "What warrior was that?"

Kjorn draped his wing over Shard's shoulders. "Walk with me, Shard."

Dawn saw them gathering to return to the Ostral Shores.

Your uncle is alive.

It pounded through Shard's skull, Kjorn's simple words, over and over. He saw the spade tail lash, saw Stigr crash to the dirt. His nightmares of blood and black feathers overlapped the memory.

"Vanir to me!" he called as the great band of gryfons rose on the wind. They all turned their faces dawnward, to the Ostral Shores.

Distantly, they'd heard the wyrms in the night, so knew they hadn't fully fled the Winderost, but Rhydda and her horde did not return for them.

Stigr is alive, Shard.

He saw the black gryfon, lying in the red mud, bleeding, his wing severed.

Your uncle is alive.

"Aesir of the Dawn Spire to me!" Kjorn's voice echoed in the fragile dawn chill. "Company of Rok, son-of-Rokar, to me!"

The sleek huntress Kjorn had been speaking to the night before called, "Vanhar to me!"

"Lakelanders!" boomed Asvander, simply.

Shard shook his head, hard. They flew in clean, divided formations so they could keep track of their numbers. The Vanir insisted to Shard they were all healthy enough to fly, and that it was time. If, in two days, no more had come to Shard's beacon, nor to the fires after the Battle of Torches, as they called it, they knew no more would come.

The outcast eagles who'd found Shard's beacon remained at the Voldsom with Hildr and the Brightwing aerie. She'd laughed when Shard expressed surprise at them coming to the gryfons' aide, and told him only that he was behind the times.

The few Outland painted wolves ran beneath the flying gryfons, for a young rogue named Fraenir seemed convinced they would be accepted into the Serpent River pack, who now dwelled near the Ostral Shores.

A warm scent drifted to him, then her voice.

"You seem pensive, my lord."

Shard flapped once, turning to see Brynja gliding neatly beside him. He'd seen and imagined her vividly so many times that it felt natural to see her there, her broad, ruddy wings brushed by cold wind, her face touched by pale light.

It seemed natural, but not real.

"Brynja," he whispered, and knew his beak remained open.

She searched his face. "I didn't seek you last night, because I knew you had much to do."

"I would've found you," Shard said, "but..." She'd already said it. Shard closed his talons, trying to remember what it was he'd said in all his daydreams of her that had worked. "I've missed you, Brynja. I can't change the way I fled and left all of you, but I am sorry for it, and I'll make it up to all of you."

Stupid. Not all of you. Just you, just you.

"You already have." Her gaze darted around to the joined flocks of gryfons, and her expression quirked in amusement. "Shard..." her ears flattened, and she looked forward toward the dawn. "Kjorn told you of Stigr?"

Shard held a breath, then loosed it. "He did."

"He doesn't blame you, you know. No one does."

"Except King Orn."

"Well."

They flew in silence. Shard could feel the host of Vanir at their backs, watching him.

I should choose a Vanir. One of my own. Accepting her would be too much to ask of them, after they've lived ten years in exile in a wasteland. Because of Aesir.

But it was not *their* mate he was thinking of. It was his own. He drew a breath, narrowing his eyes. And their exile was not because of Brynja. They needed a strong queen. *He* needed a strong queen. His thoughts flung in all sorts of useless directions, most of which were chilled with doubt.

"Shard," she said, and he looked at her. "I missed you, too."

Her eyes were bright with the dawn, with the same light he'd seen the night he told her his heart. It had faded then, overshadowed by duty and poor timing. It didn't fade now. He thought of all that he would have to ask of her. Leaving her home, her obligations, her family. He couldn't ask it of her.

"And Asvander?" he asked tightly, looking forward.

"Asvander missed you too."

Shard barked a laugh, glancing forward toward the host of Lakelanders who led their formation. "Brynja…"

"Rashard." Her eyes gleamed like dragon gold. "I'm not letting you fly away from me, ever again."

When he looked at her, he realized that the worst of his struggle had been trying to make decisions that were not his to make, and his doubts melted now in the warmth of realizing that she had already decided.

"Now," she said, when he only stared, and tucked her talons under her feathers, "why don't you tell me about that new scar on your leg?"

No one begrudged Shard flying a little faster as they approached the Ostral Shores, creeping a bit ahead every sunmark, until he outpaced the rest of the band by a few leagues, and was the first to arrive at the Ostral Shore, sunset on the second day. A lakeland sentry saw him, and would have questioned, but then he spied the distant mass of gryfons behind.

"You're Rashard?"

"I am."

"There's someone waiting for you." The sentry banked, stretching a wing toward the water, and Shard's blood beat fast in his ears as his gaze roved, searching.

Then a shout from the ground. "Shard!"

A black wing flared, drawing his eye.

With a sharp sound, Shard dove, his heart clutching, diving as fast as if he meant to attack the black gryfon who ramped and called to him from the shore of the lake.

He landed hard and graceless near the lapping waves, talons crunching the wet pebbles. He managed a breath, and looked up.

Stigr bounded to him, and stopped. Stigr. His uncle.

Your uncle is alive.

So Kjorn had said, and so, there he stood. Taller than Shard. Onyx of feather. A single, fierce green eye, like Ragna's—the other, scarred shut from his battles in the Conquering. Before Shard could form words, his gaze dragged to Stigr's shoulders. One wing was perfectly whole. Where the other had been lay a raw, gnarled scar, and a longer, thin line, still mending, ran from the base of his neck to his hip. Sorrow hollowed his joy at finding his uncle alive, for Stigr, who had taught Shard all he knew about sea flight, night flight, and the gifts of the Vanir, would never leave the ground again.

"Shard," the black gryfon murmured.

A quivering wave of nausea, a wash of the whole winter and all his trials buckled Shard at every joint. He sank to his belly in front of his uncle and touched his beak to the wet pebbles.

"Oh, Uncle. Please forgive me. Forgive my foolishness. Forgive me for running. I thought...I thought you were dead. I fell witless. I thought—I didn't think I would ever see you again. It's all my fault. Please forgive me. I would take your wound if I could."

The shush of lapping waves and quick cries of distant lake gulls thundered in Shard's ears.

Then Stigr bowed forward and thrust his brow against Shard's, pressing, warm, as if to prove he was alive. They shared breath, so silent Shard heard the strong beat of his uncle's heart. He knew in that moment Stigr had thought him dead too, and for them both, nothing mattered but knowing the other had survived.

There was no blame. There could be no regret.

"My prince," Stigr said quietly. "You've done so well. Your father would be proud of you. *I'm* proud of you."

He drew back, and Shard lifted his head. They could hear the rest of the formation approaching. There would be much to do, to discuss, to plan. Shard shook himself. "You'll tell me everything that happened."

"There isn't much to tell," Stigr said. "They imprisoned us, but Orn set his healers on me, at least. When I was well enough, Valdis and I escaped."

"Valdis?" Shard recalled that he had seen the gryfess at the Battle of Torches, but he'd seen so much, and so many, that he hadn't thought of it. Stigr glanced toward the water, tail twitching.

"We fled to the Dawn Reach, and others did too. She took care of me there." He watched Shard's face carefully. Black ears twitched back. "I suppose it will be easier, now, to tell you that I'm staying, since there's not much choice."

"Staying?" The idea didn't take hold quickly. In all of Shard's hopes for the future Stigr had been there, fishing, hunting, flying openly under the moon, and advising him. "What do you mean, easier to tell me?"

"Before the wyrm attack on the Dawn Spire, I had planned to tell you, Shard…that you were right. I have seen a different side of the Aesir than those who conquered us." His gaze twitched to the approaching bands of gryfons.

Sunset faded toward twilight.

"Valdis?" Shard asked again, feeling slow, then sure. He thought of the long autumn and winter and Brynja's strong-willed aunt, who had admired and challenged Stigr. He hadn't thought what the attention meant to his uncle, then.

"That obvious, was it? Well." He added nothing further, and flicked a pebble toward the water.

Shard knew there was no choice. Stigr could never make the flight home, and no number of gryfons could bear him over the sea for that distance. He just hadn't realized his uncle had made the decision before losing his wing.

"I'm glad for you," Shard said at last, and meant it. "You deserve all the honor that you've gained here, and all the happiness of a new mate."

Once, it might have been Sigrun, but then came the Conquering, and Caj, and they loved each other as true mates. Shard hadn't even realized what it would mean for Stigr to return with him and live among the mixed pride, if Caj remained.

"That means everything to me, my prince," Stigr murmured. "My king. And I'm still your loyal servant, whether you're close or far. Know that."

"I know. I know you always have been."

Stigr stood, stretching, and Shard tried not to flinch at the sight of the raw injury flexing with each movement. "I think it's about to get busy here," he rumbled.

"I have so much to tell you," Shard said, though now the rush of wings and laughing voices and boasts clattered down like falling rain.

"Don't worry, nephew." Stigr raised his voice over the commotion. "We have time now."

Despite their clean formations while flying, the warrior band landed haphazardly, nearly crashing into relieved family members and friends who came out to meet them, shouting, boasting, their wings stirring dust.

"Go on," Stigr said, and Shard touched his beak to his uncle's shoulder once more before turning to find Kjorn, Asvander, and Brynja, and see about building some fires.

"A new wind, a bright wind, a silver wind is blowing.
The winds will whisper, one and all,
To those they know are listening.
Raise your wings, young fledging,
and hark so you will know them.

A song of the Vanhar, a rhyme of the old Four Winds, rolled in hopeful, shivering tones through the Ostral Shores.

"Star shines bright with future light
Sun fills all bold hearts with might.
A Nightwind, fly with warning
At Dawn, with hope come singing.

But now a high wind, a true wind, a silver wind is blowing."

Shard alone stood in the shallow water of the lake shore, letting the waves slip over his feet and tail feathers. Breathing the strange salted air of the landlocked lake, he was able to pretend, for a few moments, that he stood at the shore of the sea.

Bonfires dotted the nesting hollows and hills around the great salt lake, sparks and smoke twisting high into the night. All around there was laughter, singing, bragging, the scent of meat, sparring fledglings re-enacting the battle according to the stories being told.

"Too much light for a Vanir?" Kjorn walked up beside him. "I know you prefer moonlight now."

Shard chuckled, dragging his talons absently through the sand under the water. "Not exactly." Tiny minnows, having come to investigate his legs, scattered and flashed away into the darker water.

"I would have left you alone," Kjorn murmured, dipping a foot into the cold water, then shaking it before stepping back to dry land. "But everyone is just begging to know more about the dragons, and I know for certain you haven't eaten since before the battle."

"I'll come." Shard filled his chest and held the breath, looking toward the sky for strength. There was something that had to be said, before they went on any longer. "Kjorn—"

"I know." Still, it took him a long time to say it. "There cannot be two kings in the Silver Isles."

Shard released the breath, and looked at him. He'd forgotten how large, how well built, and *kingly* his wingbrother was. Or perhaps he'd grown more so.

Be warned, with a dragon's blessing, everything you are will be more so.

"I heard rumors that you had some grand design for all that."

"I did think of something," Shard said cautiously.

Kjorn paced behind him, tail flicking. "Let me see if I have it right—you thought I could return here as Kajar's heir, unite the divided prides of the Winderost, make allies of the painted wolf packs and the eagles and all of us could drive off the wyrm scourge and live peacefully thereafter, and I could take my rightful place as king of the Dawn Spire?" He stopped, standing behind Shard as Shard looked up toward the moon. "Then, you would return with the Vanir and claim your birthright as king of the Silver Isles, make peace again between gryfons and the other Named creatures of the Isles, and all would lie happily there too?"

Looking out over the black, glistening lake, Shard said, "More or less."

"Did you have a more specific plan?"

Shard stepped out of the water. "Not really."

"Well." Kjorn drew a long breath, let it out, and glanced over his shoulder at the fires and feasting. Then he met Shard's eyes. "We'd better make one."

THE END

ACKNOWLEDGEMENTS

A S THE BOOKS GROW, SO does the list of people on whom I rely to make them happen! As always my first thanks is to my husband Dax, whose support, enthusiasm for my writing, and the occasional improvised gryfon rock ballad means everything to me. My parents, who know this is my true profession and are proud to say their daughter is an author, whatever other jobs I might be doing at the time. To my fearless and honest first readers I give huge huge thanks for your time, opinions and first impressions—Kate Washington, Tracy Davis, and my sister Jennifer Owen.

I must thank Kathy Sierra of the "seriouspony" Twitter for her inspiring images, information, and enthusiastic conversations about Icelandic horses. I'd also like to thank J.F.R. Coates of Jaffa Books for our new partnership in bringing paperbacks of the Summer King Chronicles to Australia! Thanks to the other independent carriers: the Whitefish Community Library, Cheryl and Bookworks of Whitefish, Barbara and the crew at Fact & Fiction in Missoula for all your support, the Stumptown Historical Society, Crystal Winters of Whitefish, Voyageur Books, Männerschwarm Books in Germany, and Rabbit Valley Comics.

Special thanks to Daniel Morrison of Remnant Studios for the amazing book trailer, and for helping me soon bring the first audio book to life!

To my editor Joshua Essoe, who keeps Shard awesome and my plots on course, and raises the bar for every aspect of every new book. You're worth a dragon's weight in gold. I have so much gratitude to my cover artist Jennifer Miller—for your excitement, flexibility and what I can only consider truly loving attention to detail. My layout artist at TERyvisions, for making each book stylish and professional. Richard at Crown Media for being great to work with and making the actual books so beautiful. And in the final hours, my awesome ARC readers for your early reviews, feedback, and for catching those pesky typos: Dominique Goodall, R. A. Meenan, K. M. Carroll, Kristin Yadao, Lauren Head, Eric C. Wilder of the Grimm Report, Jennifer Don and Lindsay Adams—thank you!

As a self-publishing author, I depend so much on the master mind power of many people. Thank YOU for making book 3 happen.

And now, a final thanks to my amazing, supportive, loyal Kickstarter backers for helping me turn this book into another collectible hard back. There are so many familiar names and friends on this list from my life and from previous campaigns, I'm truly humbled by your continued support. I promised to name the folks who were able to pledge generous amounts of $100 or more, but know that you are ALL AWESOME.

In no particular order of awesomeness:

Vicki Hsu	A. Parker
Herbert Eder	Kevin Wegener
Noctua Chant	Eric C. Wilder
Linda van Rosmalen	Signe Stenmark
Maddy Gralak	Nick Hennessy
Darrell Dupree	Amber Bibb
Anne "Tyrrlin" Williams	Tobias Braun
Perry Tilos	Cody R
Galit Alterwein	Jessica Thorsell

Michael Blanchard

Steve Hodgson

Kimbley

Chayla Uhl

J.F.R. Coates

Lauren Head

R. A. Meenan

The Stumptown Historical Society

Kate Washington

Laura Nix

Jay Doran

Rhonda Harms

Chrissandra Porter

Miriam "SunGryphon" Halbrooks

Ashley Johnson

Britney Brown

Almonihah

Lorsey Ann Clark

Melissa A. Hartman

Amanda Kennedy

Snow

C. McGinty-Carroll

Linda Aben-Kralowetz

Lauren "Mistywren" Wynja

Edward Fan

Charlotte Rose McCarthy (aka pandemoniumfire)

Alexander Mays Bizzell

Thaner Cox

Phelan Muirneach

Tserisa

William "VVolf" Bentley

Books by Jess E. Owen

The Summer King Chronicles

~~

Song of the Summer King
Skyfire
A Shard of Sun

PHOTO BY JESSICA LOWRY WWW.JESSICALOWRY.COM

About the Author

J ESS HAS BEEN CREATING WORKS of fantasy art and fiction for over a
decade, and founded her own publishing company, Five Elements
Press, to publish her own works and someday, that of others. She's
a proud member of the Society of Children's Book Writers and
Illustrators and the Authors of the Flathead. She lives with her
husband in the mountains of northwest Montana, which offer daily
inspiration for creating worlds of wise, wild creatures, magic, and
adventure. Jess can be contacted directly through her website, www.
jessowen.com, or the SOTSK facebook fan page, www.facebook.
com/songofthesummerking.